OCCASION OF SIN

RACHEL BILLINGTON

SUMMIT BOOKS
NEW YORK

Copyright © 1982 by Rachel Billington
All rights reserved
including the right of reproduction
in whole or in part in any form
Published by SUMMIT BOOKS
A Simon & Schuster Division of Gulf & Western Corporation
Simon & Schuster Building
Rockefeller Center
1230 Avenue of the Americas
New York, New York 10020
Originally published in Great Britain
in 1982 by Hamish Hamilton Ltd.
SUMMIT BOOKS and colophon
are trademarks of Simon & Schuster
Manufactured in the United States of America

10 9 8 7 6 5 4 3 2 1

First American Edition

Library of Congress Cataloging in Publication Data

Billington, Rachel.
   Occasion of sin.

   I. Title.
PR6052.I4028   1982   823'.914   82-19624
ISBN 0-671-45938-4

'Love,' she repeated slowly to herself, and suddenly, as she disentangled the lace, she added: 'I dislike the word because it means too much to me, far more than you can understand,' and she glanced into his face. *'Au revoir.'*

Anna Karenina
Leo Tolstoy

For Kevin, with love

Chapter One

Laura felt inappropriately happy. The sun was shining as if it were May instead of March and a carpet of wild crocuses unwound beside the train window. How could she help feeling happy on her way to the country? On her way to gloom and doom.

She leant back in the corner seat and tried to give the situation serious consideration. She was summoned by her brother to persuade his long-suffering wife not to leave him.

The sun was warm on Laura's face. She closed her eyes. Immediately she saw the cheerful face of her son as she'd waved him off to school that morning. She thought lovingly of his dark eyes and thick untidy hair. It was impossible not to smile when you thought of Nicky. She must get his hair cut.

This was shameful. Was she an entirely superficial person?

She opened her eyes and pulled herself upright with a stern expression. Poor Katie. Four children after six years of marriage and a husband who didn't understand the meaning of the word faithful. It was strange that a brother and sister should have such different attitudes. She didn't find it difficult to be faithful. On the contrary, she enjoyed the feeling of security it gave her. Perhaps, too, a sense of virtue.

Laura frowned. Occasionally she was struck by the thought of her complacency.

Suddenly the sun was eclipsed. The train entered a tunnel and she found herself staring at her face reflected in the window. She wasn't ugly. She had always liked her appearance even when she was a fat little girl. Now people told her she was beautiful. Perhaps it made no difference. Perhaps ugly people grew to like their ugliness.

She stared at herself. Hair, dark, curly like her son's. Nose, narrow, long. Eyes, blue, though she couldn't see that in the window. Skin, pale, though she couldn't see that in the window either. Shape of face, round, surprisingly round for someone her age. Long thin neck rather like her nose and large bosom rather like her cheeks.

What a long tunnel. She moved back from the window. Old and plump. After all, she couldn't be complacent.

Laura sat back and inspected her finger nails. They appeared greenish under the train's neon light. Nicky was growing up and would soon grow away from her. Her career was only a matter of convenience. Even her marriage. The level of noise changed again and the train burst out of the tunnel into the brilliance of sunshine.

Immediately her earlier pure happiness returned. She felt good. She was good. She had left her home clean and orderly. There were anemones in the sitting-room, Miles's supper simmering quietly in the kitchen, Maria, the au pair, ready to spoil Nicky when he came home from school, her own work neatly organised in clips and files. Everything neat in clips and files.

The train was slowing now. The open fields and hills closing into paddocks and gardens. Houses, gradually concentrating from the occasional to the terraced patterns of a country town. On a small rise stood a large church, the centre for the streets and houses. It glowed golden in the sun. Laura felt pleased by the symmetry of it all. She gave it a confederate smile.

The train drew in to the station. Once again the sun was shut out, though here only in a partial eclipse. There was a bridge over the railway line. Laura's carriage stopped opposite it. An elderly woman and a younger man were coming down the steps. The man carried a suitcase in one hand and held the arm of the woman with the other. They did not hurry, as most people would, seeing the train already waiting. They were a striking couple, tall and confident. Mother and son.

They were closer now, on the platform, and a pattern of light through the gaps in the station roof streaked the son's face. It was a reddish colour, with broad cheekbones, large nose, large eyes, low forehead and bristly fair hair cut short. It was the sort of very masculine face which did not appeal to Laura.

He opened the door to Laura's carriage a few yards down the platform and put the case in. The whistle blew and the porter waved his flag. They would have to be quick with their farewells. The mother held up her cheek to be kissed.

The son bent down and taking hold of her shoulders gave her

a firm kiss, first on one cheek and then the other. Laura could imagine how his mother smiled at this loving contact.

The train doors slammed shut. How would she manage with her case? Perhaps the son was not so loving after all. Perhaps he had made her late for the train and now left her in an awkward position. The train began to move slowly away. The young man's upright figure receded down the platform. He was wearing a short ski-jacket. Perhaps the colour of his face was due to sun reflected on snow.

The woman came into the carriage and Laura picked up her book.

'Is this seat taken?'

'I'm so sorry,' Laura removed her coat and the woman sat down opposite. She was wearing a tweed coat, thick with pink and mauve tufts. Her white hair had a slight tinge of mauve. She wore navy shoes and carried a navy handbag. Laura thought she was too elegant for a train journey from one country town to another.

'I had it made for me in Ireland.'

'I'm sorry. Was I staring?' Laura felt herself blushing.

'I choose a more ordinary coat for a more ordinary occasion, but then I feel so dreary.'

'I have one dress that always makes me happy.' Laura was enthusiastic, apologising for her critical thoughts.

'Clothes are a source of great happiness,' said the woman seriously.

'My husband says I pick occasions I know will be enjoyable.'

'Husbands always say that sort of thing,' the woman smiled. 'Though I shouldn't pretend to know. I've been a widow for twenty years.'

Laura thought of the young man. Of the kiss.

'That was my son who saw me off. My only son.'

Laura felt confused by the woman's ability to read her mind. She also felt that it was strange how freely they were talking.

Yet now she said, 'I have just one son too.'

'Ah.'

'He's seven. He's, he's . . . perfect!' She felt a ridiculous smile of proprietory joy crossing her face. But she didn't try to repress it for she felt this woman with her only son must understand it.

The woman didn't smile. 'I'm very proud of Martin but he

9

isn't perfect. It's not good to be too close to a son. The relationship becomes over-emotional and there is no respect.'

Laura became hot with embarrassment. She saw this woman was cold and unfeeling. There was a foreign edge to her voice she hadn't noticed before. Their talk over the coat had misled her. She picked up her book, managing, as she did so, a formal smile, 'Yes, I expect you're right. You've had more experience.'

The woman smiled too, and took up the *Daily Telegraph* from where she'd laid it on the table. Both women began to read.

The sun still shone, although pale clouds were beginning to veil the blue sky. But Laura's former exhilaration did not return. She looked at her book sightlessly. She imagined the chaos and hysterics waiting ahead. She had no doubt she would succeed. She would persuade Johnny to promise reform and Katie to stay. But it would be exhausting and upsetting.

The train was slowing for a station. The last before her own. They only stopped for a moment and then were off again, directly westwards now into the glow left by the setting sun. It had set without Laura's noticing, eaten up by a range of hills. Soon it would be dark. It was already dark enough inside the train to make the lights shine brightly.

Laura dropped her book into her bag and stood up to put on her coat.

The train had been emptying gradually and was now barely a quarter full. She walked over to the other side of the carriage and looked out of the window.

They were drawing into Newton Abbot, and there was John looking harassed on the platform with the two eldest children running circles round him.

'There she is! There! There! Not there! Oh, Daddy!'

'Johnny!' Laura called from the window. Poor John. There was not a trace of his usual ebullience. Even his hair seemed to be thinning unhappily on the top.

'Oh!' Maddy, the eldest child, a girl, crashed down on the platform in her anxiety to reach Laura's door.

'They are happy to see you.' The elderly woman came up behind her.

'They should be in bed.' Laura glanced round but then returned to watch the little girl struggling to her feet crying, tiredly. Already, the woman was a stranger again.

The train stopped.

She jumped out, as glad to be out of the train as an hour ago she'd been glad to be in it.

John hugged her. 'Thank God, you're here!'

Maddy, now recovered, and her little sister Honour bounced on her arm. Laura untangled herself.

'Would you mind getting that case out for . . . ?' The woman's case was heavy.

'Thank you so much.'

The girls became a little quieter as she stepped out of the train.

'And now I can see a porter so I won't have to trouble you any further.' She smiled and held out her hand. 'Perhaps we'll meet again.'

'Yes.' Laura shook her hand hurriedly. Behind them the train began to move away.

'Can I hold your hand, Aunt Laura?'

John put one arm round Laura's shoulders and in the other carried her suitcase. The children fought for her hand. They walked up the platform. Laura thought that however badly he'd behaved she couldn't help being fond of him. Making excuses for him. Blood is thicker than water. Was there any need for Katie to have quite so many children? Quite so quickly. It wouldn't be much fun to be a young man and married to someone who was never available to do anything, go anywhere. As far as she could remember Katie had got pregnant on their wedding night and either been nursing a baby or pregnant ever since.

Poor Johnny! Laura smiled at him. She saw a face not unlike her own, dark curly hair, rosy complexion, blue eyes, round cheeks. A jolly, satisfied face – under usual circumstances.

'I'd better tell you the worst.' The eyes shifted uneasily from her loving gaze.

'It can't be that bad. At least you're still in the house.'

'That's only because she can't do without me. As a nanny.'

'That idiot au pair's run off?'

'Actually, she's the whole trouble.'

'What do you mean?' A horrid suspicion made Laura turn to John's face again. His guilty look increased. 'Oh, no! Johnny. Not her! You couldn't be so – so stupid!'

*

The house seemed dark when they arrived. The light over the

door turned off, no light in the kitchen where the curtains were still undrawn. Usually at this time, Katie would be bustling around, baby at her hip, warming milk for one, pouring cereal for another, making supper, sorting clean clothes. And somewhere in the background, helping in a desultory way, would be the au pair of the moment.

Laura remembered Hilda, a queen of passive co-operation.

'It's such a cliché! With the au pair girl!'

Maddy and Honour stood blinking dazedly in the bright light.

'Katie's been down,' John stared gloomily at the Aga and at a pan with a little milk. 'She's taken milk for Toby. She hasn't even bothered to wash the saucepan.'

'Isn't she nursing him any more?'

'She says the news made the milk dry up. Not that she actually speaks to me. But I can tell perfectly well what she means from her eyes. I used to think she had beautiful eyes. I expect I married her for her eyes. And now they torture me. Miserable, great dark eyes!'

Laura sighed. 'I'd better put these two to bed before they wake up.'

'She'll talk to you, though. There'll be no stopping her. A whole litany of new wrong-doings, starting with the way I chew my food. . . .'

'And ending with the way you seduce au pairs.'

As Laura pushed the sleepy girls up the back stairs she could hear a cupboard being opened down below. A large whiskey for John. She wouldn't have minded a glass of something herself. No time now.

Bathroom, lavatory, bed. Stuffing the smooth pink limbs out of clothes and into pyjamas made her think of Nicky again. All children were beautiful when they were tucked up into bed. She smoothed back their long hair noticing as she did so that it needed washing. Hilda might have done that before she broke the happy news. Presumably she had broken it. Or had Katie found out?

Katie's bedroom was the other end of the house. Laura could hear the sound of a baby crying before she reached the door. She knocked.

'Who is it?' Katie's voice sounded thick with tears.

'It's me – Laura.'

'Oh, Laura!' The door was thrown open and Laura found herself enveloped by the crying baby in the arms of the crying mother. 'I did so hope you'd come. I can't tell you how dreadful everything is. Johnny is a monster, a beast. In this house – he had her here. Sneaking down the corridor. Next door to Maddy and Honour. Any one of them could have woken up and gone into them. It's too awful to imagine. It's the end. The end. I've forgiven him before. You know I have. You've even persuaded me. With me being pregnant so much. But here in this house . . . With the children!'

Katie's tears and the baby's cries finally made it impossible for her to continue. Laura put her arm round her and led her to the bed.

'Sit down, darling. Sit down and give me Toby. Has he had his feed?'

Laura felt the first step was to quieten the baby but her remark caused Katie's sobs to increase.

'He won't take the bottle. I've tried and tried. He just won't. He spits it back at me. He's crying because he's hungry. He hasn't eaten since yesterday. Oh, everything's so dreadful!'

'Sshh. Darling. Now where's the bottle?'

'I don't know. Under the bed. Or somewhere. I hate it anyway. I was going to feed him myself till he went on the cup like all the others but then when this happened my milk dried up. Oh, oh. Oh.'

'Are you sure?'

'What?' Katie looked at Laura. Her wet face showed a tiny glimmer of hope.

'You look to me as if you're bursting out of that blouse.'

'They're torture. Like rocks. I can't sleep when they're like this.'

'Why don't you try and feed him again? Go on. Get into bed and then I'll give him to you.'

Katie's face lightened further. 'Do you think I could?'

'I'm sure you could.'

'Well, I suppose there's no reason why I shouldn't try?'

Katie turned round to get into bed and it was only then Laura noticed the third little girl, Harriet, fast asleep on the pillows.

'She's keeping me company.' Katie settled into bed and unbuttoned her blouse. She held out her arms for the baby. His mouth and hands grabbed wildly for the breast and then fixed on. In a moment the wailing lump of misery was transformed into a soft pink contentment. Katie sighed deeply.

'I do love babies!'

Laura brought a chair to sit beside the bed. The peace was as strong now as the chaos had been before. Katie was beginning to look pretty again, her long chestnut hair curling round her pale naked shoulders, the brown eyes, for which John had married her, soft with love.

If only it were as easy to sort out her relationship with her husband as it was with her child. Laura began to feel a slight sympathy for John again. There was nothing so remote as a young mother. Katie should be made to see that Johnny was like a child himself and needed as much love as any of her babies. But she was so young herself and saw John as a man of the world. She looked up to him. She wanted to look up to him as a husband not mother him as a child.

'If Johnny could see you now he'd fall in love with you all over again.'

'Don't talk about that beast to me! He has no idea what love means. He never has. Never will. All he knows about is sex. And as far as I'm concerned he can have as much sex as he likes with whom he likes as long as he doesn't come near me or my children.'

Laura saw that Katie was feeling much better. Her denunciation had not altered the baby's steady sucking motion. If she felt in a position of power then the chance of her forgiving Johnny was much higher.

'Do you want to tell me what happened?'

'It's perfectly simple. Hilda had been up for her day off to London and when she came back I asked her whether she'd had a nice time and she burst into tears and said she was so unhappy because a dreadful thing had happened between her and Mr Bowles. And she didn't love him at all, at least she loved me and the children much more than him, and she didn't know how it had happened and she was so unhappy.'

Now Katie did start to look upset. Trying to disguise it she took the baby off one breast and moved him to the other. The action calmed her enough to carry on.

'At first I didn't understand. I thought she meant they'd had a row and she was giving in her notice. After all she'd lasted four months, quite a record for me. But then she made it clearer, I won't tell you what she said, I can't bear to think of it actually – but I still didn't believe her. I more or less told her to fill the washing-machine and keep her frustrated fantasies to herself. But then, of course, I couldn't resist ringing Johnny. I told him as if it was a joke. But the moment he spoke I knew. I knew it was true. So then I went down to her and screamed and shouted at her over the dirty nappies. At least she had the sensitivity to pack immediately and do a bunk.

'I knew Johnny would come down as soon as he could. So I left a note on the kitchen table saying he was to pick up the older girls from school and look after them. And that I would keep the younger ones with me and that I never wished to see or talk to him again and that I would be ringing my solicitor to start divorce proceedings in the morning. That was yesterday, Saturday, so he wasn't there and today's Sunday but tomorrow I shall do it first thing. So there you are, end of a marriage, after six years, less two days – it's our wedding anniversary on Tuesday, the children were making a lovely card – and four children. Men are beasts. Selfish, thoughtless, spoilt beasts!'

Katie finished. With a note of triumph. Laura wondered if she liked the idea of men being beasts. But then dismissed it as an unproductive thought.

'But how will you manage on your own?'

'What?' Katie's look of bewilderment told Laura that she had thought no further than the gesture of renunciation. It would be best if it remained that way. She changed her approach.

'How did John explain it?'

'I know what happened. He had sex with my au pair. That's enough, isn't it? I don't want to hear any more. I don't need to know any more.'

'Earlier you were saying about them being together in this house. Near the girls. How do you know that?'

'I can imagine, can't I?' Katie sat up straighter with a look of vehemence though at the same time removing the baby from her breast with total gentleness. 'Why are you interrogating me? It's not me who's in the wrong.'

'I'm sorry,' Laura reached forward to the lolling contented baby. 'Shall I hold Toby while you do yourself up?'

'Thanks. He hasn't burped yet.'

15

With the baby's full tummy pressing against her palm Laura tried again. 'What I meant to say was, have you considered the possibility that this was one isolated incidence? In London. When Johnny was on his own, in the flat.' Mentally Laura made a note to make sure Johnny told that story, whether it was true or not.

'Isolated incident! Isn't that enough?' But although Katie spoke fiercely, Laura noticed she leant back against the pillow as if resigned or at least weary. After all, it had happened before. She had accepted it before.

Laura stood up. 'Why don't you stay in bed now? Have a wash, put on your nightdress and I'll bring you supper in bed.'

'What about Toby? He needs changing and there's the washing and. . . .' Katie sat up anxiously.

'Yes. Yes. I won't kidnap him.'

Katie smiled. Her first real smile and fell back against the pillows again. 'Oh Laura, you are wonderful.'

Baby in arms, Laura walked towards the door.

'Even if you have got a horrible brother!' Katie smiled again and so did Laura. She shut the door well satisfied with the evening's work.

Now to inject John with the right combination of penitence and moral stiffening. Perhaps the sight of his son and heir would do the trick. He was very sweet. Laura pushed his nose and was rewarded by a wide toothless grin.

Once again she thought of her own son securely tucked up in bed. She thought there was nothing dearer to her than her son's happiness.

Chapter Two

Laura hadn't meant to stay more than a day or two with Katie. She liked being in her own home. But on Wednesday she was still there. John had left for London early on Monday morning as usual. The space between husband and wife would be healing now.

Laura's departure depended on finding some sort of home-help. Lizzie, Katie's younger sister, had just left school and was waiting to go to university. She would come in a few days.

So there Laura was stuck. Wednesday morning, the older girls at school and Laura walking round the sunny garden. Inside the house, Harriet slept and Katie bathed the baby. Around Laura the early spring warmth shone on thick carpets of daffodils and pale scatterings of primroses. The lawn was growing already, bursting with green vitality.

As Katie's spirits rose, she began to bustle round in the old way, leaving Laura with more time to herself. It was strange to find herself suddenly alone with no plans. Nothing to organise. No one to see.

It struck her that she hadn't been alone like this for a very long time. Probably before she married. Certainly before Nicky was born. Unlike her brother, she'd always prided herself on her ability to enjoy solitude. She wondered why she'd let herself lose the habit.

Laura walked through the garden and out of a side-gate which led by a short track down to the village. On the way she passed the church. Someone was playing the organ, practising hymns with a tentative touch. She stopped and listened, looked upwards at the stone walls and narrow pointed windows.

Perhaps it was the country, not solitude, she needed. She hurried back to the house and went to the telephone. Often she had a mental block about her husband's office number but today she remembered it perfectly.

'Darling. It's Laura.'

'I've got a meeting in one minute. Is it urgent?'

'No. I mean, yes. I want to stay here longer.'

'But you're expected back today. Nicky's been looking forward to it.'

'I thought he could come down.'

'What do you mean want? Is there some new crisis?'

'I just thought it would do us good. Nicky and me. The country's so lovely.'

'They're calling me. Of course you must do what you want but you know I don't approve of Nicky missing school. It's a matter of habit. If he's allowed to do it once, he'll think he can do it anytime. What is it? Are you ill?'

'No. No.' Laura felt the excitement of her idea being squeezed into dust. Only an obstinate loyalty to her feelings as she stood by the church and listened to the organ made her persevere. 'Maria could bring him down tomorrow evening. He'd only miss one day's school.'

'Obviously you've decided. As a matter of fact I've got to go up to Manchester for a couple of days. I could go on Friday.'

'Thank you.'

'Don't thank me. I told you I have to go. Goodbye, darling.'

Laura felt a ridiculous guilty excitement as she put down the phone. Her cheeks were hot and her heart pounded. She was not used to crossing Miles, even in such a small matter, she enjoyed being comfortable with people, hated rows, unpleasantness. She felt like a child who'd successfully routed the headmaster. Miles hated rows even more than she did. He thought them undignified, childish. He would only show disapproval with coldness. But he was not here to be cold.

Laura danced out into the sun again. She would pick some daffodils for the house.

A window opened above her head. Katie looked out. Her face was pink and shiny, her hair pinned up like a rosette on the top of her head. The baby's face, equally pink with bright button eyes, peered out from inside a thick roll of towel.

'You look about sixteen!' Katie called and the baby squeaked.

'I feel it!' Laura kicked her legs and swung round her arms. 'I'm staying till Monday. Nicky's coming down tomorrow.'

'How lovely! How lovely!'

'Isn't it!' Laura whirled about from one end of the lawn to the other. Katie looked out of the window and laughed at her.

'Miles is going to Manchester.' Laura stopped her wild flight and bent, panting, to pick a daffodil. She looked with concentration at the flower's frilled centre.

She began to pick more, choosing carefully, not the wide open flowers but the furled buds. She tried to guess which were the palest. She loved pale colours. She wanted to find the daffodils nearest to white and fill the house with their lightness. She stood under an old apple tree encircled in the clumps of graceful flowers. Her feet were completely hidden.

'Laura!' Across the lawn dashed a young girl in jeans and knee boots. A long scarf bobbed along the grass behind her like a tail.

'Lizzie. You're early!' Laura went to her and in her haste

18

didn't notice her feet crushing a newly opened narcissus. It lay on the earth, white with a scarlet centre.

'Have you got any money? I need money for the taxi driver. He's groaning monstrously. Think of caring about money on such a beautiful day!'

Laura laughed and went into the house with Lizzie to find her purse.

She thought how like Lizzie was to her sister. As Katie had been before she married. The same innocent capacity to love without any of the regulating controls which people usually develop to protect themselves. She supposed it was this characteristic which had made it so easy for John to take advantage of her.

Laura hoped Lizzie would have more luck. She was cleverer than Katie. More independent. Perhaps this would stop men being too important in her life.

Laura sighed, she didn't know why, and went to find a vase for the flowers.

'So what's the latest news? Has the lioness come out of her den?'

'Cubs in mouth. But minus a few skins, so be careful.'

Lizzie handed Laura the daffodils. She watched admiringly as Laura made a frothy fountain of whiteness.

'Stop staring at me Lizzie, and let's make lunch.' Laura couldn't help knowing what Lizzie thought of her and she was vain enough to enjoy it, though not so vain as to be much affected.

Now they peeled carrots, boiled water for spaghetti and fried mince. They talked of Laura's work with 'Our Agricultural Heritage' – saving old barns, as Lizzie called it – and Lizzie's determination to change from reading History to Greats. Half-way through Laura remembered the sleeping Harriet and went up to fetch her. She was cross at being wakened and clung to Laura's neck as if she would save her from a menacing world. Laura brought her downstairs. Lizzie had laid the kitchen table. A vase of Laura's daffodils stood at the centre. She looked up when Laura came down with Harriet.

'I'll get Katie.'

Laura sat down with Harriet on her lap. She thought that a period of peace in a house usually filled with the restless noise of children was unlike anything else. Was peace precious in proportion to the difficulties of winning it?

Laura thought of her own life. She seemed to have reached a stable plateau of satisfaction without any particularly difficult battles. She had been very unhappy when she was eighteen. She had been brought up a Catholic, in a convent boarding school. Her mother had died in her last term. She had been alone, shy. Sex sat on the horizon, nasty and threatening. She had hardly dared look ahead. One evening she'd got drunk and had allowed herself to be seduced by a much older married man. Afterwards she had convinced herself she was in love with him. It hadn't made her happier of course but, in a kind of way, it had been a relief. The ultimate sin. The ultimate guilt. Things could only improve. She had decided to start working immediately and not try for university. That was when she had started to feel better: work had taught her that self-analysis, concentration on the self, might help others but for her it only made things worse.

It took several years to escape from her older man. He had always been thoroughly married. Soon afterwards she met Miles. He was a barrister. He was older too, by twelve years, but he had never been married and was honourable in a way the first man wouldn't even understand. Laura liked that. Although he wasn't Catholic and by this time she was hardly more so, they married in a Catholic church.

He was tall with a pale soft-featured face. He had thick greyish hair of which he was proud and a particular way of standing with his feet slightly turned out. He wore glasses for reading. He gave his whole attention to whoever he was talking to. Laura was aware some people thought he lectured rather than talked but she liked it. She didn't feel it always necessary to listen to every word but that didn't bother her and he never noticed.

His confidence in conversation made her happy because she had gradually learned over the years that there was another anxious side of him too. It was this side that required her presence near him. In some ways she was stronger than him. But Laura didn't like to think about that too much. She would hate to discover he was a weak man.

'What are you thinking about?'

Laura looked up, surprised at Katie's voice. 'Husbands,' she replied promptly.

Harriet slipped off her lap and ran to her mother. 'Mama! Mama!'

'I'm sorry,' Laura frowned at her stupidity.

Katie bent down and hugged her little daughter. 'It's all right,' she said, 'I'm not going to be silly any more. It was ridiculous to make such a fuss. After all he's been doing it for years.' She took Harriet and lifted her into her high chair. 'I suppose it's fair in a way. He has his girls. I have my children.'

'No!' Lizzie had come in unnoticed by either of them. 'It's not fair at all!'

'Darling Lizzie. Poor Lizzie. You don't understand.'

'This is what Katie wants. Really it's best.'

Lizzie turned to Laura. 'But I can't bear to see her look so resigned, so pathetic! She should get a divorce. Why shouldn't she get a divorce?'

Katie surprised them both then. She laughed. A high clear laugh like a child's. Harriet who had been sucking her fingers anxiously while Lizzie shouted now took them out of her mouth and clapped her hands excitedly.

Katie stopped laughing. 'Of course I could get a divorce. A thousand times over. But then what? How am I better off? Less money because we'd have to split it. . . .'

'But it's not a question of money!'

'Less companionship. . . .'

'What do you mean companionship? A man who screws any girl he sees and you talk of companionship!'

'Don't say that, Lizzie. I love Johnny.'

'Love!' Lizzie sat down, deflated. 'How can you love someone who . . . ?' But Laura looked at her warningly and she did not continue.

'I do love him. Not as I used to. I know all his faults and I hate them. But I don't hate *him*. At least only sometimes like last weekend. Besides, I like being married. I like having a man in bed. I like having a husband – even if he isn't a very good one.'

'But you're very pretty. Before you were married you had boyfriends queueing down the road. I remember how impressed I was. You could easily get a man for your bed.'

'But how about a husband? Someone willing to take on four children under six. They have a right too. He's their father. They have a right to him.'

'Oh, well,' Lizzie shrugged irritably. 'If you're going to sacrifice your life to your children's.'

'But I've told you, Lizzie,' Katie spoke carefully as if she'd been thinking it all out during the days she'd stayed in her room, 'I don't just want a lover. I want a husband and I presume you don't actually suggest I chuck the children off the roof!'

'No, I don't know.' Lizzie sat staring miserably at her place mat. 'There must be something you can do.'

Laura went over to the Aga. 'How about eating?'

Lizzie tried one more appeal. 'But Laura! You don't think Katie has to be totally humiliated for the rest of her life, do you?'

Laura lifted out a spoonful of spaghetti and put it on her plate. She did not really want to answer. The truth was she thought Katie had herself created a position from which there was no way out. She, Laura, would never have married a man like Johnny in the first place. She would never have trapped herself with so many children.

'I believe in marriage,' she said slowly. 'Women function well in marriage. . . .'

'What do you mean, function well?' Lizzie screamed. 'Look at Katie. She's destroyed!'

'No. I'm not.' Katie gave her sister a sharp look. 'That's enough now, Lizzie. When you're older, you'll understand.'

Laura finished putting the carrots and the mince on the plate. 'I'm sorry. Function was a pompous word.' She smiled. 'But I do believe in marriage. Even with all this trouble, Katie and I were so happy here this morning, weren't we, Katie?'

'Oh, yes! Bathing Toby. He was so sweet.'

'But your husbands weren't here.'

'That doesn't matter. We are still married. We're still conscious of being in the married state.'

'You must both be totally cold-blooded, unfeeling. . . . Oh, I give up.'

'Do, please, darling,' said Katie turning on her a bright look, and Laura placed a plate of food in front of her. The subject was closed.

But Laura returned to it in her mind. She didn't like Lizzie thinking her cold-blooded, unfeeling. This made her realise that the steady beat of happiness in her life depended more on the admiration of friends and relations than she had previously admitted to herself. They helped to bolster up the less than glorious love affair between her husband and herself. This made her quite unhappy until she remembered Nicky and how much they loved each other.

Then she went out to pick up Maddy and Honour from school with a light heart. She would be picking him up from the station the following day. That was a happy thought. And it was only when she had the two little girls giggling in the back seat that she realised she had now put herself in the same category as Katie – a woman whose major source of affection was her child.

*

John came down on Friday evening. Although Laura had spoken to him on the phone and told him of Katie's new attitude, he arrived looking humble and nervous. Laura saw how this look softened even Lizzie.

'She's upstairs feeding the baby,' Laura said.

Lizzie took his coat and offered him a drink.

'No, no. Not yet. I'll go straight up.'

It had been an idyllic week. Johnny's arrival would change everything.

They had supper in the dining-room for the first time since Laura's arrival. Johnny opened a bottle of wine and lit the fire in the sitting-room. He was filled with London energy. Katie came down in a long embroidered robe they had bought together on their honeymoon in Egypt.

She was quiet but obviously content. Laura saw Lizzie looking at her wonderingly. So did Katie. She smiled at Lizzie calmly.

John glistened with happiness, the pale dull cast that had come over him in his disgrace was entirely wiped away. He was back to his habitual conviction that the world was a splendid place and particularly splendid to him, John Bowles.

He put his hands on the arms of his chair and, giving admiring glances at the pretty women round him, cried: 'It's a pleasure to have a harem but like all good things it must pass. I've invited Roy to stay tomorrow.'

'Oh, Johnny,' Katie murmured reproachfully. But his good humour was too charming to spoil. 'Will he be here for lunch?' She was unable to suppress the look of a woman counting chops.

23

'Roy is never precise. But at least we don't have to worry about dinner.'

'Why not?'

'We're all invited to a party. That's why Roy's left his Irish fastness. He was sitting on Roy's other side.'

'Who?' Laura, questioning, thought how her brother loved to surprise and organise.

'Martin Keane. It was his mother you met on the train. She worked out who we were. She's staying nearby. And tomorrow night there's a little opera and dinner. It's for charity. Martin's involved in the production in some way.'

'Well, I can't go.' Katie looked down at her plate. Tears started in her eyes. 'I'm feeding the baby and, besides, I've no baby-sitter.'

'I can stay!' cried Lizzie.

'No, no,' Katie gulped. 'I don't want to go. I don't want to do anything. I just want some peace. Like there was this morning. And now there's Roy and an opera and heaven knows what else.'

'I give up!' John scraped his chair back and stood up. 'I thought it would be a treat. And you like Roy, at least so you always say. I find him rather a bore, as a matter of fact. Always banging on about some impossible theory. As a matter of fact I asked him for you!' He felt in his pocket and pulled out some strips of paper. He flung them onto the table. 'There you are. Do what you like with them! Burn them! I don't care. After all, it's only a hundred pounds!'

'A hundred pounds. Oh, Johnny!'

But Johnny had already swept out of the room. The role of unappreciated husband suited him much better than that of the humble penitent. He marched through the kitchen where he collected a cigar and a knife to cut it with. He then proceeded at a slightly slower pace to the sitting-room where he settled down comfortably to watch the late night news.

Still sobbing, Katie helped Laura and Lizzie to clear the table. 'I'm such a drag. Such a bore. But I feel so exhausted. Knowing I have to get up in the middle of the night. At the end of the day, I just want to sleep.'

'It's nursing,' said Laura kindly. 'It's perfectly natural.' But she turned her back on her sister-in-law.

Katie blew her nose on a paper napkin. 'Sorry. Post natal

fountain. To be discounted. I'll make it all right with Johnny. Don't worry. You'll go.'

'An opera,' said Lizzie doubtfully, though her eyes were bright. 'It sounds awfully grand. I only brought jeans.'

'We'll find you something,' Katie picked up the tickets and handed them to Laura. 'You keep these. I'll only flush them away with the nappy liners.'

Laura smiled. She was glad Katie had decided to pull herself together. There was nothing to be gained by sinking back into despair. She handed Lizzie the pepper and salt to put on the kitchen shelf.

'You must wear my long evening dress,' she cried impulsively. 'It's cream with lots of old lace. You'll look beautiful in it and it doesn't matter a bit what I wear.'

*

Roy was obsessed by the idea of pig swill. He arrived at twelve thirty and, despite Katie's protestations that lunch would be ready at any minute, insisted on immediately going out again to see if there were any interesting pig farms in the area.

It was raining, the kind of heavy drizzle that cancels out days of sunshine in a few hours. Nicky, who was still at an age to be excited at the prospect of mud, followed him out. So did Lizzie to whom he was excitedly explaining how the recycling of household waste via the pig sty could solve one of modern civilisation's greatest problems.

Laura knew she should stay to help Katie with the lunch but went along too. After all, she had spent nearly a week being helpful. Besides, she felt like walking in the rain. She was excited, restless, energetic. It was unusual for her who usually was so tranquil, her energy so productively directed.

'All I know about pigs comes from P. G. Wodehouse,' Lizzie grinned at Laura.

'Wait for me! Wait for me!' called Honour and Maddy, determined to go now their Aunt Laura was going.

Roy strode ahead. He was exceptionally tall and thin with wide shoulders and a long pointed forehead decorated by thin strands of dark hair. His glasses were held together by sellotape. He had arrived wearing huge green gum-boots and a buttonless tweed coat which flapped wide like the wings of a bird. At a casual glance he looked gormless. In fact he was constantly agitated by new theories to better the world. He was that odd, though not so odd, combination, an intellectual farmer.

Laura had met him through her brother. They had been at university together. In an obvious sense they were an unlikely couple, the intellectual and the sensualist. But Roy admired John's easy way with life. The way he had found a pretty girl, married her and had four children while he, Roy, had hardly begun to answer fundamental questions of love and sexuality. Being humble and intelligent, Roy always assumed other people knew the answers better than he did which was one of the reasons why his cast of theories ranged so wide and changed so often. During the long evenings on his farm he would ponder on and read about the great problems and then bring his answers to be tested by his contemporaries in London.

Usually their worldly cynicism, made impressive by well-cut suits and an intimate knowledge of current affairs as seen on the television (the reception wasn't very good on Roy's farm) and in the papers (which Roy received a day late), made him look ridiculous, even in his own eyes. And he gave up his idea of the moment. But occasionally strong criticism or, contrarywise, someone's interest made him keener still.

Thus pig swill.

Laura hurried to catch Roy up. She liked dogmatic men. That's why she had married Miles. She felt safe round men with ideas, men, when you came to think about it, who were not really very interested in women.

'*Mud, mud, glorious mud,*' sang the children, sloshing and stamping.

'And the testament of success would be the first pig sty actually in a front garden,' said Roy grabbing Lizzie's arm in his excitement.

'*So follow me, follow. . . .*'

The children chased wildly towards a puddle which linked up two little streams flowing on either side of the lane.

'*And there let us wallow
In glorious mud!*'

Laura looked at Nicky. He was usually a pale little boy with a head too big for his body accentuated by his thick dark red curls. Simply by thinking of his pigeon shoulders and ribby chest she could bring tears to her eyes. But now his face was flushed and his body in its short jerkin looked aggressively confident. He turned round, obviously to look for her, and, seeing she was watching, kicked a huge spray of water straight at Honour.

'Ow! Nicky! You've soaked me!'

'Cry baby! Cry baby!' Chanting happily, he ran off down the road.

'What a killer!' remarked Roy who had temporarily run out of pig swill steam. His voice was admiring.

'He's not usually,' said Laura defensively.

'Aggression's natural in boys that age. In fact it's attractive.' Lizzie continued to watch Nicky's steaming progress while Laura turned back to console the girls. 'I love tough little boys. The problem comes when they turn into tough big boys.'

'Or men.' Roy looked suddenly gloomy as if the discussion affected him particularly. 'Women prefer tough men.'

'You don't mean actually physical toughness, I mean, bashing up, do you?' Lizzie found this a much more interesting topic for discussion than pigs.

'That can be part of it.'

'You can't be serious!' cried Lizzie enjoying the chance to be assertive about something. 'No woman likes being bashed up. That's male-propagated codswallop!'

'It's not primarily a case of physical violence. It's more an instinctive wish in the woman to see her man strong. Probably it all comes from the biological facts of the male–female relationship. . . .'

'Oh, honestly, Roy! How can you believe such old-fashioned nonsense? Women's Lib disproved that biological junk years ago. Everyone agrees there's absolutely no inherent psychological superiority factor in the male female partnership – anyone could tell you that!' Lizzie's indignation coupled with her fluent use of long words made Laura smile. It seemed such an unlikely argument to be holding on a wet country walk.

'What?' Roy had asked her a question. 'Do I like strong men? It depends how you define strong.'

'Don't be so careful!' Lizzie and Roy had now reached the same plateau of excitement.

'I define strong as someone who bases his life on firm principals. I'm not impressed by the sort of strength that commands the attention of the world.'

'Is that so? Do you really believe that?' Roy swung round and stared closely into Laura's face. It confirmed her impression that the reason he was so interested in the subject was that he felt himself to be, at least in the world's terms and in the estimation of most women, a weak man. He fell back again. 'Well, if you really feel that, then you're exceptional. An exceptional woman.'

'An exceptional human being!' cried Lizzie. 'You mustn't think in terms of separation by sex.'

But this time Roy didn't rise to the bait. He became silent and thoughtful and Laura, looking at her watch, suggested they turned back for lunch.

*

Lizzie became awkward before they were to leave for the opera. She said she couldn't leave her sister alone with all the children. But to Laura it was clear that she didn't like the way she looked in the lace dress. Laura picked up the discarded dress from the bed and put it on. Lizzie who was standing at the window staring at the already dark garden turned round in surprise.

'It didn't suit you,' said Laura calmly. 'Now put on your jeans and your silk shirt and let's go.' She remembered how she'd felt at eighteen before she went to a party. The nervous excitement, the feeling that fate was waiting to crown her with happiness or cast her into gloom, the fantasy that someone waited across a crowded room.

She sat at her dressing-table changing her earrings for the amethyst drops that went with the lace dress. She was glad to look beautiful.

Lizzie snorted. 'Whoever heard of an opera in a private house? And dancing. It's absurd. An anachronism. Like a hunt ball or something. I'll be totally out of place.'

Laura didn't like the idea of being an anachronism. She, too, despised hunt balls. Yet opera had seemed to her a wonderfully romantic idea. She now admitted to herself that she had been looking forward to it all day.

'Everybody won't be old and married.' She paused. 'That man whose mother I met on the train, he can't be very old.'

'Martin Keane,' Lizzie came behind Laura and piled her hair on top of her head. She surveyed herself critically. 'We play tennis sometimes.'

'I didn't know you played tennis.'

'In a mixed doubles. I'm not very good. His girl-friend plays.

She's not very good either. So she likes me to join.'

'I didn't know he had a girl-friend.'

Lizzie looked surprised and Laura thought what an odd remark it had been since she knew almost nothing about him.

Lizzie let her hair fall and moved towards the door. 'She's kind of his secretary or something. Martin's a micro freak.'

'That doesn't sound much fun.' Laura watched her own eyes in the mirror. They were very wide.

'Actually, I think he uses Philippa as a protection against other girls.' She went out of the door and then suddenly put her face back in. 'Girls like me!' Laughing at herself she dived away again.

Laura didn't smile but after a pause called after her, 'So you are coming?'

'Of course!' came the cry, bright and confident, quite unlike her previous indecision. 'How could I resist!'

Chapter Three

The rain had cleared by the time they arrived at Lullington House. It was a black starry night but moonless. As a Londoner, Laura was used to a sky smudgy with reflected lights. This clean black and silver dazzled her. She walked along the driveway with her face turned upwards. The air was cold and fresh. She breathed deeply and felt her body fill with a weird sense of home-sickness except she wanted to be nowhere else, of nostalgia except she looked forward, of déjà vu but she had never been there before.

'Laura, Roy!'

There was a cry behind her. Roy and Lizzie who were walking ahead of her turned round. Unwillingly, Laura stopped.

'I'm stuck! I need a push!'

John had let them out on the driveway while he drove the car into a field designated for parking. But they were late and the tyres of many cars had churned up the wet grass.

Roy didn't look at all cross at the prospect of pushing a car. 'I'll help. You two go on ahead.'

'If you're sure.' Laura was not normally selfish but at that moment she felt she'd rather go home than wade in mud. She had cast herself in the role of Cinderella.

Lullington was a sixteenth century manor house composed of three wings round a wide courtyard. It was not particularly large and, as Laura and Lizzie waited behind some other guests to show their tickets at the door, they could hear the sounds of a small orchestra warming up.

Out in the fields a cow mooed. Laura laughed.

A fat and harassed lady wearing a dress painted with monstrous roses took their tickets. 'Oh, dear,' she groaned as she tore them in half.

'But it seems such a success!' Laura encouraged her. 'So many people.'

'Personally I prefer horses. Coats to the left please.'

Laura and Lizzie handed their coats to another fat, but jolly, woman and hurriedly recrossed the hall. For the sound of music had died from the room beyond. The rose-enveloped lady was standing in the doorway staring into the night, imagining presumably when it would be filled with her departing visitors.

Suddenly she was impelled backwards into the hall. Three tall men, talking and laughing, came out of the night. Their faces were wild, their hair curled from the damp night air.

Their hostess, agonised, put a finger to her lips. Lizzie rushed to greet them. 'Hurry! Hurry!'

Laura watched. Martin Keane stood between Roy and Johnny. They all had the look of men who had successfully pushed a car out of a bog. She couldn't imagine how they would settle down and listen to a spinet.

A stage with a painted backcloth had been constructed at one end of the great hall. It waved in an unsettled way. The orchestra sat to one side and the audience, confined to neat rows of gilt chairs, stared straight ahead with already mesmerised faces.

There was a noise behind her and the three men appeared waving gilt chairs above their heads.

'Your chair, m'lady!' Martin Keane held the back of a chair and bowed towards Laura. Laura went to him graciously and sat down.

'Thank you.'

He sat beside her. 'Do you only smile at people you've been introduced to?'

'Sshh. They're starting.' Laura thought how young he was. She pulled a piece of hair in front of her ear and felt glad that she had a good profile.

The opera began. It was called *La Serva Padrona* by Pergolesi and had a cast of three: master, mistress and serving maid. The singing was confident, the orchestra lively.

Laura felt Martin watching her. She did not look at him. Her face burned but the room was hot. Trapped.

It seemed like hours, days, weeks before the master chased the serving maid for the last time and the music concluded with a satisfactory chord.

Laura jumped to her feet.

'I had no idea you were an alcoholic,' Martin still sat.

Laura put a hand to her cheeks. She looked at Martin and saw his admiration. There was nothing wrong in admiration. Nevertheless she noted his defects for future reference, low forehead, rough skin, frizzy hair and crooked teeth.

She said, 'Has no one told you? If I don't have a drink in two seconds, I'll do something disgraceful.'

Martin laughed.

Laura realised his laugh was characteristic. It pulled back his mouth and showed his crooked teeth. It was loud and unselfconscious, it made yellow streaks appear in his eyes. She was irritated that it made her observe so acutely. At the same time she was pleased to have caused it.

'I'd better take your arm before you get the DTs.'

He took her arm and put it over his. Laura saw that, although outwardly a masculine man, he was also friendly, brotherly. He liked women as well as loving them.

They walked to the supper room.

Roy and Johnny strode ahead. Lizzie circled them chattering. Every now and again she glanced back at Laura and Martin. Laura gave her matronly, motherly smile. Martin's arm burned her side.

From that first moment in the station she had known it would be like this. She fought a grotesque urge to fling her arms round his neck and press her mouth on his.

Luckily she was used to hiding her feelings. She walked slowly, smoothly, giving her calm wide look. Her head turned sideways to Martin's talk.

Martin talked about the opera, about Pergolesi's relationship to Mozart, about the place of small orchestras in civilised life, about the relationship between music and computers.

Around them, women in long evening dress and men in suits or dinner jackets pushed enthusiastically.

'Isn't that your mother?' said Laura.

Martin's mother was distinguished by the elegance of her dress. Laura remembered her tufted coat on the train. An elderly woman who loved clothes struck her as unusual. Women, she knew, had moved their priorities long ago to work, children, husbands. Mrs Keane was a widow. Her son had kissed her lovingly.

The dress was made of crimson silk. Sleeves and skirt swirled with sharp-edged pleats.

'Who could miss her?' Martin sounded both ironic and affectionate. He let go of Laura's arm. She felt it like a sharp coldness.

Mrs Keane was a worldly woman with a worldly woman's critical eye.

'Good evening,' Mrs Keane greeted Laura before she spoke to her son. Laura noted this mark of favour to her or of disfavour to Martin. 'So you have met him for yourself?'

'My brother knew him. They met in London and planned all this.'

Martin bent to kiss his mother. 'The belle of the ball.'

'Ha. Ha.' Mrs Keane had an unfeminine laugh. A derisive snort. She turned to Laura. 'How can he say that? With you. Like a bride.'

Laura didn't think this was a compliment. Talking of antique lace, they moved again towards the supper room.

Lizzie saw them from a distance. She waved. Laura went to her, hoping to leave Mrs Keane behind. But she had hooked her arm into her son's. Laura looked to see if he resented it but could not tell. She put her hands to her still warm cheeks.

Round platters of food were spread across a long table. Rigid patterns of piped mayonnaise and regimented salad. Laura was reminded of dolls' house food that would not chip with a chopper. She found herself entertaining the peculiar mental image of throwing one of the plates against the wall.

'The red looked safest.' A glass of wine was handed to her. Martin's fingers touched her wrist. She looked beyond him and saw his mother was talking to their hostess. It was difficult to imagine them friends.

Martin noticed that she'd seen. 'They were at school together,' he said. 'My mother's half French. She came here as an eleven-year-old. To a boarding school. She tried desperately to be English.'

'That explains it.'

'What?'

'She's different.'

'Don't tell her. She thinks she was completely successful.'

Martin stood close to her.

Laura guessed he stood close to every pretty woman.

Lizzie, Roy and John arrived. They had collected another girl. A very pretty girl with straight golden hair. Young. Coupling Laura with Mrs Keane. Very slim. Dressed in what seemed to be an extended man's suit.

'She's a model. But she wants to be a jockey.' Johnny's face beamed with the satisfied look of a man in his element. Over his shoulder Roy's face, devoid of his glasses for the occasion, blinked benignly. He too was enjoying himself, happy to move as a satellite to Johnny's sun. Laura thought it was John's enjoyment in people that led to his being unfaithful to Katie. Poor Katie. Perhaps the baby slept.

Martin was pulling the young girl's golden hair, swearing it was a wig. She laughed. She had a very affected laugh. Laura turned away.

'I'm starving!' cried Lizzie.

'Why are you looking like that?' Laura felt fingers gripping her arm, Martin's lips were close to her ear. She handed him her glass.

'I'd like another drink.'

'Oh, Mummy! I've been looking for you everywhere.' The girl's voice was ugly, shrill. She held out her arms to embrace her mother. Laura watched. Her mother was the flower-strewn battleship.

Laura turned round to face Martin. She smiled at him, frankly. 'Did you help organise the opera?'

'No. I was going to record it. But I didn't. My mother bought me a ticket. Made me come. She thinks I don't know enough of the right people.'

'Don't you like opera?'

33

'Yes. Sometime I'll show you *The Magic Flute* on a synthesiser.'

'I hope there's dancing,' she pointed her toe. Still Cinderella. Roy brought food to her. But she was not hungry. She handed it over to Martin. He ate hungrily, looking at her over the edge of the plate. At first she was put off but then admitted she liked the confidence of his appetite.

Roy returned. He tried to give another plate to Laura. Then he stayed to eat it himself and talk. Without his glasses he couldn't see very well. He dropped pieces of lettuce all round him on the floor without even noticing. He wanted to try out on the professional his theory that music operated on a different part of the brain from any other sensation. He argued that it actually altered the physical order of the cells setting up a vibrating reflection which is a kind of music in its own right. He called it music of the mind. Modern music was nearer this music than music of the air which is why it was so unsatisfactory. For the brain had been done out of a job.

Laura stopped attending.

She knew that Roy was tone deaf but that wasn't why. She didn't want to interrupt the purely physical sensations of happiness she was enjoying. Let Martin and Roy argue. She liked the smoke-screen to thought that the wine had caused in her.

'I hope there's dancing,' she repeated as if to herself.

She looked about and saw Johnny stroking the young girl's arm. She saw Lizzie talking to a small man in a mauve ruffled shirt. She was swilling wine round and round in her glass. Noticing Laura looking her way, she raised her eyes heavenwards. Laura smiled serenely. She wanted to dance. But the orchestra were stuffing themselves by the table.

'Where are the singers?' asked Laura. 'I'd like to congratulate them.'

'We'll go and look,' Martin took her hand as if she were a child to be led. There was no need to feel frightened. Roy stood back.

Martin pulled her through the crowds. They reached a door at the far side of the main room. 'They're changing.'

'Should we disturb them?'

'Of course.'

They came out into a dark stone-flagged corridor. Martin

34

held her hand tightly but he didn't slow down.

'Here we are,' he pushed open a small wooden door. It was very bright inside. Two faces turned to look at them. They were pale, greasy and surprised. One broke into a smile.

'Martin! How dare you show your face.'

'You would have been much crosser if I'd done a bad recording. It would have been very very bad.'

Laura noticed the shine of confidence Martin put over everything.

'I loved it,' Laura said. They looked at her.

'This is Laura – who loved it.' He was making fun of her. But only mildly. 'We're not staying.' They kissed their fingers at him.

Laura and Martin stood outside in the dim corridor. He took her hand up to his chest. He pulled her towards him. Laura stiffened nervously and glanced over her shoulder.

'I'm not going to rape you.'

He laughed. Laura bared her teeth and made a noise.

'Shall I show you the priest's hole?'

'Yes.' Her voice hissed.

They were off again. Martin's hand was warm and leathery. It was a long time since Laura's hand had been held by anyone except a child's soft curled paw.

Laura thought that Martin must be five or six years younger than her. When she was younger she had identified more years with more maturity. Like wine or cheese. Miles was mature.

Laura took her hand from Martin. He looked at her ironically but said nothing. He stopped.

'Here we are.'

'But it's just a door!'

'It used to be a well. A three-foot thick stone had to be removed. It slid out without affecting the others. Quite an engineering feat.'

'Can we go in?'

'Why not?'

Laura turned the handle.

'Mind the steps!' Martin shouted just in time. Laura rocked on the edge of three steep steps into blackness. Martin grabbed her arm. His fingers pinched but stopped her from falling.

'It's so very dark,' she said breathlessly.

A light filled the room with glaring brightness. Laura felt herself pale and cold. She looked around.

'What a large, plain, ugly room!' she said.

'Where you expecting a romantic hole?'

'Yes.'

'It has no windows.'

'That doesn't make it a hole. It has a desk and carpets and pictures.'

Laura felt furiously angry with him. It was clear that he had no sense of occasion. Flooding her with light in an ugly room.

Shaking his fingers off her arm Laura swung round and ran back down the corridor. Cinderella. The clock struck twelve.

She felt silly. Baffled. By herself as much as by him. Why hadn't he made some brutish lunge which she could have snapped off with a sophisticated quip? Why drag her down dark corridors if only to show her a dreary room? She had been enjoying the party. Why had he forced her away?

Laura raced back for the warmth and wine. Martin didn't follow.

*

Laura was giving Lizzie her full attention. The corners of her eyes were pinned to the front. She was sipping at her wine with pursed lips. She was standing very straight.

'And then,' said Lizzie, 'he took off his coat, shouted "Whoopee!" and went from the vertical to the horizontal in a perfect ninety degrees.'

Laura didn't laugh.

Johnny appeared. A train of chattering men and women spread round him.

'Hey, Laura, I thought you were with that scoundrel, Martin. And if it comes to that, where's Roy? If you don't watch Roy at a party, he'll sneak off and do something depressingly dull.'

'Martin is just coming in,' said Lizzie, 'with a girl on either arm.'

Laura stared ahead.

She felt remote and dignified. Phrases like 'Let the young things enjoy themselves' composed themselves in her head. She imagined the nape of Nicky's neck and his soft sleeping breath. She thought of Miles staying in some marbled hotel in Manchester.

'They're going to play,' cried Lizzie excitedly. 'Let the dancing commence.'

Laura, who had been longing to dance, heard her as if from a distance. She watched the dining-room empty and then saw Roy sitting on a chair in the corner. She went over to him. She hadn't had a chance for a real talk. She would ask him about the farm.

'You look so. . . .' she stopped. Roy was asleep.

The musicians were playing Strauss waltzes. Earlier in the evening this would have defeated the dancers. But now they jogged around uncaring.

Lizzie waltzed. Laura sat on a gilt chair, and watched critically. Lizzie was dancing with Martin. Not particularly well, though not particularly badly. Martin's feet, Laura noticed, were long and narrow, unusual in such a bullish sort of man.

Lizzie was laughing as she spun round. Her legs, in their tight jeans, criss-crossed with Martin's. John was dancing extravagantly with the golden-haired girl. He threw her from arm to arm. Oddly, he was a more graceful dancer than Martin.

Laura sipped her wine and half closed her eyes. She could hardly remember the excitement of the early evening. She felt comfortably old and perfectly glued to her chair. The relief of escape, she told herself. Flirtation had never suited her.

Roy came to sit by her. 'I was asleep.'

'I know. I resisted the temptation to wake you.' They sat in silence. Then Laura said abruptly. 'Why don't you marry?'

'Oh, Laura!' He looked reproachful.

'I was just thinking about marriage in general and wondering why some people resist the pressure.' Her voice faded away. She had actually been wondering why Martin was not married.

'It's difficult to explain. It's very important. I believe in marriage. I want children.'

Laura assumed an encouraging expression. Martin and Lizzie were now dancing close. Laura wondered if Lizzie was a virgin. With all their affection for each other, they had never discussed that.

'Now take Lizzie.' Roy paused again and laughed loudly. 'Actually, that's just what I'd like to do.'

Laura stared.

His voice rose passionately. 'I'd like a young innocent Lizzie to come to me and give me love and children and stop all the arguments buzzing in my head.' He frowned deeply. 'Of course it's only a dream.'

'Why?'

'Look at me.' Under Laura's gaze Roy took off his glasses and stuffed them into his top pocket. His eyes were large and dark but blinked weakly. The naked lack of self-regard was too painful. Laura looked away.

'Have you ever asked a young innocent?'

'Apart from my appearance, there's where I live. Nine-tenths of the year on a muddy farm in Ireland. And then there're my moods. I'm very moody. Very opinionated.'

'So you've never asked anyone?'

'How could I?'

Laura returned to watching Martin and Lizzie. They were dancing slower, their hips and thighs pressing together. Congratulating herself on the matronly numbness which feels no jealousy, she finally asked Roy. 'And what about Martin. Why isn't he married?'

'I expect lots of girls would like to marry him.'

'So why isn't he married?'

'Perhaps he's more interested in things that flash and go beep beep.'

Laura almost pointed to Lizzie in Martin's embrace but then realised Roy wouldn't be able to see without his glasses. He had never understood people. That was the real reason he hadn't married.

She stood up. 'I think I'll see if there's anything left to eat. I wasn't hungry earlier.' She left Roy. He looked happier. As if semi-blindness relieved him of one kind of pressure. He stuck his long legs onto the dance floor and folded his arms.

In the hallway, between main room and dining-room, Laura found the outside door open. Some guests were leaving. There was a pattering on the gravel driveway. It had started to rain again. Laura thought with nostalgia of the dazzling night sky of their arrival.

The dining-room was empty but the dishes still stood on the long table. Laura found a spoon and started ladling yellow stuff onto her plate.

'Would you like some cream with it?' The hostess appeared behind her.

Laura had a fleeting image of Lizzie's slim hips pressed against Martin's. 'Yes, please.'

'Go along to the kitchen then. I popped it back into the fridge.'

Laura walked slowly along a stone-flagged passage. Her mood dropped lower. Inside the kitchen a woman was fishing out a tea bag from a cup. She was wearing a long candlewick dressing-gown. She looked up and Laura, to her surprise, recognised Mrs Keane.

'I don't stay up late any more. The price is too high the next day.'

'I'm just getting some cream.' Laura opened the fridge door. 'Actually I don't want it any more. Nor this trifle.'

'I wish you would.'

'Why?'

'We'll get it for lunch tomorrow.' Mrs Keane gave her loud barking laugh and with a sense of disillusionment, Laura realised that was where Martin had got his unrestrained roar.

Laura decided she wanted to go home. She went back to the dancers and handed Roy her trifle. He ate it sleepily.

'Where are the others?'

'Aren't they dancing?'

'No.'

Roy put down the trifle and found his glasses. 'No, indeed.'

Their hostess appeared behind them. 'Some people are playing ping pong.' She was despairing.

'I'll get them.' Laura stood decisively.

'Through there,' pointed the hostess.

They were playing progressive ping pong. Dropping bats and running round. Glasses of wine perched precariously on the shelves behind them.

'We're going home,' said Laura like a schoolmistress. Martin put down his bat immediately. He came to her.

'Where have you been? I haven't seen you for hours.'

Laura didn't look at him. She wouldn't be taken in a second time.

He took her arm. 'We never even danced.'

'No.' She tried to take her arm away but since he held on firmly she merely turned her head with a cold expression. She found it impossible to behave normally close to him. She wouldn't even have noticed if someone else held her arm. This made her angrier.

'We must go!'

Out they went. Found their coats. Martin followed them to the door. He kissed Lizzie and then turned to Laura.

'Oh dear, it's raining,' she said, putting her face deliberately into the night.

'Allow me.' Martin whisked off his jacket and held it over her head. She walked on, he came with her. The others followed.

His body was very hot from playing table tennis. He was all round her. She sensed he wouldn't go unless she made a scene.

She walked briskly. He talked into her ear. 'I've never seen anyone as beautiful as you. I've never met anyone like you. All I want to do is hold you. All I want to do is kiss you.'

Laura felt herself spinning with the closeness and warmth of him. But she continued to walk as fast as she was able. This would all be forgotten. Even the way he was saying it was not serious. Intense but not serious. They would both forget in the morning. As long as she made no acknowledgment. His behaviour during the evening was inexplicable. She tried not to think of hers.

They reached the driveway where the car had eventually been parked.

'You're soaked,' said Laura in a high stilted voice. As if he had said nothing. She wondered what the others thought of his intimate Walter Raleigh. 'Thank you.'

He said nothing. But when she had got into the car, put on his coat unhurriedly. As they drove away Laura turned and saw him walking back down the driveway. The rain was falling all round him like silver darts.

Chapter Four

Katie had had a bad night.

Laura went into her bedroom and found her feeding the baby for the third time since midnight. She thought the bright sunlight might have cheered her up but, when she pulled the curtains, a lump under the bed clothes grunted and burrowed protestingly.

'Don't please! Poor Johnny's head is torturing him. I should have fed the baby in another room.'

'Of course you shouldn't.' Laura dug her brother in the back. 'It's entirely his own fault if he's got a headache. I'm taking your three and Nicky to church. If your ungodly husband tells me where the car keys are.'

'Overcoat pocket.'

It was a clean sunny windy day. Laura drove along the narrow country roads. She was resolved to live up to her image of herself.

She thought there was no better way to start Sunday than taking a car-load of children to church. Human beings need ritual. Nicky had protested but the girls had rushed happily to find their best coats. The Sunday joint, newspapers, Sunday walk or Saturday football all stemmed from the same need. Of course religion could answer a deeper need than a leg of lamb. But, on a superficial level, it could be compared to these modern holy cows and come up trumps.

Exhilarated by her mixed metaphors, Laura looked into the mirror and saw the row of four round childish faces.

'I spy with my little eye something beginning with . . . W-W.'

'Windscreen-wipers.'

'You saw where I was looking!'

The family was another ritual. She was glad she had a husband who felt about marriage as she did. An indissoluble bond. It was unusual these days. In her case she supposed it came from her Catholic background, in his from a deep need for order. Like a child's. Feeling herself becoming muddled, for Miles was very unlike a child, Laura began an habitual exer-

41

cise: counting her friends who had become divorced. Honestly she asked herself the usual question. 'Are they better off?' and honestly she answered: 'No, they are not!'

The sun was high. The grass on the banks waved gaily. The children had opened the windows; their hair blew behind them.

'Nearly there!' cried Laura.

She thought that form had an absurdly bad name at the moment. What was the Catholic saying? 'The outward sign of inward grace.' That's what she wanted her life to be. 'Outward sign.' Outward show, if that was right the rest would follow. We are not naturally spiritual beings. Concentrating on the inward self was as likely to lead to selfish introspection as higher spirituality. That's what had happened to so many of her friends. It was pride to think anything else. Who deserves a psychiatrist?

The church, built of heavy Victorian stone with a bell on the top, appeared on their right. Laura parked the car and sprang out. A sudden throb in her head reminded her of the night before. But she took a child's hand on either side and forgot again.

She was there, clean, smiling, good. As she walked up the aisle, she was conscious of the world's approbation.

A few high clouds had gathered by the time Laura and the children returned to the house. Laura had noticed them momentarily darken the stained-glass windows of the church.

They returned with palms. Laura was ashamed of herself for not realising it was Palm Sunday. Yet glad that she was there with her flock. She drove slowly as she approached the house.

'Hurry up! We want to play!' shouted the children. When she stopped they exploded out in all directions. She stood and watched them. Only the smallest child, Harriet, came back and held her skirt.

Johnny appeared at the doorway. 'You look virtuous!' He had not been to church since his schooldays.

Laura gave him a smug smile. 'I am. You look – better.'

Johnny had the several-layers-missing look of a man who has had a very long shower in the hopes it will wash away the excesses of the night before. His face was pale, his hair was plastered flat against his head, his movements were slightly shaky.

'Do you think we can sit out?'

42

'Why not? With overcoats.'

'What about the oldies?'

'What oldies?'

'Mrs Keane.'

Johnny began to carry out deck-chairs and put them on a patch of lawn beside the house.

Laura whisked up Harriet and carried her into the house. 'Time for a rest, darling.'

Then she went to the telephone to see if Miles was back from Manchester. He wasn't. The phone rang in an empty house. She went along to Katie's room. On the way she met Lizzie who was wearing purple sneakers.

'I thought we might have a game of tennis,' Lizzie said, seeing where Laura was looking.

Laura found Katie struggling into a crimson dress with a wide belt. The wide belt wouldn't do up.

'It looks pretty. As a smock.'

'I'm fed up looking pretty in smocks. I've looked pretty in smocks ever since we married. I want a waist!'

Laura didn't answer. She drifted out and wandered across to her own bedroom. The house was quiet but filled with restless sunlight. Outside she could hear the older children playing. She leaned out of the window and saw Johnny complete a neat circle of deck-chairs. The children burst out of the shrubberies and threw their coats into the deck-chairs. She thought it impressive that they had not flung them on the wet ground but Johnny shouted after them crossly.

A tall dark figure came striding down the driveway. It was Roy. He made for a deck-chair and took out a wedge of newspapers from a large inner pocket. He must have walked into town for them. Laura realised that for all her virtuousness she hadn't thought of saving someone a journey and bringing back the papers.

Her virtue had slipped away. She felt unsettled, dissatisfied with herself. Even her appearance no longer pleased her. The pleated skirt and jacket which had seemed so right, so gay and glowing, now seemed dull. She envied Lizzie's purple sneakers. She was irritated by the childrens' shouts. She felt like shouting at someone herself. She realised she had better go and put the joint in since Katie almost certainly had not. She thought critically of Katie.

Laura did not try and analyse her change of mood. She wouldn't think about Martin.

A car drew up in front of the house. Laura had just finished peeling the potatoes. She put them carefully round the joint. She listened to the voices. Johnny was leading them round to the deck-chairs.

'They're here!' Katie put her head round the door.

'Shall I get up Harriet?'

'No. No. Not yet.' Katie, looking horrified at the idea of waking a sleeping child, disappeared.

Laura dried her hands methodically. She could have just stayed there but that would be admitting defeat. She walked out with a stern brave face.

The grass was very green. Still spongey from all the rain. Johnny was standing in the middle of the deck-chair circle handing out drinks. Everybody else except Lizzie was sitting down. They were all there.

Roy stood up and Laura found herself sitting next to Johnny's young girl, who looked completely untouched by the night's festivities. Her golden was hair tied back and she was wearing cream jodpurs and a hacking jacket. She turned out to be called Bianca.

'My mother couldn't come,' she said in her cawing voice.

'What a wonderful evening!'

'And Helen Keane. And Martin.' Martin was hidden behind Bianca.

This gave Laura a mixed pang of disappointment and relief. She listened to the conversation about the night before but felt unable to talk herself. The sun was surprisingly hot, shining directly into her eyes. She felt a sense of languor, a temptation to shut her eyes. She thought she heard a buzzing as if it was high summer. When she did shut her eyes the world was filled with scarlet patterns like paisley on a black shawl.

'You're tired.'

Martin was leaning forward, talking to her across Bianca. His explanation of her mood did not suit her. She sat up crossly.

'It's the sun. I love sun. I like to give myself up to it.'

This came out sounding absurd. It was absurd. Martin wore an indulgently ironical expression.

Laura allowed herself to remember his words in the rain and darkness of last night. She thought his present expression might help to wipe them out. Taken with irony they were no threat. They were meaningless.

At that moment Nicky appeared. This was an added help. He came to her and tried to sip from her glass. Laura talked round the side of his head.

'This is Nicky. He would like to be grown-up.'

Martin appeared reasonably interested. Not as interested as Bianca who said she would love to have a son if only you could do it without being pregnant.

Katie frowned unhappily and Roy said gruffly, 'What about a husband?'

'Oh that!' Bianca made a face.

Everybody laughed. Except Roy. He looked affronted.

'You certainly need a man.' Martin gave a smile not unlike a leer. It was not directed at anyone in particular but Laura felt disgusted.

'What's wrong with a test-tube?' Everyone looked at her. She was surprised at herself.

Bianca cawed triumphantly. They had become the modern women against the rest. Roy and Katie were particularly irritated.

'I must go and look at the lamb,' Katie stood up.

'It's fine,' said Laura reassuringly. 'I put it in.'

'I'll go in anyway.'

There was a pause. The children shouted.

'I see the strike's ended,' said Johnny.

A discussion began about the strike that had ended and the strikes that were about to begin.

Nicky swung on his mother's arm. Sensing her agitation, he tried to provoke it out into the open.

Eventually, she cried out, 'Oh do go away, Nicky!'

He ran off with an air of self-righteous indignation. Laura sat back.

She was amazed that one man, one ordinary young man, could upset her so much. She remembered all the stories from her friends of love and desire. Sometimes sympathy had only just risen above disapproval.

It seemed impossible that sitting on her sister-in-law's lawn she was feeling the same uncontrollable emotion. Last night she had longed to throw dishes of food at the wall. Now she could barely resist hurling over the deck-chairs, so that their occupants sprawled on the grass. Then she would snatch up Martin and press him to her bosom. Or alternately slap his face. Such exaggeration gave her new determination. Of course she could control it. Face it out.

She stood up. She said to Martin and then to Bianca, also, because otherwise it seems odd, 'Come for a walk.'

'Not for too long!' Mrs Keane pulled at her tufted coat as if she was growing cold.

Laura led them through the garden and over a stile and into a large field. Despite all her good intentions, she was aware of a feeling that she was acting out of character. It seemed impossible to behave naturally now Martin was here. Her calm self had disappeared into this person she hardly recognised, tense, energetic, aggressive. She wondered that no one seemed to have noticed.

'Look at the primroses!' shouted Bianca. She began to run down the long sloping field.

Laura wondered if this was her way of attracting Martin. If so, it was not very successful. He hardly looked, remaining at Laura's side with a sober expression.

His hand slipped down her side and took hers.

Laura told herself this was what she had wanted. An opportunity for a simple rebuff. Unfortunately no sophisticated quip came to mind.

She snatched her hand away. 'Don't!'

'What?' He stopped and looked at her with a surprised expression.

Laura floundered, 'Don't hold my hand.' It sounded ridiculous.

'Oh. Sorry. I didn't know you were one of those people who despise manual contact. Shall I kiss you instead?'

Laura thought that if she could laugh all would be well. But her face refused to form the appropriate lines. There was no alternative but to continue her enactment of the shocked matron.

'Anyone could see us!' This was quite the wrong thing to say. Not at all what she meant.

Martin laughed heartily. 'I thought there was a much more serious reason. About your husband not liking it or something. If it's only a question of not being seen, we can head back to the rhododendrons and no one will see a thing.'

'Don't be silly.' He had now totally preempted any warning moral words about her married condition. He had made her look silly.

As if reading her thoughts, he mocked, 'I only want to hold your hand.'

'Please leave me alone.' Laura tried to flee, walking, almost running, down the hill. She felt tears in her eyes. Martin strode behind, humming. Bianca had reached the bottom of the hill, she was stooping down like a flamingo picking primroses.

Laura let Martin catch her up. 'I'm sorry. I over-reacted,' she said. Why did everything she said to him sound ridiculous?

'I forgive you. Where's your husband?'

'In Manchester.'

'For long?'

'Why?'

'I'd like to invite you to dinner.'

Laura saw her opportunity. 'I'm sure he'd love to come. He'll be back tonight or tomorrow.'

Whatever Martin meant he did not look discomposed. 'I'll telephone.'

They reached Bianca who offered Laura a posy of primroses.

'Manual contact with flowers?' Martin gave his loud guffaw.

*

Laura and Nicky took the 4.35 p.m. train back to London. It was very full and the afternoon sun slanted into the carriage making everyone hot and bad-tempered. Laura got a headache. Nicky fell asleep with his mouth open as if he had caught a cold.

They queued for half an hour to get a taxi across London. But when Laura saw the house her spirits rose. It had recently been painted white. The magnolia tree had opened in her absence and now spread across it, pale and pink. She looked forward to being at home again. In command. There would be letters and messages and work and Miles.

Miles opened the door. He had obviously been waiting for them. He looked pleased, even relieved, as if he had thought they might be delayed.

'Here we are!' said Laura, giving him a kiss. 'Go on, Nicky. Give Daddy a welcome home kiss.'

'We're the ones who've come home.' Nicky ran past them and up to his bedroom.

47

'When did you get back?' Miles brought in their cases and carried them upstairs. Laura followed behind him.

'Before lunch. I thought you might ring.'

'I did. But there was no answer. About twelve.'

'I got in about twelve.'

'We must have just missed each other.'

Miles dropped Laura's case on their bed. He had already unpacked his own. His clothes were stacked in neat piles, underclothes, shirts, sweaters, dirty clothes. Laura wondered that, having taken this much trouble, he could not have put them away in his drawers. But she knew it would be pointless to argue. All his actions were based on some sort of principle.

She suspected this one was to do with the duties of a wife. It would be ridiculous to be irritated. She also believed a wife had duties.

'It must have been a real holiday.'

'That wasn't the object in my going,' Laura began, and then relented. 'But it was a holiday. And the weather was so lovely. Mostly.' She remembered the rain as they left the party. 'We went to an opera.'

'How extraordinary!'

'Rather well done, actually. In a house.'

'Anyone interesting there?'

'Johnny brought Roy McNeil back from London. The house belongs to a Mrs Lindsay who hated the whole thing. She had a daughter called Bianca who was a model and a jockey. And there was a drunken producer.'

'It doesn't sound your sort of thing.'

'No.'

Laura could hardly believe she had not mentioned Martin's name or his mother's. He was going to telephone with his dinner invitation.

She opened her mouth.

'Mummy. Mummy! Someone's been fiddling with my model.'

Laura turned round. 'Where is Maria?'

'Maria?' Miles gave a special look of boredom which he reserved for mention of the current au pair.

She went across to Nicky who was making a fuss. 'Anyway it's time for bed,' she said, seeing that she could offer no consolation.

Nicky became more biddable once he was in pyjamas. More
ready to be kissed and cuddled. Laura looked forward to that
moment, trying to hasten it.

He sat in bed and they said prayers together.

'We shouldn't say prayers on Sunday.'

'It's the most important day.'

'But we've said them in church already.'

'Do you know who I love most in the whole world?'

'Me.'

'Don't sound so bored.'

'You've told me so often before.'

'Have I really?' Laura laughed. Nicky burrowed down into
bed.

Laura was reminded of her brother hiding from his hangover. Where was the man in Nicky? She tended to think of
boys and men as a different species.

Laura kissed her son good-night and went downstairs to
make supper for her husband. She thought now of pimentoes
and tomatoes and lamb chops. For several minutes she considered whether to mash the potatoes or serve them plain.

Laura and Miles sat in the kitchen eating their supper. They
each had a large glass of Rioja. They looked contented.

'So Katie realised which side her bread was buttered?'

'Don't be so vulgar!'

Miles was surprised at Laura's vehemence.

Laura sipped her wine. 'You're perfectly right of course. I
just didn't like hearing it said.'

'I expect you're tired.'

'I thought we agreed I'd had a holiday.'

'Sorry.'

It was unlike Miles to apologise, particularly when it was she
who was snapping. Laura realised how much he must have
missed her. She didn't know why it was such an effort to talk to
him civilly. Sitting there silently with her wine, she really had
felt perfectly content.

'Have some more?'

'No thank you. It was very nice.'

'Good.' A pause. 'Are you busy this week?'

'Going to Manchester set me back.'

Laura knew Miles liked talking about his work. When they'd
first met it had been one of the things that most attracted her.

English men did not as a rule take girls to expensive restaurants and talk exclusively about the short-comings of the jury system. She remembered on their first meeting going through every range of reaction, beginning with a sense of insult, moving through boredom and ending with admiration. She had despatched her current boyfriend that evening, saying firmly they had out-grown each other. Though what she had meant was that she had outgrown him. It struck her only then that her older married lover had never talked about his job at all.

Miles was a barrister. A QC. He had become a QC at thirty-five shortly after they married. Now he wanted to be a judge. No one but Laura knew how much he wanted it. If you tapped his brain, JUDGE would come out like treacle. A Judge in the Criminal Division. One of the forty at the top.

This difficult ambition naturally made him work very hard. But he also brought work home, more to stay close to his obsession than because he needed to do the work, Laura thought. Although she still encouraged him to tell her about it, she no longer took much pleasure in listening.

She could remember the evening when she had realised he was not talking about a particular case because it interested him – as an idea interested Roy, for example – but because it was a brick in the edifice topped off by a shoulder-length wig. He became impatient with her, too, if she showed any signs of not treating his remarks with absolute seriousness. It had taken her five years to suspect she was married to someone with no sense of humour.

When they were on their own, she accepted it and became passive, hearing him with deference, not even tempted to prick his balloon of importance. But when they were with friends, she was more sensitive, ashamed, whether on his behalf or hers, of his self-importance.

Oddly enough, she seldom did see a flicker of irritation. He was treated everywhere with as much deference as he could wish. Then Laura had realised the world likes important men.

Laura put down her empty glass of wine. Across the table Miles was still talking. He had a high brow, domed as if waiting for that wig. A good-looking man, Laura thought. And was pleased to be thinking it. Not handsome perhaps, but good-looking.

'More wine?'

She smiled. 'Thank you.' Better looking than Martin. Though totally unattractive.

Laura jerked herself upright, surprising Miles. He looked offended. 'I was telling you about adjudication.'

'I was listening.'

They were interrupted by a key rattling in the downstairs door.

'No wonder Maria can't make the keys work when she uses them like that.'

'Don't take it out on her.'

'What do you mean?' Miles stood up. 'She's wrecking that lock.' He stamped off to open the door.

Laura sighed. She felt tired. She felt as if she had never been to the country.

Maria was uglier than she remembered and slightly drunk. 'You have a good time, away, yes?'

Laura wondered whether she could do without an au pair. The trouble was that as long as she kept up any semblance of a working week she must have somebody to pick up Nicky from school and give him tea.

'Oweee!' Maria squealed. She had managed to trip on the bottom stair, proving that she was a lot more than a little drunk.

Laura said, 'Oh dear. Have you hurt yourself?' And thought that she would have to spend half an hour convincing Miles that she was responsible enough to take care of Nicky.

Miles had gone to work in his study. Maria had gone to bed, giggling. Laura cleared the kitchen. This gave her pleasure. She laid for breakfast. She put a chocolate biscuit in Nicky's cereal bowl and a vase of daffodils she'd brought from the country in the middle of the table.

She put more daffodils in vases and took them into the drawing-room. She could sense Miles next door working yet hoping she would come in. He loved her. His love was always there, unwavering, unrelenting. Laura went in. He turned from his desk.

'Off to bed?' He held out an arm. Laura went to it and kissed his cheek.

'I'll have a bath first.'

'Don't go to sleep before I come up. You've been away for a long time.'

This statement of intent aroused ambiguous feelings in

Laura. She was both pleased that she had the power still to attract her husband and irritated by the mixture of deference and certainty in his approach. The clumsiness deadened her own desire.

'I promise not to,' she said, smiling.

Laura lay in bed.

When she was first married, she'd lie in bed for an hour waiting expectantly for Miles' touch. Now she had to make a conscious effort not to fall asleep. Yet she loved him. And when he came to her, any earlier irritation disappeared and she turned to him eagerly.

Laura stroked her husband's cheek. She tested the bristles against her palm. She ran her hand over his shoulders down his back, to his buttocks. His skin was soft as if there was a little too much fat under the skin but not unpleasantly so. Miles was more impatient than her. He grabbed her breasts and her hips. Laura liked him to take the initiative. When he encouraged her to take over she felt her energy draining away. She wanted him enough to receive but not to take.

Miles stretched on top of Laura. She felt her body soft and centred like a flower. She was glad when he took her and cried out. Only for a fractional moment did another face pass in front of her closed eyes. There was no need for guilt.

*

Laura and Miles lay in each other's arms. Quiet, content. Laura was thinking of Nicky sleeping next door. Miles was thinking of Mr Amadeus Bagley who he was to defend the next day.

Chapter Five

It was Monday morning. Laura sat at her desk.

She had a small office in a large block of offices. In fact she preferred to work from home where everything was within her control. An office made her feel vulnerable. Almost single-handed she ran an organisation called 'The Association for the Preservation of Our Agricultural Heritage'. She never could make out how she'd got into such a thing. Desperate for some job with flexible working hours, she supposed. At the moment she was organising an appeal to save a tythe barn being turned into a block of flats. The previous week she had spent days composing a letter suitable for fifty prominent people. Now she had to photostat, address, stamp and post.

Laura sat at her desk considering whether to go out for lunch. The fifty letters were stacked up in front of her. The phone rang.

'Association for the Preservation of our Agricultural Heritage.'

'What a mouthful!'

'Who is it?'

'Martin Keane. We met over the weekend.'

'Sorry. I didn't recognise your voice.'

'Why should you?'

Why indeed? Laura had been behaving perfectly normally. So why had she been apologising?

A strong instinct told Laura to slam the phone down. But that would be idiotic and cowardly. Instead she said stiffly, 'Can I help you?'

'Not about our agricultural heritage, if that's what you mean.'

'I didn't mean. Necessarily.'

'You had an agricultural heritage sort of voice.'

Laura actually made the receiver hover over its base. When she returned it to her ear, Martin was saying, 'I rang, as I said I would, to ask you to dinner.'

'I thought you'd ring my home number.'

'So you remembered.'

Laura struggled to put nothing but friendly interest in her voice. 'I like going out to dinner.'

'Good. What about April 14th?'

This was over two weeks away. Laura did not want to sound disappointed. She said, 'Oh, I don't know.'

'That doesn't sound very enthusiastic.'

'I'll have to look at my diary,' she gulped. 'And ask Miles.'

'I'd better give you my number then.'

'Yes.' Laura felt her voice fading. Her heart was beating hard and her cheeks flushed. However she wrote down his telephone number.

'I'll hope to hear from you, then.'

'Yes.'

He put down the phone. Laura leaned back in her chair. Her heart slowed and her flush subsided.

She realised he had said nothing. Nothing. He had invited herself and her husband to a dinner party. She received invitations like that every week. His behaviour over the weekend had been meaningless. The first time he had been drunk. The second time he had been joking. Teasing her. Because she was not used to being treated in such a lèse majesté manner she had been disturbed and put too much importance on it. It meant nothing to him.

Laura went out to lunch. She wandered into a large department store where she often shopped and looked through some evening dresses. She took one off the rails and went into the changing-room. She took off her green jersey dress and dropped it onto the floor. She saw she was wearing a very old petticoat. If someone had asked her when dressed what underclothes she was wearing, she wouldn't have known what to answer. It was a long time since underclothes seemed important.

The changing-room was small and had mirrors on three sides. She couldn't avoid her reflection. The neon lighting gave her face a shadowy pallor.

She seldom worried about growing old. Now that struck her as odd. She looked and saw no grey hairs, few wrinkles and skin as bright and smooth as it had ever been. She had been braced to see a middle-aged face.

After her face she looked at her body and that was thinner than she expected. Her bosom was still big but her hips which she had always considered unfashionably wide seemed quite average and flesh seemed to have dropped from her shoulders and arms.

Laura put on the dress she had chosen from the rails. It was white chiffon printed with small scarlet carnations. The neck was scallopped and embroidered with scarlet thread. Her winter white skin and dark hair gleamed.

'Well, madam, you can't resist that.' An assistant arrived and made highly recommending noises. Laura felt vaguely affronted, her private communing disturbed, but had to admit the assistant was right. She couldn't resist it.

'I haven't even looked at its price.'

'Quite a pricey dress, I believe.' The assistant fished for the ticket at the back of Laura's neck, 'but then you must expect it with something so special.'

Laura who hadn't planned to buy a dress at all knew she would pay any price.

Laura walked back to the office. It was raining slightly, but she didn't notice.

Laura was not an introspective person. She had principles of behaviour which were little different from those she'd followed as a child. The anxieties and worries had been eased out of them over the years. Guilt, which had been one of her major preoccupations, hardly troubled her at all now. She was kind to herself, recognising she was not a very good person, certainly not as good as people thought her, but not very bad either.

This easy conscience gave her that air of calm which was so attractive. It also made her able to help other people without becoming too upset, too involved. She had sorted out Katie's problems because she believed in marriage. She had not allowed either of them to consider the psychological problem involved. She saw no point.

This made her strong. Not hard, because she was kind to people and cared about their suffering if not its cause. She had many friends who loved her, looked up to her and were sometimes envious. She knew that. It was one of the reasons why she felt no need for self analysis. She was doing all right without.

But now, walking along crowded London streets with her carrier bag banged against her legs by the passers-by, she tried to think of herself. The process reminded her of examining her conscience when she had been a better catholic and gone regularly to confession. It was not easy. Her concentration kept veering off herself and onto a shop window – or a bus advertisement or a passer-by. But she determined to persevere, telling herself that spending £180 on a dress must reflect a central disturbance. She never spent money like that on clothes.

How would she explain it to Miles? She didn't have to tell him, of course. They had separate bank accounts. He would see the dress but he would never imagine how much it cost, he would never ask her. He trusted her. He trusted her in everything. He had no reason not to. She hid nothing. She had nothing to hide.

Laura began to think about money. She knew this was

cheating, avoiding the issue of herself. But, after all, it was important. She earned two thousand pounds a year, Miles earned over thirty. These were the facts. They were rich. They could afford the occasional £180 dress. There was no reason for guilt. Miles, though strict about regular household expenses, loved her enough to forgive such a spur of the moment wildness.

Forgive? Why should he have to forgive? Because he earned £35,000 and she earned £2,000? Laura realised that she was being drawn into the kind of feminist way of thinking that she had heard so often from her friends but never applied to herself. She had always had everything she wanted so why should she worry or complain?

But forgiveness. She didn't want to be forgiven for something that wasn't a sin. She had a perfect right to spend her whole £2,000 pounds on one dress if she felt like it. She had a right to choose how to spend her money. And a duty to spend it wisely.

Duty. This was a whole other concept. She had noticed few of her friends ever talked about duties. They talked about rights, about freedom. Laura believed in duties. For one thing it made life a whole lot simpler. Her wifely duty was to look after her husband, their child and their home. His was to look after her. So where did that leave her in the matter of the £180 dress? Looking for his forgiveness. She wanted to stamp her foot like a child. The whole argument seemed circular. Pointless.

Laura noticed that she was wet. The rain was now falling steadily. What extraordinary weather it was. One minute brilliant sunshine and the next a monsoon. She stood under an awning and remembered Martin whispering in her ear under the umbrella. She didn't try to remember the exact words, the memory of his breath and his closeness was enough.

With a feeling both of dread and excitement she pictured herself as she looked in the new red and white dress. Her previous argument which had been leading round to the return of the dress was now completely forgotten. She hugged the carrier bag to her bosom.

*

Miles and Laura sat in their living-room. Miles put down his coffee cup and turned off the 10 o'clock television news.

'I don't know why I watch it. They're just parasites, feeding off the newspapers.'

'Surely the pictures add something.'

'Distract.'

'Even in court you have faces, witnesses, exhibits.'

'I wasn't referring to courts but since you've brought it up witnesses, exhibits, jurors, the whole fancy dress parade does more harm than good. Drama, that's all it is. It gets in the way of a true verdict. A true verdict would best be reached by a single judge in possession of the evidence. The written evidence.'

'You don't really believe that.' Laura was shocked.

'Yes, I do.'

'I can understand the judges. . . .'

'You mean because of self-interest,' Miles interrupted her sharply. 'The judge's role is entirely disinterested. He is put in the position of God.'

'Surely he brings his usual old prejudices. . . .' Laura's voice faded away. Miles's face had become rigid. He hated the idea of his wife arguing with him over the judge's role. The rationality or not of her points was irrelevant. Laura knew this. She understood, even sympathised. She admired him for caring so much about something.

'I think I'll have a bath.'

'But you can't just go when we're in the middle of an argument.' He said that, almost shouted it, but Laura knew it was best that she left. 'The trouble with the world now is that it's enslaved by the emotional nonsense of the communications industry. The quality of jurors has steadily fallen since television took over from the written word. They no longer think rationally, they simply emote. The most delicate of instruments, the human brain, is being turned into a reactor. Like an animal reacts to the smell of its enemy.'

'Or the smell of its mate!' Laura laughed. She had reached the door so the teasing was irresistible. She heard Miles's explosion of fury as she ran up the stairs.

As a matter of fact, she agreed with most of what Miles said. It was his bitter tone she disliked. As if the degeneracy of the human species was a personal attack on him. Perhaps her attitude was indication of an easy-going, superficial character. She couldn't care so personally about the state of the world.

Laura went into her bedroom more slowly. She collected her things for the bath. Her laughter would have made a division between Miles and herself.

She saw her new dress hanging in the wardrobe.

There were two things she had meant to bring up with Miles that evening. The £180 dress and the invitation to dinner on April 14th. Instead she had engineered a division. A reprieve.

Laura pulled out the dress from among her clothes and smiled at it. She went along to the bathroom and lay steaming in the hot water.

She would make it all right with Miles when he came to bed.

*

It was Good Friday. Laura and Nicky had just come back from The Station of the Cross. Laura got Nicky's tea. She took pleasure in it, buttering the bread smoothly and applying exactly the right layer of marmite.

'I want peanut butter,' said Nicky.

'You can have that afterwards.'

The telephone rang. It was Roy. He was speaking from Ireland. 'I thought you were coming to stay with me.' He was hurt, aggrieved, lonely.

Laura was horrified. 'But Roy, when did you ask us?'

'Surely you haven't forgotten?' Laura wondered whether she had forgotten or whether Roy had forgotten to ask. He lived such an intense cerebral life that sometimes he forgot to make the transition from thought to words.

'It was when we were sitting watching them dancing. On the opera evening. You said you could think of no better way to spend Easter.'

'Of course that's true.' A dreadful stirring of memory made Laura hesitate. How could she be sure of anything that evening? Out of the corner of her eye Laura saw Nicky scooping out half the jar of peanut butter. She grabbed his hand and cried into the receiver, 'Oh, how dreadful! I'm so sorry, Roy.'

'Let go, mummy!' shouted Nicky, shaking free.

'It's not your fault,' said Roy gloomily. 'You can't help forgetting. Other people have before. It's just I never thought you would.'

'Perhaps tomorrow. . . .' Laura faltered. They both knew it was impossible. After many apologies and promises to come soon she rang off.

'Can I have some ice cream?'

'It is fasting and abstinence.'

Laura thought very badly of herself. She hated the sensation.

Leaving Nicky to pig it in the kitchen, she rushed upstairs to write a loving letter to Roy. She found a sad photograph of herself to include in the envelope. She went out immediately to post it. After that she felt much better.

Nicky was watching television. Laura went and sat beside him. She took his hand. Sometimes he wouldn't let her but today he leaned against her comfortably. The programme didn't interest her much.

She had never gained the habit of television. There was something about the features of its image that failed to excite her.

Nicky was watching a film about snakes. He had his thumb in his mouth.

Although it was Good Friday, Miles had gone to his office. But over the Easter weekend he would stay with them and make a family. They would join with other families and search for chocolate eggs. Nicky would eat too many and be sick.

It was not hard to be happy, Laura thought, as a female bootlace snake was mated by a hundred lesser males.

*

Laura usually sat in the same place in her sitting-room. It gave her the best view of the window and was furthest from the television and telephone. For some reason after supper on Tuesday evening she was sitting in a corner of the sofa nearest the telephone. Miles was sitting at the other end reading the *Sunday Times*. He was methodical about things like newspapers. If he had not finished a paper one day he returned to it the next or the next. There was a neat pile of unread papers at his feet. Laura held a colour supplement on her lap. But she was thinking of her new agricultural heritage project, a summer meeting at one of the best preserved fifteenth century farm complexes.

The telephone rang. The telephone didn't often ring after nine o'clock. There was a rustle of disapproval from Miles. Laura picked up the receiver.

'Hello.'

'Could I speak to Mrs Knight please?'

The formality mislead her. 'Yes. Speaking.'

'Martin Keane here. I was hoping to hear from you.'

'Oh. Oh, yes. About the dinner.' Such was Laura's confusion

that she picked up the magazine, trying instinctively to hide her face.

Miles who would have noticed nothing was attracted by this odd behaviour.

'Who is it?'

The name Martin Keane would mean nothing to Miles. Laura had never found the right moment to mention with appropriate casualness his invitation to dinner. Now she was trapped. She wanted to faint, scream or run out of the room. She also was just enough in control to know that all these actions were quite unnecessary. Miles trusted her completely. He could have no idea what she was feeling. If she sounded odd he would put it down to anything but such mad stifling emotion.

Nor would Martin guess. He was merely asking her and her husband to dinner. He was surprised that she had not rung back. She lowered the magazine and, instead of answering Miles, half turned her back on him.

'I'm terribly sorry. It seemed so far away. And with Easter coming in between.'

'You mean you forgot.' He sounded surprised but not too unbelieving. Laura began to calm a little.

'Well?'

'Who is it?' repeated Miles, not cross but keen for the facts.

'Hold on,' said Laura. 'Miles is here beside me. I'll ask him now.'

Laura turned back to face her husband. In order to explain her agitated expression, for she was still finding it difficult to breathe, she said, 'Oh dear! Isn't that dreadful! That friend of Johnny's I met over the weekend invited us to dinner. April 14th.'

'Who is he?' enquired Miles, not without interest. He enjoyed going out to dinner.

'Martin Keane. He's in computer programming.'

'God! Married?'

'I don't think so.'

'Who will cook the dinner then? I'm not going to a bachelor flat to sit on the floor and eat spaghetti.'

'He's hanging on. I can't keep him hanging on.'

'It seems you've kept him hanging on for days.'

'But I hardly know him!' cried Laura. This was certainly

true. At this point Laura felt like saying 'No' very firmly into the receiver. No to everything. 'I'm sorry,' she said, 'Miles can't find his diary and he thinks there may be a Bar dinner that evening.'

'I have to know ahead because I'm holding it at the Garrick, and the ancient waiters need to know numbers ten days in advance or they fall down in a dead faint.'

'Is it your birthday?' said Laura for reasons she couldn't fathom. Miles was mouthing furiously.

'Certainly not. It's pure pleasure.'

'Hold on. I think Miles has found his diary.' Laura put her hand over the receiver. 'It's at his club,' she said to Miles. 'The Garrick.'

Miles was himself a member of the Garrick. 'Funny sort of computer programmer.'

'We'd love to come,' said Laura into the receiver with more relief than excitement. Her hands had only just stopped shaking.

'Seven thirty for eight and if you're even a second late the waitresses will pour a crock of potàge nourissante over your head.'

*

Laura sat at her dressing-table. She was wearing her red and white dress. She put on a crystal necklace and crystal earrings and then turned for Nicky's admiration.

He lounged on the bed avoiding Maria's efforts to put him into his bed. Laura found his presence calming. He reminded her constantly she was a good mother. Why shouldn't she be a good mother and a beautiful woman? An admired woman?

Miles came into the room. He was already dressed.

'Nicky still up?'

'I'm sorry. It's my fault.' Laura stood.

Miles looked at her astonished. 'You look splendid! Nicky, look what a beautiful mother you have!'

Laura took the compliment for the dress instead of herself. 'Oh, I'm glad you like it. It's new.' She had long quietened her conscience over the price of the dress and now enjoyed his admiration without any guilt. 'I hope it's not too smart for the Garrick.'

'I shouldn't think so.' Miles turned away. His interest in her appearance had already passed. Generally he liked appear-

61

ances for what they represented rather than what they were. Laura thought she must look truly beautiful for him to comment.

They travelled to the club in a taxi. Miles disliked driving. Usually Laura offered but tonight she didn't feel like it.

'He must have money,' said Miles reflectively. 'This Martin Keane. Our host. You can't give dinners in the Garrick if you haven't got money.'

Laura looked out of the window, at the passing traffic. She wanted to remain in the cocoon of her own self-satisfaction.

'I don't know. I suppose so.'

'What sort of age is he?'

'Younger than you. Younger than me too.'

'Must have private money, then. Can't have made that sort of money at his age. Though they say quite unlikely people are making fortunes out of the computer explosion. Could be very successful, I suppose. And, of course, a dinner like this could be set off against expenses. Impresses business connections, a dinner at a club like the Garrick.'

'I hope not,' said Laura suddenly.

'What?'

'That there're not too many business people or whatever you called them.'

'You mustn't be prejudiced. Business connections can be useful in all walks of life. I wouldn't mind making a few links there myself.' Miles resumed his reflective tone of speech, and Laura returned to the window trying hard not to listen.

'I wonder who will be there. You say he's a friend of Johnny's. Perhaps Johnny will be there.'

This possibility hadn't occurred to Laura. In fact she hadn't considered the matter of other guests at all. She had simply pictured her meeting with Martin. Now it occurred to her that she would have to make conversation with other people just as she did at any dinner party. She might not even be sitting next to Martin.

'The interesting thing to consider is why we've been invited. You scarcely know the man and I've never even met him. There must be some reason for it.'

Laura's heart beat uncomfortably hard. She knew the reason for the invitation. However she said in a bright if slightly breathless tone, 'He's just a sociable sort of person, I think. And a great friend of Johnny and Roy. It's quite natural, really.'

'A great friend, you say. University days, do you think?'

'Oh, I don't know!' Laura allowed herself to sound cross. 'What is this, an interrogation by the prosecution? I hardly know the man, I told you.'

Laura knew she sounded emotional. Miles' methodical investigation of everything surrounding Martin was too sharp. She wondered if some instinct had made him probe. But he always liked to analyse. It was the lawyer speaking. Normally she didn't notice or didn't care.

'I'm sorry.' Miles smiled and squeezed Laura's hand. To Laura's distress she found herself pulling away her hand. Quickly she put it back. Turning against Miles was no part of her self-image.

'I'm sorry too. It's because I'm nervous. I'm always nervous before big dinners when I don't know the people very well.'

'No one who looks like you should be nervous.' Miles squeezed her hand again and this time Laura turned right round to face him and then gave him a warm smile.

She saw its effect on Miles. Admiration, love and then desire. She even felt a response in her own body. She enjoyed the power of being beautiful.

'He probably fell for you. That's why we're invited,' Miles said suddenly. And laughed.

Chapter Six

Laura sits on Martin's left. Across the large table she can see her husband and her brother.

She is in a state of exhilaration. She feels no need to talk or for him to talk to her. No need to test the power of her physical reaction to him. The moment she saw him, she knew he felt exactly as she did.

Martin is concerned with seeing that the wine and food flow at the proper rate and that the distinguished older woman on his right is amused. Occasionally he turns to Laura. He makes ordinary remarks about ordinary things, but at those moments Laura feels faint, as she did that evening when he telephoned.

Laura cannot eat. She does not even try, taking a small portion and pushing it round her plate.

'You're not eating,' Martin notices when they reach the second course. 'Are you ill? Are you slimming? Or do you just hate duck?'

'Everybody else is eating,' says Laura, 'so it can't be the duck's fault. Don't worry about me. I'm drinking.' She lifts her glass.

'I agree that's better than nothing. But think of ageing waitresses' pride. Not to speak of the ageing kitchen staff.'

Laura lifts a fork of potato to her mouth. She doesn't want to make an issue of it.

Martin is diverted again.

The man on Laura's left says, 'I believe we've met before.'

Laura tries to focus. She puts the fork of potato down. 'No. I'd say not.' Laura sees he is large with a red complacent face. She doesn't want his admiration.

'How do you know our host?'

'Through my brother, John Bowles.'

'Oh, so you're Johnny's sister! Well, that explains it!' He rocks on his chair with satisfaction.

'What do you mean?'

'You look just like him. In a feminine sort of way, of course. Ha! Ha!'

Can this idiotic man really be one of Martin's friends? Laura's contentment is shaken. 'What do you do?' she asks.

He is taken aback. 'That's a direct question.'

'Why not?' Laura looks at him boldly.

He capitulates as she knew he would. 'I suppose you'd call me a business man.'

'A business man,' Laura gives him an approving smile. He is one of the business connections Miles had imagined. Not a true friend. 'So you're not proud of your profession?'

'Who said that?'

'You wanted to keep it hidden.'

The man decides she's flirting with him. 'I'll talk about anything. Just turn the programme and press the button.'

Laura finds she can carry on this level of conversation without losing her awareness of Martin. When he glances at her, she feels it like a touch. Carrying on the silly flirtatious conversation with someone she dislikes on one side and reacting to Martin's presence on the other, Laura loses track of what is happening over the rest of the table.

She has no idea what stage the meal has reached. Whether they sit there hours or minutes.

Suddenly there is a coffee cup in front of her and she realises that this evening which had caused so much anticipatory dread and excitement is nearly over. Martin has said nothing to her. The certainty she had felt at the beginning of the dinner, that he shared her emotions, begins to drain away.

Laura stops talking to her uncouth neighbour and falls silent. Her exhilaration oozes out of her like air from a balloon. She feels her beauty go with it.

'You were getting on very well with Tim.'

'Oh, him.' Laura is too sad to hide her feelings.

Martin laughs. 'Didn't you like him? He obviously more than liked you.'

'He's boring. Sorry. I suppose he's a friend of yours.'

'For years and years. Since we were children. I had a very conventional background.' Laura records this contradiction of her theory of the business connection, but doesn't care any more. For as Martin bends towards her, saying nothing important, but bending close, she feels the glow of happiness and beauty return like a puff of warm air. She keeps her head down a little so he shan't see. She half expects him to whisper in her ear as he did under the umbrella but he only says, 'I even tried to be an insurance broker for a while.'

She replies, not knowing what, and is surprised as Martin leans away from her. She makes an effort not to sway towards him.

'Would you say our waitresses are feeling their legs?'

This makes no sense to Laura until he pushes back his chair. Then she realises with horror that he is signalling the end of dinner.

'That's one good thing about these dinners,' says Martin generally, 'you don't get hangers-on.'

The distinguished lady on his right nods happily. Is she thinking of a good night's sleep before her distinguished work first thing in the morning?

Through her despair, Laura finds a relatively appropriate comment, 'Don't you like giving dinner parties?'

'I never can decide. If I give enough I might find out. Perhaps it's because I'm not married.' He pauses. He stares at Laura who is trying to narrow her eyes from the wide and forlorn. 'If I was married to you I'd never want to see anyone else. And I certainly wouldn't let you see anyone else. Your husband is a brave man.'

Although Martin's tone is light, Laura knows at once he is saying exactly what he means. Once again she is blown up with happiness.

Miles is standing. He has come round to talk to Johnny. Johnny has a cigar in his mouth and his arm round the girl, Bianca. Miles is smiling as if he's had a productive evening. She wants to ask Martin who he chose for Miles's neighbours but doesn't like the idea of even to that extent discussing her husband.

Deciding this one second, she finds herself saying the next, 'Miles is a remarkable man!' But that is more of a statement and expects no discussion.

'I'm sure he must be to have married you.'

Laura is annoyed with herself. While his remarks before had been spoken truly, this was the sort of platitude made to any pretty woman.

Nor could they say more, for people began to approach with

thanks and goodbyes. Laura sees Miles shaking his head at Johnny and looking towards her. He wears a husbandly expression, which means, we've had a good time but let's go now, at once, immediately.

Laura returns it docilely with a little nod. It is a marital code being repeated all over the room. Security, the pull of the lungeing rein.

'Darling sister. If I had you would I ever wander!' Laura feels herself surrounded by cigar smoke. Her arm is taken and her hand carried to someone's lips. 'Is incest the crime dry old legal sticks like your husband make it?'

'Johnny, you're drunk!'

'Of course I am! It would be an insult to our host's wine to be anything else! You are coming dancing, I presume?'

Laura and Miles never went dancing. It would never occur to either of them. Laura vaguely felt it was something Nicky would enjoy in a few years. But now she looks at her brother with a surge of envy.

'Where are you going?'

'Whichever club will have me. Are you coming then?' Laura sees he doesn't really want her. She represents the settled marrieds, good behaviour. Her presence would make him feel old. And guilty about Katie, left behind in the country.

'Of course I'm not. Miles would hate it.'

'More's the pity! More's the pity!' He moves away in what she can't help seeing as relief.

Laura is overwhelmed by restlessness and dissatisfaction. When Miles takes her arm, she shakes him off. She pretends to be picking up her handbag from the table.

'It's time we were off.'

'I suppose there's time to say thank you to our host.'

Miles looks with surprise at her cross face.

'Didn't you have a good time? You looked as if you were having a good time.'

'That's why I don't want to go. Why are we always so boring? Always thinking about how we'll feel in the morning. Johnny's going dancing!'

These remarks are so obviously the result of bad temper rather than logical thought that Miles doesn't bother to argue.

'I'm sorry you had a bad time,' he says trying to take her hand.

'I didn't! I've just told you!' At this childish display Miles becomes cold. He decides Laura has drunk too much. Very occasionally she does. He allows himself a mild quip, 'Sometimes you have exactly the same expression as your brother.'

'And why not? At least he's alive!'

Again Miles doesn't argue. Johnny's weaknesses are so obvious that they are not worth pointing out. Miles has had a good evening impressing the publisher of a magazine and does not want to be seen sniping with his wife.

He approaches Martin. 'Thank you for a most enjoyable evening.'

'Johnny hasn't persuaded you to go dancing then?'

'Unfortunately. I'm in court tomorrow.'

'What about your wife?'

Laura comes up in time to hear this. She has had a second or two to calm herself and feel ashamed of her rudeness to Miles. But when she hears Martin asking Miles to let her go dancing, for that is how it seems to her, her agitation returns. She decides that if Miles, like a Victorian father, says 'No, she will not!' then she will defy him, crying out, 'Oh, yes I will! I still have my free will. I didn't give that up when I married you. I choose to go!'

All this runs through her mind while Miles pauses and Martin waits politely. Then Miles smiles, 'You'll have to ask her yourself.'

Laura sighs. She feels a mixture of relief and disappointment. She won't go dancing. She thinks of getting up early to get Nicky off to school and a meeting she has with an under secretary from the Ministry of Agriculture at 10 o'clock.

Now she is safe, she looks at Martin directly. 'I'd spoil Johnny's fun,' she says, with partial honesty. 'Big sisters are a dreadful dampner.'

'You're not Johnny's big sister!'

'Yes,' For some reason Laura wishes to clear this up. 'Three years older. I expect that makes me older than you.'

'Hardly the same generation.'

'We must be off,' says Miles.

Again Laura's mood changes. She can't go quite yet. Can't manage to separate herself from Martin. Although she says nothing nor even looks at him, he must sense something for he leans forward suddenly and kisses her.

It is a mere peck. A perfectly conventional peck on the cheek but for Laura it says enough.

Miles and Laura leave the club. They pick up a taxi quite easily because it really isn't very late and Laura listens as Miles tells her about the magazine publisher. 'Until I am a judge,' he says, 'it would do me no harm to write the odd legal feature. Under a pseudonym, of course.'

When they get home, they make love. Laura, virtuous in her renunciation of the dancing, feels only slightly guilty in picturing Martin.

*

Over the next few days Laura made a sustained effort to analyse her attitude to Martin.

She admitted that she had conceived for this man, whom she hardly knew, lustful passion. She liked the biblical sound. She would not call it love. This was the case. The question was, what should she do about it?

That it was on a totally different plane of importance to her marriage hardly needed to be expressed. At this point she remembered all the excellent advice she had given her love-sick friends and applied it to herself. However, she told herself, it was hardly necessary, she would never do anything to endanger her marriage.

Both on moral grounds and pragmatic. Pragmatically speaking then, would it not be best to cut herself off entirely from the dangers of Martin by never seeing him again? This might be a little difficult, a little awkward since Miles had obviously decided he was a good thing. (Was that Martin's plan?) But not impossible. They were all busy people. There were many possibilities for excuse.

It took several days for Laura to force herself to face this line of action. It was the thing she least desired. The idea of it made her feel sick with misery. As it was, the unaccustomed process of self-analysis had taken the joy and satisfaction out of her days. Even Nicky asked her why she drooped around all the time.

For three days Laura stuck with the inevitable decision that she must cut Martin out of her life. Then she went to stay for the weekend with a friend. This friend lived in a tiny cottage in the middle of Dartmoor. She had been divorced two years ago and, since both her sons were at boarding school, she was alone much of the time.

She did have lovers but none of them was allowed to stay with her for long. She had determined to find out what she was on her own. She had married when she was nineteen. She was trying to be a potter.

Miles made fun of her. He said she was playing games, supported by her husband's alimony. But Laura suspected he thought her friend, whose name was Nell, a bad influence. In his terms, he was probably right. But they had been friends together for so long now that she must have gained some immunity.

Besides she didn't believe you had to share principles to be friends. It was important not to become narrow and dogmatic as Miles sometimes seemed to her.

The weekend she went to visit was sunny again. Nicky was staying with a friend and Miles had a meeting on Saturday morning, a game of golf Saturday afternoon, and she would be back after lunch on Sunday. One night with Nell twice a year or so was a tacit agreement between them.

*

The moment Laura sees Nell squatting outside her cottage examining a row of her pottery mugs, she longs to tell her all about Martin. Nell is wearing her usual tart's uniform, black shiny trousers and skin-tight T-shirt, which she has affected since her divorce. Laura assumes it is an affectation because she can't reconcile it with the pudgy self-effacing schoolgirl and adolescent she had known so well.

She is aware that to many people it reflects Nell's true character. Perhaps even to Nell herself who enjoys boasting about her love-affairs.

'They've all cracked,' she cries as soon as Laura steps out of her car. 'Some place right along the line. Bloody hell, I need a drink.'

Nell has also started swearing since her divorce. This upsets Laura more than her dress or her morals. She supposes it is a reflex of her convent education. She is even slightly ashamed of it and tries to hide the inevitable rigidity that comes over her face.

The two women kiss. Nell has a mass of henna-red hair. She has small round dark eyes and a snubbed nose. She wears no make-up. Her face hardly looks different from her schoolgirl self. During her marriage, she had appeared sophisticated for a

71

while, even matronly. Now she seldom brushes her hair and doesn't shave her legs. Laura tolerates this, like the tight trousers, as a kind of pantomime.

'Oh, it's so lovely to be here again! So free!' Laura sighs, throws off her coat and takes a beaker of red wine from Nell.

'I'm always telling you,' says Nell leading them outside again, 'that you lead the most imprisoned existence of anyone I know.'

This is true but usually Laura hardly notices or if she does think vaguely it shows Nell's jealousy of her happy marriage. She has never really believed in her protestations about freedom. But now she finds herself taking in the idea of her life as an imprisonment and considering it. In case Nell guesses she says, 'Miles' work means we have to live in London.'

'I didn't mean just London,' says Nell. But she doesn't press it further. She lies back on the grass and stares at the sky. Laura would like to do the same but she is wearing a pale-coloured blouse and the grass is damp.

'Extraordinary how important responsibilities seem till you chuck them,' says Nell to the sky.

Laura thinks this is the kind of remark that infuriates Miles. It is a silly thing to say. 'I chose my responsibilities,' she says. 'I like having Nicky at home. I don't want to send him to boarding school.'

'Nasty, nasty.' Nell sits up and looks at her row of mugs. 'Actually, despite my brave words I'm very depressed. First, I've got varicose veins. Can you imagine? At thirty-five, varicose veins. Second, Lyndon, you remember Lyndon, he's my young lover who owns a caravan site, has left me for another. Third, worst of everything, my cups have cracks!'

'Are you sure your legs haven't got cracks and your cups varicose veins?' Laura laughs at Nell's miserable expression. She decides to lie back on the grass after all. Now their conversation has fallen into the usual pattern. Nell, despite leading her life entirely for her own convenience (as Miles sees it), always has a dozen fascinating problems both mental and physical which she likes to unburden on her friends. Laura doesn't flatter herself that she is Nell's only confidante, despite their long-lasting friendship, and knows that Nell very seldom takes her advice. This allows her not to be deeply upset by what, in Nell's telling, seem the most soul-destroying events.

'When did Lyndon go?' she asks quite gaily.

'Ten o'clock.'

'What do you mean? This morning?'

'Yes.'

'Then he'll be back again.'

'That's not the point. He insulted me. He told me about this girl he's employing whose boobs won't fit in a caravan kitchen.'

Laura wonders for the first time what level of affection Nell feels for Lyndon or indeed any of her other lovers. Do her legs tremble and her face grow hot when she sees one?

'Do you love Lyndon?' she blurts out, interrupting Nell in mid-flow.

Nell looks delighted at considering such a fascinating question.

'My love for Lyndon is purely physical. It started as an experiment. I'd never had a purely physical lover before.'

'Does he . . . does he . . . ?' Laura struggles to describe her reaction to Martin without giving herself away. 'Does he make you feel very self-aware?' This sounds feeble even to Laura. She adds. 'Of your body, that is.'

Nell doesn't pay much attention. 'The experiment is totally successful from my point of view but unfortunately he feels the need to bring in this other girl. For puerile reasons of jealousy.'

Laura stops listening to wonder whether she could seriously discuss Martin with Nell. She realises now that it is entirely for that reason that she has arranged the weekend. She had thought it would be perfectly easy to slip some reference into the conversation. Then later, perhaps in the evening over slightly too much wine, she could return to the reference, elaborate and question.

But now that she is face to face with Nell and her romances she realises what a gulf has grown between them. She was used to thinking about Nell in a patronising term. She saw herself as the strong successful secure woman, Nell as the brave but misguided loser. If she is to reveal her present confusion, she will sacrifice this position and lower herself to Nell's level.

Yet she can't believe her feeling for Martin is on a level with Nell's for Lyndon. Pride. Is that what she had to lose? Or self-respect?

'I'm starving,' says Nell. 'I've made a huge stew. I thought we could eat it at every meal. It improves with re-heating.'

Laura laughs. It was on this level that she envied the freedom of Nell's life.

*

It is late. Laura and Nell are sharing a bedroom just as they did twenty years ago at boarding school. Nell is sitting cross-legged on top of the bed. She is wearing a long striped T-shirt and a pair of out-sized glasses. The glasses are new and under the thin cotton her breasts droop lower than before. Laura stands in the tiny bathroom putting cream on her face and neck. She is wearing a white nightgown. She calls.

'I've always meant to ask you. What was it like the first time you were unfaithful to Joe?'

Nell puts down the pamphlets on Our Agricultural Heritage, in a way that suggests she will not pick them up again.

'It wasn't a sudden dive into vice. The strange thing was that I stayed faithful to Joe for so long. I suppose that was babies. I was pregnant when I married him and then I had Seth two years later and then I wasn't very well. I had that miscarriage. In fact it was only after four or five years of marriage that I began to feel any sort of lust for Joe or anyone else. And he encouraged me to have friends, men friends. Not exactly lovers, but very nearly. It took me years to realise that he'd been having it away all along. Once I realised that it would have been quite ridiculous for me to say no. It wasn't as if I had any religious scruples like you. I used to go out and have good lunches with some bright young man, or not so young, slightly drunk, more than slightly on occasions, and then we'd sort of end in bed. It really wasn't very serious. But very nice. It made me much better tempered with the children and Joe. I don't know about the first time. I'm not even sure I can remember who it was. They're a group, in my mind, five or six or seven. Really it was a good time.'

'Then why did you get divorced?'

'All those lies. Hypocrisy. I hated it in the end. After a couple of years. One evening I walked into a party and there were four men who'd been my lovers. One of them had only left my bed a few hours before. And I walked in on the arm of my husband and talked to them as if they were nothing more than friends. They were no more than friends. And I knew it must have been the same for him. Suddenly I felt quite revolted. Perhaps that's too strong. I felt silly, part of a silly meaningless game. And I didn't feel excited any more. I just felt very very depressed. Not ashamed. Just sad. Depressed. That's when I determined to divorce. When I told Joe he was quite understanding. He knew about my lovers by then, of course. Not who they were, but that they existed. He said he didn't mind much about a divorce either way. There was someone he might marry, he said. That was pretty depressing too, his lack of passion, though it convinced me I was doing the right thing. It didn't last, of course. You know about the rest. All the battles and hysteria. Over the children. And money. At least it showed we still loved the children. And money. Though he was quite generous in the end. Anyway, I suppose what I'm trying to say in answer to your question, life isn't like that, big yes or no. You just slide. In marriage you slide. First time I was unfaithful? Who knows? Who cares?'

As Nell stops talking Laura walks through from the bathroom. She is trying to see how Nell's life relates to hers. But she can find no point of contact. She sits down on her bed.

'Do you mean, you never felt guilty? Surely when you first married you wanted to stay faithful to Joe. Whatever you say now about being pregnant, I remember you had all kinds of ideals about marriage.'

Nell turns her back on Laura. 'I expect so. I was filled with silly romantic ideas.'

Laura sees that she will not get any relevant discussion about her own situation unless she is more open. 'But there must have been a moment when you were aware of temptation and knew that you must either consciously resist it or else risk the gradual slide, as you called it, into sin.'

The word slips unplanned from Laura's mouth. Sin. She is surprised at herself. None of her friends, not even her Catholic friends, uses that word these days. Except, perhaps, to their children. And not much to them. It makes her realise even more clearly that her love, her lust, for Martin is a good old-fashioned sin. A mortal sin, a purely wrong, self-destructive act. In terms of 1980s morality, it might be nothing, it might be just what Nell described it, but for her it would be a sin. She remembers childhood catechism lessons. 'Avoid the occasion of sin.' Agreeing to the occasion of sin was as bad as the sin itself. She must not see Martin again.

Meanwhile Nell is not reacting to the idea of sin with the surprise and horror she'd expected. Instead she is silent. Eventually she murmurs, 'Sometimes I wish I did believe in all the paraphernelia of Catholicism. It'd make life so much easier. You're lucky, you know.'

'No, I'm not.' Laura stands up. 'I mean I'm a very bad Catholic. With a very easy conscience. I've used birth control for years and I haven't been to confession since I married. I only go to church on Sundays because I like it. I don't always go anyway.'

'But you seem Catholic,' insists Nell. 'You don't believe in the moral free-for-all like everyone else.'

'I don't know what I believe in.' Laura feels genuinely confused. 'All I know is at the moment I'm suffering from a terrible temptation to go to bed with a rather ordinary not very good-looking young man.'

So it had popped out finally. This terrifying bombshell Laura had been carrying round with such trepidation. Now it was out in the open, it was transformed into a tiny firework.

'Oh, are you!' Nell laughs. She seems relieved that the conversation, as she thinks, has become less serious. 'Anyone I know?'

'Honestly. It's important,' protests Laura. 'I shake whenever I see him.'

'It's good to know you're human, at least.'

'Of course I am.'

'Aren't you going to tell me who it is?'

'Certainly not. You're much too much of a gossip. Do you remember the nuns telling us about avoiding the occasion of sin? That's what I'm doing. Making sure I don't see him any more.'

'Oh, really. Laura. You are a baby. If you start avoiding every attractive male you might as well become a nun or at least go into purdah.'

Laura knows it is not a case of every attractive man but is made to feel ridiculous. She laughs. 'Still, the nuns did have something. I mean if this man asked me to go to lunch and I accepted, it would be as good as saying I wanted to go to bed with him. Wouldn't it?'

'You are impossible! What do you think Women's Movements have been fighting for? A woman can do anything with a

76

man, do a striptease if she wants, but that doesn't mean she has to make love to him.'

Laura feels the argument slipping from her grasp. It isn't that she would feel a duty to go to bed with Martin but that that is what would inevitably happen. On the other hand, the whole idea seems much less threatening now that it is in the open.

'Anyway,' adds Nell, 'I don't think much of anyone's moral principles if they crack up under the odd lunch with a sexy man. Surely you meet some sexy gentlemen in Our Agricultural Heritage. Tall, healthy men of the soil, uncorrupted by city ways.'

Laura sees that the conversation is again hindered by her unwillingness to state the whole truth. Of course she had often met attractive men over the ten years of marriage, she had felt their surge of emotion and reacted at least partially before suppressing it. But never before had she felt as she does about Martin. With a breathless sense of terror she realises that what she feels for him is not lust. It is more like the total love she feels for her son.

With this realisation comes an immediate instinct to change the subject. What does Nell know about love?

'I'm exhausted,' she says, trying to yawn. 'Talking about my irresistible man has made him seem perfectly resistible. How could I be serious about a man who says "super" and wears lace-up shoes?'

Nell laughs. 'I never thought you were serious,' she says and Laura sees that is true. In Nell's eyes she is some sort of plaster madonna. 'Let's sleep now. I'm planning a four-hour walk for the morning.'

*

Laura drives slowly back to London. She is physically tired after all the moor trekking but she is scared of arriving in London. Usually she looks forward to coming home, to hugging Nicky, seeing Miles, to re-entering her well-ordered life. But now she sees it as a battle-field. The phrase 'occasion of sin' runs continually through her mind. She entertains idiotic ideas like taking a holiday or moving house. She even thinks of throwing up her job. She remembers Martin's telephone call to her office. She remembers every word he has ever said to her and replays them in her head.

On the long journey she goes through every sort of emotional response, from delirious excitement when she recalls how he whispered in her ear under the umbrella and how he wanted to kiss her in the fields to miserable depression when she admits to herself how little he said at his dinner party. At this point it strikes her that she has never written to thank him. This for Laura, a punctilious thank-you writer, is extraordinary, showing only too clearly how he has upset her usual behaviour. Worse, it gives her an opportunity to contact him. Occasion of sin. Occasion of sin. No. Here at least, she will stand firm. No thank-you note. That is decided.

This decision brings a faint calm as Laura nears her house. She notices now the pink blossom in the streets and the trees, still so spring-like in their fresh green. Her usual joy in living begins to surface so that by the time she opens the front door, she is able to shout, 'Nicky! Nicky!' in quite a naturally light-hearted tone.

'He's not back yet.' Miles appears on the stairs. He looks tired and grey. He rubs his eyes and clears his throat. 'I'm afraid I've got a bit of flu.'

Laura feels a sharp stab of revulsion. 'Poor thing. When did it start?'

'Yesterday. I didn't ring you. I didn't want to spoil your fun.'

Laura carries her case upstairs. She looks at his clothes, 'You didn't go to bed?'

'I got up to get the papers. Then I lay on top.'

Laura has another uncontrollable thought: That it is better to be tortured by unsatisfied love than sunk into the depression of virtuous old age. Miles looks very old. Then she remembers that he is often unwell when she returns from visiting Nell.

'You look wonderful. Did you have sun there?' Already he is starting to look better.

A new thought crosses Laura's mind, something that has never struck her before. Does he live off her optimism and strength? Does he cling to her like bitter ivy round a sturdy bright-leafed tree? But that is ridiculous. He is strong, successful, dogmatic. He earns the money to run the house. Clever, interesting. Deadening.

'Yes. We walked for four hours this morning and the sun shone all the way. Where's Nicky?'

'They're bringing him back at six.'

Laura unpacks and tries to remake her fragile cloak of

78

happiness. Miles sits on the bed and watches for a while. Usually Laura finds his presence, so admiring, so affectionate, reassuring but today she wants to be alone. Eventually, perhaps sensing her resistance, he goes downstairs.

Soon afterwards Nicky arrives home and Laura runs to him, swings him lovingly in her arms.

'We went in a landrover and I was allowed to steer and we fell into a stream!'

Over supper at which Miles shows no lack of appetite, he complains about Nicky's habit of sucking his thumb. 'He's just too old.'

Laura smiles without answering. Apart from choice of school, Miles has left Nicky's upbringing entirely to her and she sees no reason why he should suddenly interfere. At least he must earn the right first. 'You should take him to the courts, sometimes. Show him where you work. Get to know him on his own.'

Miles looks coolly at his glass. 'The courts are forbidden to anyone under thirteen.'

Laura feels silly and ignorant. After a pause during which they both finish eating she goes over to Miles and kisses him. 'I'm sorry,' she says. 'I know you don't have much time for Nicky. I'll have a go about his thumb.'

Miles looks pleased. He puts his arm round her waist and then pulls her down to sit on his lap. He puts his hand on her thigh under her skirt. 'Let's leave the washing up for Maria.'

Laura feels his hand hot and heavy on her skin and shuts her eyes. His hand moves up her leg. They go upstairs holding each other closely.

Chapter Seven

The next day is dark and cloudy. Laura gets up feeling indefinably ill. Perhaps Miles really did have a sickness and she has caught it. She has a shower after breakfast and puts on one of her favourite dresses. She feels unable to pin her hair back from her face as she usually does and instead lets it fall round her cheeks. She is not well enough to contemplate the possibility of sin which is some relief.

Laura believes in mind over matter. If the body is weak then the mind must show double strength. She therefore spends a particularly hard-working morning at the office.

She emerges just before one with the ache in her head outweighed by the satisfaction of her work. Nevertheless the hours of concentration have left her feeling weak and curiously removed from her usual self. She walks along the pavement under a light drizzle, hardly noticing where she is going. She knows she should eat. On the other hand, now that she has risen above her illness, she might allow herself to go home to bed. Then again, she needs to buy cornflakes and lavatory paper and coffee.

Laura wanders along in the rain, not thinking. She reaches the point where two large roads meet opposite a park. Shall she walk across the park and then home or turn left for some lunch and then return to the office? Or even turn right to a row of shops and buy some summer sandals? Her trance-like state increases.

The pavements are quite uncrowded here. She is in the hiatus between busy shopping areas. One or two people pass her. A man's long step approaches. A voice says, 'Standing on street corners?'

Laura looks up to see Martin in front of her. He is smiling broadly. He holds an umbrella with a broken handle, over his head. 'Do you often linger in the rain?'

'I hadn't noticed.' Laura tries to shake off her sense of paralysis. This is the man who has been the centre of her thoughts ever since she met him. Here he is standing in front of her. Asking her why she is standing in the rain. There must be all kinds of responses.

She stares at him and notices he is very smartly dressed in suit and broad-striped tie. He is not wearing a mackintosh. She thinks he looks like a prosperous American business man. He is still smiling and she can see his crooked teeth.

Checking her heart and pulse, she feels no change. That, at least is the benefit of paralysis. Or perhaps she is already recovering from her infatuation.

'I was trying to make up my mind where to go,' she says slowly.

'Why not take pity on me and come for a drink?' says Martin. 'You can't really like getting soaking wet.'

'Where are you going?'

'Home. I've just been stood up for lunch. A businessman's lunch. His plane's late.'

Home. Laura looks round. Trying to remember what his home looked like. Then remembers they were given dinner at his club. A flicker touches her as she remembers her emotions that evening. 'That was a wonderful dinner you gave,' she says in a dutiful tone of voice.

'Do come and have a drink?'

'Where?' Laura recalls her determination never to see him again. Why had she thought it so important? She has drinks, lunch, with men all the time. Even so, if he says, 'Home,' she will refuse. She doesn't analyse why.

'The Garden Hotel,' says Martin, pointing.

'OK.'

They walk. The rain stops and Martin puts down his umbrella. Laura feels no need to talk. She doesn't feel happy or unhappy. She simply feels removed from the whole experience.

Martin talks enough for the silence not to seem strained. Once he holds her arm as they cross a side-road. Laura takes her temperature again at his touch but finds she is still calm.

They reach the Garden Hotel. It is a modern building on the edge of the park. Martin looks up at it. 'Perhaps we should have lunch. But then if we're going to have lunch we shouldn't have it here.'

'I haven't long,' Laura says. Though really she can't see much difference between lunch or a drink.

Martin turns to her. Without warning he puts both hands up to her face and pushes her damp hair back from her cheeks. 'You look so pretty. The rain on your hair and your pink cheeks.'

Even though his hands were there for only a moment Laura continues to feel their gentle stroking. Her hair stays where he has pushed it. In one movement he has brushed aside the protection of her previous mood. She can feel her colour heightening, the blood rushing fast, her headache beating and her hands shaking. It is now impossible to go and have lunch or even a drink.

She looks at him with startled, pleading eyes. 'I haven't long. I'm late. I shouldn't have a drink at all.'

'You can't be the second person to let me down today.'

Laura hesitates. If she refuses, he might guess the reason. Why has she ever allowed herself to come this far? She remembers she's ill.

'I'm not feeling very well,' she cries desperately.

Martin comes closer to her. He puts an arm round her. He leads her into the hotel. Laura puts her head down but gives up fighting. She wonders how he can fail to guess what she is feeling.

'What you need is a drink.'

They go to a small, heavily carpeted, dimly lit bar. Martin fetches Laura a sherry. She begins to feel better immediately. She takes off her wet coat and feels happy that she is wearing her pretty dress. She sighs, then crosses her legs.

'I did feel ill,' she says. 'I'd been working so hard all morning.'

'But now you feel better,' Martin sits attentively but not particularly close. Laura begins to relax. She looks at Martin again and is able to see an ordinary young man. She sighs again.

'Is all this work for Our Agricultural Heritage?' he asks. 'Lucky tractors.'

Laura embarks on a long explanation about ancient tythe barns and cattlesheds.

'Have another drink.' Martin stands up.

Laura leans forward with an aggressive expression. It seems a good cover for her emotional condition. 'You should care about things like this.'

'Oh, I do care. Show me an earth-work and I'll cry.'

Reluctantly, Laura lets her anger go.

Martin brings back another beer for himself and sherry for her. Laura doesn't want it but says nothing. Martin looks at his watch. Laura notices with a traitorous stab of anguish. Can he be bored?

'I shall have to eat,' he says. 'If no carbohydrate passes my lips by two o'clock I turn into a werewolf.'

Laura laughs with relief and new terror. She determines not to eat with him. 'Beer is stuffed with carbohydrates.'

'You know what werewolves live off, I presume? Beautiful women with wet curly hair.'

Laura's mind remains clear enough to see the ridiculous flirtatiousness of his tone. But her physical self continues to react helplessly. With no Agricultural Heritage aggression to syphon off her emotion she feels the tension building again. She shivers. Her palms sweat. Occasion of sin. The phrase re-appears.

'I think I'm going to faint.' This is no pretence. The room is going black and swimming round.

'Put your head between your knees,' Martin springs to his feet. He stands over her.

Laura lifts her head tentatively.

'I'd better go home.'

'Yes,' Martin puts his arm round her and helps her up. This is all right. Her illness has taken over the situation.

They leave the hotel and look for a taxi. Laura begins to feel better but says nothing. I was ill, and I bumped into Martin who helped me home. The situation has a rational explanation. She can imagine herself mentioning it to Miles over supper that evening.

They arrive at Laura's house. She had imagined Martin would de-materialise, as the house materialised. She had not imagined the two together. But there he is still, helping her out of the taxi up to the front door.

Laura searches for her key. She finds it eventually and holds it up like a rabbit out of a hat. She needs him no longer. A look of desolation crosses Martin's face. Laura notices it and is confused. Embarrassed. Happy. She half turns her face away.

Martin takes her by the shoulders. She looks sideways beyond him and notices the sun has come out. It cuts across the road but doesn't reach them where they stand under the doorway.

'Thank you for the drink and bringing me home,' she says formally, eyes still slanting from his.

'You can't just disappear.' His voice sounds different. Hoarse, higher-pitched. Laura hears the appeal. She mustn't acknowledge it.

'I'm sorry,' Her voice is neutral.

Martin is still holding her shoulders. So near escape she can allow him that.

He leans slowly forward and kisses her. Anywhere else she

would have fled. But they are parting and her house is solid behind her.

She doesn't kiss him back but she lets him kiss her. As he does she thinks this is the first time she has let a man kiss her on the lips since she was married. She is filled with a terrible sadness. Like the home-sickness of a child. But she still doesn't pull away. She feels like crying, the tears full behind her eyes.

At the same time the gentle pressure of his lips against her closed mouth give her a sense of tranquillity, contentment. He loves her.

When he draws away, she looks at him and says quietly, 'Goodbye.'

He can't look at her now. He tries to smile but fails. He runs from her.

Laura watches him out of sight and then lets herself into the house and goes upstairs to bed.

Laura lies in bed. The sickness has descended again. She feels hot, her head aches, her limbs shiver. She tries to read, she tries to sleep. She turns from side to side. Finally she turns on her stomach and buries her face in the pillow.

Maria knocks at the door, and comes in before Laura speaks. There is a crackling and a rustling. She cries excitedly, 'Just look, look. Flowers like I never. Roses. So many.'

Laura doesn't want to look. She can't bear it. But Maria insists, thrusting the giant bouquet under her nose.

'Here's the card. Who knows what a lot!'

Laura reads the card though she knows perfectly well who it's from. She thinks, it's the first time he's written to me. It says, *Get well soon, Martin*. Nothing. So ordinary. Even so how will she explain three dozen red roses to Miles. She begins to laugh and cry at the same time.

The warm-hearted Maria is concerned. 'You not well, a bit.'

'No. No. Please collect Nicky for me.'

Laura feels her fever increasing. She wants Maria to move the huge vase of red roses. She has never liked those tall dark-leaved shop roses. Gloomy, forbidding, malignant. She feels them taking over her light pretty bedroom.

She sits up severely straight and says, 'No taste. Absolutely no taste.' This makes her laugh and surprises Nicky who comes in to ask if he can watch television.

He looks at her as if she's mad.

84

'I'm not well,' says Laura sinking back.

Miles arrives home late. He comes up to her at once. He sits on the bed and takes her hand. Laura snatches it back.

'I'm so hot.'

'Shall I get you a drink? Have you taken anything?'

'No. No. It's nothing. I just need a rest.' She sounds irritable. She hates the way she sounds. It makes her feet hotter and sicker. 'A drink would be wonderful. Very cold. I'm sorry.'

Miles knows how she hates being ill and he will think that is why she is cross. He gets up again. On the way in he had seen nothing but Laura huddled under the blankets. Now he is amazed by the vase of towering roses. Laura often buys herself flowers but nothing on this scale.

He picks up the envelope nearby but it is empty. 'Whoever sent you these?' he says.

'What?' Laura's head is muffled.

'Roses.'

'Martin Keane.'

'Who?'

'Martin Keane. He gave us dinner.'

'How extraordinary.'

Miles stares at the roses. 'There're thirty-six of them. Three dozen.'

'He brought me home. We bumped into each other on the street.' Laura's face is completely hidden, her voice even more muffled. 'There's a card somewhere,' she says.

'How extraordinary,' repeats Miles. 'He must be very rich.'

Laura raises her head a little. 'I think he's just that sort of person,' she says. This sounds true to her and therefore will sound true to Miles.

Yet he stands a moment longer. Laura, eyes shut, head throbbing, can sense his hesitation. She has a sudden strong urge to throw off the bed-clothes and scream out: 'Save me! Save me! Ask about him! Question me! Make me break down and admit what I'm feeling. Destroy this silly love before it destroys us!' But she says nothing, for after all perhaps the truth is as she told him. They met by accident. He brought her home. They parted. But the kiss. The kiss. And his look of desolation as she said goodbye.

Miles turns from the roses. He has decided to accept them.

Nevertheless, as he reaches the door he says critically, 'I thought you hated shop roses.'

'I do. I do. They're ugly,' Laura cries. 'I told you. Martin Keane sent them. He doesn't know me. He doesn't know I hate them. Take them away. Throw them away!'

Of course Miles will do no such thing. He shuts the door quietly behind him.

Laura begins to cry. She imagines Martin choosing the roses with loving care. She hears herself shouting how ugly they are and how she hates them. She imagines that their crimson heads are already drooping on their artificially forced stems. The dark green leaves hanging limply, the whole a mockery of beauty and happiness.

When Miles returns with a glass of lemon she implores him to take them away and throw them into the dustbin.

'Promise me!' she sobs bitterly, 'Promise me.'

*

Laura was feverish for several days. And after that she was weak for many more. Miles was very kind to her. It was as if he enjoyed her enforced captivity. He did not urge her to get well quickly. He put up with Maria's cooking and company without complaint. On several days he took Nicky to school or brought him home. He carried supper up to Laura and ate it with her. He told her endlessly about his latest case. His deep voice with its lawyer's solemn cadences flowed above her comfortingly. At night he held her in his arms.

After the fever subsided Laura did not allow herself to think of Martin consciously. But she could not control her dreams. They were so long and vivid that she was afraid she would give herself away to Miles, crying out Martin's name.

On the sixth day of her illness Miles made love to her. Laura accepted it with gratitude for all his kindness. She would not let herself use Martin's image to arouse passion in herself. But Miles was happy anyway. She had often suspected he preferred her passive to passionate.

*

Laura went to recuperate at Katie's. Nicky came too as it was his half-term. Lizzie, still without a job, was also staying. So they were all there as they had been earlier in the year.

The daffodils had passed but the tulips were still flowering

86

and the roses beginning to dot the old walls with pink and yellow. A clematis flung a veil of starry flowers over the roof of a shed Laura could see from her bedroom window. She stood and looked at it as she dressed in the morning. She wondered at it. The beauty, the perfection, thrown over a rough shed, careless whether it was noticed or appreciated. Sometimes it made her feel sad, sometimes she thought it magnificent.

'Why do we care so much about our relationships with other people?' she said to Katie one evening. 'Why can't we just be!'

'But that's just why you're so wonderful,' sighed Katie. 'Other people get all tangled up but never you. You're so strong-minded.'

'Do I really seem that?' Laura looked at her feet. She was wearing sandals through which her long toes, neatly painted with pink varnish, protruded.

'You have everything. Husband, job, child, beauty, money. You have to be strong-minded to have that.'

'Couldn't it just be luck?' Laura thought that she was in the middle of the worst crisis of her life and no one had noticed. At the same time she saw with satisfaction that the pink varnish on the toes had been applied with total accuracy. Perhaps this was the definition of strong-mindedness. The ability to apply un-smudged varnish to the toe-nails when under stress.

On Friday the weather which had been cool suddenly switched to a May heat-wave. Laura and Lizzie made a picnic and set off with the children for a day at the sea.

They arrived after a twenty-mile drive at about midday. The beach was shingly, the deep sea a dark green. A north-east wind which had not previously been apparent blew white spray off the waves. But the sun was bright overhead and the sky a clear blue. The children tore off their clothes and begged to be taken into the water.

Laura was cold. Ever since her illness she had suffered from the cold. Even the briskest walks didn't seem to warm her. Now she watched gratefully as Lizzie stripped off her clothes and ran down to the sea.

They all seemed so happy, bounding and splashing. Guilt-less. She made a pillow of towels for her head, a swaddling of coats for her body, and cuddled down into the smooth pebbles. It was surprisingly comfortable. The noises of water and voices were far enough away to be soothing rather than disturbing.

Now that she was protected from the wind, the sun seemed actually hot. She closed her eyes.

When she opens them again she assumes she is dreaming. Standing above her, expression blacked out by the sun, is Martin. Because she is dreaming she does not move, merely smiles lazily.

'You must be fatter than you look. Or are those rubber pebbles?'

Laura realises he is real. She squints and blinks into the sun. 'However did you get here?'

'Johnny brought me. It was such a beautiful day. We decided to give London a miss. Katie sent us on here.' Martin crouches.

Laura can see his face clearly now. She still doesn't sit up, feeling that she hasn't properly entered the situation while she continues in her attitude of sleep. 'You're lucky to be so free,' she murmurs.

'Actually, I'm wooing a potential client in the area. I might combine business and pleasure.'

'Visit him you mean?'

'Yes.' Martin puts out his hand and gently strokes her warm face. 'You could come with me.'

Laura jerks herself upright. 'My son's here,' she says in a rush. 'Nicky. I don't think you've met Nicky. . . .'

'That Sunday morning in Johnny's garden.'

'Oh, yes.' Laura straightens her clothes and smooths her hair but does not jump up as she means to do. She can see Johnny at the water's edge. He is making the children laugh by pretending to get his shoes wet and then jumping back at the last moment.

'We can't go on like this,' Martin's voice has the strained high-pitched sound Laura remembers from the doorstep.

'Like what?' A lurching sickness makes her whisper.

'I think of you all the time. That's why I came with Johnny. I rang him and suggested it. I knew you were staying. I spy on you. I follow you. When you were ill, I couldn't bear it. It's so painful. I must have you. I must be near you. You must let me hold you. I can't bear not to touch you.'

Laura looks straight ahead but makes no other attempt to resist his words. Her feeling of a dream returns. They are the words she most wants to hear and most dreads. She wants to smile, to laugh, to dance round with her arms above her head, exulting. But she also wants to throw the towels and sweaters over her head and tunnel deep down into the pebbles.

When he stops, there's a silence. Then she says quietly, 'But I'm married.'

He snatches her hand. 'I know. I know. Just come with me this once. Let me be with you for an hour or two. That's all. Come with me. Now. Please. Please. It's not much. I won't be a bother. No one will think it odd. Johnny and Lizzie are here with the children. Just come with me to the factory. What's wrong with that? Please, Laura. Please.'

Laura doesn't answer. She watches Johnny coming up towards them. Martin hears his step on the stones and drops her hand. He stands up.

'I've persuaded Laura to come and charm the awful Mr Leatherhead for me. We won't be long.' His voice sounds very strange to Laura but Johnny seems not to notice.

'Bet we gave you a surprise.' He burrows into a carrier bag standing nearby. 'If you two are deserting, I'm having the first drink of the day.' He pulls out a bottle of white wine and a cork-screw.

Laura finds herself standing up. She doesn't look at Martin. She walks down to the water and calls to Nicky. 'I'm going off for a little while. You'll be all right, won't you?'

Nicky hardly bothers to look round. He is pouring water over a happily screaming Maddy.

Martin and Laura walk up the beach to where he has parked his car. The pebbles make their progress slow and awkward, giving Laura every opportunity to return. But although she lags behind, in some childish way refusing to acknowledge whom she is with, she plods steadily on, eyes cast down to the rolling crunching shingle.

Thinking about pebbles is preferable to thinking about what she is doing.

Martin has an expensive car. Laura doesn't know about cars, but she recognises its expense. It is dark green, shaped like a sports car although it has four seats. Martin opens the door for Laura.

'The sun has made it very hot,' he says, 'I'll wind the windows down.'

He leans in front of her. Laura stands outside waiting. She looks back at the beach but the figures are too small to distinguish certainly. There are more people now. The wind has dropped and the air feels very hot.

Martin steps aside and she gets into the car. So does he. He puts a folded map onto her lap. 'We're here.' He points. 'And we want to get there. Are you any good at map-reading?'

Laura comes out of her trance. She is relieved. They are going on business. Standing in the hot sun, she'd decided there was no Mr Leatherhead. Even so, she'd got into the car.

Martin touches her hand as he takes it away from the map. He turns the ignition and drives off.

Laura starts thinking again and thinks that every moment of this is a new experience of being unfaithful to your husband. She bends her head over the map. Occasion of sin.

'Would you like a drink?'

'Oh, I thought Johnny. . . ?'

Martin points an arm backwards to a bag on the back seat. 'White wine. Iced. I'm never without.'

Laura thinks that he has planned all this. And yet when he had made his declaration to her on the beach he had seemed so uncertain, so terrified that she wouldn't come. It couldn't be a silly seduction. Could it?

'I thought you had a girlfriend?' she says out of the blue.

'Oh, I have,' he says. 'Lots.'

'I meant one particular one.'

'Philippa. She's not particular.'

'Oh.'

'She's a product of my laziness.'

Laura realises that by asking about his other girlfriends, this Philippa, she has put herself into a comparable position. She pulls herself more upright which is difficult in the very slung-back seats and studies the map.

'It's not far,' she says. 'About five or six miles. What does Mr Leatherhead do?'

'He makes mezzanine floors. He desperately needs me to sort him out. That's what I'm going to tell him.'

'I don't understand what you do.'

'No one of your generation understands. Particularly women.'

'Thanks.'

'I'm only teasing.'

They drive on for another mile or two without speaking. The

sun is burning in on Laura's left shoulder. It comes from above the sea which runs beside the road, green and glittering. Laura feels thirsty.

'I would love a drink now.'

'I'll stop?'

Laura looks at Martin. It is the first time since she agreed to go with him. He looks hot. His face is red. There is sweat on his forehead. He is wearing jeans and a khaki coloured T-shirt. It strikes her that they are not the sort of clothes for impressing potential clients.

'Don't stop. Johnny taught me to open bottles of wine when I was eight. He was six.'

Martin slows down as she twists around and finds the bottle, the opener and the two glasses.

When she is about to pour, he stops the car.

'Don't stop.'

'I think we've overshot our turning.'

Laura retrieves the map from the floor. 'I warned you I was hopeless with maps.'

'We might as well drink our wine in peace.'

Martin gets out of the car, leaving Laura to follow with the glasses and bottle. He strides off in the direction of the sea. Beyond the wide green verge there is a track leading through shrubberies and fields to the beach.

Laura hesitates. He looks back. 'Come on! There's a track!'

Laura follows him. She tells herself it would be rude and hurtful to refuse. She walks slowly, and finds, despite everything, she is enjoying the sun and the air and the prospect of cold white wine, in a totally simple childish way. It doesn't seem wrong. If Miles dropped from a tree, she would smile and wave and invite him to join the party.

Laura walks faster, swinging the bottle cheerfully.

She catches up with Martin on the edge of the last field before the beach.

'This is far enough, don't you think?'

There is no one on the beach but Laura agrees. Grass and sea and white wine. Her sense of innocence persists.

They sit down together. The grass is long and slightly damp. Laura remembers sitting on Nell's lawn drinking red wine.

'Won't Mr Leatherhead be waiting for you?'

'It wasn't a firm date. Anytime will do. One o'clock.'

'Do you always arrange your day just as you want it?'

'No.'

'How did you come to be a friend of Roy's?'

'At Cambridge. He got into the habit of trying out his arguments on me. And I got into the habit of listening.'

'I admire him very much.'

'So do I. Have some more wine?'

Martin and Laura sit quite close to one another, talking naturally about normal things. In a moment or two they will move and go and look at the home of mezzanine flooring.

Laura feels very adult. It would have been cowardly not to come. She smiles, almost beams, at Martin. She sees a whole series of sun-filled déjeuners sur l'herbe stretching ahead.

Then Martin kneels up. His position is ridiculous, the eternal attitude of supplication. 'Please, Laura!'

Laura's world of innocent happiness shatters. Tears spring to her eyes. She clasps her hands round her empty wine glass. 'What can I do?' she cries. 'I'm married! I love my husband. I love my child. They trust me. I believe in marriage. I shouldn't have come. I should never have come!'

Martin shuffles across the grass on bended knees. The absurdity makes the intensity in his face even more painful. Laura thinks wildly of grass stains and children.

'Don't you understand. I love you. I love you. I love you. I've never loved anyone before. Never. And you love me. I know you do. You love me. Me. You must admit it. You must!'

Laura stares dizzily. Still separate for a moment, she thinks that none of the descriptions of passion she has heard or read got it right. This demand for subjugation.

But now everything has turned round. It is too late to analyse or reject. She is already along the road. It would be wrong to withdraw. Cowardly, childish. Wrong. Here is a man, offering her his whole self. And she loves him. He knows that anyway. What's the point in denying it? She loves him. He loves her.

Laura touches his face gently. He is quiet. She touches his hair, his shoulders. Runs her hand over his chest. She feels the heat and passion. But she still holds him away.

This brief time with Martin ridiculously on his knees and Laura touching him so gently and the sun bright overhead and the glittering sea beyond and the long damp grass beneath

92

them stays with Laura always afterwards as the purest expression of their love.

Martin and Laura made love and afterwards lay in each other's arms.

Though the one person in the world Laura doesn't want to think of is Miles, she can't help comparing his soft, pale, dark-haired body with Martin's – strong, hard, fair. He is younger, of course, by fourteen years but she doesn't think of that. She merely loves everything about him. The feel, the smell, the shape. And, loving him so much, she can't help but turn against Miles.

Before this she had never even thought of Miles's body, critically or uncritically. It was the body of her husband. That was all. But now that changed. He was another man. Dark, pale-skinned, plump.

Laura and Martin make love again. They cry and sweat and groan. They seem like people in agony. When they roll back into each other's arms, they comfort each other for their passion.

Martin wipes the tears from Laura's eyes, 'Are you unhappy?'

'You know I'm not.'

'Then why are you crying?'

'You know.'

'Tell me.'

'Because I love you. And because I never thought it would be possible.'

'What?'

'To feel like this.'

Martin cradles her proudly.

The sun pours down on the lovers. Their minds are entirely wiped out. Gone to blackness. They can't hear or see. Eventually they can do nothing but sleep.

They both wake at exactly the same time. It is a terrifying moment of realisation. They snatch at each other's hands and hang on fiercely. They can hear the sea again and the birds and even the cars passing by on the road.

They see the sun still high.

Martin kisses her. 'I love you.' Then he looks at his watch.

Laura kisses him. 'I love you.' Then she feels for her petticoat.

93

They sit up slowly. The green sea gives Laura an idea. 'I'm going to swim.'

'It'll be cold.' Martin looks at her adoringly. But his fingers do up the buttons on his shirt.

'Otherwise I won't be able to walk or speak.'

Laura tries very hard not to think as she crosses the long strand of pebbles. Her legs shake so much that she nearly gives up.

The shock of the ice-cold water makes her cry out. At the same time she realises that she is trying to wash away the sin. She wishes she hadn't gone to the sea and goes panting back to Martin. She throws herself at him, 'It wasn't just for fun! It's more important than that. It means something, doesn't it?'

Martin stops combing his hair. He holds her closely. 'I love you,' he says, soberly, 'And you love me. Love is the most important thing in the world.'

Laura calms down and tidies herself. As long as she is close to him all will be well.

They walk arm in arm back to the car and Martin picks up the map.

'Did you overshoot the turning purposefully?' Laura smiles.

'No,' Martin replies with a look that means 'Yes'.

He starts the car.

Chapter Eight

Martin goes back to London that same evening and Miles comes down to join Laura in the country. Laura meets him at the station. She is a little late and Miles is standing alone, looking pale and exhausted, in the ticket hall. Instead of being sorry for him as she would normally, she is filled with loathing. Why does he have to look like that, his dark, pin-stripe suit, his white shirt, his dark thinning hair, his white face? Then she feels a longing to tell him everything, to describe every moment of how she has spent the time between twelve and one. To make his white face white for a reason.

Instead she runs up to him, smiling, apologetic, 'Oh dear! Was the train early. Or am I late?'

'The latter, I believe.'

Such pomposity! Laura feels it ridiculous and somehow humiliating to her. Yet she kisses him warmly and even likes it when he puts his arm round her. He is always so pleased to see her, so solidly admiring. He is not cross that she is late. He loves her.

After all, the dark suit and pale face are not his fault. They are the badge of his success as a lawyer.

'You look well again,' he is saying delightedly. 'Glowing. Did you get to the sea?'

Laura had told him they might drive to the sea. His warmth, his question are too much for her. The loathing which had been replaced by affection is now blotted out in such a black misery of guilt that she cannot answer him at all.

They have reached the car so she hands him the keys wordlessly. They get in. He doesn't notice her silence but talks about his week. He is not very interested in finding out about the sea-side.

Laura's feelings of guilt continue. She thinks this is the first time that she has felt like this since she was a child. The overwhelming blackness of sin. She remembers the first time she lied. She had denied taking a biscuit from the biscuit tin. She never told anyone and it was days, even weeks, before she recovered. Since then she had told so many lies, little lies, polite, smoothing lies, the lies everybody tells. Yet no worse than taking the biscuit. But the blackness had never returned.

With a mixture of relief and shame, Laura realises that this dreadful guilt of the moment will gradually soften. She will get used to it and the blackness will lift.

'We had a marvellous day at the sea. Johnny and Martin joined us there.' Already she can speak. And speak about him.

'Doesn't Johnny ever work?' Miles claps his hands on the driving wheel in disapproval.

Laura thinks of a judge's gavel. Normally she would have defended her brother but today she is merely glad that Miles has made no comment on Martin.

When they reach the house, Miles goes up to have a bath and Laura wanders round the garden. She tries to be logical about what has happened. But the memory of their passion floods her mind and makes it impossible to reason coherently.

After she has walked round the garden, round and round like a horse on a lungeing rein, she realises they have made no plan for another meeting. This throws her into such a state of terror that calm consideration recedes even further. She hardly knows Martin. Men protest undying love all the time without meaning it. She is cast back to thinking about her married lover before she became married. She hasn't thought of him for ten years but now she tries to remember if he talked to her as Martin had, yet then returned always to his wife.

The blackness of her despair, for she soon feels certain that Martin never intends to see her again, now wipes out the blackness of her guilt. All she cares about is that Martin and she should be together again. She walks into the house, head bowed.

'I'm afraid the day was too much for you,' says Katie, looking up from chopping parsley. 'You'd better get to bed early.'

The roles are reversed. Katie is the strong one, taking care of her.

'Here, let me do that.' Laura takes Katie's place at the table. The chopping movement soothes her. She likes the way the bright green springs from under her knife.

Katie turns to making gravy at the stove. She has stopped nursing the baby and Laura notices she has suddenly become much slimmer.

Laura says, 'Can you remember when you fell in love with Johnny? How it felt?'

Katie continues to stir the gravy but answers without hesitation, 'Oh yes, I think of it often. I went down to see a friend at Cambridge. It was Sunday morning, about twelve. Johnny burst into the room to borrow some coffee. He was wearing pyjamas. He said he had a hangover, and felt dead. But I thought he was the most alive person I'd ever seen. I wanted to be near him all the time. But I never thought I stood a chance. He was so popular. He was always surrounded by people and I could tell they felt the same as I did. I was amazed when he asked me out. I think he just happened to have an odd evening when no one more exciting was around. And then he couldn't help seeing how I loved him, being flattered by it. He likes being loved. And loving. He's very good at it, you know. He loves me. He loves the children. He loves us very much. He just loves lots of other people as well.'

All this time Katie has been stirring the stew. But now she puts the spoon down and turns to Laura. 'You didn't ask for all this, did you? I'm sorry. But you see, although I know exactly when I fell in love with Johnny, when I tell you what it felt like, I have to tell you the rest. Because I still feel it, just the same. When Johnny is here, I'm alive. It's so simple. That's why I'll forgive him everything. It's not the children, really. They only come first when he's not here.'

Laura hands over the parsley to Katie. She forces her voice into the cadence of reassuring sister-in-law. 'Of course, Johnny loves you. And the children.'

'Oh, well,' Katie smiles. 'There's no use worrying. I feel calm tonight. He's pleased with me because I've stopped nursing.' She pauses and sighs only slightly. 'It must be strange, having someone who loves only you.'

Laura gasps, her heart beats fast and then, looking at Katie's calm reflective face, she recovers herself. For a second she had thought that Katie was referring to Martin. The madness of such an idea shows her how far she is from a normal frame of mind. Katie could not know about Martin and would not refer to him in that way if she did. Miles is the man who loves only her. Her husband who shares her bed. Who is about to share the supper table with herself, her brother, her sister-in-law. An intimate family evening.

Laura wants to scream and run away. Instead she takes the stew pot from Katie's out-stretched hands and places it on the table.

'Supper!' she calls in the loud and firm voice of a woman who has called 'supper' for ten years. Katie comes near and kisses her cheek.

'Don't think I'm jealous,' she whispers as the men's feet come closer, 'Your happiness makes me happy too.'

*

Laura sleeps badly. Dreams without substance enough to dispell press round her. Several times she leaves the bed. Once she goes to Nicky where he lies in a tiny room, almost a cupboard. She thinks she might have been punished by his catching her fever. She imagines his forehead burning, his hands sweaty. But he is cool and comfortable, his mouth open, snoring slightly. Later, towards dawn, she goes to the window and peers through the curtains. The sun is not yet up. There is a grey mist all around like a reflection of her dreams. Then, quite suddenly, a bird begins to sing. Then another, and another.

The noise seems deafening and she can't imagine how anyone in the house can sleep through it.

She closes the curtains and slides back into bed. Miles, like his son, is snoring. Usually she pushes him crossly on his side but tonight she doesn't want to touch him. She lies stiffly, doing nothing as positive as waiting for day but unable to sleep.

After an hour or so she is seized for the second time by a longing to tell Miles everything. He is so close to her, the room is dark like a confessional. She can tell him everything, he will forgive her, and it will all be over like a bad dream. She thinks of the words used in confession, 'Bless me Father, for I have sinned. It is –' how many years? She can't remember, fifteen, twenty? – 'since my last confession.' She can't, of course, begin like that to Miles. He is no priest. She didn't, however, consider his reactions as if he was a man. She only thought of herself and how she could tell him. 'I have sinned exceedingly in thought, word and deed . . .'

Laura stretches out her hand and says, 'Miles, listen to me.' Her voice seems loud to her but he doesn't stir.

She hears a movement from next door. Nicky, who always wakes early, is getting up. She listens as he runs to the bathroom and then to the girls' room. She thinks lovingly of his love for her.

Disturbed, Miles rolls towards her and presses his face close to hers. Still only half-awake he puts his arms round her and a leg over hers. He wants to make love.

Laura lies rigid. Then she thinks that letting him make love to her is far worse than forcing herself to tell the truth. As for the confession, she can make that to a real priest later that morning. She puts her arms round him and helps him on top of her.

'I'm glad you're feeling better,' he says, as he rolls away.

*

Laura doesn't get to church that day. It would have seemed too extraordinary to go on Saturday. Besides the day passes by as Saturdays usually do. Children, cooking, walking. The suffering of the night before seems to have taken place in some separate part of her mind which is closed now. She even manages to enjoy their picnic lunch on the lawn and the sight of Nicky racing Maddy across a field. She knows she looks tired but that can be blamed on her illness. The day passes without the need to tell a single lie and, although Martin is in her mind all the time, she never actively thinks about him. It is a day off.

On Sunday she tells a lie in order to avoid taking Nicky to church and sets off, earlier than usual, on her own.

The confessional is the old-fashioned sort, very small and dark with a thick grill between her and the priest. She imagines an old man, sensibilities dulled by years of accepting the burden of sins far worse than hers.

'Bless me Father for I have sinned, it is many years since my last confession.' She pauses.

'Yes. Go on.' His voice is soft, encouraging, neither old nor young.

'I love a man who is not my husband. We have made love. He loves me.' She stops abruptly. She feels there is nothing more to say. She waits.

She feels the priest leaning forward. 'Is that all?'

'Yes.'

'Ah. Well. You say you love him?'

'Yes.'

'Love is a wonderful thing. Perhaps the greatest of God's gifts to man.' He pauses. 'Do you have any children?'

'A son.'

'And you love him?'

'Of course I love him!' Laura realises that this is not an old priest who will accept her sin and pass absolution. This is a young, questing priest who wants to help her examine her conscience. She has not expected this. She is not prepared for it. She does not want it. 'I love my husband too!' she cries defiantly.

The priest leans away again. As if now he's aroused her beyond the bald statement, he's satisfied.

'Love,' he murmurs in his soft voice which Laura now hates. 'There's a lot of talk about love these days.'

'It's not talk. I love my son. I love my husband. I love my . . . I love him too.'

'Oh, yes. I'm not denying it. The human capacity for love is infinite. God meant it to be so. He loves all of us.'

Laura stops listening. She thinks that all over the countryside there are ancient pillars of the church who would have given her absolution without question and with it the strength to renounce the sin. And she has to find the one young argumentative priest who wants the price of her soul to forgive her. She had entered the confessional in humble penitence, as she thought, but now she rages with rebellious thoughts.

'You must ask yourself,' says the quiet voice, 'what sort of love you feel for this man. Is it the same sort of love you feel for your son?'

'Of course it's not!' Laura bursts out. 'No woman feels the same love for a boy as she does for a full-grown man. For a lover!' She hopes she has shocked him.

But after a pause he comes back calm as ever. 'And is it the same kind of love you feel for your husband?'

Laura feels the question close like a trap round her neck. And because it is a trap, she fights to get out. 'All love is good. You yourself said it's God's best gift to man. There're all kinds of different kinds of love. Love is never bad. Love is never a sin.'

There is a much longer pause.

Then Laura hears the priest shifting on his chair. It sounds as if he is about to stand up.

'I must prepare for mass now,' he says. 'Perhaps the mass will help you to prepare yourself for a true confession and repentance.'

'What?' Laura doesn't understand. She had come to him for absolution, for a pure new heart. Surely he is not turning her down.

'You are not ready yet to receive the sacrament of penance. I am sorry. I will pray for you. You also must pray. Think about love too. About the different sorts of love.'

'But Father, you can't send me away!'

'I will bless you now. In the name of the Father, Son and Holy Ghost.'

The priest gets up and leaves the confessional. Laura stumbles after him. She kneels at the back of the church. She feels angry and humiliated. Again, she thinks with longing, of a venerable old priest who would have done his best to help rather than antagonise.

The congregation stands as the priest and servers enter. Laura looks to the robed figure and sees, to her amazement, that he is old. White-haired, as venerable as any testament saint. She jumps up and flees out of the building.

*

Laura looked so drawn that Miles tried to persuade her to stay longer in the country. But Laura protested about her work and her son. She tried to protest honestly but inside herself she was thinking only of a meeting with Martin.

It rained and she walked in the garden.

*

Laura is at her desk by nine-thirty. She has dressed carefully in a plain dark dress. She has lost weight from not sleeping for two nights.

A lot of letters have collected in her absence and she begins to open them mechanically. She puts those needing an immediate answer to one side and the less urgent to the other. She has a strong sense she is incapable of answering either.

The phone rings. Outwardly Laura remains impassive. She lets it ring twice and start a third time.

'Hello.' Her voice sounds husky.

'Good. You're back. The invitations have come through. Pick them up at twelve and then we can talk.'

This is work. The man on the telephone is called Ben Casey and he is referring to the great summer Agricultural Heritage meeting. Laura doesn't answer.

'Hello? Are you there?'

'Yes. Sorry. I'll be there at twelve.'

Immediately Laura puts down the phone, it rings again.

'Hello?'

'Laura.' This time it is Martin.

They have not spoken for three days. They are both breathless at the other's presence, even across telephone wires, and say nothing.

'Darling.'

Laura laughs, a hysterical but happy laugh. She's his darling. Nothing else seems of the slightest importance.

'Yes, I'm here. I'm all right.' Then she remembers that she mustn't see him ever again. She stops laughing.

He says, 'I'm coming over to pick you up at twelve-thirty.'

'No. You can't.'

'What do you mean?' He sounds disbelieving. After all she has welcomed him with her laugh.

'I've got a meeting at twelve. Not here.' She can hardly believe this is true.

'Cancel it.'

'I can't.'

'Laura, I've got to see you.' His voice takes on that strained, passionate tone she cannot resist.

'I know. I know. But what can I do?' It is not clear whether she is referring to the particular problem of the meeting or the impossibility of the whole situation.

Martin decides to believe in the meeting. 'I'll pick you up when you've finished. Where will you be?'

Laura thinks she must end it in daylight, in the city while she is thin and wearing her clean, plain dress. After her meeting when her brain is active instead of her body.

'Inverness Terrace. Off the Bayswater Road. I should be finished by one.'

'I'll see you then. Darling. Darling Laura.'

The rest of the morning passes and Laura finds, to her amazement, she has quite without conscious thought answered a dozen letters.

The meeting is not so easy. Ben Casey notices her abstraction and is irritated. He is even more irritated when she won't come to lunch. He is young and confident, and not used to being turned down.

'I can't.'

'Why not? You need to eat. You've lost weight.' He wanders over to the window and looks out. The office is on the fifth floor. 'There's a man standing on the pavement waiting. Is he giving you lunch?'

'I don't know.' Laura doesn't want to look. She can't understand Ben's sudden interest in her. They work together, they've been to lunch a few times but otherwise they hardly know each other. He's behaving as if he's got some kind of proprietory right.

Inside herself she has a scared feeling that he had sensed a change in her. That by making love with Martin, by falling in love with Martin, she has lost the bramble hedge growing round the secure and faithful wife.

'I must go,' she says, standing up as calmly as possible. She takes the wrapped pile of invitations. 'I'll start on these tomorrow.'

'He's attractive, I suppose,' says Ben, still looking out of the window, 'if you like that "I-could-have-been-in-the-SAS-but-I-chose-the-City-look." Not supple enough for my tastes.'

Laura manages something approximating a caustic laugh

though she recognises Martin from Ben's description. 'I'll see you in the next day or two. Don't ring me at the office. I'll probably do quite a lot at home.'

She doesn't know why she says this, covering herself for not being in the office. She leaves quickly, imagining Martin on the pavement and longing to be with him.

He comes to her. She goes to him. She means to stop him, warn him of Ben up above.

Coming home, she thinks foolishly as he holds her tight. Coming home.

They get into Martin's car. Laura loves the car too. They sit there holding hands, looking at each other. Laura remembers she must never see him again.

'I'm taking you back to my flat,' says Martin. 'You look pale. You need looking after. You look tired.'

Laura is afraid she is not as pretty as he remembered.

'Kiss me,' she says, in contradiction to everything she has planned.

When they let each other go she smiles and cries. 'Do I look better now?'

'One hundred per cent.'

She laughs and he starts the car.

The traffic is lunch-time blocked, giving Laura time to reflect again. Gradually, Martin becomes a stranger. She still loves him but she hardly knows him. His profile and his hands on the wheel and gear-stick look alien. He concentrates on driving and doesn't speak.

When they arrive outside his block of flats, she says in a cold voice. 'Now I must go. I'm sorry. I should never have come. I'm sorry.'

'This is impossible!' Martin swings round on her. 'You can't change like this. You're coming up with me. I've left you alone all weekend. I need you now.'

Laura is frightened. He seems so angry. She tries desperately to stop tears reaching her eyes. 'I'm sorry.' Her voice is weak.

'It's nothing to do with being sorry.' He grabs her and pulls her out of the car. 'I love you! Don't you see! No one's ever been loved as I love you. I don't care about your husband. I won't hurt him on purpose but he doesn't love you like I love you. And you love me. You don't love him.'

He is standing on the pavement shouting at her. Laura sees

she will have to go up to his flat. They can't part like this. She goes into his arms quietly. He stops shouting and they walk into the building.

Martin's flat is decorated by machines. They sit with watchful television eyes on every flat surface.

'I do have an office but things seem to work their way back here.'

Laura gives herself an unspecified time before she must walk out forever. This means that she can accept Martin's kisses and soothe his anger. For a second she is reminded of her son when he was smaller. It is the only time she can remember being involved in such a loving and unstable relationship. Tears and laughter, crossing each other unpredictably. It had shocked her then for her nature was happy in tranquillity.

They kiss and they touch until Martin breaks away and pulls her towards the bedroom. This is the moment she must wave her halt sign. Unfortunately she can hardly speak, let alone speak commandingly. She finds herself in the bedroom. Martin hasn't even noticed her hesitation.

The room is warm and made dark by heavy curtains not properly pulled open. The bed is much larger than her own and covered by a duvet put on slightly askew. At this point Laura gives up trying to resist.

Martin says, 'I never expected this. I never expected to fall in love. I'd give up everything for you.'

'Yes. Yes. I love you too.' The relief of surrender makes Laura feel giggly. Her head floats like a balloon. But her body is hot and heavy. They undress quickly.

*

A telephone rings in the bedroom. Martin and Laura are dazed, half asleep. It rings again. They stir. Martin mumbles.

'I won't answer it.'

The telephone goes on ringing. Laura moves. 'I think you'd better.'

'Hello.'

As Martin rolls away to pick up the receiver, Laura opens her eyes. She stares at the ceiling trying not to hear that it is a woman's voice on the other end.

Martin is brief. 'No,' he says, then 'Yes,' then 'I don't know.' He sounds irritated and cold. The woman's voice sounds agitated. 'Well you shouldn't have,' he says, exasperated. 'I asked you to leave them here.'

The voice becomes so loud that Laura can hear a few words, '. . . you need me . . . I don't care if you think you're in love . . . I look after you. . . .'

Laura longs to bury her head under the pillow. She feels totally humiliated although she doesn't analyse why her displacement of a rival should have that effect. Until this moment she has quite forgotten the existence of a girlfriend. Surely Lizzie had said she was living with him? Her eyes move round the room and she notices a feminine hair-brush on the top of the chest of drawers. She realises that the duvet cover has a sprigged flower pattern on it that no man would have chosen.

Martin slams down the phone. He doesn't turn towards her. They lie side by side tensely. Laura wants to go to the bathroom but imagines it hung about with floral sponge-bags and dressing-gowns.

Martin takes her hand. 'Sorry.'

'It's not your fault.'

'I told her to clear everything out yesterday. But of course she couldn't resist leaving some things behind.'

'Poor girl.'

'Not at all!' Martin sounds irritated again. 'I never promised her anything. She moved in because she wanted to. I didn't ask her. I always told her she'd have to go sometime.'

'I don't expect she believed it.'

'That's her problem.'

Laura is upset by his coldness even though it's not directed towards her. She gets up silently and goes into the bathroom. There is no floral decoration but the air seems perfumed. She turns on the shower and as she stands under the fiercely pounding water, recalls their first love-making by the sea. It seems a very long time ago. Something that had happened in a different world in a different time. It had an innocence which this meeting did not. It was right they should be interrupted.

Laura feels sick. She goes into the bedroom where Martin is still lying in bed and dresses quickly. He says nothing. If he doesn't speak she will be able to go. She brushes her hair and goes to the door. But when she reaches it, she turns. It would be too cruel to part in silence. On the other hand there's nothing to say. She stands looking at him, helplessly.

'Say goodbye then.' He stares at her, sullen in defeat.

'Goodbye.' She runs away. Out of the flat, out of the building, into the streets.

A chemist's clock tells her it's half-past three and she decides to collect Nicky from school. She picks up a taxi.

Nicky is surprised by her appearing. He pulls on her hand excitedly.

'Let's walk back by the adventure playground.'

He doesn't mention and Laura forgets that Maria will come to collect Nicky and find him gone.

Laura sits on a wooden bench watching her son swinging on a rope from one platform to another. She finds herself curiously split as she had been over the weekend. One part of herself is enjoying the sight of this healthy little boy bravely swinging in the late afternoon sunlight. Another part is screaming in total despair. This part cannot understand how her body sits there composedly with smiling mouth.

After half an hour she feels cold and calls to Nicky. He comes reluctantly, only lured by the promise of an ice-cream.

They arrive back at the house to find Maria trying desperately to reach Laura. She has already had time to imagine Nicky dead, abducted or absconded. Laura who is normally sympathetic to others' anguish – particularly when she is the cause – reacts coldly. She goes to her room, saying she has a headache.

She lies down on her bed, first taking the phone off the hook. It is the first time in her life she has taken the phone off the hook.

She is roused two or three hours later by Miles's voice.

'I hear you overdid it.'

She lifts her head slowly. 'You're back early.'

He studies his watch. 'Not particularly.'

'Why. What time is it?'

'Seven-thirty.' He goes to the phone. 'You mustn't take the phone off the hook.'

'Why not?'

He looks at her curiously. She doesn't usually question his statements. She usually wishes to please, particularly when he's just come home. 'I tried to ring you several times. I was worried.'

'I'm sorry. I'd better get some supper.'

'If you're not feeling well. . . .' he lets the sentence trail away.

Laura knows he enjoys their supper together, that he doesn't eat much at lunch-time in order to enjoy it more. That he gets up early and works hard all day. Guilt breaks through her misery.

She puts her legs out of bed and sits sideways. Miles comes to her. He puts a hand on her knee. 'Maria says you picked up Nicky and then disappeared with him. She burst into retrospective tears.'

Laura stands up sharply, throwing his hand off her knee, 'Maria cries easily.'

Miles's voice loses its sympathy. 'I think you should apologise to her.'

'I'm not a child!' Laura goes to the bathroom. Her anger comes as a relief from guilt and misery.

'You're certainly behaving like one!'

Laura slams the bathroom door. She has probably slammed the bathroom door three times in their married life.

Miles stands outside. Laura can feel him trying to understand what it's all about. She is hoping he will lose his temper, shout something horrible, put himself in the wrong. But although he is fairly often reproving or sarcastic he never loses his temper. He considers that undignified. Laura who had thought she agreed about this and admired him for it, now finds it unforgivable.

If he shouted at her she might break down and tell him everything. Then they could cry together and all would be made right again.

This fantasy is interrupted by Miles's level tones, saying, 'I think you should stay in bed. I'll send Maria up with a couple of aspirins and perhaps you'll apologise to her then.'

'Oh. Fuck off!' Laura never swears. She smiles as she imagines Miles's stunned expression. He occasionally swears with a self-conscious emphasis when he feels the situation calls for it. She never does.

Laura cleans her teeth viciously, scrubs her face and hands. Then she follows Miles downstairs. She determines to make him supper and sit with him as he eats it. If he will not fight with her then an icy silence is better than a calm reconciliation.

This armoured resolve even allows her to bare her teeth apologetically to Maria. Their relationship has always been perfectly adequate without any help from Miles.

It is only as she sees Nicky's empty cereal bowl on the kitchen table that her hardened heart turns over with the thought that. he has gone to bed without saying goodnight to her. 'Did Nicky say his prayers?' she asks Maria.

'Indeed yes. He was so tired that boy.'

'I like to hear them myself when I'm in.'

'But you were asleep.'

Laura is angry again but manages to hide it. She thinks about Nicky. How he curls up into the bed. She struggles against the saddest feeling that he will have grown up and gone away from her in the morning. She knows it is irrational but it is reinforced by the depressed look of a plant which has not been watered while she was away, by Maria's ugliness and by an ant which she sees crawling by the sink.

Her anger with Miles turns into this sadness which she relates only to her son. She goes upstairs to find him. It is faintly annoying to find Miles calmly concentrating on a volume of International Law but she does not allow it to deter her.

'I'm sorry,' she says humbly, kissing his cheek.

He doesn't look up but she can feel his pleasure and restored confidence. He pats her hand. 'I know you're not well. I should be more tactful.'

This is an apology. Laura tries to be glad. But she can't help feeling his patronage. She forces a smile.

'I've put the supper on. It'll be ready in about five minutes.'

'Good.' He looks up now. 'What is it?'

Laura suddenly laughs. 'I don't know.' It is quite true. The day has been full. All day filled with passion. Yet the thing that strikes her as most extraordinary is that she, Laura, who manages so efficiently house, husband, child and career can't remember what she's cooked for supper.

Miles looks at her, surprised, as she laughs again. Then he smiles. He is glad to see her restored to happiness.

'I'll go and see,' she says, still laughing. 'Whatever it is, we wouldn't want it burnt.'

Chapter Nine

Lizzie arrived to stay with Laura. Still trying to fill in time till university, she had found a job selling buttons in a department store. She insisted on giving a part of her salary to Laura as a contribution towards her upkeep.

Her presence made Laura feel old. It was like having a grown-up daughter in the house. She had to be pulled out of bed in the morning, advised not to wear luminous false eye-lashes for work and persuaded to eat something sensible in the evening.

'You're worse than Mummy,' Lizzie groused, not seriously. 'I'm sure you never used to be like this.'

This was true. Laura was exaggerating her motherly role as a weapon in her struggle against loving Martin. She had not seen him since that day in his flat. She had not gone into the office, working instead at home, where she assumed Martin would not ring her. Imagining herself mother of a teenage daughter made the idea of a lover, himself hardly older than Lizzie, more unlikely.

However, Lizzie left the house at eight-thirty which meant Laura had a long solitary day ahead. Worse, she discovered that Maria, fat, ugly Maria, had a lover who she was accustomed to entertain in her room over the lunch-hour. He arrived one day and refused to be turned away. Obviously the abstinence caused by Laura's daily presence had finally become unbearable. After much shuffling and whispering Maria let him stay, and for half an hour there were muffled thumps and giggles from her room.

Although Laura saw it was a sensible line of action and much better done when Nicky was out of the house, she found the thought of it disgusting. She imagined Maria and her lover in the most intimate postures. The idea of sex revolted her. She not only remembered her performance with Martin with shame but also couldn't bear to let Miles touch her. She pleaded her period and headaches and exhaustion. Miles was sympathetic. He asked if Lizzie was too much work. Laura denied it vehemently.

Ten days passed.

*

Lizzie is lying on the sofa in the sitting-room. Laura is trying to read. Miles has only just come in although it is late and eats his supper off a tray.

Lizzie says casually. 'Guess who came in to buy some buttons today?'

'Who?' Laura puts down her book. Miles continues to eat.

'Guess.'

'Your mother.'

'All the way from Cirencester?'

'Who else knows you sell buttons?'

'Half of London, it seems. Did I tell you Philippa, Martin's girlfriend, called in the other day?'

Laura stands up abruptly. 'Who wants coffee?'

'Who came in today?' asks Miles.

'Martin,' cries Lizzie. 'He bought some shirt buttons. Then he asked whether I'd have a game of tennis sometime. And I said did he need a fourth, assuming Philippa was the second and I was the third. And he said he needed a third and a fourth since Philippa wasn't around any more. So I said surely she was because she bought four yellow buttons off me only the day before. To which he made no comment. Wasn't that odd?'

Miles pushes his tray aside. 'I wouldn't mind a game of tennis this weekend.'

Laura has reached the door. She wants to leave but has to hear the end of the conversation.

'He suggested we play Saturday morning. At his club.'

'I'm taking Nicky swimming!' Laura shouts.

Miles and Lizzie look up in surprise. 'Bring him along. He can be ball-boy.'

Laura goes out and makes the coffee. She realises that she cannot discuss the question of tennis and Martin without sounding inappropriately emotional. She cannot bear the thought of arousing Miles's suspicions. She has been pressing him to play tennis for weeks. It will seem very odd indeed if she refuses this opportunity. The best thing, she decides as she carries the coffee upstairs, is to say nothing, play and make sure they part as soon as the game is over.

Later that evening she registers with satisfaction that Philippa has not moved back into Martin's life.

In the night she wakes up to the realisation that Philippa must have told Martin where Lizzie was working.

At dawn she becomes convinced that Martin is going to use Lizzie to humiliate her. Whatever happens, the tennis game must be cancelled.

But when she sits with Miles and Nicky over breakfast, and Lizzie dashes in for a coffee, her courage fails. Silent acquiescence is the only course.

*

Laura plays tennis well but her figure, with its deep bosom and long rather heavy thighs is not suited to a tennis dress. This has never worried her. However, when Lizzie appears in sawn-off shorts and a T-shirt she sees herself in unflattering contrast.

Yet again she considers a variety of excuses and then says nothing. As she ducks into the car it strikes her that the more matronly she looks the better.

This conviction gives her the courage to follow Miles into the tennis club. The sight of him is infinitely depressing. His legs, in particular, the pallid plumpness, the lack of muscle in the thighs, disgust her. They are well paired, a depressingly middle-aged middle-class couple. She wonders that Nicky, so beautiful and lively, can bear to acknowledge them as parents. As she walks besides Lizzie's long slender legs, she sees years of physical decay ahead.

Laura has never till now felt the need to compete on some common scale of the body beautiful. Nor has she expected Miles to do so. At thirty-five, she is behaving like a silly eighteen-year-old.

At dawn there had been clouds in the sky. Now the sun shines out of pure blue. The club-house is stuffy and quite dark. There is a bar and a lot of tables and chairs.

'You're punctual!' Martin springs up from one of the chairs.

Miles says, equally jolly, 'How're the machines?'

'Buzzing. I thought you might have trouble getting them all out of bed at this hour.'

'I know you mean me!' cries Lizzie flirtatiously.

'Of course I mean you,' Martin bends to kiss her cheek.

III

Laura stands back watching this charade and trying to turn love into hate. She sees by Martin's manner that he is nervous. Even without looking directly at him, she knows he is not looking directly at her. When he kisses Lizzie she feels certain he only wants to hurt her. She draws back even further.

'Let's get onto the court,' says Martin. He still has not said hello to her. She follows them out.

The court is red and gravelly and already desert hot. Martin spins his raquet. 'Rough or smooth.'

They spin their raquets and look. Laura and Martin are paired together. Laura thinks they will have to speak.

They walk together over to the far side of the court. He says quite suddenly, 'I can't go on without you.'

She says, 'Don't say that.'

On the other side of the court Miles is swinging his arms around. He shouts 'Play!' A ball comes low over the net.

Martin and Laura look at it stupidly. Lizzie laughs loudly. She sends over a ball.

'Hit it!' cries Laura.

Martin looks at her and smiles. He hits so hard that Lizzie doesn't even attempt to play it.

'There's no reason why we shouldn't play tennis,' she says, keeping her eye on Miles who is preparing to send another ball.

'That's what I thought,' Martin grins and bounces. 'And if you're playing you might as well smash your opponents.'

Miles has a good tennis style but is unfit and out of practice. Lizzie is very energetic but can't serve. Laura is steady though not fast and Martin wants to win.

Laura knows the whole thing is ridiculous, but as the game progresses and the sun rises higher and even Miles gets red in the face, she can't help seeing it as some ancient rite for male dominance. She is certain that Miles has no suspicion of her relationship with Martin. But his undisguised aggression makes Miles want to stamp him down. He had liked him at his dinner party in the club, when he, Miles, had been the successful barrister in his pin-stripe suit. But now on the hot red gravel with Martin young, glowing and determined to win, he does not like him at all.

Lizzie also wants to beat him. In youthful optimism, she feels this would make him take her more seriously.

Laura thinks she is watching all this, that she doesn't mind who wins, that she only wants it to be over. But when Nicky, who is ball-boying in a hit-and-miss fashion, drops a ball when she is serving, she shouts angrily, 'If you can't do it properly, don't do it at all!' She feels no guilt that she had promised to take him swimming.

It is a relief not to think. The physical effort reduces the brain process to the simple aim of getting the ball back. She is able to treat Martin as a partner and Miles and Lizzie as opponents. The pairing of husband and wife is broken down.

Laura begins to play well. They are all playing above their usual game, breaking the tennis-for-fun rule that execution constantly disappoints expectation. They are surprised by their success.

Laura's body throbs. Her chest hurts and sweat runs down her back. She hasn't been so happy since she lay beside the sea with Martin. Her only problem is to restrain herself from throwing herself into his arms whenever they win a point. They brush past each other and, as they pass over balls, their hands touch.

The score stands at one set all, three four in games – to Martin and Laura. Miles is serving. Laura has avoided looking at him as far as possible. Suddenly as he follows up to the net after his service, he gives a weird grunt and drops to the ground.

It flashes through her mind at once that he is having a heart attack. The unaccustomed exercise, the heat, his age. He is a decade older than any of them. A thought follows too quickly to stop. *If he dies I can marry Martin.*

She runs forward shouting 'Quick! He's having a heart attack!'

But Miles is not lying, nor is he unconscious, he is crouching, bent double. And as she circles round the net and approaches him, he puts up his head and says between clenched teeth, 'Of course I'm not having a heart attack, you silly fool. I've simply pulled a leg muscle. What a damn stupid thing to do!'

There is silence. Lizzie and Nicky run up. Martin comes closer but stays the other side of the net. Miles sits on the ground holding his leg. 'Damn stupid. Playing like that when I haven't played for weeks.'

By the rules of the ancient rite game, this should have been the moment of victory. Miles vanquished, down if not entirely out. But his words, his sensible regret for the childish foolishness that had led to his downfall, put the game back into the ordinary world again.

They had all been behaving idiotically. And he, an important barrister-at-law, had paid the price. 'I've got an important case on Monday,' he says, making the point.

'Do you want an ambulance?' asks Martin in a voice without emotion.

'No. If you give me an arm, I'll hop. It's just a matter of rest and strapping it up. Laura can strap it up. Here Nicky, pick up my raquet.'

He is more of a husband than ever. Laura watches as Martin comes round the net and helps him up. They form into a little procession.

The sentence comes into Laura's head. *You can't live with a man you want dead.*

*

Laura was not a dramatic person. She did not like dramas. If she suspected someone was going to cry or shout or otherwise upset the calm, her instinct was to flee or, if that was impossible, ignore the whole episode in the hope it would go away. She distrusted drama, feeling it rightly named and linked to dramatic fiction. She therefore discounted her own emotions at dramatic moments. She was acting as much as anybody.

So when the tennis game was over and Miles was strapped up, hobbling and cross, she wiped away her thought. *You can't live with a man you want dead.*

She expunged it from the record without examining it further. The reality of the situation was Miles – his duty to his work and hers to him. Duty was a word that came to her again as all important. She noticed that it seemed not to exist for present-day writers and journalists. Being particularly sensitive to any writing on the woman's role of which there was a great deal she became aware that it was all based on the need for self-fulfillment, an entirely selfish object.

Unable to talk about it to Miles from whom she felt increasingly remote and unloving, she wrote a long letter to Nell. It turned out to be more like a lecture. Nell replied with defensive fierceness: *One of your nicest characteristics used to be your refusal to judge. Duty is easier for some than others. . . .*

Laura couldn't say that it was herself she was judging.

*

It is at this point, about a week after the tennis game, that Laura goes once again to confession. This time she chooses a church in a part of London which is predominantly Irish. Here, she feels, there will be hell-fire rather than polemic. Happily she joins a long queue of old ladies waiting for absolution. They will not stand for a prolonged discussion.

'Bless me Father for I have sinned. It is four weeks since my last confession. In that time I have committed adultery which I now regret.' She rattles it off decisively and then waits, tense, head bowed. If it is necessary she will flee again. The priest takes a wheezing breath.

'You have committed one of the gravest sins, my child, but you say you have repented. To repent of a sin is a wonderful God given joy. Pray that you may never repeat your failing and that this sacrament may give you strength to follow the path of right. Now as your Act of Penance, say one "Hail Mary" in honour of the Blessed Virgin.'

Laura walks outside the church with a childish feeling of spiritual purity. White-wash or true inner cleanliness, she doesn't consider it or care. She has confessed and been forgiven. Every cloud has a silver lining. Her adultery has brought her back into contact with the church. She is the lost sheep back in the fold. She will go to church every Sunday, she will go to confession regularly, she will be a better, healthier, more unselfish person.

First of all, this new strong God-filled person will take herself to work, at her office. No need now to skulk and hide. She has the Holy Spirit within her and fears no temptation.

Laura sits at her desk. Replies are coming in to the invitations for her Agricultural Heritage Day. She looks at her calendar and sees it is only three weeks away. One of the replies is from the Minister for Agriculture who promises to come and make a speech. The Minister for Environment is already expected. Suddenly it's an important event. There'll be no problem now getting a wide press coverage.

Laura is pleased and excited. She is half convinced that the Minister has only accepted because she is this pure new soul. The truth which she also knows is that he has a country house five miles from where the party is to be held. She rings Ben Casey to tell him the good news. He is delighted but also anxious about the protocol for managing two ministers.

'Politicians are worse than Princes.'

'At least they're both members of the same party.'

'I'll tell you what, let's have lunch to celebrate and plan.'

Why not? Laura can think of no reason. Life is so easy when you're virtuous. She can't imagine why she had ever needed more than an interesting job, a happy family. In her new purity and in Miles's absence, she feels confident that she will, at very least, like him again as she used to.

She thinks, fleetingly, that if only she had found this morning's priest first time round, what a lot of misery, and sin, would have been saved.

Laura and Ben sit in an Italian restaurant drinking white wine. Ben says, 'Of course, he'll probably cancel at the last minute.'

'Probably. But by then we'll have everybody there we want.'

'Yes. Use his name like mad. I hope the marquee is big enough.'

'I'll go down there this week to check the barn and the display. Of course the old tractors won't get there till the day.'

'How have the photographs come out?'

'Not bad. But we need some much bigger. I'll try and get to the photographers this afternoon.'

Laura finishes her artichoke vinaigrette and notes with satisfaction that she is a busy woman. She may be earning no more than an honorary salary, but her work is important and she does it well. She thinks that she has been taking it too much for granted. Perhaps this is the moment to push herself further into a real career. This meeting is throwing her into contact with all sorts of influential people. Even Ben, for example, younger than her, piling Parma ham on melon, he could be useful if she did decide to branch out.

'I must say,' says Ben, wiping his full red mouth. He has a round attractive face and thick curly hair. 'You'd never make a civil servant.'

Laura is piqued.

He laughs. 'Never admit you can do anything today or even this week. It gives the impression you don't have enough to do.'

Laura smiles. 'Actually I'd make a very good civil servant. I'm good at getting on with people and I'm good at getting things done.'

'A disaster. If you don't act, you can't fail.'

'You don't really believe that.'

'I believe it's a sensible way to behave.'

'It's immoral!'

'Whatever's morality to do with it?'

'There's a moral code for every sort of behaviour.'

'You'd certainly be a disaster in the civil service.'

Laura doesn't mind him joking any more. She's interested in the conversation. 'But you don't behave like that. The whole jamboree is a tremendous risk.'

'I said it was a sensible way to behave. I didn't say I behave like that. Working in the civil service's like that. Wearing a balaclava back to front. I often think of leaving.'

'What would you do?'

'I did think of going into the film industry. Till someone pointed out they're even more afraid of action than we are. So I expect I'll grow old in the service of the Queen.'

Laura laughs. His face pouts comically. 'You look far too young to grow old.' She hasn't felt so happy for a long time. It strikes her that this conversation between colleagues and perhaps friends is reality in the same way Miles and Nicky and their home is reality. Despite her feeling of love and total intimacy with Martin she has never had a proper conversation with him. The emotional tenseness between them right from the beginning put sensible thought out of the question.

Fantasy, she says to herself, drinking more wine. That is fantasy. This interesting discussion with an attractive young man who could help my career and who finds me attractive but within bounds, in other words he will not fall on his knees and declare his undying love for me, is reality.

At this point, as the waiter brings them some elegantly grilled veal, she recognises that Ben Casey has become distinctly more attractive to her as the meal has progressed. Indeed if, over coffee, he asked her to go to bed with him, she would be definitely tempted. She would resist, of course, without much difficulty, but the temptation would be there.

Laura finds this alarming. She has had lunch with Ben several times, though not at such impressive places, but she has never before felt the slightest urge towards adultery. So why should she feel it at a time when firstly she is deeply in love with another man and secondly she has renounced this man a mere two or three hours ago, for a life of virtue? It's enough to make you believe in the devil. Laura smiles to herself.

The devil is a relatively consoling explanation. The truth, she suspects, in psychological terms, is that her new virtuous armour has not yet completely encompassed the state of physical arousal which her love for Martin had induced. The image of a dog in heat enters her mind. She looks at Ben's mouth and imagines kissing it. Luckily this image is blanked by a large slice of veal.

'You're very quiet,' he says, between chews. 'Don't you like your food?'

'It's delicious.'

'What food are we offering our eminent guests?'

Laura pulls herself together. 'Cheap food. Barbecued chicken and chips.'

'It sounds very American. Shouldn't it be a bullock?'

'Too expensive. Unless we get frozen New Zealand stuff. That's not very English either.'

The meal continues. Laura decides that she is not degraded to the level of a dog in heat. But that it is difficult for a mature woman to drop suddenly from an unusual pitch of physical excitement to absolute celibacy. The answer is to turn to Miles again. That had seemed easy only an hour ago. The shaming truth now is that she'd rather sleep with this relative stranger who she had only started liking half an hour ago than with her own husband.

'Coffee?'

'Yes, please.'

A cold fixed look has come over Laura's face. It baffles Ben who, ever since he'd seen the boyfriend waiting on the pavement, had assumed her available. He watches her sipping her coffee.

'I should be going soon,' Laura puts down her cup.

Ben leans forward. He starts to say something. But instead he grasps her hand convivially.

'I've enjoyed our lunch.'

'Thank you.' Laura sighs with a mixture of relief and disappointment. She has seen what was in his mind. But now he has decided to place her as the faithful wife.

She gets up. She thanks him again. 'I'll see you soon.'

Ben looks into her eyes again, 'Very soon.'

But the moment has passed. She turns away impatiently. She

feels certain she will never feel that particular temptation again. She remembers her confession and makes an inward sign of the cross.

Ben, waiting for the bill, regretfully watches her hurry from the restaurant.

*

Miles had been mildly cross ever since he pulled his leg muscle. He was busy, his leg hurt and he had no time to rest. Laura didn't mind his ill-humour, she even welcomed it as appropriate punishment for her infidelity. Besides, it made it an excuse to stay away from him. There was no point in making herself available with winsome airs and invitations when he growled and groused.

But after her confession, with theories of duty matched to a new purity of soul, she determined to go towards him. It was his right to rebuff her. She couldn't help hoping he would. But it was her duty to approach him.

Laura and Miles sit on either side of the kitchen table. Maria pops her head round the door to say goodnight. 'Have a nice evening,' says Laura warmly.

Nicky puts his head round to say he forgot to do his homework. 'Do it in the morning,' says Laura encouragingly.

'Would you like a stool for your leg?' she asks Miles who is staring either thoughtfully or glumly at his plate. She arranges this quickly, hoping he will notice she has changed into a dress and brushed her hair.

She serves a generous helping of risotto for him and a less generous one for herself. She doesn't want to put back the weight she has lost. With a pang she thinks the only person whom she wants to see her body must never come near her again.

'How is the leg?' she asks brightly.

'I've got five days I could make free next week. Let's go off somewhere. Just us.'

Laura is taken aback. She is making the overtures, not him. Automatically she responds, 'What a marvellous idea! I can't remember when we last had a holiday together.'

'I've got to get this leg right. It must be somewhere I can rest.'

'How about Ireland. With Roy?' As Laura suggests this she remembers the Agricultural Heritage party and her resolution to take her work more seriously. How can she go off and leave it for five days?

Miles is pleased with the idea of staying with Roy. He has a good library and is unsociable. 'I might be able to get away Tuesday night,' he says. 'Back on Sunday. Nicky will be all right with Maria and Lizzie. She can take him down to your brother's on Friday.'

Laura says nothing.

*

It rained while they were in Ireland. Not heavily. Just a soft wetness more like mist than water. Sometimes the sun came out and shone through it like stage lights through a gauze. Since Miles would not move beyond an armchair and a pile of books and legal journals, Laura took long walks.

Alone in the weird green wetness, she had all kinds of strange thoughts. She decided that Miles was having a breakdown. The pulled leg muscle was not bad enough to make him drop out so completely. It was against his nature. Perhaps he was having some sort of male menopause crisis – more to do with work than anything else, she assumed – at exactly the same time when she was facing the biggest crisis of her life. This idea increased her sympathy for him though not enough to want to question him with a view to help. She felt theoretical sympathy as she walked the fields. On the other hand it made him seem less attractive. She had never been attracted to failure.

It never occurred to her that his unusual behaviour in taking them away into isolation might be because he suspected her own state of mind. She did not wish to credit him with so much understanding.

She also thought of Nicky. She had always taken motherhood for granted as an unselfish fulfilling experience. But now she found herself wondering what purpose she actually served in Nicky's life. He had not appeared at all upset by their departure. He had merely made certain he could watch his favourite television programmes and that his pocket money would be forthcoming on the proper day. It struck her that he seldom talked to her now. He seemed to assume that she wouldn't be interested. In a way he was right. The cheerful ramblings of a four- or five-year-old were much easier to enjoy than a seven-year-old's description of a football game, or his explanation of the internal combustion engine. They were growing apart because they had little in common.

Laura sighs and stamps the mud off her gum-boots. She usually takes the same route through the fields. About two thirds of the way round she reaches a clump of large oak trees. Here she stops to rest for a minute and to contemplate the damp beauty of the pastoral scene. Here she reaches the point in her thoughts when she can no longer keep out Martin.

Some cows, black-and-white-patched, move slowly through the lush grass. They swish their tails lazily at the flies who cluster in the warm wetness. Love. Why did she think she loved Martin? Or he her? Love was putting someone before yourself. Love was not this obsession she felt with herself in relation to him. When she pictured him, tall, strong, loving, she immediately pictured herself, glowing, giving, loving. She was excited by the thought of herself with him, her body with his body. She thought more of her body than his. This was obsession, not love.

Yet it was love that made them one. When she was with him she felt one with him, peaceful, good, secure, happy, at home.

Tears start in Laura's eyes. When she's apart from him she feels totally alone, abandoned. Laura comes out from under the trees and starts up the steep slope that leads to the house. Usually the hard climb dispels the worst of her self-pity and allows her to enter the house with pink cheeks and a cheerful enough disposition to offer Miles drop-scones and tea. But today she turns left and goes down to the farm buildings which are set away from the house.

Roy goes there each morning, returning for lunch and sometimes for tea. She has never thought of following him before. Most of the buildings are old, built of stone with slate roofs, but she can just see a large modern barn behind and what looks like a silage drum. It has a modern prosperous look about it. It makes her feel happy that Roy's mental anguish is cushioned by a worldly prosperity. She thinks of those fat black-and-white cows and the wide fields soon to turn golden with summer crops. She looks eagerly for Roy to congratulate him on fertility and order. The anguish of love has been smoothed into the pattern of nature.

Roy comes out of a shed. A farm worker follows behind him.

They are frowning. Laura waves. Roy smiles, says something to the man who turns back, and then comes to Laura.

'I was going to congratulate you on, well, everything,' she throws an arm expansively around, 'but you look anxious.'

'All farmers do. In case it's suspected they're making money. Actually, it's a ridiculous problem. A bit's dropped off our incredibly expensive new bailer, rendering it a hundred per cent inoperative. I'm just going down to the fields to look for it. Want to come?'

Laura puts her arm through Roy's. She feels incredibly fond of this tall, ungainly man whom she has known for so many years. They have hardly talked, the chair-bound presence of Miles hindering them.

The sun sprays light through the clouds. They walk briskly back the way Laura came.

'I shall pray to St Anthony,' she says.

'Who's St Anthony?'

'The patron saint of lost things. He's only failed me once and that was after I'd failed to put a pound in the poor box when he'd found me my engagement ring.'

'I didn't know you were that sort of Catholic?' Roy looks at Laura seriously.

'I believe in St Anthony. I've been thinking about Catholicism lately. I even went to confession.'

'In one of those sinister little coffins?'

'You can do it out of the box, if you like now. And they've instituted some sort of communal confession and absolution. I like the box. But I'm old-fashioned.'

'That's why I like you.' Roy stops to undo a gate. He clicks the bolt up and down and then forgetting what he is doing starts to climb the gate.

Laura is about to laugh when she sees his intense expression. 'I wish I could believe,' he says just as he gets astride the gate.

Laura is embarrassed although at the same time she wants the conversation very much. So few of her friends will talk seriously about religion. Roy sits on top of the open swinging gate, his huge green gumboots kicking against the bars.

'If you want to believe, then you will believe. It's as simple as that.'

'Nonsense! For a start, why do I want to believe?'

'Why?'

'Because I want to be happy.'

'What's wrong with that?'

'Oh Laura!' His face droops reproachfully.

'I'm sorry. I know that's not good enough reason, for you – though it is for most people. You have such high standards.' She frowns. 'I can't think with you sitting on that gate. Come down and I'll try to be more intelligent.'

Roy looks down at his perch with surprise and descends abruptly the other side. He holds it open for Laura. 'If only I was a cradle Catholic like you, then I wouldn't need reasons to believe. I just would. You're so lucky.'

They walk but no longer arm-in-arm. Laura watches Roy's way of thinking with his body. He twists and turns in front of her. 'I don't find it difficult to believe,' she says. 'In God, in the church, in dear old St Anthony. But I'm not very good at translating it into everyday action. I'm an emotional Catholic. What do you find it difficult to believe in?'

'Everything.' Roy becomes totally dejected. He kicks his toes on the ground like a child and tugs his hair. 'I'll tell you where I stand now.' He wrenches on the sleeves of his jacket. 'I can see no possible position between being an atheist or a priest.' He stops and stares at Laura balefully.

'So you're an atheist?'

'Yes.'

Laura feels unable to argue him from such a rocky fastness. She wonders whether to suggest he sees a priest. But she knows no priest to suggest. After all, he is in the land of priests if he wanted one. She looks past him at the large open field.

'Is this the moment to pray to St Anthony?'

Roy descends gradually from his unassailable position. Laura wonders if she has failed him totally. Then consoles herself with the thought that the simple fact of talking to a sympathetic listener is often more important than dialectical argument. He can get that from books.

'This is the field.' Roy looks round him. 'So you see why I don't get married.'

'Atheist now, priest later?'

'I don't know. I don't know.'

Laura turns from him. 'I'm going to pray to St Anthony.'

'On your knees?'

'No.' She smiles at him. 'It's too wet. But you ought to think of a reward.'

'Church mercenary?'

'The church isn't proud.'

'Pride? Is that what you think it is?' As Roy looks as if he's going to get worked up again, Laura clasps her hands. 'Ssh. I'm beginning.'

'Aren't you going to do it aloud?'

'No. I couldn't concentrate with you listening and staring.'

Laura prays. She prays not only to St Anthony but also to Jesus and Mary His Mother to intercede for her. Halfway through, the prayer changes from a prayer for a piece of iron to a prayer for herself and her immortal soul. The sensation of prayer fills her heart in a way it hasn't since she was a child in her convent, praying at early mass on no breakfast. She stands for several minutes till Roy stops watching and wanders off.

The sun goes in again and the air is pale and clinging.

It seems to Laura that if her prayer is answered, her life will become pure and happy again as it was before she met Martin. Except she will be stronger because she has known and resisted temptation.

By now Roy has reached the middle of the field. He shouts, 'I've found it! I've found it! Long live St Anthony and the one Holy Catholic Church!'

He runs towards her holding up the little circle of iron.

Chapter Ten

The morning after Laura returns to London, Martin rings her at the office. That afternoon they leave together for New York.

She takes no luggage and says goodbye to nobody, not even Nicky. It is such a wild action that it would have seemed like fantasy were it not for the bursting glowing happiness that makes every detail of life around her more than ever vivid. His presence transforms the taxi ride to the airport, the wait when they arrive, the cup of tea, the bus across the tarmac, the aeroplane. She can hardly believe she had done the same things only a few days before with Miles. She has no memories of it. Then had been the dream. Now is the reality.

Martin's arm around her gives her a feeling of total intimacy. They might be in bed together. She can't understand how they have survived apart. She wishes the aeroplane journey would last twenty seven hours instead of seven. She doesn't think of what she has left behind.

*

That morning she had seen Nicky off to school. He'd been irritable, fussing about an unironed football shirt. He'd wanted to leave for school too early and shouted rudely when Laura delayed. She'd even wondered whether he was punishing her for going to Ireland without him. She thought not. It was just that their separation had made her more aware of his imperfections. He was going through an unattractive phase. Since she had no idea of not being there when he returned she had made no particular effort to get close to him.

Miles had also been suffering from Monday morning. He had risen early, turned and twisted, grunted in a subdued way which nevertheless had woken Laura. Then he had wanted to make love. But she had pushed him away, pretending to be more asleep than she was. So he had put on his dressing-gown and gone down to his study to work. He was dressed by seven and out of the house by seven thirty. Laura had kissed him goodbye from her bed. She had no thought of leaving.

Lizzie had been more cheerful. She had brought Laura a cup of tea and had sat on the edge of the bed. 'It's been miserable without you. The house seemed so gloomy. I only had one good evening.'

'What was that?'

'Martin took me out. We went to a film, then we had a pizza and then we went to a night-club.'

Laura went to her office after dropping off Nicky. She didn't know what she'd expected but it disappointed her. It seemed small and cold and drab. Ever since her lunch with Ben Casey she had been keeping in mind an image of herself as a career woman. It was a cheering idea. But now it seemed unlikely and uninspiring. She rang Ben Casey to tell him she was back but his secretary said he wouldn't be in that day. He had left a message for her. The Minister for the Environment had already

125

cancelled his acceptance to the summer fair. He would be sending one of his assistants.

Laura sat at her desk looking out of the window. She saw the back of a large concrete building across the street. She decided to go out and pick up some more blow-ups from the photographers.

When she returned the phone was ringing. A girl from the next door office popped her head in. 'It keeps ringing but since you tell me not to answer it, I haven't.'

'Sorry,' Laura lifted the phone. 'Hello.'

'I have to see you.'

'Martin.' Laura sat down on the chair. She was shaking. She tried to remember how long it was since they've spoken. Since the tennis game.

'I have to see you now.'

'No. No.' Laura remembered about Lizzie. 'Why did you take Lizzie out? You mustn't take Lizzie out.'

'It's the nearest I can get to you.'

'You mustn't.'

'Then you must let me see you.'

'That's blackmail.'

'I love you, Laura.'

'Yes.' Laura whispered.

'I'm going to New York in two hours.'

'Oh.' He was leaving her. He had rung up to tell her he was going away. He no longer loved her.

'But I can't bear to be without you. I love you.'

'I love you too,' Laura whispered.

There was a pause. Laura could feel his breath. She had said she loved him.

'Laura?'

'Yes.' He had sounded gentle. She wanted him so much.

'Come with me to New York?'

'Yes.' She hadn't hesitated. She had simply said 'yes' as if it were the easiest thing in the world.

*

Now they are sitting together on an aeroplane on their way to New York.

Martin orders drinks. He takes out newspapers and magazines from his brief-case. Laura looks at the case. 'I haven't even got a tooth-brush.'

'New York's five hours behind us. We'll go on a shopping spree.' When he smiles and bends to her, Laura can think of nothing. 'I'll use yours!' she cries.

'You're beautiful.'

'That's because I'm happy. I've never been so happy before. I've never been happy at all.'

'Never?'

'Never!' Laura puts her cheek to his and wipes away husband and son.

Time goes so quickly. They have no time to look at the newspapers, no time to talk. They get mildly drunk and think of nothing but each other.

When they get to Kennedy Airport it is still afternoon and warmer than in England. Laura suddenly stands still. 'I haven't got a visa!'

Panic-struck, she looks at the grey-shirted, thick-set man in passport control. What is she doing here? How did she come here, with no case, no visa?

Martin puts his arm round her. 'Give me your passport.' He opens it, smiles at the photograph. 'At least it's not out of date.' He flicks through the pages. He stops. 'What do you mean you haven't got a visa? There's one here. Valid Indefinitely.'

'But I haven't been to America for years. Six or seven years.' She doesn't say 'before I had Nicky' but she thinks it.

'Well when you did, they gave you a visa valid indefinitely. The Gods are on our side.'

Laura tries to control her trembling. They won't cross-question her, turn her back. But she has thought of Nicky for the first time since leaving England. He will already be out of school, wondering where she is.

'I must send a telegram.'

'First moment we're through customs,' Martin is comforting. 'They always like a good look at my computer bits and pieces.' She becomes calmer. They queue under the neon lighting.

Laura writes out the telegram. *Gone to New York with Martin. Quite safe. Will be in touch. Tell Nicky I'm on holiday.* She wonders whether to put in Martin's surname. It seems inappropriately formal. Yet otherwise Miles may not know who he is.

Laura had been unknowingly pregnant when she last came to New York. She had attributed her feelings of malaise to jet-lag and the strangeness of a strange city. Miles had spent all day at his conference so she had either been on her own or with wives who made her feel inadequate with the energy of their ambitions.

Now as she sees the yellow taxis outside the airport she remembers the nausea and the depression. When Martin had said 'Come to New York' she had pictured a new glittering city.

Martin opens the door of a taxi and helps her in. 'Do you come here often?' she asks when they are sitting close together.

'Yes,' he says briefly. He looks at her closely. 'I learned my trade here.' He brings his face to hers and kisses her. 'I didn't know you had been here before.'

'Don't let's talk about it.'

'No.' They are silent, trying to restore the loving warmth and excitement.

They approach Manhattan. The taxi driver is racing, the roads half empty. Tolls and bridges fly towards them and then suddenly the spires and turrets of the city rise up in carved silhouette.

Laura cries out 'Oh look! Oh look!' Her exhilaration returns in a rush. They swoop inwards, downwards and along beside the river.

'We're staying down-town,' says Martin. 'In the middle of nowhere.'

'Will you be with me?' Laura tries not to sound fearful.

'Of course. All the time. We'll never be separated. You can come to all my meetings. If anyone doesn't want you, then I don't want them!'

They smile at each other. It all seems easy again.

Martin has never stayed in the Downtown Hotel before. It stands in an old district designed like a London square but within walking distance of the Village. Their room is large but dark. Laura is struck by the thought that she who has always placed so much importance on the support of objects, of possessions, is here entirely on her own.

This makes her bold. What has she to lose? She winds herself round Martin.

'I thought you wanted to buy a tooth-brush?'

'There's only one thing I want to do.'

They make love.

Thin strips of ideas float through Laura's mind. 'Dispossessed.' 'Possessed.' 'Freedom.' Her limbs tangle in his with a suppleness that surprises her. As if her body has thrown off shackles as well as her mind. Was it for this she came to New York?

They lie together in bed hearts still loud, skin still wet. They stroke each other tenderly.

'I love you.'

'I love you.' Love? Laura remembers the confessional for a moment and then forgets.

They sleep.

When they wake, they feel thirsty, hungry, happy.

'I don't care where we are or what time it is!' cries Laura.

They shower and go out. The light evening warmth wraps round them. They walk hand in hand like young children. Laura who is usually fastidious about clothing wears her crumpled travel-worn dress as if it's an honour.

Martin insists on taking her to a dress shop in the Village. He sits there while she tries on silk shifts in rich colours. He chooses three and a pale jacket and underclothing. The assistants enjoy the scene, making helpful suggestions and flirting mildly with Martin.

They walk out carrying bags on either side. 'My trousseau,' says Laura.

'Oh my God!' Martin looks at his watch. 'We're supposed to be there at eight.'

'Where?'

'The restaurant.' He looks surprised. 'Didn't I tell you?'

'No.'

'Jeannie and Hal Gluckman. I usually stay at their place. We're meeting them for dinner.'

'Oh.' Martin has made no calls since they arrived in New York. His friends won't know she is coming too. Pride stops her from saying anything.

Martin holds her, squeezes her waist. 'Don't worry. They'll fall at your feet like everyone does.'

Laura moves away a little. That's not the point. She feels vaguely humiliated. She still says nothing. They walk on. The large carrier bags bump against their legs.

Martin takes her arm, stopping her. 'What's the matter?'

'Nothing.'

'Don't say that. Tell me. You can't keep things away from me.'

Laura pulls away, avoiding his eyes. It is their first quarrel. So soon. She is not used to being pressed. Miles is glad to avoid problems, confrontations. She is not used to so much concern. Honesty. Does he want honesty? Here in the middle of the street. She feels hot and tired. She puts down the bags. She looks at him.

'You must ask me before you make plans.' Foolish tears start in her eyes. She blinks.

'Darling.' He puts his arms round her. Several people stop to stare. 'I didn't think. I'm sorry. Of course we won't go out to dinner. I don't care about them. Not at all. They're nothing. Nothing compared to a moment's unhappiness for you. I suppose I just wanted to show you off. I'm sorry. I didn't think.'

Laura becomes calm again in the face of his concern. She puts out her hand to him. Whenever they touch, they recover. Touching base. 'It's all right. I want to meet your friends. Just let me go back to the hotel first.'

'Of course. I'll ring the restaurant from there and explain you're with me and we'll be late.'

*

Jeannie and Hal are unconcerned by their late arrival. They drink wine and argue about the Russian involvement in the Middle East. Hal is a lecturer in Japanese History at New York City University. Jeannie is a doctor. They look alike. Thin and dark and tall. Laura is surprised to find these are Martin's closest American friends. She remembers her first image of him. Standing on the country railway station in his anorak. And how she had placed him as a dull product of the English upper class. She would have expected him to know correct round-faced men who take only slightly more interest in their jobs than their tennis.

'We're so glad to meet you,' Jeannie holds out her hand. 'I can't say I've heard so much about you because the first I heard of you was ten minutes ago.' She smiles broadly revealing long discoloured teeth. 'But I'm very pleased to start.'

She is assuming they are lovers. Laura had listened as Martin telephoned. He had merely said she was a friend of his visiting New York. But now Jeannie and Hal are assuming they are lovers. In the nicest possible way. For of course they don't know that Laura is married and has a son. Even if they did know it, she has no doubt they would still be ready to like her.

Laura tells herself that she is in a world where women leave their husbands all the time. They see nothing shameful or reprehensible in her behaviour.

Yet that is the worst of it. For she is not like that. She believes in marriage. She has been faithful to her husband for ten years.

Laura acknowledges Jeannie's greeting and shakes hands with Hal. She feels disturbed and unsettled. Why is she sitting down at this check tablecloth in this darkly lit restaurant? Hal pours her a glass of red wine and she immediately takes a drink. She is there as Martin's lover. That's why she's there.

'Is this one of your two days in, two days out visits?' Hal asks Martin.

'I don't know. NBC want to discuss a series on Computer Programming. I don't know how long we'll stay.' Martin looks at Laura. They have not discussed time in relation to the visit. It has no end. An end would involve looking to the future. They cannot do that yet. Laura sees that Martin is suddenly wondering about this dinner. Perhaps it wasn't such a good idea after all. Laura decides to make an effort. The wine is making her feel good. Powerful. She only has to look at Martin to feel him regain confidence and joy. He feels for her hand and holds it under the tablecloth.

'I'm going to England in a couple of days' time,' says Hal. 'To deliver a lecture.'

'He's got so grand now,' says Jeannie, 'I hardly see him. His students, never.'

'She knows I don't have students anymore. The last thing postgraduates want is a pet professor.'

'I'd love a pet husband.'

Hal looks at Laura. 'Jeannie decided to be a working doctor instead of a theoretical one. Half a bottle of wine and she regrets it.'

'Only when you swan off to foreign parts leaving me with Sam due for a twist of the OrthoDontist's screw and Eleanor on the first day of her grade examinations.'

'My. . . .' Laura starts a sentence. Her mouth hangs open. She was going to say 'My son may have to wear a brace.'

'My work takes me to muddy tractors and cowsheds,' she says instead, taking another gulp of wine.

'Laura runs something called Our Agricultural Heritage,'

explains Martin. 'She's very big in the world of historical cow-sheds.'

Laura is glad she didn't mention her son. She feels a right to be herself. Why should she react to everything as a mother? Wife and mother. A little sprout of grievance begins to grow. Kindly, subtly with her own connivance, Miles has schooled her to be the accepting wife and mother.

Laura begins to enjoy the evening. She deserves time off. Martin's love encloses her again, barring out all doubts. She doesn't care what Jeannie and Hal think. They are clever. Let them work it out for themselves. She owes nothing to them. She has no responsibilities here.

*

Martin and Laura make love through the night. They sleep, they wake, they talk. They talk about themselves, about their childhood, about things they haven't thought of since they happened.

Laura tells him about horses and school and the death of her mother.

Martin tells her about school and boredom and the moment he first touched a computer. 'I shook and went hot all over. At last I was alive.'

'Like falling in love.'

'Exactly.'

Laura's self-revelations stop before her marriage. Neither says anything but it is understood that it is a danger area.

They make love and sleep and wake and talk and time, dislocated anyway because of their removal from one country to another, and, in Laura's case, from one life to another, loses all pattern.

They wake up and the sun is shining brightly through the net curtains.

Martin leaps out of bed. 'What ever time is it! I've got a meeting at ten-thirty.'

Laura watches him lazily. He bends over a case filled with mechanical nuts and bolts. He is naked. His body is thick and strong and golden in the sun. She loves him so much that it dissolves her body. She clasps herself and smiles.

'What are you grinning at?'

'Do you love me as much as your computer?'

'What a question! When I think of all the energy I've spent

on you. Enough to keep this whole city warm for a year.'

Laura watches him run to the shower. She won't move all morning. Just lie there, hugging herself as she is now. Then they'll have lunch together and look at the city. Then they'll come back and make love again. Her body responds to this idea with a very positive tingling of excitement. She hugs herself closer and shuts her eyes.

Martin moves round the room, dressing. She doesn't look at him now. He bends over her. 'I'm going now. Here's my number in case you need me. I'll ring about twelve-thirty to tell you where to meet me for lunch.' He kisses her. 'I have a strong feeling I'm not going to make much sense at this meeting.'

Laura kisses him and lies back snugly. The door closes behind him.

For an hour she lies, drifting in and out of sleep, listening to alien city sounds. The hotel itself is quiet as if everyone has left it for the day. Laura is glad to be alone, to admit to her tiredness. Her body dominates her thoughts, making happiness easy.

Gradually she awakens and her mind begins to take over. She works out what time it is in England. Five o'clock. Tea-time. With a sudden sense of loss she pictures Nicky sitting at the kitchen table, eating burnt toast made by the ugly Maria.

She jumps out of bed and runs to the bathroom. She showers, putting her whole head under, letting the warm water run and run and run. But when she comes out she finds she is shaking, her teeth chattering. She towels herself dry vigorously and outwardly, at least, she stops shaking.

She puts on her new underclothes, getting some pleasure from this and then deliberates over her new dresses. The sun is not so bright now but she can sense the heat of the day even through the window. She chooses a turquoise blue dress.

She sits at the dressing-table. Her hair makes wet epaulettes on her shoulders. Laura gazes at her face, in the mirror, and waits for the terror of loss to strike again. She wonders what time it is. When did Martin say he would ring? Twelve or twelve-thirty. She hurries to her watch. Only eleven-twenty. It can't be. She throws it down, knocking the telephone.

She comes back to the dressing table slowly. As she sits down the telephone rings, making her start. She picks it up.

'Hello.' But there is nobody there. She holds the receiver,

hoping perhaps for a friendly voice. She is about to replace it when someone speaks.

'Operator.'

'Oh.'

'Did you want to call?'

'No. I . . . Sorry.' She puts the reciever down hurriedly. And almost at once is struck by the realisation that she could call Nicky. Miles would not be home yet. Nothing could be easier. She could reassure him. He would reassure Miles. He would not ask where she was. She picks up the phone again.

'Hello.'

'I have a call for you.'

'What?' She doesn't understand. She wants to make a call.

'Hi. Laura.'

'Yes. Speaking.'

'It's Jeannie. How are you?'

'Fine. I'm. . . .'

'Martin said you might like to have some lunch.'

'But we're having lunch.'

'He hasn't contacted you yet then. He's got stuck with a business lunch.'

Laura doesn't speak.

'We could go somewhere really nice. Posh nice. Or weird nice. Or you could just come to my apartment if you'd prefer that.'

Laura wants none of these things. She only wants Martin. She feels afraid of Jeannie's directness and energy. She wants Martin. She wants Nicky. She wants her son. Laura realises she is about to cry uncontrollably. She must get off the phone.

'I'm sorry. Thank you so much. But if Martin can't make it, I think I'll look up an old friend.'

'Of course. It's just if you had nothing better. . . .'

'Thank you. Thank you so much.'

Laura puts down the phone. The tears roll down her cheeks. She manages not to scream and bang her head.

The phone rings again. Martin. She doesn't answer it. She hates him. She stops crying and is about to pick up the phone when it stops ringing. The tears start again. She goes and lies on the bed. She rolls on the bed in self-pity. She hasn't cried like this since she was sixteen. She despises people who cry.

The phone rings again. She surprises herself by stopping

134

crying instantly and picking it up.

'Laura.'

'Yes.' He hasn't called her darling. Her anger builds. She has always thought of herself as an unemotional person.

'I'm in a meeting.' He hasn't called her darling because he's in a meeting. Laura tries to reserve her feelings. 'And I'm afraid it's going to go on through lunch. I'm sorry.'

'Jeannie rang. I didn't know what she was talking about.'

'I asked her to. I meant to get to you first. But you were engaged. Who were you ringing?'

'No one.'

'Oh.' He sounds anxious. Laura is glad he sounds anxious. 'I can't talk now. I'll see you at the hotel at 3.30 p.m. Have fun with Jeannie.'

'I'm not seeing Jeannie.'

'What? Look I've got to go. What do you mean you're not seeing. . . .' He puts his hand over the mouthpiece and she hears him apologising to someone.

'See you later!' she calls loudly and puts down the phone.

She strides about the room crying and shouting. She has thrown aside husband and beloved son for him and he cannot even break a business appointment. A lunch.

There is a knock at the door. She stands completely still. She thinks it is Martin. She is gloriously happy. He has rushed back to comfort her.

The door opens. A maid puts her head in. Seeing Laura's face, she retreats hastily.

'No hurry! No hurry!'

Laura sits down on the bed. She is cold now. Face set. After a few moments she picks up the phone.

'Front desk please . . . Would you check out flights to London . . .? Today.'

Laura walks out of the hotel. She has been in New York less than twenty-four hours. She hasn't walked on the streets in sunlight. The noise and sun makes her feel dizzy. A yellow cab passes. She hails it and gets inside hurriedly.

'Where to?'

Where to? Laura tries to think of a place where she would be less than completely miserable. 'The Metropolitan Museum, please.'

'You from England?'

'No.' Laura hunches in the corner.

The driver turns round to get a better look. 'You sick?'

'No.'

'I don't like sick people in my cab. Particularly women. They're liable to miscarriage on my clean seat.'

Laura sits up straight and shouts, 'I am not sick. I was miserable and I'm now angry. I didn't know you had to pass a health test to pick up a taxi.'

'OK OK.' The driver relaxes forward over his wheel. 'You're not sick.' A pause. 'But you are English.'

Laura gives in. 'Yes.'

'What part? Jolly good show London?'

'Yes.'

It is a long drive up-town to the Metropolitan. As the driver tells Laura about his experiences on a cab driver's tour of European cities, Laura considers her position. On the whole she is proud of herself for shouting out that she was miserable and angry. She had never admitted such a thing in her life before. It even makes her smile to think how happy it would have made Nell to hear her. She has become part of the sisterhood of suffering women. The little seed of grievance started against her husband now spreads to include Martin. Yet she is not despairing. Her own description of herself was correct. Miserable and angry. Deep inside. She still thinks it will be all right. A life-time of happiness and confidence sustains her.

Laura walks blindly through the Metropolitan Museum. She tries to concentrate but the surfaces remain meaningless. However it soothes her, even the lack of meaning has a glazing distancing effect. The long smooth galleries pass one after the other. She walks for an hour as someone might along a country road. Every now and again she stops to admire the view.

Laura leaves the museum and finds she is very hungry. She considers where to eat and decides on an expensive restaurant. Martin had given her money the evening before when they were buying clothes and it will give her satisfaction to spend it. She buys a copy of the *New York Times* and goes into the first restaurant with a clean canopy.

It is very expensive. The head waiter bows her to a corner table. Most people are nearing the end of their meal. Laura realises she is conspicuous but enjoys the feeling. She is no longer miserable. She is a free spirit, alone in a great city. She will fly home in an hour or two.

The wine waiter appears and she orders a bottle of Pouilly Fuissé. She picks the most expensive item off the menu which is smoked Scotch salmon mousse followed by English lamb. The only problem is the *New York Times* which is bulky and dirty. She shovels it under the table and sits back contentedly sipping her wine.

The head waiter appears again. Bowing again. He hands her a slip of white paper. Laura looks at it with surprise. She has a moment when she thinks it the bill, that she is being turned out as if a prostitute. Actually it is a message.

'From the gentleman in the other room,' says the head waiter encouragingly.

'The other room. How can he see me?'

'Mirrors. When you came in.'

Laura reads the short note. *Why are you here? I will be at the hotel in an hour.*

Laura cannot understand. Martin is here. She is bewildered. Her confidence ebbs away. She wonders whether to reply. It is unnerving that he can see her but she cannot see him. She pushes away her salmon mousse.

'Anything wrong, madam?'

'No. No. It's delicious.' The plate is borne away by a waiter with an air of injury.

Laura looks down at the table cloth. She thinks perhaps she will leave.

A tall figure stands in front of her. Not quite still, as if moving by. Laura looks up.

'Oh!' she gasps. To her surprise, a gasp of pure happiness. It is Martin and at the sight of him everything seems resolved into love and joy. She can see and feel how he loves her.

'Hello, Laura,' he says and then turns back a little. 'Pat, this is Mrs Knight. An old friend from old England.' He turns back to Laura. 'What a surprise to see you here!'

Laura hardly looks at Pat. She sees she is young and attractive but it does not interest her at all. The bond between Martin and her is so strong. She feels no jealousy.

'You over for long?' says Pat.

'No. Not long.'

'Martin's been filling my ears with GOTO, GOSUB, GCOL, HIMEM. Does he ever talk normally?'

'Oh, yes.' They will meet at the hotel in an hour.

Laura finishes her meal in peace and happiness. She wonders vaguely if Martin thought she had followed him.

The restaurant is air-conditioned cool. When she steps out the heat radiates off the streets. She realises she drank too much wine but is glad that she did. She breasts the heat, walking down Fifth Avenue with sweat tickling her arm-pits. She stops occasionally, looking at shop windows much as she had stopped in front of paintings in the Metropolitan, except that now she pin-points the minutest detail, noting colour, shape and line, as if it was her own face or finger.

When she picks up a taxi, it is because she doesn't want to keep Martin waiting, not because she is tired or hot.

But Martin is already waiting, standing in the middle of their bedroom with an anxious expression.

She runs into his arms. He seems about to stop her but then relents and holds her tight. They don't kiss although their bodies strain to be close.

He pushes her an inch or two away. 'You're so hot.'

'I walked. Oh darling, I want you so much.'

Even in this moment of passion Laura is surprised to hear herself saying such things. She has never told any man she wanted him.

Martin frowns. 'How did you find out where I was?'

'I didn't. What does it matter?' Laura is impatient. She drags at him.

'Don't you want to hear about Pat?'

'No. No. Not now. Please, darling.'

Martin doesn't know she is going back to London that evening. She hasn't changed her mind about that. But he doesn't know and can't understand her impatience.

'I'm sorry about lunch. It was a business meeting, whatever it may have looked like. She's a producer at NBC.'

'It didn't look like anything, Martin, I love you!' Laura saw she was begging a man to go to bed with her and she didn't care. She was begging because she would leave him in an hour or two. But she didn't want to tell him with his mind full of Pat. Didn't he understand? She didn't care about Pat. Then why was she leaving him? Because this being in New York together no longer seemed right. It was not the vacuum she'd imagined. She had to go home. She had to think. There was Nicky.

At last Martin takes off his jacket and lies down with Laura. They lie still for a little and then undress each other gently.

Afterwards Laura cries tears of happiness and Martin kisses each place they fall. Then she tells him she is going back to England that evening.

He becomes corpse-like, cold, rigid, heavy. She is frightened. Frantically, she tries to explain. Frantically, she whispers in his ear. 'Too sudden, too harsh. I must think. I must think. . . .'

He says in an ugly leaden voice. 'If it's not Pat and it's not your son then it must be cowardice.'

Perhaps he knows she won't go if he hates her. She couldn't bear to leave him hating her. She wants to tell him it won't be forever. But that would be unfair. She must think without promises.

'I love you!' She whispers over and over again. As if she was making up for all the years she never said it.

Eventually he accepts it. 'So why are you leaving me?'

'I've told you over and over again I'm not leaving you. I could never leave you. I'm leaving the situation. Now I know. Now I know how I love you I need to think.'

'You're going home,' Martin says in a bitter voice. 'You're going home to your husband and son. Why should you be able to think with them?' But his bitterness has a tinge of resignation. Laura hears it and kisses him again.

'If I go to Johnny or Roy it will just be more complicated, involve more people.'

'What about a girlfriend?'

Nell. Nell would be on Martin's side. She can hardly like Miles when he makes his disapproval of her so obvious. She could go to Nell.

'No.' Laura thinks she cannot be in England and not be with Nicky. She doesn't tell Martin this. He has no children. He cannot be expected to understand.

She gets up slowly and goes to the bathroom. Martin watches her. She remembers how she had watched him that morning.

Chapter Eleven

It was early in the morning when Laura arrived at London airport. She picked up a taxi. It was a cold grey day, made colder and greyer by her feelings of sadness, guilt and fearful anticipation. She longed to see Nicky. Although she had only been away two days, less time than her visit to Ireland, the decision of separation had been made as if forever. She longed to see him well, cheerful, unaltered by her faithlessness. As the taxi drew near her house and she realised she would arrive at breakfast time, her fear increased. Nicky, Lizzie, Maria, Miles staring at her with harassed morning faces. What would she say?

'Stop here, please.'

She wanted to walk the last five minutes. She had little to carry even though she had decided to bring with her the New York shopping. She was cold, shivering, her teeth gritted together. She stopped about four doors away and put her bag down. She swung her arms around, flexed her waist, touched her toes. A postman passing, looked at her oddly. It was their regular postman who had delivered their letters for ten years. He hadn't recognised her. She was an alien. In two days she had put herself outside normal human contact. She had destroyed normal happiness.

This was no good. If she went on thinking in such over dramatic terms she'd never go home. It was already eight-thirty. She picked up her bag and walked a few more paces. Now she could see her own front door. How extraordinary! She'd always imagined it was painted crimson but now her new alien self could see quite clearly it was pink.

The door opens. Laura darts behind a tree. Miles and Nicky come out. She circles the tree, watching. Nicky is talking excitedly, waving his hands around. Laura has forgotten how tall and strong he is. Miles also is taller than she remembered and better looking, more distinguished. As they reach Miles's car he speaks sharply to Nicky who shakes his head and runs back into the house. Miles gets into the car. Laura hesitates. Miles is facing away from her. Should she follow Nicky? But then he is out again, swinging his forgotten satchel. Laura can't resist.

She calls 'Nicky!' He doesn't hear. She calls again louder, 'Nicky!'

He looks without stopping his run to the car. He sees her, smiles broadly, waves, 'Hi! Mum!' He jumps into the car. They drive away.

Laura comes out from behind the tree and stares after the car. It crosses her mind that Miles may see her out of the rear view mirror but she doesn't care. Besides presumably Nicky will tell him she is back. Although on the other hand perhaps he will not consider it important enough. Laura is bewildered. She abandons her son and when she returns he merely smiles and waves.

She walks up to her front door and lets herself in. Maria stands hand to heart.

'Oh. Aiee! I thought a burglar.'

'Only me.'

Laura who was always concerned to see contentment in all around her, doesn't bother to give Maria an explanation. She goes to her room. It is untidy, bed un-made, men's things around. It smells of a man on his own. This at least has changed. She starts to tidy it.

As she folds Miles's pyjamas she realises the obvious fact that Nicky didn't know he had been abandoned. She herself had suggested he should be told she was on holiday. He had known nothing but family security. Why should he suspect? As far as he was concerned she might as well have been spending a couple of nights on some Agricultural Heritage project.

This reminds her that it is still a full week from the big summer meeting. She had abandoned that too, without thought, but now she was back it would still be waiting. She ought to ring Ben Casey.

This is a very odd idea. Is that why she had come back? To start life as usual. To ring Ben Casey before talking to Miles would be wrong. Would it be wrong? Were there correct ways of behaviour for the returning wife? Was she the returning wife?

She finishes tidying the room and goes down to the kitchen.

She says to Maria coldly, 'I'll finish cleaning here, you go and turn out Nicky's bedroom.'

Certainly she was the returning wife. But not the repentant wife. No. Not that. No temptation to the confessional. She had come back to think. Seeing the empty fruit bowl and the empty bread-bin, she thinks she'd better put a big shop-up on the day's programme.

She plugs in the kettle and the phone rings.

'Hello.' She is here in the house. There is no point in disguising it. A woman asks to speak to her. It is not an American operator.

'Speaking.'

'So you are back.' It is Miles.

'Yes.'

'I'm very busy this week.' This seems a non sequitur.

'Oh,' Laura pauses and since he says nothing, adds, 'I'm sorry.'

'I don't have much time. I won't be home much.'

Laura feels like saying 'Good' but merely waits for him to continue.

'I don't want you to upset Nicky.'

Upset Nicky! She has looked after Nicky for all his seven years and now Miles talks about her upsetting him. He wouldn't have an idea what would upset him. He barely knows the child. Laura controls her voice with difficulty.

'I have no intention of hurting Nicky in any way. When I saw him this morning he looked extremely cheerful.'

'He asked me what you were doing hiding behind a tree.'

'Oh.' Laura was not prepared for this.

'What were you doing hiding behind a tree?'

Laura begins to feel hysterical. 'Avoiding the dog shit,' she giggles. It feels better to be laughing at Miles's solemn, magisterial voice. 'You'll make a wonderful judge!' she cries wildly.

Miles allows a short pause before he says even more coldly. 'This is not the moment for discussion, I am merely making certain that you will not involve Nicky in your problems since I will not be at home when he returns from school.'

'What do you want me to do? Promise not to hurt my own child?'

'That would be a start.'

Laura becomes angry. She shouts, 'And what about upsetting you? Don't you want to know where I've been, who I've been with, what I've done!'

'I know who you've been with. You told me. And I can guess what you've done. It's not very original. Women do it all the time. I had always thought you were different. Special. I was wrong. I'll see you this evening. Between nine and ten. Goodbye.'

Laura is left holding the telephone. She is shaking all over. He is absolutely right. That is her only thought. He is absolutely, totally, one hundred per cent right. She has joined the ranks of other failed women. She has lost what was special about her. She is hurting everyone, including herself. She huddles in the chair, feeling, on top of everything else, very sick.

She runs to the lavatory and throws up. When she comes out, the telephone is ringing again. She doesn't pick it up but it goes on and on. Eventually she hears Maria answering it. She knocks at the door.

'Mrs Lyons for you.'

Laura picks up the phone. 'Nell.'

'Whatever is the matter with your usually well-organised household?'

'I'm sorry.'

'Something the matter with you?'

'I don't know.'

'I was just ringing to say I'm on my way up to London and would you like to have lunch?'

'Oh yes, I would!' Laura shouts into the phone. She sees a lifeline.

'Well, that's better.'

Nell had a meeting in the West End so they agreed to meet at a restaurant in Soho. Laura was glad to get out of the house. Perhaps Martin was right. Her own home was no place to think. There seemed no place between life as normal or total rebellion.

'I've been seeing my solicitor,' Nell begins even before Laura sits down. 'What a bastard that husband, ex-husband, of mine is!'

'Oh dear.' Laura wonders as Nell tells a tale of grievance whether she will listen too.

'Someone and I'd like to know who told him firstly that I was making a fortune out of my pots and, secondly, that I was living with another man so now he's refusing to pay proper maintenance. I mean who has the children ninety per cent of the holidays? If you saw what they consumed! It's more like werewolves than human beings. And I'm expected to pay half of it out of some imaginary profits. It was all because I won that award. You knew I won that award, didn't you? That's what put him on to me, I'll bet. Well, awards don't buy peanut butter. Do you know a pot of peanut butter which is a mere hors d'oeuvres in Jack's gastronomic needs costs 65p?'

'No.' Laura didn't know. As Nell picks up her menu, she takes her chance, 'I need to ask your advice.'

'Problems, problems,' Nell says without putting aside the menu. Laura's problems are notoriously undramatic. 'Do men have problems like women do?'

Laura is not to be diverted but she hesitates over the choice of words.

Nell, about to introduce the subject of garlic at lunch-time, suddenly notices she is seriously upset.

'What's the matter? Tell me. I'll try to help.' She leans forward encouragingly.

'No one can help me.' Laura bursts into tears.

Nell looks with amazement. She has never seen Laura cry. She has never seen her ugly, her face blotchy, screwed up and running with water. Although essentially sympathetic, she cannot repress a twinge of satisfaction. Laura is human too.

'Oh dear. I shouldn't cry here.' Laura gulps.

'Nonsense! Everyone likes to see women reduced to tears. Particularly men. Very good for business. You'll probably be given a free meal.'

Laura smiles a little and gradually stops crying. Nell hands her a paper napkin and she blows her nose.

'So?'

'I've fallen in love with a man and I ran away with him to New York but now I've come back.'

Nell looks deeply shocked. But she realises she mustn't show that to Laura so she asks almost brusquely, 'Is he married?'

'What? No.' Laura can't think why Nell asks such a silly, irrelevant question. The bald statement of facts has depressed her beyond tears. She stares at the menu and decides to order chicken. She doesn't like chicken much. She waits for Nell's judgment.

'That's a good thing anyway.'

'What?'

'Him not being married.'

'But don't you see,' she puts down the menu, 'I've ruined my whole life and probably Miles and Nicky's too. For what? Why? Because I fall in love. I think I fall in love.' She stares beseechingly at Nell. Is there some better interpretation?

Nell avoids her eyes. She had always admired Laura's marriage, believed that it would last forever. Although she did not like Miles, she recognised he loved Laura, and would do anything within his nature to make her happy.

Nell says, 'Do you still love him?' She doesn't really believe Laura capable of the deepest kind of love. Perhaps it is because Laura has never had to endure the deepest kind of suffering.

'Love! Love!' Laura cries wildly. 'How do I know? I thought I loved Miles. But this. This. This takes me over. It's everything. It blots out. It blots out even Nicky.' She throws her arms on the table, knocking a knife to the floor and lets her head crash down on top of them.

Nell watches a strand of hair fall into the salt.

She sighs. 'What does Miles say?'

'Miles?' Laura looks vacant as if he too is irrelevant. 'I don't know. We haven't talked about it.'

'What?'

'He rang me this morning but he only talked about Nicky,' Laura pauses suddenly. She realises this isn't true. Miles had said he used to think her 'special' and now he no longer did. That was what had precipitated her worst misery. Obviously she had tried to wipe it from her memory. Was that particular misery mainly composed of hurt pride?

But Nell has fixed on her remark about Nicky. 'Only talked about Nicky. That's typical. Probably trying to make you feel guilty. That's a typical husband's dirty trick. As if love for a man has anything to do with love for your son!' Nell is glad to be able to defend Laura against Miles's bad behaviour. 'You mustn't let him bully you. And don't let him even discuss Nicky without someone else there.' Nell grows quite fierce in her defence. 'You love Nicky just as much as him, don't ever forget that!'

Laura is bewildered. 'What do you mean "someone else there"?'

'A solicitor. Whatever.'

Laura becomes very quiet.

Nell notices it and realises that her righteous indignation had carried her too far. 'But you probably haven't thought of divorce yet.'

'No,' says Laura in a small voice. She has a feeling of total unreality. It is impossible that she is sitting in a restaurant talking about divorce, her divorce, with Nell. Their food arrives.

Laura shreds her chicken.

Nell says, 'I suppose you don't want to tell me who it is?'

Laura supposes she owes Nell a name. But she is beginning to regret talking to Nell. Before their conversation she had only thought of love, of virtue and sin. But now she feels obliged to consider her action in terms of the world.

She ducks her head. 'It's no one you know. You wouldn't even like him.' She stops. Tries to eat some meat.

'So what are you going to do? You can come and stay with me anytime you need space. Bring him too if you want.'

Laura is disgusted by this friendly offer. She tries not to let it show in her face. 'I've got to think,' she says.

'I've never found thinking helps much,' Nell now tucks in to her food quite greedily. She sees Laura has withdrawn and doesn't want to step where unwanted. Poor Laura. She is looking calm again and beautiful, on the surface the old Laura. But, Nell thinks sadly, nothing will ever be the same again. It's almost enough to make you believe in the apple and the Garden of Eden.

Laura hurries from the restaurant. She is going to be at least a quarter of an hour late for picking up Nicky. On this day of all days. When all she was doing was exchanging self-indulgent soul-baring. Two nearly middle-aged ladies swopping stories of life and loves over a bottle of wine. The scene disgusts her. She feels as she did when Nell suggested she took Martin to stay.

Laura picks up a taxi and tells him to hurry. 'Ever heard of the tortoise and the hare?' he says imperviously.

Nicky sits in the school cloakroom. He is all on his own and the lights have been switched off. Unlike that morning when she had been surprised by his height and strength, he now seems small and pale.

'You're very very late.' His voice is defiant but she sees he is near tears. 'Even the teacher had to go. She tried to ring home but no one answered.'

Laura runs to him. She hugs and hugs him. 'I'm so sorry, darling. I had lunch with Nell and then I got stuck in the traffic.'

Nicky's body is stiff. 'I don't like Nell.'

'Oh you do, darling! She gives you wonderful presents at Christmas.'

'She doesn't give me anything for my birthday.'

They walk down the street together. Nicky relents slightly and lets Laura hold his hand. She bribes him with an ice lolly and a string of liquorice. He ties a bow in the liquorice and says testingly, 'Daddy told me a lie. He said you were in America for a holiday. But you couldn't have got there and back so quickly.' He pauses and a flash of attention, more than paid to lolly or sweets, brightens his face. 'Unless you went by Concorde.' He shakes her hand hopefully. 'Did you go by Concorde? You must have gone by Concorde!'

Resisting the temptation to lie Laura pulls him and cries, 'Come on. I'll race you home.' She knows if he runs with her he'll forgive her. And he does, shouting and boasting at his supersonic speed. Having questioned once, he almost certainly will not try again. Laura lets Nicky win and catches up as he hammers on the door.

Before she can get out her key, the door opens. Miles stands there.

'You're late.'

'Are we?' Laura lets Nicky hurtle off towards the kitchen. 'We stopped at the sweetshop.'

'You shouldn't bribe him.'

'Why not?'

Miles gives her a scornful look. 'I want to talk to you.'

'OK.' Laura stands, refusing to be intimidated, refusing to repent. Let them talk, but on equal terms, not the judge to the defendant, not the righteous to the guilty.

'Come into my study.'

'OK.' Laura never says OK. She knows it will irritate. She follows him across the hallway. 'I've never known you home at this time.'

'I should be working.'

Laura decides not to feel guilty about this either. However, this proof of his concern makes her frightened for it gives a reality to what she has done. On the other hand she is pleased at his interest. What she most dreaded was an attempt to pretend nothing of any importance had happened. At least he is taking her seriously.

'Well?' She stands in his study. 'Shall I tell you all about it?'

'Laura!' It is an appeal, breaking through her defiance but she does not dare hear it. However she does sit down.

'I suppose I should apologise.'

Miles sits down too. He looks tired. He looks old. Laura hates him. He looks at his toe-cap. She says, 'What are you going to do?'

He looks up surprised. 'Nothing. I've never done anything. I'm not going to do anything.'

Laura thinks that is true. He has become a nothing in her life. 'You said you wanted to talk. And I've offered to apologise.'

'So you're staying?' Miles finds the words very hard to say. His mouth becomes small.

'I don't know.' Laura crosses her legs. For a moment she is shocked by herself. Then she says loudly, 'I'm here now anyway.'

Miles gets up. He stands stiffly. 'There's no point in talking.' He hesitates, looking at her. 'I think you've gone mad. I can't talk to a mad woman. I'll go back to chambers.'

Laura sees he is going to walk out of the room and is suddenly afraid. 'Don't you want to talk about it?'

He goes to the door. 'No. You're grown-up. It's your choice. But if you ever leave Nicky and me again, even for one night, I'll make sure you never come back. You'll never have Nicky again.'

He goes out of the room, carefully closing the door. Laura sits enclosed by his study. She is trembling all over. Before meeting Martin she had never trembled in her life. This untapped capacity amazes her. As if her whole body is altering. Perhaps she is mad.

The front door closes and she hears Nicky calling from the kitchen, 'Mummy! Mummy! I've spilt the lemon!'

Laura wants to talk to Nell again. Can Miles really keep her away from Nicky? It seems inconceivable. But it starts a new kind of terror. She plays games all evening with Nicky until he is exhausted and irritable with so much attention.

Then she goes to bed. As she lies down she pictures Martin for the first time as he was in their New York bedroom. Immediately the telephone rings. She knows it will be him.

'My darling sister! Whatever is all this? Don't move. I'm coming round immediately.'

Johnny. Laura is exhausted. Johnny has inexhaustible energy. Laura pleads but he is adamant. He is only round the corner. He will be there in a moment.

Three quarters of an hour later, he arrives, brandishing a bottle of wine. 'There's no point in being gloomy about it, is there? Now, let's try and sort it all out.' Laura realises he is at least half drunk.

'I don't want to talk, Johnny. I've got nothing to say.'

'Nothing to say! Running off to New York with your brother's oldest friend and then having nothing to say. I feel responsible you know. As far as I can remember I actually introduced you. If it wasn't for me you'd never have got yourself into such a twist. A brother responsible for his own sister's downfall. It's shocking, tragic! Reminds one of Greek at school.

'Bella, horrida bella,
'Et Thybrim multo spumantem sanguine cerno.'

'That sounds like Latin.'

'Greek, Latin – it's all the same tragedy-wise.'

'There is no tragedy. I'm here, aren't I?'

Johnny is stopped short. 'That's true. Yes. So you are.'

Laura presses her offensive. 'Who told you about "my downfall"?' She manages what she hopes to be a satirical smile.

'No one exactly told me.' Johnny puts down his glass to concentrate. 'Philippa, Martin's erstwhile girlfriend, told me he had gone to New York and then Lizzie said you'd gone and then Miles nearly snapped my head off when I asked him where you were, so it wasn't very difficult to put two and two together. After all, I'm not blind, not about things like this anyway, I'd seen the way you two vibrate whenever you get within a hundred yards of each other.'

'You're drunk,' Laura moves further into the attack. She takes the bottle from him though he isn't actually attempting to pour from it. 'Your imagination's got the better of you. I'm here. I was in New York. So was Martin.' She manages the name bravely. 'Nothing odd in that. Lot's of people go to New York. Now apologise to me and go home.' She hardens her heart against Johnny's bewilderment. He had come, after a drop too many it was true, to comfort and counsel. He had not expected this assault. She sees him beginning to doubt. Certainly he had always considered his sister a woman, indeed the only woman, inviolate to the temptations of the flesh. Perhaps he had been envious, glad after her many lectures to him, to see her fall.

Laura is pushing him onto his feet. 'I'm sorry, I. . . .'

'It's all right. Just go. I'm tired.'

Johnny goes humbly. He kisses Laura's hand and tells her he is glad that he is wrong and that all is well. 'Once you start, you know, it's endless. One falls first time for the great love. And then when it finishes, there's another and another. It's endless. No way to lead a life. I often wish I'd stayed completely faithful to Katie, from the start. After all, what is love? "Proculhinc, procul este, severae!" which means "Get out of it, you grim old bags!"'

He goes, apologising once more. But Laura suspects that he is not altogether convinced. He is warning her. She does not try and go to bed again but sits waiting for Miles.

As she sits, she remembers again her work and that she has not been in touch with Ben Casey. She remembers how much more attractive he'd seemed after she'd made love with Martin. Was that what Johnny meant? He meant well. She could only hope that he would not tell anyone else what he suspected. Gossip, which previously she'd seen as a perfectly respectable entertainment for people who had nothing else to do, suddenly seems a horrible threat.

She pours herself a glass of wine and tries not to imagine the possibilities.

An hour or more later she hears Miles's key in the door.

She hurries to meet him in the hallway. 'I won't see him any more,' she says taking his coat.

Miles says nothing but kisses her briefly on the cheek.

'Have you eaten?'

'No, I wouldn't mind a sandwich.'

'I'll make you one.'

She is relieved to be away from him. Relieved to be in service. With a moment of self-dramatism she thinks she perfectly understands how those renouncing great love become priests or nuns. Devoting their lives to those they cannot love.

She makes perfect sandwiches, neatly salting the meat and trimming off the crusts. Martin and she had not been long enough together to know whether theirs was 'great love' or some tawdry counterfeit.

That night she is so tired that she is hardly aware of Miles's presence in the bed.

Chapter Twelve

It is a perfect summer morning. Laura stands in the middle of a wide sloping field watching farm implements come slowly through the gateway and circle into position. In the next door field the crest of a marquee appears over the hedge. A loud-speaker van drives fast towards her. Ben Casey is sitting beside the driver. He jumps out, and says in anguished tones, 'We'll never be ready in two hours!'

Laura looks at him calmly. She has never seen him worried before. She remembers his civil service admonition about action. It is strange to see him in a wide open space. She compares him unfavourably to Roy, who looks his best against a background of a few hundred acres. Then, inevitably, she thinks of Martin. The tractors had distracted her for quite five minutes.

'We'll be ready,' she says firmly. 'And if we're not, we're not.'

'Where do you want the speakers set up?' The driver doesn't bother to get out of his van.

Laura looks at his bored face shouting through the window. She is sure people once were not so unattractive. Is it because she no longer likes people as she used to? Because, while she is separated from Martin every action, every word is a conscious effort. She tries to remember what it was like to be spontaneously happy, and fails. She tells the driver where to put up the speakers and then walks with Ben Casey to the marquee.

'Once that's up we can get the displays and the food in,' she says in a strong bossy voice which quite surprises her.

They inspect the barbecue which is already in operation and

then go over to the field to be used as a car park. 'We're lucky with the weather,' she says. 'We'll probably get a huge crowd.'

Ben Casey cheers up a little. 'Thank heavens, the minister's not coming till twelve-thirty.'

'Don't worry. It's all going to be a huge success.' Laura believes this and wishes she cared. At nine o'clock in the morning she has a strong desire for a strong drink. The day stretches ahead interminably. Perhaps in the evening when all the work is over she will get drunk.

At the last minute they had decided to turn the marquee into a disco after seven o'clock. People would have to pay. They might even make some money. Laura had invited any of her friends she'd spoken to in the last week. At the back of her mind is the terrifying hope that Martin will appear. She has not seen or spoken to him since they parted in New York, nor has anyone else mentioned him. But she feels he must have returned to England. She tells herself that she never wants to see him again.

Just before eleven when Laura is in the confusion of the first arrivals before the display is finished, Katie drives up with a carful of children. She hoots merrily.

'You're not supposed to bring cars here,' Laura shouts.

'I said the children couldn't walk so far and the man waved me through. Maddy's been sick.'

Looking at Katie's pink and happy face surrounded by shouting, waving children, Laura wonders why she had got into the habit of saying 'Poor Katie.' It was because of Johnny's unfaithfulness, she supposed. And yet Katie was not pathetic. She was a determined woman, living life as she wanted it. The man at the gate had strict orders to let through no one except the minister.

'Park behind the marquee. The tractors are in the next field. I'll be with you in about half an hour.'

Katie has Nicky in the car and Lizzie and a new au pair. She drives away shouting. 'We only took an hour to get here, can you believe it?'

Laura who had been staying with her the night before and had driven over herself taking at least an hour without children being sick would prefer not to believe it. She watches Katie narrowly missing a guy rope and remembers how she had been before she married. A jolly schoolgirl.

Laura likes the minister. She has met him before over drinks in the House of Commons. He is small and tubby with sharp features and eager ambitious eyes. He has no real interest in agriculture but likes doing a good job. Despite his unprepossessing appearance, he has a reputation for liking women, particularly a lady on the other side of the House. He also likes to drink. This combination makes him cheerful company in the unusual circumstances of a marquee in the middle of the Somerset countryside. Laura flirts with him and apologises for the wobbly crate he'll have to stand on to make his speech.

'As long as you wait nearby with your arms open.'

Laura catches herself thinking that life is just about worth living. She introduces him to Nicky who looks impressed and handsome.

The press begin to arrive.

She has the minister, Ben Casey can have the press. She notices Ben looking at her with what she decides is admiration. Crowds begin to collect round the wobbly box. The loudspeakers announce that after the speech which will take place in five minutes there will be a children's Fancy Dress Parade. Katie has been working hours to turn her children into a farm-workers' family circa 1750. Nicky had refused to be involved.

The minister finishes his drink and steps onto the box. A satisfactory number of cameras click. His private secretary who'd stayed discreetly in the background now comes to stand beside Laura. 'He's very good at this sort of thing,' he whispers to Laura. 'He'll do ten minutes to the dot, opening with a laugh and closing with a sob.' He speaks with pride and Laura thinks, as she does periodically, that what she lacks is 'job satisfaction'. It gives Miles such an unfair advantage.

The minister is now getting his laugh. He smiles contentedly and then lowers his voice. Laura wonders what his relationship is with the MP from the other side of the House. They are both married to other people. They are both ambitious, successful. Is that thing called a 'relationship between equals' something allied to 'job satisfaction'? Do they swop politics before sex?

Miles only talks about his career to impress her. He does not put her fully into the picture. If he did she might be able to understand and help. But then he would seem less impressive. He wants to make a speech to an admiring audience, not have a conversation.

Laura's attention is drawn to Ben Casey who is trying to stop a photographer from taking pictures during the minister's speech. The strange thing was that she had not chosen to fall in love with someone who would treat her as a working equal. Someone like Ben Casey. She knew almost nothing of Martin's life, his working life. Software meant as little to her as Miles's legal jargon. Perhaps she was at fault. She had never considered the problems in her marriage until she had fallen in love with Martin. She had thought herself happy. She had been happy. Laura sighs. No. She wasn't going to take the blame. Miles had trapped her, turned her into what he wanted her to be and now it was too late to change.

She would never have 'job satisfaction'. Silly phrase. Laura looks at the minister now building up towards the sob and thinks how ridiculous he seems, uttering as if deeply moved, ideas he had been spoon-fed by his private secretary that morning. She feels ashamed of her flirtatious flattering of him earlier.

At least Miles is a real human being. She tries to picture her husband's pale tired face with wifely pride and does not altogether fail. Miles has been nice to her since her promise to remain with him. He has declared his intention of paying a visit to her 'old tractors'.

He arrives shortly after the minister's departure in the middle of the afternoon. Although it is Saturday, he can only interrupt his working schedule for an hour or so. Laura thinks she detects a shading of patronage and martyrdom under his warmth and encouragement. She is sure of it when he looks round and says, 'So the minister didn't make it after all.'

'He was here for hours. He made an excellent speech.' She refuses Miles's offer of a cider and watches him drink a pale ale with disgust. She might have wanted a vodka and tonic.

She says in a firm voice, 'I'll have to stay for the dancing.'

Ben Casey comes up. She introduces them. Ben Casey makes some flattering remarks about her organisational ability. Like a form-master talking about a child to her parent, Laura thinks irritably. The civil servant is obviously impressed by the Queen's Counsel in his suit and they begin to talk about Law and the Environment.

Laura leaves them together, noticing with satisfaction that as she goes both men falter and watch her out of the corner of their eyes.

'I'll try and find Nicky.'

Miles doesn't stay long. He has registered his presence and official encouragement. Although Laura wants him to go, this annoys her too. She pecks him on the cheek, telling him to drive carefully and unfreeze the fish pie before cooking it.

She regrets this meanness as soon as he has gone. After all he had driven over a hundred miles to support her. If only she could believe it was out of love not out of duty. This thought stops her a moment for she realises that it would be more unbearable if she really thought he loved her. She would be cruel then, not just unkind. In his absence, she can be such a good wife.

Laura sighs and then is immensely cheered to see Nell coming towards her with her two teenage sons and a third youth she doesn't recognise. She runs towards them crying, 'Friends! Friends! I hope you're staying for the disco.'

The third youth turns out to be Nell's boyfriend. The one who works on a caravan site. Laura remembers Nell telling her about him in that remote era before she'd met Martin. At that time all Nell's stories of love had the ring of fantasy. Now she believes and looks at him considering. He is very beautiful, in a disconcerting way not unlike Nell's sons who are blonde and tall and gruff-voiced. He is sunburnt and wears turquoise beads round his neck. He also has a discreet gold hoop in his ear. Up to a few weeks ago Laura could never have taken seriously a man with a gold hoop in his ear. Now she looks at him as she might a golden apple in a bowl and wants to touch.

He says, 'Got no caravan stand, then?' His name is Lyndon.

'I'm afraid this whole thing's rather against caravans,' Laura apologises. 'It's more about the past. You know, preservation and that sort of thing.'

'People love caravans,' says Lyndon, peering over the hedge to where the vast ancient machines sit idly. 'Take Nell's kids, they'd much rather live in a caravan, than a house. Wouldn't you?' He turns on the boys who mumble and shuffle embarrassedly.

'I'm not against caravans,' says Laura which is not true since she hates them as much as anything inanimate, 'I was just explaining why there isn't a caravan stand here. It's not an ordinary fair.' She stops, disconcerted by the blankness of

155

Lyndon's beautiful blue eyes. She glances at Nell who smiles encouragingly.

Nell takes Lyndon's arm. 'He's planning to make his first million before he's thirty. Come on, it'll do you good to look at the past.'

'Twenty-five,' says Lyndon, giving her a cool stare. Laura catches it too and finds herself blushing as if it was meant for herself.

As the four of them walk off towards the tractors she wonders whether the boys accept the situation easily. They seem unchanged, unmoved. Silent, pale blue eyes staring intelligently. They were very good classicists, Nell had told her once. Perhaps the study of Greek and Roman drama had given them a mature detachment. What was Johnny's line, *Get out of it, you grim old bags!*

Laura makes a half-convinced mental note that children are not easily made into sacrificial victims.

The sun is beginning to turn golden now and lose its heat. Families with children are leaving. Picnics and papers are stuffed into empty oil cans round the fields. The barbecue, endlessly churning out sausages, stops for a rest. Laura says goodbye to Katie and Nicky and the other children and then goes to the marquee for a rest. Soon she must begin organising the evening's entertainment.

She sits on a fold-up chair drinking tea from a cardboard cup. Ben Casey comes and squats beside her. 'You look sad.'

'I'm not,' she says sharply.

'Tired?'

'Not particularly.' She wants to be alone. Perhaps Martin will come that evening.

'It's been a huge success.'

'So far.'

'The dancing's only the icing on the cake.'

Laura stands up. 'I'm going to find a quiet patch of grass for a moment's peace.'

Ben Casey stands too. 'I thought you looked done in.'

'I am not done in.' Laura walks away.

Ben Casey watches her go affectionately. He has never seen her like this. Willful, almost rude. She is thinner now and the backs of her legs are white although the fronts are sunburnt. She used to seem perfect.

Laura lies in long grass on a hill above the fair. The grass, too steep to cut or plough, is filled with wild flowers, poppies, buttercups, scabious, daisies. Red, yellow, orange, mauve, blue, white. The colours blur in front of Laura's eyes. She half-sleeps, dreaming of Martin's face, his touch on her body. 'What angel wakes me from my fairy bed?'

Laura sits up and looks around. She feels better, fresher. She opens her handbag and gets out her mirror. Her eyes are bright, her face glowing from the sun of the day. The sun is behind her head ready to dip behind the hill she sits on.

She brushes her hair, makes up her face and smooths her silk dress. One of the dresses she bought in New York. She stands up and feels strong and brave. The night is ahead.

Coloured lights strung round the marquee glow in the dusk. Someone is experimenting with the disco.

'Where have you been? We've been looking for you everywhere?'

'I had to have a rest.'

'So that Casey man said. But you seem to become invisible. Johnny's here with some girl and several other people who say you invited them.'

Laura smiles at Nell. 'I hope Johnny's brought that crate of wine he promised.'

Johnny has not only brought the wine but also Martin's girlfriend, Philippa. Before Laura can properly react to this Ben Casey arrives, agitated.

'The man at the gate and the man at the car-park have gone off. They say they were paid for a day not twenty-four hours. No one will buy tickets. It'll be chaos.'

'Never mind about the chaos. Just have someone sitting guard in front of the drink. They'll buy tickets if they need one to buy a drink.' Johnny is in ebullient form as he always is at parties.

'That sounds sensible.' Laura volunteers to sit at the table.

Ben Casey relaxes. 'I suppose it doesn't matter much about parking. Most of them are arriving on motor-cycles anyway.'

The new visitors are young. Suddenly Nell's three young escorts are appropriate. So is Nell in her dungarees and her long red hair. Laura sits at the table selling tickets and wonders whether she feels old and sad. She drinks some wine.

Philippa is young. Johnny always feels younger than the

youngest at any party. Laura's other friends look a little lost. Three couples surprised to find themselves in a marquee under a darkening sky.

The music starts. It is magnificently loud. It fills the whole space, shutting out the ordinary world, making conversation impossible. Ben Casey arrives with a young man. He drags up Laura and pushes the young man into her chair. He takes her over to the slatted wood of the dance floor.

She realises he is smaller than her. She dances tentatively, holding Ben's outstretched arms, swaying backwards and forwards. Then he begins to move faster, shouting above the din, 'You're not old yet!' For a moment Laura hates him. Hates him for being familiar, hates him most of all because he is not Martin. He pulls her arm about and tries to swing her. All around them people are bobbing and bouncing, faces already flattened into vacuum by the deafening noise. Philippa's face passes. Laura remembers seeing it at Martin's party given in his club. Then, too, it had been a vacuous face, across a table, unknown and unknowing.

Laura wonders if it will approach her during the course of the evening and throw accusations. Johnny and she must have talked about her as they drove down. She is a pretty girl, with small features and straight silky hair. As she passes her face suddenly screws up into a pekinese mask. She sneezes violently. She doesn't look capable of passion. Laura remembers her telephone voice as she and Martin lay in his bed.

She dances by and her eyes register Laura. Laura wonders what she sees. A tired middle-aged woman, listlessly swaying. She is behaving as Miles would.

Laura begins to dance, throwing her body around with more energy than anybody, bending and stamping and twirling. She does it for Philippa and to prove she is not Miles. She does not feel ridiculous because Ben Casey is delighted and starts to do the same. Besides it is dark and the noise, one tune following another without break, blots out any normal self-consciousness.

They only stop for a drink and to pump more breath into their bodies. Gradually Laura is filled by the exhilarating feeling, that nothing matters. She is floating, flying, drowning on a sea of noise. She notices Ben Casey has started to touch her body as she twists and circles around him. He, presumably, thinks she dances for him. But she dances only for the dance. Ecstasy. Standing outside her body. Pure ecstasy. She hardly feels his fingers on her body. Let him touch, it means nothing to her.

Even Philippa's face, swimming past, no longer affects her. Poor Philippa, let her dance too, if she can. Another pekinese mask, another sneeze. Nell comes near with Lyndon. Lyndon has taken his shirt off. Laura remembers he is her golden apple and wants to touch him as Ben Casey touches her.

Suddenly they have swapped partners. Nell and Ben locked in heaving embrace, Lyndon and Laura circling each other, warily at first, performing at a distance, then closing in till their bodies slither past each other as they turn. Laura thinks that this slithering past, not quite touching is, after all, the thing. Contact would be so ordinary, so to be expected, so all over.

They slither and slide past each other. Her body is burning, heart thudding, yet inside she is still cool, distanced. She has a flash memory of when she last felt like this, the tennis four which ended with Miles pulling his tendon. Martin was at her side then, yet Lyndon, with his sweating torso and gold earring, is more real. Martin is a shadow; she no longer cares if he comes.

'I need some air!' Lyndon mouths and grabs her hand.

They are outside the marquee before she can think. He pulls her a little further away and begins to kiss her.

Laura is limp, trying to summon up the strength to push him away. This is not what she wants. It may seem fantasy now but it will be shaming reality in the morning. Yet she can't bear to become sober again. She pushes him off, 'Let's dance.'

'I've had enough dancing.'

'I want to dance.'

He grabs hold of her and kisses her again.

'No.'

'Yes.' He touches her breasts and puts his hand at the back of her neck.

Laura shivers. 'Nell,' she says, weakly.

'What about her? She's got off with your chap, hasn't she?'

Laura pushes him so hard that he nearly falls over. She runs to the dance floor and seeing one of Nell's sons standing watching takes him by the hand. With his customary silent embarrassment he comes obediently.

They begin to dance. He dances better than Laura would have expected. His stiff shyness only lasts a few minutes. Laura doesn't find it hard to get back into her rhythm. She is surprised at herself. Is she so hardened now as to be unmoved at her near seduction by a too beautiful youth with a naked torso and gold earring?

Seth. She remembers the boy's name now, dances in front of her. She half closes her eyes. What is the difference, she thinks, between one young man's body or another's? Where is the morality in it? The morality ties her to her husband. To Miles's ageing pallor and distinguished career. Martin could have been Lyndon or Ben Casey or even this boy, Seth.

Laura begins to feel tired but not unhappy. Martin is still a ghost. She sees the evening will end now without him and doesn't care. Her body is her own. She is a wife and mother. But her body is her own. Her thoughts become muddled and she realises that she has reached a point of total exhaustion.

Johnny appears beside her. 'The London lot are going back,' he mouths. 'I'm ready to drive you whenever you want.'

'Now,' she says dropping the boy's hand. She asks no questions, says goodbye to no one. Philippa, she assumes, is included in the London lot.

'I'm exhausted and drunk,' she says to Johnny as she gets into his car. There are only the two of them.

'So you are,' Johnny used to this condition in himself, sounds pleased at the idea.

'It was a great success,' she says tipping her head back on the seat and shutting her eyes.

'Certainly was,' Johnny begins to drive and talk. Laura remembers how they used to go to parties as children and Johnny prattled all the way home, infuriating their mother.

'. . . So you didn't even notice Lizzie's absence or wonder where she was . . . ?'

Laura half hears his words but feels no duty to respond.

'. . . whatever you may say and I must admit you were pretty convincing the other night and I can't say he's giving anything away, but all I can say is he looks perfectly miserable. Perfectly miserable. And if there wasn't anything between you two why else should he flatly refuse to come tonight? It's just not in character. Whatever she thinks, he doesn't fancy Lizzie. As a jolly companion perhaps but never more than that. I suppose you're going to pretend to be asleep now. All I can say is I've never seen a man look more miserable. He isn't dancing. Whatever happened in New York . . . At least you should see him and clear it up . . . or something . . . poor old Martin. I'd always thought he was more sensible. And you! When I think of the lectures . . . I may say I haven't breathed a word to Katie, which I think pretty good of me, considering.'

Laura sits up suddenly. This is not fair. 'Considering what?' she cries out angrily.

Johnny is flustered. 'I was just talking. I was worried. Poor old Martin. . . .'

'Considering what? Considering what?' Laura screams.

'Nothing. Considering nothing.'

'Then shut up!'

There is silence. Laura puts her head back on the seat. To both their amazements she falls instantly asleep. But his words repeat endlessly in her sleep, making a pattern of sorrow and regret. When they arrive at the house, she kisses Johnny and stumbles upstairs.

All she wants is peace. Peace.

*

Laura wrote to Martin.

Darling Martin,

I owe you an explanation, I cannot ever leave Miles. Although I love you. I believe in marriage. Nicky is very important to me. I could not make him unhappy. I would be unhappy. I would make you unhappy. I love you so much. Laura.

She wanted to write more but each time she came to the point of telling him she loved him she burst into tears. She felt like an old woman weeping over the death of a child. She seemed to have no will. But at least she posted the letter. She thought as she did so that the letter box on the corner of the road would always be a place of misery. Even this absurdity did not make her smile.

She went home and taught Nicky how to play draughts. When he was slow to learn, and whined, she smacked him, viciously. Four days later, a letter arrived from Martin. Miles handed it to her at the breakfast table. Laura saw that he knew instantly who it was from. This surprised her. She didn't know he had such strong instincts. But she met his gaze guiltlessly.

She had written, *I cannot ever leave Miles*. The old formality still sounded appropriate.

Even so she was not brave enough to open the letter at the table. She pushed it aside among the cereal packets as if it wasn't very important.

In the end she carried it unopened to her office, opening it there quickly with trembling hands.

Darling,
I must see you. You must let me see you. Martin.

Laura jumps up from her chair. She paces round the room. This is not fair. He has not said he loves her. He's given her no beautiful words of love for her to perfume and fold away for the years ahead. What does he mean, *must? I must see you. You must let me see you.* Was something seriously wrong? Of course, everything was seriously wrong. But was there some outside reason why he *must* see her? Was he ill? Had she left something in New York? Was he leaving England forever?

And why had he not called her by name? Only *Darling*. At least she was his darling. But people write 'darling' to their mothers. He had not written 'I love you'. Perhaps he wanted to tell her that it had all been a mistake. That he had never really loved her. And that now he would happily release her back to her husband and child. Perhaps her letter had seemed ridiculous, melodramatic. Perhaps he had only been having a fling with her, a petite affair, knowing always she would return to Miles.

I must see you. You must let me see you. Now she studies the writing, trying to see if it expresses passion or resolve or desperation. She remembers Johnny's words . . . 'He looks perfectly miserable. Perfectly miserable.'

Laura sits down on the chair again. She realises it was all a delusion. You can't finish love with a letter like hers. Even if Johnny was wrong, if his liking for emotion had led him to exaggerate; she still had to see him. '*Must*' see him.

With totally contradictory feelings of dejection and failure and radiant happiness, Laura makes the decision to see Martin just one more time.

Wondering at the simplicity of the action, she picks up the phone and dials his office number.

He answers.

'Oh, darling, darling.' At the sound of his voice, Laura

realises that she has been deceiving herself. There was no sensible reason to see him again. Even her letter had just been a trick to get a response from him.

She should put the phone down again. She has heard him say 'Darling. Darling Laura.' But it is not enough. He still has not said, I love you.

'I've missed you so much.' His words, so absurdly unoriginal, seem wonderful to Laura.

'Oh, darling. I love you. I love you. I love you.'

Now she should put the phone down. Now she has no excuse. Three times. I love you. I love you. I love you.

'I love you too.' How can you put the phone down on a man who is giving you everything?

'Come to my flat now. We've got to meet now. It's been nearly two weeks. You don't know what it's been like. I can't work. I can't think.'

Laura doesn't dare speak. She can't even remember why they mustn't meet. 'I love you!' she whispers. In the back of her mind she still has a feeling that if they both love each other enough and declare that love, they need not actually meet.

'Can you come now?' he cries impatiently. 'I can't really but I will. What's the point of sitting in an office when I can't do anything!'

A tiny memory and warning registers with Laura. In New York he had not been able to break a business lunch to be with her.

'I can't come now,' she says. And immediately feels mean, as if she is counting the points of his affection.

'When?'

'I don't know. I can't start it off again. I just couldn't bear your letter. I couldn't bear to end like that.'

'Oh.' Martin goes completely quiet. If there had been a click she would have thought he'd put the phone down.

'Martin?'

'Yes.'

'I'm sorry. But what I said in my letter is true.'

'Why did you ring me?' His voice is accusing.

'Because I had to know you were all right.' Laura decides to be more honest. 'That you still loved me.'

'So now you know, that's that.'

'Yes. I'm sorry. It was very selfish.'

163

'Yes.' Both their voices have become coldly, formally polite.

Laura realises that she has achieved nothing. He is not loving her now. He is hating her. Even despising her.

'You can't put what we've got into a box and tie it up with a pink satin ribbon and label it love.' Martin's voice sounds weary now. He is talking to her as if she was a child. 'Whatever you do it's not going to end happily ever after.'

Laura recognises that up to this moment that was exactly what she had thought was possible. She thinks of the confessional and the purity of forgiveness.

'Happiness is not the only thing in life.'

'Quite. I wish you hadn't telephoned.'

'Oh, Martin! Don't say that.'

'What am I supposed to do? You have a husband and a child to go to. What have I?'

Laura thinks, A job. He has his computers. Yet he is right. She has not thought from his point of view. At least only in relation to her. To her happiness.

'I don't know you.'

'You don't know me!' Martin suddenly sounds very angry.

Laura tries to explain, 'I don't know how you live, how you work, what was important to you before you met me.' She feels like crying. She had often thought about this before but had never imagined telling him so in the middle of an argument.

'I don't know anything about you either.'

'No.'

Laura thinks dully that this must be the end. An angry denial of knowledge.

There is a long silence. It seems to Laura to last for hours while she sinks further and further into despair.

'But I love you!' Martin's voice is strong and warm.

'Oh, Martin. I love you too!' Laura now does burst into tears, overwhelmed by his generosity.

They arrange to meet at his flat in an hour.

*

Miles knew as soon as Laura started seeing Martin again. She could see it in the way he looked at her. It was worse than when she was deceiving him for she could never quite shake off his presence. Even when she was in bed with Martin, she felt his watchful eyes. Miles did not try and make love to her or talk to her more than necessary.

She waited for him to strike. He had said if she ever left him again he would never let her return nor let her see Nicky. She had not left the home, but she had left him. He must know she would not be able to carry on as she was.

She began to hate him.

*

One afternoon Laura has a call from Katie. She says she is coming up to London the next day for the dentist and would Laura be free for lunch. Laura invites her to the house but she says she's already booked a table at a restaurant. She sounds more nervous than a visit to the dentist warrants.

Laura agrees, though wondering at her unusual initiative.

Laura is a little late. Hurrying along Soho's crowded pavements she sees a familiar figure ahead of her. She catches up with him just before the restaurant.

'Roy! What are you doing in London? Why haven't you phoned me?'

'I've only just stepped off the plane, I. . . .'

'But how lucky! I'm just going to have lunch with Katie. You must come too!'

'As a matter of fact. . . .'

'You were going anyway. That's wonderful!' But now Laura can't help noticing that he is looking inappropriately embarrassed. 'There's nothing the matter is there?'

'No. No.'

'Come on, then. What a treat!' Laura puts her arm through his and pulls him gaily into the restaurant but her feeling that there is something wrong remains.

She is certain of it when they find Katie so distraught that she hardly manages to return Laura's kiss.

They sit down and order their meal. When waiter and menu have gone and wine comes, Katie looks at Roy and then starts in a clear high voice like a schoolgirl reading her lesson, 'I think I should tell you that there is a special reason for this lunch and for Roy coming along too.'

Immediately she starts speaking, Laura knows what it's all about. She can't think why she'd been so slow to guess. Perhaps because she had always been the one to advise both Katie and Roy.

'You want to discuss my private life,' she says in a bright false voice. 'I suppose I might have guessed Johnny wouldn't be able to resist telling you.'

'It's not just Johnny. Everyone knows.' Katie bursts out, tears in her eyes. 'Oh, Laura! How could you? I always thought of you as so perfect. Above it all, I looked up to you. I admired you so much. And now this! It's so awful!'

Roy clears his throat loudly and Katie subsides. 'Oh dear,' she murmurs. 'That's not at all what I meant to say.'

'Never mind,' Laura still uses her bright cool voice. 'I get the point.'

'We come to you because we are your friends. Because we love you,' begins Roy with a valiant attempt to control his emotion. 'We want to help you.'

Here Katie nods energetically. This strikes Laura as comical. She tries not to smile but cannot restrain a giveaway twist to her mouth.

Roy sees it and looks hurt. 'Of course if you're determined to marry the man, there's nothing we can do.' This is clearly not what he'd planned to say either. He drinks a gulp of wine.

Katie wails, 'Oh, no!'

This time Laura finds her not funny but irritating. She says, 'Divorce is legal in this country, you know. People do it all the time.'

Katie gives another wail. Laura takes a sip of wine. Martin and she have never discussed divorce or marriage.

'I thought you were Catholic,' Roy looks at her with a sudden almost intellectual interest. 'I thought you believed in a moral code and that moral code included marriage.'

Laura has no answer to this. She looks down. 'I do,' she says, losing that hard knowing voice. 'I haven't decided on anything.'

Katie heaves a huge sigh of relief. 'I knew it would be all right. Well, if not all right, not the worst.'

Laura ignores her and looks at Roy. 'Do you think love is important?'

'What is love?'

'You sound like a priest. Did you come over especially to lecture me?'

'Sort of. I wanted to see how you looked as a fallen woman.'

'How do I look?'

'Beautiful. Sad.'

Laura shakes her head and takes another sip of wine. 'Well, now we've got me out of the way, we can enjoy our lunch.'

'There're so many things I want to say,' Katie is anxious, as if she has not done her duty.

'Keep them. It'll make an excuse for another lunch.'

'Oh, Laura, it's no time for joking. The point is Martin isn't right for you. He never will be. He's younger.'

Laura turns on Katie. 'I don't want to talk about it. Do you understand? I've forgiven you for getting me here under false pretences. But if you try and talk any more I won't forgive you and I'll walk out of the restaurant. So you won't have achieved anything anyway.'

Katie sits completely crushed. She doesn't dare eat or drink. Laura finds her hands are shaking and hides them under the table. She has always loved Katie and cared for her like a younger sister. She has never lost her temper with her before even when she's been most irritating.

The waiter brings their food into a bleak silence.

*

Laura wondered why people concerned themselves with what was surely her business and her business alone. It did not strike her that Johnny might have thought the same when she had persuaded him to go back to Katie. She never thought of their situation as in any way similar, although they were brother and sister. She did not think of herself as the unfaithful wife.

*

'I love you,' Laura says to Martin, one afternoon. 'And I'm better for loving you.'

'Better happy or better good?' he crosses her hair under her chin like a tie.

'I don't know. Just filled with love. Love for the whole world.'

'A bow tie and boobs,' he tugs on her hair, 'I hope that whole world excludes husbands – particularly your own.'

He has never mentioned Miles before. Laura is silent.

'Or perhaps a beard and boobs?' he suggests, pulling out her curls.

Laura wants to cry out, I hate him! I hate him! She shuts her mouth and her eyes. What would Martin say if she told him that? Would he say, Come and live here, I want you my own and always? Even to herself she doesn't pronounce the words divorce and marriage. She doesn't want that because she can't leave Nicky and because she believes in marriage. Laura sees nothing ridiculous in believing this. She is in a state of love, a state of sin, but she still believes in marriage. On the other hand if Martin did not respond with a 'Come live with me and be my love', she would be in despair, able only to assume he hardly cared.

How could he let her live with someone she hated?

Chapter Thirteen

Laura had always liked to sit in her living-room, calmly, doing nothing. For years she had been in the habit of going there after Nicky was in bed. She might go with a newspaper or sewing or a book or perhaps intending to watch television. But she knew, in truth, she would do nothing. She loved her drawing-room, the pictures, the flowers, the bits and pieces of bric-à-brac, the leaves of the plane trees outside dancing sunlit on the walls. She used to sit for an hour or more waiting for Miles.

Miles used to enjoy finding her there. He sensed this passive contentment was the source of her day-time energy and good humour. He joked about it, calling her his buddha, his meditating mystic. And it was a kind of meditation.

But now this favourite hour of the day is destroyed. Laura, restless, dreading her husband's return, wanders about the house. She cooks, she tidies, she telephones Nell.

Nell says, 'You can't go on like this.' She often says this kind of thing which Laura usually disregards as not being relevant to her. She has to go on like this. But for some reason on this occasion, she listens. It gives her an idea.

'I shall go to Italy,' she says. 'It's Nicky's summer holidays in a week or two.'

'That does sound a good idea.' Nell is enthusiastic, as she is for any positive action, but Laura doesn't let her into her full confidence. Suddenly her mind is bursting with brilliant images. The Italian coastline, Sorrento, bougainvillea, sun, blue seas breaking on rocky cliffs crowned by pale temples. Churches, piazzas, picture galleries, Pompeii. Restaurants, al fresco, white cotton tablecloths, bread-sticks, an ice-cold bottle of Verdiccio, Martin.

She and Nicky would be joined by Martin. And later, when she could persuade him to stop working for a moment, Miles would take Martin's place.

Laura has a vision of how she will manage a husband and a lover.

At the back of her mind, unacknowledged, is the memory of when she was last in Italy. With her married man. It had been only there that she had felt a lifting of guilt. Even before that, she had gone there as a schoolgirl. She had spent hours in the Uffizi staring at fourteenth century madonnas which, in their richness of colour and detail yet purity of intent, seemed to combine all she most admired in the world. Her first kiss had taken place on the Ponte Vecchio. As the man, whose name she could never remember but whose face she would never forget, leant forward, she had a magic sense of stepping off a pedestal, out from a picture frame. She had become the madonna who could give birth and remain a virgin, kiss and yet stay untouched. This feeling has never quite left her.

Italy. Laura puts down the phone to Nell and goes quickly to the kitchen. Miles will be back any minute. She will mention it to him immediately. Lies are not so difficult any more. As long as she is doing something while she tells them. Sometimes she can't believe Miles doesn't guess when she bends suddenly to pat a cushion or lift a book to straighten its uncreased cover. She does not want to think that he does not want to know.

Laura looks at her watch. She longs to ring Martin. But she doesn't like the idea of Miles coming in during their conversation. That would be far too crude, too unaesthetic. Already the distinction between what is a matter of good taste and what is a matter of morals is becoming blurred.

Laura lays the kitchen table neatly for supper. She gets real pleasure from the smoothness of her white sauce. The front door opens upstairs. Miles calls as he always does, 'I'm home.'

Laura goes up to meet him which she has not done lately. Her step is light with thoughts of Italy. 'Did you get that big blackmail case you wanted?' she asks with hardly simulated interest.

'I did indeed,' Miles rises quickly to her mood. 'Let's open a good bottle of wine to celebrate.'

'What a lovely idea!' Laura thinks that this will be an excellent chance to break the news of her holiday plans. She must emphasise Nicky's wan London face, his need for sun and sea.

*

Martin and Laura walk hand in hand through Hyde Park. They are in Hyde Park because no one they know will be there. It is a glorious summer's day – the trees dark with leaves, the sky bright, birds singing, grass warm. If it had not been so perfect they would have stayed in Martin's room, huddled close, making up for and storing up for all the times of separation. Even now, hand in hand, hardly a breath of air between them, they feel almost unbearably apart.

They sit down on a bench. There, Martin can put his arm right round Laura and she can lay her head on his shoulder. If she shuts her eyes she can imagine they're in bed together.

'How can I work?' Martin speaks into her hair. 'I've got my reputation to think of.'

'What's that?'

'A thrusting dynamo of energy and ambition. That's how I earn my living. If I'm not there, thrusting away, nothing happens. Nothing happens, no business. No business, no money.'

Laura takes none of this seriously. 'Thrust away. As far as I'm concerned, you're perfectly free.'

Martin smiles. 'Free?'

'You're quite sure of me. You don't have to worry what I'm doing.'

'No, I know that.' Martin's voice is lightly ironic. She goes from him to her husband. But Laura is unsympathetic. She knows she is Martin's totally, night and day, parted or together.

Now she pulls away from him and opens her handbag. She takes out some aeroplane tickets. She opens the top one. 'Mine,' she says. She opens the next. 'Nicky's. This must be yours.' She hands it to him happily. 'Your flight is exactly the same time as ours but a day later.'

Martin looks down at the ticket. 'How old is Nicky?'

Laura is surprised, flushes. The question upsets her. Nicky is so much part of her that Martin's lack of knowledge implies a lack of knowledge of her. The fact that she has hardly talked about Nicky does not help because it is rooted in the same

170

feeling. She cannot give information about a part of herself. Martin should somehow know. This confused feeling makes her brusque.

'He's seven.'

'I'd thought he was younger.'

Laura tries to cut through her sensation of discomfort. 'Mothers always make their sons seem younger.' Laura suddenly thinks of Martin's mother, so formidable and elegant. She would like to change the subject to her but Martin is still questioning.

'What will he do in the evenings?'

'Baby-sitters. He's quite used to baby-sitters.' Laura speaks airily although her heart turns suddenly. What will he actually do in the day? For one second she sees that she is using her beloved son as a cover against Miles's suspicions. That she has not thought of his interests at all.

But Martin, with the bachelor's conviction that it only takes a proper attitude to keep a child in its proper place, has satisfied any worries he might have. 'Can we go home now?'

Laura at once thinks of nothing but touching him, holding him. 'It can't be for long,' she says, failing to sound practical and in control.

*

Nicky's suitcase lies open on his bed. Bulging with the goggles, flippers and snorkel, the games, toys and books that he had insisted were essential, it is rather bigger than Laura's. Soon he will be back from school and Miles will be back from court. He is going to drive them to the airport.

Alone in the narrow room, Laura stands rigidly staring. Up till this moment everything she had done seemed inevitable, even forced on her. She had not been strong enough to refuse. But now she is taking a step herself, in cold blood, that is entirely her own idea and involves the only person over whom she has complete responsibility, her son.

She is interrupted by the telephone. It is Katie ringing to wish her a happy holiday. 'Forget everything,' she says two or three times, 'and have a really good holiday. You deserve one. We've all relied on you too much in the past. Really enjoy yourself and you'll feel quite different when you come back.'

Laura sees that Katie, partly out of Christian charity and partly because she cannot bear to see her idol defiled, has decided that she, Laura, is having some sort of nervous break-down which sun and sea air will cure. Laura, who has always hated upsetting people so much that she'd buy a packet of despised fish-fingers rather than disappoint a shop-keeper, now feels a cruel urge to shout at Katie: Martin's coming to Italy! Don't you see? That's the only reason I'm going. So we can sit in the sun together. Away from prying people. Prying people like you!

Instead she says, 'Thank you' and promises to send a postcard. As she puts down the phone she thinks fleetingly how much easier it would be if Nicky was going to stay at Katie's and she was going for a holiday alone with her lover. But she doesn't entertain the idea in any serious way.

*

Miles, Nicky and Laura wander round the shops at London airport. Nicky holds Miles's hand. The small bright-faced boy and sober, dark-suited man make an odd contrast. Laura fights against a feeling of revulsion. She wants to break their hands apart. As they buy newspapers a man approaches them.

'Miles,' he says.

They stop in a row politely. Miles introduces his wife and son. He pushes forward Nicky and watches with pride as he shakes hands. Laura catches the man's eye. He smiles and she sees there his admiration for such a happy family scene.

'Going on holiday?' he asks.

'I'm following later,' says Miles. He takes the man aside. 'In fact I wanted your advice. I've got a big blackmail case coming up. . . .'

The man is a barrister on his way back from the international court in the Hague. The two men talk. Nicky drags Laura over to buy a comic.

Nicky is getting more and more excited. As they reach Customs he tries to run ahead. Miles grabs him for a farewell kiss.

'Don't forget, I'll expect a swimming otter by the time I come.'

Laura wonders if he will kiss her and when he lets Nicky go she raises her face obligingly. Miles looks at her but makes no move towards her. She therefore finds herself staring straight at him from a close quarter, something she has avoided for weeks. What she sees in his face, the simple suffering makes her literally flinch backwards. She blinks and tears start in the back of her eyes. She bends her head downwards.

'Have a good trip,' Miles says in his solid voice above her.

'Yes. Yes. We will. Look after yourself.' Without turning her head, Laura takes Nicky's hands and almost runs towards the Customs.

*

'This is Italy.' Laura puts her foot on the tarmac of the airport runway and breathes deeply.

'How do you know?'

Laura looks down at Nicky and can't decide whether to smile or be irritated. The moment she'd stepped from the aeroplane, she'd felt herself in a completely different world. She could already smell the warmth from the ground at the end of a hot day. She could hear the cicadas, or imagine she could, and see the brown-skinned bodies around her. She had relaxed. She was happy.

'Because a sign over there says Pisa Aeroporto, which means Pisa Airport. Pisa's in Italy.'

'Italian's a very easy language, isn't it?' Satisfied, Nicky boards the bus for the terminal.

Laura thinks how lucky she is to have such a well-balanced child. Only children, she decides, are either insufferable, pushed into the vacuum of being neither adults nor children, or they come out like Nicky. Sensitive, self-contained, and charming. In the new jacket she has bought him for the journey he looks astonishingly grown-up. She can see that if they had been going to spend the holiday on their own it would have been very enjoyable. She can almost regret it.

He chats gaily as they drive towards the coast in the small white car she's hired.

'What will our room be like? Can we swim the moment we arrive? Why does everyone wear sun glasses? Why do you have to pay to go on a road? The trees look as if they're cut out of cardboard. Why are there so few of them?'

*

They do swim the moment they arrive, negotiating a permanent place with an umbrella on the sandy beach.

The sea, dark green and cool, floats about Laura's body like

173

shifting mirrors. The sun, already low, casts shadows into every dip in the sand. Their limbs, so English pale, seems green-tinged as they stand, finally, at the water's edge.

Laura looks down at Nicky. He is small and boney, hair flattened against his skull. 'You won't be lonely here, will you? With no other children.'

Nicky turns to Laura as if affronted. 'I'm going to swim all day. There'll be no time to be bored. Anyway I saw a whole lot of children in the hotel.'

Laura is surprised. 'That is a good idea. We'll look out for them tomorrow.'

'They were English too.'

The hotel is large but not particularly grand. Nostalgic memories are stirred by the number of beautiful youths standing casually in the Reception area as if part of the management. One standing near the bottom of the staircase, steps forward as they pass. He looks into Laura's eyes. She stops.

'Mrs Knight?'

'Yes.' She feels he will announce some forgotten relationship, some past Arcady.

'There's a message for you at the desk.'

Laura laughs. A dazzling sense of anticipation hurries her to the desk. Nicky waits, trailing his damp towel on the carpet.

'Ah.' Laura reads the message. He is catching an earlier flight. She clutches the piece of paper tight.

'What's the matter, Mummy?'

'Nothing. Nothing.'

'Was it Dad?'

'No. No.' She looks down at him as they mount the thickly carpeted stairs. 'Just a friend. He might come and see us tomorrow.'

Nicky turns his head away, uninterested.

'You can have supper with me in the restaurant, tonight. As a treat.' As she says this, she imagines tomorrow night, Martin and she together over a dinner table. They have never had dinner alone before.

Laura and Nicky are sharing a bedroom. Miles had suggested it and Laura could think of no reasonable objection. That night she lies beside him, unable to sleep. He snores slightly, his body twisted into the warm sheets. The room is stuffy with the heat of an Italian night. Laura feels herself beginning to sweat and runs her hands over her skin. It seems to rise under her fingers. Tomorrow night she will go to Martin.

*

'Mum! Mum! Look at me!' Nicky's face, protruding awfully with his snorkel, surfaces above the green waves and then submerges leaving only a few glistening bubbles. Laura sits up on the beach. She wears sunglasses and holds a book in one hand.

'Well done!' she applauds. She has told the hotel where her friend can find her. She is waiting, dressed in pink and mauve, wearing a straw hat against the glaring sun. She feels herself as taut as plastic but she looks quite lazy.

'Go on! Try again! I'm watching.'

She thinks of that first time they had made love. On an English beach with a cool English sun overhead. Then, the moment of ecstasy had been before, the guilt of the first fall casting a terrible glare over their passions. She had run for the cold sea water to cleanse her. Here, the water, warm and thick, will only compound the act. It is too late to think of sin. She has lost a sense of general morality. Her only responsibility is to her son. And there he is in front of her eyes, tumbling and shouting with happiness. At any moment she will have beside her the two beings she loves most in the world.

'Gelati, gelati Motta!'

Laura has always had a sensation of falling asleep at the points of greatest happiness in her life. As she hears teasing Martin's voice in her ear, she actually closes her eyes. He crouches down beside her.

'Vanilla, Arancia, Limone, Cioccolata?'

They haven't seen each other for three days. Martin is wearing bathing trunks and a T-shirt. His legs are covered with thick blond hair. Their nakedness which she only associates with making love causes her to flush. She moves away a little, though giving him a close look.

'There's Nicky. In the water.'

'Ah. Your son.'

There is a note in his voice she can't quite fathom. He stands up and goes to the water's edge. After a moment she goes to join him.

'Nicky! Here's my friend. Come and say hello.'

Nicky splashes out of the water. 'You can't swim in that

175

T-shirt,' he says to Martin. 'That is, if you want to swim.'

'Oh, can't I!' Martin runs into the sea sending up glittering sprays of water. After a few yards he hurls himself face downwards in a gigantic belly flop.

Nicky is delighted. He runs after him, shouting, 'Can you snorkel? I'm learning to snorkel!'

But after his exhibition, Martin's mood seems to change. He turns his back on the shore and wades into deep water. From there, with a strong stroke, he swims directly out to sea.

'Wait! Wait for me! I can't go as deep as that.'

'He'll be back.' Laura calls. 'Come in now and I'll buy you a drink.'

Laura and Nicky sit on a concrete square under a striped awning sipping drinks. Laura thinks she understands why Martin had left them. She in his place, might have done the same. She watches him, wet and beaming, come up the beach towards them.

'I feel different. Wonderful. What are you drinking? Bacardi and rum?'

'Oh, Martin.'

'And where are we eating? I'm starving. Dawn travel takes it out of you.'

'So far we've only eaten in the hotel. I had chicken and chips.'

Laura glances at Nicky, slightly surprised at his easy acceptance of this take-over by a stranger.

'I happen to have bought a guide to the best restaurants in Viareggio.'

Laura now dares to look at Martin. His hair is still wet, plastered back darkly. The pale forehead revealed above the reddish nose and cheeks divide his face in a strange unflattering way. His eyes look small and close together. His mouth is open slightly so she can see the start of his crooked front teeth. She remembers how that first day she had seen him on the railway station. Then he had seemed too handsome in a manly regular way. Now he seems almost ugly. Now she loves him.

He stands up scraping the steel chair across the concrete. 'I'll have to get some trousers from the hotel.'

'We must change too.'

It is very hot. The beach is almost empty. Only a few foolish foreigners lie prone under the dazzling sun. Laura feels sticky and slightly sick. They cross the road and enter the cool darkness of the hotel. Laura suddenly notices that Nicky has burnt his shoulders. She lays her hand on him and he flinches away.

He had been an image of carefree happiness as he played in the water. She had not looked after him as a mother should.

'Oh darling. Is it very painful?'

He shrugs. 'Can I have coca cola for lunch?'

Upstairs Martin shows them his room. It is identical to theirs. Laura tells Nicky to run along and find a cool white shirt. Quickly, if he wants a coke.

Martin and Laura hold each other. The heat and awkwardness forgotten. They embrace, standing in the middle of the room. 'I'm sorry,' Laura whispers.

'What do you mean?'

'About Nicky.' She looks at the bed over his shoulder.

'You can't apologise for your son.'

'No.' Laura breaks away. 'This evening.'

'Yes.'

The restaurant is pale, green-tinged, only the thinnest strips of sun slide through closed venetian blinds. It is rather like being under water, noises muted, actions slowed. Through this quiet, Nicky's childish voice cuts suddenly.

'Are you staying long?'

'That depends.' Martin seems undismayed. 'What you mean by long.'

'We're staying for two weeks. And my Dad's coming out for the last few days. Perhaps even a week. He works very hard. Do you work?'

'I play about with machines.'

'So you don't work.'

'People pay me to do it.'

'Have you ever seen the Acorn Electron?'

'I've got one.'

'Do you make lots of money?'

'Yes.'

'So does my Dad.'

Nicky stops talking as suddenly as he started and returns to concentrating on his food. Laura wonders if he realises that Martin has evaded his question about how long he was staying. His introduction of his father into the conversation, as if in rivalry to Martin, had worried her but now she relaxes again.

'When we're bored on the beach,' she says, 'we must drive to Siena.'

'I am bored.' Martin snaps a bread stick. 'You don't mean you were thinking of going back there?'

Laura laughs. 'Nicky's planning to swim every day. All day.'

'I don't mind swimming. But I can't bear hanging around with sand between my toes.'

Laura turns to Nicky. 'Would you like to visit one of Europe's most beautiful towns?'

Nicky has a large mouthful of food. He chews and swallows and at length answers politely, 'No, thank you.'

Martin gives a great bleat of laughter. Laura thinks that she has not heard that sound for a while and remembers how, early on, she had identified it with his mother.

'Then we'll have to find something else for you to do.'

Nicky sits up straight and pays more attention. 'I did tell Mummy about this English family in the hotel.'

Laura is amazed at their practicality. For her the clash of personalities drowns any ordinary ideas of organisation.

When they get back to their hotel Martin says to Nicky in a firm voice, 'Do you know what a siesta is?'

Nicky looks wary. He stops at the top of the grand staircase. 'What?'

'A post-prandial nap.'

'What's that?'

'A rest. After lunch. In the heat of the day. Your mother will put cream on your shoulders and then you'll lie down. For precisely an hour. I'll lend you my watch.'

'I have a watch.'

'Mine has a musical alarum.'

'What will you be doing?'

'That's nothing to do with you. Your mother will return on the dot, I assure you.'

Nicky turns to Laura who smiles weakly. She is afraid to break the spell of Martin's command. She thinks what a good prep school master Martin would make.

Later she tells him so. They sit on his bed, side by side. Now they're together, alone, Laura finds herself oddly nervous.

'I did teach as a matter of fact. After university. Before I decided to make money. My mother, of course, wanted me to be a don.'

'A don!'

Martin laughs. 'A less confident man might be insulted by your tone.'

'You seem so modern. So extrovert.'

'My mother's an intellectual snob. As well as a social one. My father ran the Centre for International Studies till his death. And I always seemed very clever to her. Actually I was clever, scholarships and that sort of thing. She thinks what I do now is degrading. Like being an engineer. On the other hand she likes me making money. I buy expensive presents for her. She's very materialistic, my mother, corruptible. It's her French blood.'

Laura smiles but feels this is probably true. They both become silent. Laura assumes Martin is thinking about his mother. Without warning infinite depression descends. He has a whole other life she can never enter. She doesn't want to enter.

'I love you and I want to kiss you.' Martin's voice, oddly formal, barely reaches her remoteness. 'That is, if you want it?'

'What time is it?' Words fall flatly.

Martin looks at his watch. 'Three o'clock.'

'I must go back to Nicky soon.' Actually, she is locked into position on the bed.

Martin stands up. 'I suppose you're regretting I've come.'

'It's not that. I'm sorry.'

Martin looks down at her, saying nothing. She wishes he would act. Slap her face, perhaps. Take responsibility.

She manages to stand up and goes slowly to the window. She draws back the curtains. The white light makes her recoil. She brushes Martin's arm but still he does not touch her. She moves near the wall and leans against its solidity. She feels a faint vibration along her side and realises it is the effect of a telephone ringing in the next door room.

It takes her several seconds to realise that the next door room is her bedroom.

'My telephone's ringing.'

'I presume Nicky will answer it.'

'It's probably Miles.'

Without looking again at Martin, Laura leaves the room. She shuts the door quietly behind her and enters her own room. Nicky, red-faced, is talking animatedly.

179

'All morning. From the time we got up till lunch-time. I never even rested. But tomorrow I've got to wear a T-shirt even in the water because the sun's so hot.'

As he pauses, Laura hears Miles, voice questioning.

'Oh, yes! Masses. We had spaghetti, real Italian spaghetti . . .'

Laura hears no more, for at the word 'we' she feels head, limbs and body diffuse into nothingness.

'We' meant Nicky, herself and Martin.

For the first time she realises that Nicky must tell Miles that Martin was here staying with them.

She sits down on the end of the bed. Why had this never occurred to her before? It seems so terribly obvious. She cannot tell Nicky not to mention him. She can do nothing. If Miles finds out it will be the end of their marriage.

'We might go to some city or other. Do you want to speak to Mum?' A negative mumble. 'All right then, I'll tell her. The day after tomorrow. Bye, Dad.'

Nicky puts down the phone. 'That was Dad.' Despite everything his look of satisfaction makes Laura smile.

'I thought it might be.'

'He's going to ring the same time the day after tomorrow.'

Two days. Two more days. Nicky had said nothing. Laura feels life returning. She jumps up energetically and only then remembers the scene she has left behind in the other room. It seems inconceivable, in the face of catastrophe so barely averted, that she could waste, so childishly, precious time together.

'Here! You get dressed,' she throws Nicky his shorts. 'I'll be back in a moment.'

Martin is lying on his bed reading a newspaper. Momentarily disconcerted by his calm, she nevertheless snatches away the paper and cries. 'Come on, we're going to Siena!'

'Was it Miles?'

'Yes. Yes.' Laura pulls on him impatiently like a child. 'I had a sudden terror Nicky would tell him you were here. But he didn't. And now we must enjoy ourselves.'

Martin gets up slowly. 'I thought you must have allowed for that. For him knowing.'

'No. I. . . .'

Martin interrupts her. 'Come here.'

At last they kiss. They draw apart. Laura finds tears in her eyes. They smile at each other.

There is a knock at the door.

'That'll be Nicky. I'll take him on down.' She looks at Martin. 'I love you.'

Nicky has become rather cross. His T-shirt rubs his burnt shoulders. 'We don't really have to sit in a hot car do we? We spent all yesterday travelling.'

He begins to whine and snatches at his mother as they go down the stairs.

'I shall be sick in the car, I know I will.'

'You're never car-sick. You must be fair. You had your way this morning.'

'You liked the beach too.'

The foyer is crowded, people setting out on expeditions as the siesta period finishes. Several couples, several family parties. Laura is diverted by another childish voice raised insistently. It stands out because it too is speaking English.

'Why shouldn't I ask? At least ask?'

'Because we don't know them.'

Laura hears the mother's low voice and, looking directly at her, smiles.

'There.' The voice triumphs. 'She smiled. Now you can ask her.'

'It's them,' whispers Nicky with a heavy nudge.

Laura hesitates. In the past her self-contentment had encouraged her to a certain remoteness. She did not speak to strangers. In the past she would have turned away. Now she takes a step forward.

The boys meet before the mothers. Clasping hands as if they were long lost friends. 'We're going to a fun-fair. Will you come too? My sister's only a baby and there're bumper cars!'

By the time Martin descends the negotiations are complete. Nicky will stay with them for the rest of the day. The mother is clearly responsible, temporarily husbandless, wearing a middle-class badge of anxious smile, cotton head-scarf and red nose smeared with Nivea.

Even the awkwardness of her assumption that Martin is Nicky's father does not dim Laura's satisfaction. She who has made Nicky the centre of her life for all of his seven years now hands him over to a total stranger without a qualm.

Chapter Fourteen

The car is small and hot. The white motorway to Siena is crowded. The glare and noise seem to enter the car. But instead of spoiling Laura's mood, it increases her sense of release and exhilaration. Usually someone who relied on air and space, with a tendency to claustrophobia in crowds or cramped conditions, she now has the feeling of flying through endless light. The problems of parking in an unfamiliar Italian town, bringing sweat to Martin's brow, causes not a frown. She hops out of the car – even her actions are not typical, having lost their usual calm strolling effect – and cries in equally lively manner, 'A promenade to the piazza and then a long drink while the crowds pass and the sun goes down!'

'I certainly need that.' Martin wipes his face with a pale blue handkerchief. In all Laura's exuberance, he is quiet, watching, waiting for her excitement to turn from herself to him. She seems hardly aware of him.

At length they reach the central square, the perfect fan-shaped piazza where each year the horses of the Palio race round the cobbles. They choose a café, sit down at a small table and order drinks. Laura's fantasy of Italy is fulfilled. Martin has brought an English paper on their walk. As he opens it Laura registers surprise that he should show any interest in the world outside. Men are never so passionate in their involvement, she thinks without criticism.

In fact he shuts it again, smiling. 'I read it this morning. On the flight. It's unbelievable. I only left England this morning.'

Laura is glad then that he too has lost his sense of time.

'We don't seem to be doing much sight-seeing.'

Laura flourishes her arm. 'What better sight could we see!'

'I wonder if Trafalgar Square has the same effect on foreign visitors?'

'There's nowhere like Italy. They've been learning how to enjoy themselves with style for centuries. The English have been coming here for about as long.'

'Dolce far niente.' Martin sips at his drink. 'This is pretty good.' He looks at it reflectively. 'Being here, I mean. But there is one place I can imagine that would be even better.' He covers Laura's hand with his hot, heavy palm.

For a second Laura withdraws, not physically. Just a momentary sense of affront to her dream of romance. Then as he stands, she rises too, goes close to him, eager to be in his arms. Of course he is right. Why are they behaving like tourists when they could be lovers?

'I saw a respectable but not too respectable hotel just before we entered the piazza.'

In every way it was better to make love here in this city out of time and space than in a room barely divided from her son. From her son talking to her husband on the telephone. Laura looks at Martin, at his eyes bluer and more intense than she remembered, his hair already fairer in the sun, his red rather dry mouth with the crooked teeth. They walk briskly to the hotel.

They walk out again an hour later, giggling guiltily like children. 'The face of the receptionist!' cries Laura clinging onto Martin's arm. 'I thought she was going to call the police.'

'The Pope more likely.'

Laura doesn't hesitate. 'In Catholic countries they cheat even more. Do you know, I might get quite a taste for deception.'

'If we can't find the ruddy car you might have to develop a taste for walking.'

They have forgotten the street where they parked the car, even forgotten what it looked like. They walk along the uneven streets, pushing through the crowds dressed smartly for their nightly parade. They pass heavy church doors open for the evening, candles flickering. For a second Laura is stabbed with a memory of her own Catholicism. But this ornate darkness is so different from her quiet English experience that she quickly discounts it.

They look up and see the sky darkening with a few pink clouds wafting high. They smile and nudge each other at an old woman singing Verdi beside a spring gushing from a wall. Laura slips on a curb and Martin catches her, arm round her waist. Their drink in the piazza now seems to have taken place between strangers.

'When you're old you must dress entirely in red velvet,' says Martin.

'Red velvet?'

'It came to me suddenly. Laura will look superb in old age as long as she dresses entirely in red velvet.'

'Like a cushion. I'll look like a cushion. Or a chaise-longue,' Laura jeers.

'I've always been very fond of chaise-longues. That may have been what inspired me to red velvet. With tassels. With tassels everywhere!'

'Now you're turning me into a table-cloth.'

They go on like this until almost by chance they find the car again. They have already walked past it twice. By now the light is darkening and Martin bends to look for the lights switch.

As the lights make two pale triangles on the road, Laura thinks of Nicky for the first time.

'It must be late.'

Martin looks at his watch. 'Nearly eight.'

'Oh God. We won't be back till after nine.'

'No.'

It is entirely dark by the time they arrive. The hotel foyer is empty but noisy chatter comes from the brightly lit dining-room. Laura stands at the door and, seeing no party of young English children, goes swiftly upstairs. Martin she has left behind, standing at reception, asking for something, taking a white slip of paper.

This image stays on her retina as she hurries along the corridors, chasing ahead of her panic. It is only when she reaches her room that she realises she has not brought a key. She stands by the door, panting. Her haste, the claustrophobia of her fears, of the hot windowless corridor, makes it really difficult to breathe. She wants to sit on the floor leaning her back against the smooth wall.

What if something has happened to Nicky? She will have deserved it. She will have caused it. Guilt. Black wings of guilt.

Martin appears walking evenly. He hands her the piece of white paper and her key. Without looking at her, he opens the door to his own bedroom and goes in.

Laura unfolds the paper but is unable to concentrate on the words there. After a second she opens her own door. The room

184

seems at first completely dark. But as she stands a faint line between the drawn curtains begins to show. At the same time her own heart-beats slow and become quieter.

She can see and listen. In Nicky's bed there is a white hump and the hump breathes. Laura falls across him laughing.

'Oh, don't Mum. Go away. You're hot.' Nicky pushes her off irritably.

'Oh, darling. How was the fun-fair? Was it fun? Were they nice?'

'Mm.' Nicky won't answer and rolls away into the sheets.

Laura kisses him and stands up. She breathes deeply, smiling. Then she remembers Martin and the unread note. Not wanting to disturb Nicky by putting on a light, she goes into the bathroom.

She sits on the side of the bath thinking for a moment. She still can't get used to her sudden and constant changes of mood. Was that calm balanced person she used to be always a façade, a flimsy stage set put up as a protection and distraction from this other woman at the mercy of every emotion? She looks down at her hands and seeing the white note, opens it without urgency.

We had a wonderful time. Nicky behaved beautifully. I do hope we can borrow him again. While I was putting him to bed your husband telephoned. He'd like you to call back. I hope you had a good day. Mary Stevenson.

So it had happened. Laura felt a curious mixture of relief and terror.

She stands up and then, with a self-consciously dramatic gesture, throws the note down the lavatory. She pulls the plug. Images of movie heroes divert her attention from her situation. She walks briskly from the room, so briskly that in the darkness she runs into Nicky's bed, banging her knee. This also is an acceptable diversion. She hops about holding her leg.

Nicky stirs and grunts.

She leaves the room walking past Martin's door without a glance. She leaves the hotel going into the blackness and lights of the sea front. Without plan, she nevertheless feels perfectly directed, not breaking her stride until she has walked for a full ten minutes in an easterly direction. She then stops and looks for a telephone kiosk. She hasn't brought her handbag but she doesn't hesitate. The Italian operator would make a reverse charge to England. Aside from this she has no conscious thought; makes no decisions.

The kiosk is hot so she leans her foot against the door, letting a draught of salty air slide through. As she waits for the call she stares at the sea through the dirty panes of glass. At the endless blackness as it merges indiscernably with the sky.

'Hello.'

'Pronto, signora. Your call.'

The 'hello' is not Miles. It takes Laura some time before she realises it is Maria speaking.

'Is Mr Knight in, Maria? It's Mrs Knight.'

'Ah, no. He is leaving an hour ago. Two hours perhaps. You are well?'

'Yes, yes.' Impatiently. 'Did he say when he'll be back?'

'Next week. The week after.' Maria laughs. 'You see him before me. His case finish early. He come to you.'

This time Laura runs along the sea front. What had Mary Stevenson said to Miles? Had she said, *Mrs Knight. Oh, yes, she's gone to Siena with her husband?* Or had Nicky? *Mum's gone to Siena with Martin.* Yes. Surely one of them had said that.

She reaches the hotel, hot and panting. Martin sits in reception reading a magazine. He looks very cool and handsome. Almost as she first saw him. He's wearing a pale blue and white striped jacket. She looks at him with tenderness and sorrow. He is already in the past. Her husband, the inescapable present, has come to supplant him.

He comes over to her quickly and takes her arm. 'What's the matter?'

'Miles is coming.'

'What?'

'His case finished early. He's coming here.' She stares into his face.

'You're hot. You're exhausted.' He leads her along. 'What you need is something to eat.'

Laura is surprised. 'You don't understand! He's coming.'

They have reached the entrance to the restaurant. Martin turns to face her. 'What do you expect me to do? Fall apart? Explode? Vanish into a black hole?'

'Oh.' Laura tries to concentrate. She realises that was just what she'd expected would happen.

'Anyone can tell you haven't been unfaithful before.'

186

Laura allows Martin to lead her to a table in the corner of the large restaurant. The waiter seats them opposite each other and spreads pink linen napkins on their laps. Laura is completely trapped. She feels as if she's on an aeroplane. She has a sick feeling in her stomach, as if the plane had just dropped fifty feet. Is all this just that? Being unfaithful for the first time.

'Isn't that your baby-sitter over there?'

Laura looks and sees Mrs Stevenson sitting some distance away. She is on her own but has her back to them. 'She wrote me a note.'

'I read it. Your husband won't be here for hours. He telephoned at eight. Eat, drink and be merry for tomorrow you die!'

Laura wants to say, I don't know what I'm doing here. This is not me. It's all a dreadful mistake. I don't know myself. But at that moment the waiter arrives with a bread basket and Martin, taking it from him, holds it out to Laura. The gesture, his hand curled round the wicker, the protective yet firm expression on his face, reminds her that this is the man she loves. The only man she has loved, without whom her life has been and would be empty.

Still incapable of speech, she takes a bread roll.

Martin nods approvingly. 'Now you're behaving more rationally. Now we can talk. What do you think? Shall we run away into the night before he arrives?'

Laura tries to laugh, to assume he's joking but is not at all certain. She realises that whenever she is with Martin she cannot make Nicky seem real. 'Running away into the night,' she murmurs, stupidly.

'So you agree?' Martin clasps her hands in his. She thinks he will raise them joined above her head in a boxer's salute. Avoiding his eyes she sees Mary Stevenson stand up and turn in their direction.

Laura drags her hands from Martin and gets up hurriedly. 'I must thank her.' She catches her up by the door. 'It was so kind of you. So kind.' She hesitates. She sees a coldness in the woman's face quite different from the morning. She realises that she has run over in order to explain that she is not like that. That certainly she is having dinner with her lover, that her husband is on the way with retribution, but all the same it is not like that. Again she has the feeling that it is all a terrible mistake. Perhaps Martin will have disappeared when she returns. She interrupts Mrs Stevenson who is explaining the joys of their afternoon by saying in an urgent tone, 'My husband is arriving soon.' Without waiting for a reaction she turns and goes back to her table. She is struck by her extraordinary need to appear virtuous in the eyes of Mrs Stevenson.

Martin sits waiting, eating pieces of his bread roll. 'Well, have you decided?'

'What? What do you mean?' Laura feels tears of self-defence springing ready. Why is he bullying her?

'Have you ever taken a decision in your life?' His tone is loud, hectoring.

'No. No. I don't suppose so.'

He looks at his watch. 'I'll give you an hour. After dinner.'

'I can't eat.'

'Drink then.'

He has ordered for her, melon and ham, which arrives now in chilled silver bowls. He eats his, looking serious. Laura takes up a squared chunk and feels it rest on her tongue more like glass than food. She swallows with difficulty.

'You never think about me at all.'

'I'm in love with you!' she cries out.

'Exactly. That's to do with you. Not me.' He says this in a rational matter-of-fact voice. 'What do you think I feel like?'

'I don't know.'

'I'm a perfectly ordinary man.'

'Don't. Please don't!' Laura doesn't know why this is so painful. She looks at him imploringly. 'Please can we go upstairs.'

'We haven't finished eating. I ordered spaghetti al le vongole. My favourite.'

'Please.'

He pushes back his chair suddenly. The waiter approaching to take away their melon, jumps back nervously. Martin gives him a severe look. 'My friend doesn't feel well.'

As they speed up the stairs, along the corridors, Laura feels the warmth of release. Soon they will lie in each other's arms. She cannot be expected to think when she's lying in his arms.

'So now what?' He takes her by the shoulders and forces her to sit down facing him on the end of the bed.

'No, Martin.'

'You have to choose.' He stares at her, inexorable. His fixed look could express hatred as easily as love.

'I can't. I'm so tired.' She glances longingly at the bed. 'I just want to sleep.'

'No. You don't.'

'Yes.' She pleads. Whispering. 'Please, Martin.'

As suddenly as he had lifted her from the restaurant, he now capitulates again. He snatches her into his arms.

Laura feels the lift of victory and then a tinge of fear. He should not have given in to her weakness. They kiss desperately, lungeing and pulling at each other's hair and limbs. They twist and turn on the bed, throwing coverlet and pillows to the floor. They roll right out of bed and land tangled up and bewildered in the dark. They clamber up and begin again, struggling against each other as if searching for something.

Despite all this effort, Laura does not manage to blot out Martin's question. At last, when they groan, relax and fall wetly apart, she lies, waiting, wakeful.

She lies on her back. Above her head she can just see the outlines of a particularly ugly lamp fixed rigid to the ceiling. The gilt rim and plastic centre stare down at her like a terrible giant's eye. She recalls with dread the Victorian 'Eye of God' which follows virtuous and sinner everywhere. She is about to point out the plastic orb to Martin, to diffuse its power, when she hears a faint sound. It is so still in the room that she immediately assumes it is Nicky next door, turning, dreaming, waking, looking for her.

She sits up, clasping her hands madonna-like, across her bosom. Martin doesn't stir. The sound is repeated. Louder. Under her elbow and she realises that it is Martin snoring. The sound is so ridiculous, so out of keeping with her tense position and dramatic thoughts, that she bursts out in a snorting giggle, suppressed before it can wake him.

He has had a long day. It is not his husband flying over with retribution. He has no beliefs, no responsibilities, no duties. The eye of God is not for him. Why should he stay awake?

Laura settles down at his side again. A curious feeling of peace descends. She remembers Martin accusing her of never taking a decision, and realises he is right. As long as she does not have to act she can cope quite well, whatever the situation. Even now with the thing she most dreads about to happen, she can feel her body compose itself to rest. Even to sleep. On the other hand, if she tries to gird it up, out of bed and into her own bed next door – which is the obviously sensible action – she feels she will fall apart, become a gibbering hysterical creature. As she had been earlier.

Let Miles find her where she lies, at peace. Laura lets her eyelids fall and the 'Eye of God' disappear.

Hours later she becomes aware of several noises. They enter her dreams and because of that she cannot be clear how long an interval passes between each one. First there are voices drifting into each like a duet and becoming in her dream the continually breaking and returning flow of small waves on a sea-shore. Then there is a sharp ugly sound, a penetration, frightening, knife into bone. Then a dragging, scraping, thudding, so corpse-like that she hardly needs an image to match. Finally a squeezing, hissing, breathing as if an animal, large and fur-covered in her dream, has settled into sleep.

At dawn she wakes entirely. She goes to the bathroom and washes efficiently, using Martin's tooth-brush to clean her teeth. He uses spearmint-flavoured toothpaste which she's never liked. She comes back into the room and is surprised to find her dress laid neatly on a chair. She puts it on quickly not looking at Martin who lies comfortably curled round a corner of sheet. She brushes her hair and noticing her face is red from the sun goes back to the bathroom and pats it gently with talcum powder.

Then she goes over to the bed. Martin is watching her.

'What are you doing?'

'Getting ready.'

'What for?' Martin takes her arm. She sits down beside him on the bed.

'I thought I should be ready.'

Martin says nothing.

'For one thing I want to say good morning to Nicky. I can't go in naked, can I?'

There's a long pause. Martin gets out of bed and winds himself in a sheet. He stands facing Laura. Laura notices abstractedly how handsome he is, how upright and young. She has a weird sensation that he has sprung from her loins. A strong golden arrow, leaving her heavy and flaccid behind.

'You know your husband came in the night.'

'I dreamt. . . .' Laura breaks off.

'He's there now. Next door. With your son. His son.'

'How do you know?'

'I woke up. I got up. I heard.'

'I didn't know. . . .'

'I'm going for a shower.' Martin turns about swinging the sheet like a toga and strides to the bathroom.

Laura has a strong urge to get back into bed again but instead bends forward to pick up pillows and coverlet. The moment of decision has come and she feels no more prepared.

Soon there will be noises next door. Nicky's light high voice answered by Miles. Nicky will be questioning.

There is still time to go back.

She is surprised by a sudden sharp tap on the bedroom door. She jumps round and goes to it obediently, almost glad to be diverted from her thoughts of the scene next door. A bell-boy stands there, probably only twelve or thirteen, but his sleek brown face already marked by a Mediterranean sexual innuendo. He holds out a note to Laura.

'This for you now at seven-thirty.'

'Seven-thirty!' Laura is taken aback. 'How could it be seven-thirty?'

'Oh yes. He leave an hour ago.'

Laura jerks the note from the boy but finds he has come in with it. He stands insinuatingly and it is only after a few seconds that she realises he is waiting for a tip. She rushes to Martin's jacket, feeling through his pockets with shaking fingers. She thrusts several lire into the boy's palm, barely avoiding his bony little fingers that seem to want to close on hers.

'Thank you. Thank you.' She thrusts him out of the room.

There is no need to read the note. It is all quite clear now. Even her dream is clear. She had not woken to Miles's entrance but to his departure. With Nicky, their two voices rippling like waves on the sea shore.

Laura opens Martin's bedroom door and looks to her left. Her bedroom door stands open, brilliant sun spreading from the window even to the corridor. Martin's room had been in semi-darkness, curtains still drawn.

'Buon giorno.' A maid stands at the door to the bathroom.

Laura enters the room and looks around. Apart from her case the room is completely empty, not even bottles on the dressing-table, a belt hanging on a chair. Surely she had left something of hers around the room? She goes to the case and opens the lid. There was everything, jumbled, warm, a little sandy. Had he put them there, throwing them in with anger and then slamming the lid on them? Had Nicky been asleep or had he watched, uncomprehending, terrified?

She sits down on the bed, throat horribly blocked and sore.

'Mi scusi, signora. . . .' The maid goes to the case and starts taking out the bottles. 'Pensato . . . scusi.' She stands in front of Laura apologetically.

So he had not put them there. 'That's all right.' A small relief. What had the maid thought? A little boy abandoned by his mother? Abandoned. Impossible. No mother could abandon her son, such a son. Perhaps she had thought her drowned. A tragedy. The husband come to take his poor motherless child home.

Laura stands up and takes the bottles from the maid, then gestures for her to leave. She goes quickly but closes the door very gently. As if on illness.

Laura goes into the bathroom and sees hanging on the shower rail Nicky's bathing costume. Not even hung by her own hands for Mrs Stevenson had put him to bed.

Laura reaches up for the still damp trunks and crushes them to her. She rushes into her bedroom and, falling onto the bed, begins to cry convulsively. A sense of miserable defeat envelopes her.

She is still crying when Martin comes in.

'Making no decision can still be a decision in itself,' he says.

She doesn't answer but her sobbing decreases.

'So are you going to rush after them? Or come down and have a nice crisp croissant.'

'Oh, Martin! If only. . . .'

'We had met earlier?'

'No. Yes. Nicky. . . .'

'If only we had never met, do you mean?'

'No! No!' She jumps up and clasps herself round him. 'I didn't know about anything before I met you. I wasn't alive at all!'

Martin pats her back gently as if thinking. Then he says quietly, 'Of course, he can't possibly keep Nicky from you.'

'Can't he! Can't he!' Hope rushes up. Miles is not a court of law. Miles cannot punish her. No one deserves to have their son taken away.

'Oh, yes. You'll have him the moment you want him. The only question is, do you want to run after him now or stay with me and have a crisp croissant?'

Laura looks up at Martin and sees that he is slightly apart from her. If she is not careful she will lose her husband, her child and her lover. Of course he is right. No mother can be separated from her child. Those days of guilt and retribution have long been discredited as inhumanitarian. As Old Testament eye for an eye, rather than New Testament christianity. She shivers a moment remembering the plastic orb then smooths her hair back from her face. 'Just give me a moment to wash my face and I'll be ready. A car chase across Italy would be far too melodramatic. And too hot!'

She even manages a small smile.

Chapter Fifteen

Later Laura thought that the intense heat of Italy in late July and August was one of the important reasons why she accepted the separation from Nicky. They had moved immediately from the hotel in Viareggio to a house Martin discovered in a small village in the hills above the sea. In the morning they were woken by the warmth of the sun slicing through their latticed blinds and the harsh crowing of a cock in a farm below.

They ate breakfast, even at that early hour, under the shade of a vine clustering with reddening grapes. They looked across a valley to dark wooded slopes above which the sun rose glowing triumphant day after day. Below them the village spluttered and coughed and bleated. After breakfast they drove down to the beach where they spent more time in the water than on the sand. They swam long distances, racing sometimes, sometimes setting themselves goals of far distant points along the shore, giving themselves a sense of virtue, rewarded by an ice-cream or a lazy flop under the umbrella.

Soon after midday when even the sea seemed to have taken on the dazzling glitter of sunshine they left the beach driving slowly upwards, ate salad in their dark stone-flagged kitchen and then, as all around them sounds muffled into a heat-dozed siesta, they too dropped into sleep. Limbs splayed exhausted across the bed as if they had spent the morning working in the fields. Often when they woke, an hour or two later, they made love, happy to think of the climax of heat overcome and the warm comfortable evening ahead.

They showered then, dressed more formally, read under their vine, shopped for fat peaches and juicy green beans. Sometimes they drove to Viareggio or Camaiore or Siena or even Florence. They stayed up late, drinking stregas under a black star-lit sky, pleased with having created another perfect day. At last, half drunk, they dropped once more into sleep, prepared, even in their heavy dreamlessness, for the sun's challenge on a new day.

They did talk. About Italy, its history, its politics. Martin had bought several books about Tuscany which inspired him to theories and late-night plans for extensive travel which always seemed impossible in the morning eye of the sun. Laura was reading Mrs Gaskell's *Wives and Daughters*. She found it comforting. The Victorian saga of family life and loves, so remote in every way from her present situation, gave her, contradictorially, a sense of security and continuity. Martin joked about her intense concentration as she read it and called it her 'soap opera'. Not wanting to finish it, she read slower and slower, until Martin spotted the unlikely sight of Trollope's three Palliser novels in a beach store, which he produced with a flourish. 'And for our next rich story of lively human interest . . . !'

She accepted them gratefully and managed to close Mrs Gaskell without too much regret. She had not read so intensely, with such a will to lose herself, since she was a teenager.

As soon as they had settled into their house Martin took a 'poste restante' number at the Viareggio Post Office. He picked up letters every couple of days and although Laura did not ask directly she gathered they were to do with his work. She knew that, until they had met, his work had been the most, probably the only, important thing in his life, but now she did not question how he could leave it for several weeks. Perhaps at the back of her mind was the feeling that his work was at least some exchange for her son.

Laura had kept Miles's note given to her that morning in the hotel. It had said simply, *It's better Nicky comes with me – Miles.* Miles had never been an elaborate writer of notes. In the early days of their marriage they had been separated fairly often as he sat in courts round the country. He had sent her notes, on country court note-paper. They began *Dearest* and ended *Miles*, just 'Miles' as this final note had done. No love. Yet even Laura could never pretend that love was lacking. She was his centre, his one and true love. He wrote, *Jackson v. Jackson turned out to be a shambles*, but his heart was filled with love. Words he distrusted, perhaps because as a barrister he used them daily to express a legal truth which was only some of the time a reality.

Years ago Laura used to go and watch him perform in court as she might go to a theatre. At first she had been impressed by the majestic ceremony, the wigs and robes, the bombastic language of tradition. She had been excited, too, by the closeness of it all, the judge, the barristers, the accused and the witnesses all crammed together in a space hardly bigger than her living-room. In that way she had felt as if she was on the stage herself.

Then came a case when Miles was acting for the Crown, prosecuting a group of four men accused of cutting up a plain-clothes policeman in a night club. Laura was close enough to touch them, three nondescript youngish men and one hugely fat, almost as wide as he was high. She left at the end of the day, caught the underground train home. Arriving at her station, still thrilled by the inside view of such gangsters who, according to Miles would probably get prison sentences of at least twelve years, she stepped out of the train and made for the lift. It was only as she reached the small dark box that she saw directly ahead of her, already entering the lift, the unmistakable figure of the hugely fat accused. She then saw the other three with him.

Too late to stop her entrance, she edged into a corner, eyes turned away, hoping like a head-in-the-sand ostrich, that if she couldn't see them, they wouldn't see her. For in her surprise, even panic, it seemed quite likely that they would reach for a knife and slice her about as they had the unfortunate policeman. She was a witness to their evil, a voyeur, she had been watching greedily, enjoying their course to justice. She had been protected by the arms of the law, now she was alone, four to one, out in the world. She was frightened, ashamed, uncom-prehending.

Later when she told this to Miles he was amazed at her reaction. 'But surely you know about bail,' he said. 'Criminals are walking around all over the place. Until they're con-victed.'

'Yes. But.' This didn't seem to explain to Laura what seemed to her her perfectly natural reaction. She saw that the law was a game, a charade, in which barristers played as devious a role as criminals. Miles did not represent righteousness but one side of an unreal argument. This feeling which reduced Miles in her eyes, was increased soon afterwards.

Once more she went to court. But this time Miles was defending. His client, strange word, was a small smartly-dressed youth with a clean pimply face. She had come at Miles's suggestion since he was winding up the case with an impassioned speech over which he'd worked very hard. Indeed he was impressive, colour rising in his cheeks, his wig flaring jauntily on his shoulders, words mostly long and of latinate construction, pouring from his lips.

Afterwards as they sat outside waiting for the jury's judg-ment, she congratulated him. He smiled, pleased, squeezed her hand and then said quite nonchalantly, 'Of course he'll go down.'

'Oh, I'm sorry,' Laura sympathised.

'He's so obviously guilty.'

'But everything you said . . . ? You said he wasn't there. He couldn't have done it.'

'I did my best for him.' Miles began to look impatient and Laura realised that her continuing failure to understand the process of the law annoyed him deeply. In fact it wasn't that she couldn't understand it intellectually but that she couldn't reconcile it with her own inner morality. Lawyers, she felt, must be deceivers.

From then on she no longer went to court and her confidence in Miles's superiority to herself began to drain away. She felt constricted in his presence. She stopped telling him her inner-most thoughts. It was then she became pregnant with Nicky.

In the dark hot Italian night she understood that she married Miles out of admiration, never love. That when admiration had lessened it had been replaced by affection, the affection of a long close association between friends. An outward casing. Never love.

But mostly, she did not analyse herself, terrified of facing her own deep-seated belief that a wife does not leave her husband, a mother does not leave her child.

She was grateful to Martin who no longer questioned. She did not even care to find out whether it was out of tact or casualness. Still their love dazzled her too much to see beyond.

*

One morning they are sitting having breakfast on the terrace of their little house. Laura puts up a hand and touches a bunch of grapes. 'They're almost ripe.'

'Pity we'll miss them.'

Laura looks at Martin, surprised.

'We only took the house for three weeks.'

'Oh.' Time is an enemy. Linked to inescapable facts. 'I've lost count of the days.'

'Look at this.' Martin takes a letter out of his pocket and hands it to Laura. Then he looks away. It is written in neat flowery hand-writing curling across expensive air-mail paper.

Well, my darling, you have surprised us all, running away with the wife of an eminent QC. It makes all those, like myself I must admit, who profess not to believe in romantic passion, look quite silly. I make no comment except to say that I miss you and that she is older than you and has a child and a good husband. Bon voyage but don't make it too long. Like the most conventional of mothers (which I am not) I too look forward to a daughter-in-law and many charming children just like my charming if sometimes misguided son.

Félicitations, ta maman.

Laura finishes the letter and looks up at the faraway line of trees and the shocking blue sky above. The contents she can hardly take in, it is Martin's motives for giving the letter to her that makes her skin freeze. She feels her eyes water and before the worst should happen and she burst into blubbing tears, she quickly hands the letter back. She cannot think what to say and the lump in her throat makes it difficult even if she could, so she says nothing.

Martin takes the letter almost abstractedly and then looking down at it suddenly gives his screech of laughter. 'This is my mother's letter!'

197

'I know. She doesn't seem very pleased with you.'

'I didn't mean to give you this,' he laughs again.

His laughter, enormous relief though it is, makes Laura's tears even more dangerously close. Martin doesn't seem to notice, saying with ebullience, 'Mother should have learnt her lesson by now. She first tried to marry me off when I was eighteen. To the daughter of a Russian princess she admired. The letter I wanted to show you is quite different.' He digs fruitlessly in his pockets and then stands up. 'I must have put it down inside.'

Left on her own, Laura revolves maman's phrases. *She is older than you and has a child and a good husband . . . I too look forward to a daughter-in-law and many charming children just like my charming if sometimes misguided son.* Martin's laughter, genuine enough, could not wipe away the sting of those words. If he did not take them seriously, she did.

Martin returns waving a piece of paper. 'Here you are. I'll read it. *Dear Mr Keane, With reference to . . .* dum dee dum, dum dee dum, *therefore we are pleased to inform you that your application for a contract . . .* ta ra . . . what the pompous ass wants to say is that they need to sort out their whole computer system, which is in a godawful mess . . . Signed, *Yours very sincerely, Herbert C. Craddock – for Mathieson, Craddock and Humbert, of San Francisco, Boston and New York.*'

Martin throws the letter towards Laura. 'It's actually Brooklyn. But what does it matter. Two or three months in New York. Being paid. It's a triumph of bringing coals to Newcastle!'

This business exultation is unexpected. Coming straight after his mother's letter. Laura feels herself amazed, unable to cope. 'What does it mean?'

Martin stops his crowing look, like their cock in the morning Laura thinks, and says simply, 'It means we'll have to go home.'

'Home?'

'That's what I meant to tell you in the first place. But first of all,' his enthusiasm picks up again, 'but first of all we're going to Petra.'

'Petra?' Laura finds she has stood up hand to bosom, as if a maiden poised for flight. 'Petra.' It sounds like a girl's name to her. She imagines a rosy-cheeked beauty with black ringlets. Daughter of a Russian princess.

' "A Rose-red city, half as old as time." I've booked us flights tomorrow. My treat.'

'Final treat,' Laura murmurs. But Martin swoops towards her with the sort of demonstrative hug which the heat of the day usually discourages. Laura wonders if she is right in feeling a note of falseness. Was he trying literally to sweep her off her feet? Until he dropped her. *She is older than you and has a child and a good husband.*

'I'll clear away breakfast.'

'Yes.' Martin lets her go without showing disappointment at her reaction.

Just as, an hour ago, Laura could see no end to this summer of love, now she can see nothing but the end. The end in the coffee cups, shining cosily in the wooden rack for someone else, the end in the greenish flagstones waiting to cool off other hot feet, the end in the large square bed, the coarse pale blue sheets which she would have to pull off in the morning.

'What's the matter?' She feels Martin's large solid warmth behind her and despite herself leans backwards into his arms.

'Nothing. I'm sad.'

'Because we're leaving?'

'Yes.' She whispers. Let him judge how much more she means.

'That's the whole point of Petra. To make you feel excited not sad. It's not the end.'

'Of course not.' The words spoken now and in the open, Laura feels able to pretend she has never felt it. She gathers their bathing things with a cheerful expression and listens attentively as Martin explains that he had been to Petra as an undergraduate and had always wanted to return there.

By the time they arrive at the crowded beach and the surprisingly uncrowded sea beyond, she has begun truly to think it is not necessarily the end. Time begins to liquify again, as easy to push aside as the clear water through which her body cuts a path. She swims far out and then lets herself drop, pointed down like an arrow, till her toes touch the sandy bottom.

She breaks surface to find Martin's head bobbing nearby her, watching. 'Why did you do that?' he says.

She smiles, happier now than she had been all day. 'Do what?' As they tread water side by side, she imagines they look like two bobbing otters, with blinking eyes and watery snouts.

'Sink like a stone. It makes me nervous.'

'I don't feel like a stone at all. I feel marvellous. I can't explain. Everything falls away. Come on let's swim in now.'

'But you do it often. Suddenly disappear.'

'I'm sorry. I hadn't realised.' Secretly she is delighted that he cares.

They decide to have their last Italian lunch in a restaurant. Since it is the best restaurant in Viareggio, they end up in the same place as they ate lunch with Nicky. Laura says nothing but is slightly surprised Martin should have chosen it.

He begins to talk again about Petra, the colour, the shapes, the mystery. There is an Agatha Christie story set there which he has found in the same book-store that uncovered the Trollope novels.

Laura is suddenly struck by the thought that they are going to travel a long way in the opposite direction from England, where, as far as she knows, Nicky is. She feels a dreadful wrenching pain, worse than anything she has felt since they were parted. He had left her here in Italy where she had remained, ready as it were, even though it was totally unlikely, for his return. But now she was leaving, striking out from his point of departure for somewhere much further. Now she was leaving him. She pictures his face, pale, pinched, tearful. Abandoned.

Her food, a lightly and most deliciously grilled fish, becomes a mess of bones. The sauce, a froth of whipped eggs and herbs, looks sickening.

'Why aren't you eating?'

Time again, strapping her up with terrible fears. He hadn't told her how long they were going for. 'It's too rich.' She pushes her plate away.

'Yes. I prefer our salads.'

Our salads. A shared past. She will go to Petra because she has no choice.

That night she curls into Martin's arms with a childlike confidence that makes him feel strong and gratified.

'I feel lonely.' She admits, as always, only a little part.

'You mustn't.'

'No.'

'I want you with me all the time.'

She lets his words mean the everything she wanted from them and lifts her face to his.

She slowly stops being a child and stretches out along his body.

*

A simple action at Pisa airport raises Laura's spirits. She sends a postcard to Nicky. She sends it to their London address, in perfect confidence he will receive it, amazed she has not thought of doing it before. Martin seeing what she's doing, smiles. 'I shouldn't put a cross and "our bedroom".'

'Don't be vulgar. It's a picture of the Leaning Tower of Pisa.' She smiles too. She draws many kisses on the bottom of the card. Contact has been restored.

*

It is raining in Jordan. Lashings of ice-cold water hissing and spitting on the small hostel outside Petra. Laura and Martin, exhausted by their long journey, dig out crumpled sweaters from the bottom of their cases.

'It's most likely,' says the proprietor, anxiety defeating his English.

'It's raining on my dreams,' says Martin, lifting a glass of beer. There is no wine.

Laura doesn't return his smile. The chill enters her bones. She goes to her narrow bed fully dressed. She can't think what she's doing half way up a wet and rocky desert.

In the morning they wake to the sound of dripping. Martin goes to investigate. The dripping comes from a tap.

'We have a dawn!' He throws open the door. Laura sees a perfect purity of light glimmering through a veil of pink and mauve. 'Hurry! Hurry! We must be at the city as the sun rises.' They go on horse-back. Single-file, treading a sandy track through ever narrowing boulders.

'You look like a boy scout,' shouts Laura. Fair-weather friend, she thinks to herself. Fair-weather friend and lover.

Martin's horse is more eager than Laura's, bumping him along ahead. He turns round, holding his hand up against the sun just beginning to slant up between the rocks. 'I can't tell you what you look like.'

Laura laughs. She is wearing a pair of his trousers, shamingly tight round her hips and bottom, but bagging hopelessly round waist and leg. 'I can't help it if I'm all woman.'

201

Their guide, a little boy riding the largest horse of the three, turns round and grins cheekily. Laura, about to give a cool look, suddenly changes her mind and gives him an open smile. After all, she has nothing to hide. She has declared herself correctly. Woman, all woman.

The boulders on either side begin to close in and take strange shapes. Crevices, carved deep and oblong, mark ancient burial grounds.

> *'Match me such a marvel save in Eastern clime,*
> *A rose-red city "half as old as Time"!'*

recites Martin. His words echo back to them as the rocks close in a smooth dark tunnel above their heads. Slowly a thin bright-coloured line widens at the end of their vision.

'I'd like this moment to go on forever!' cries Laura. But the gap spreads wide spilling out its treasure.

They enter the city, carved hundreds of years ago out of the living rock, long abandoned, a mysterious and only half-discovered dream. A main track is bounded by lacey palaces and temples but other smaller tracks lead upwards into wilder parts.

They slip off their horses, arranging for the guide to bring them back an hour before sunset.

'I can hardly believe it exists,' Martin stands still, looking around him, 'even though I've seen it. It might have been a *Grand Meaulnes* out of my feverish youth.' He turns to Laura. 'It reminds me of you.'

'What? Old? Stoney?' She stands looking at his face. The sun makes it exactly the same colour as the rock behind.

'I couldn't believe you existed. And then when I saw you, so placid, so certain, so beautiful, I knew I could never have you. You were my dreams. You are my dream.'

The sun that day was different from the sharp Italian sun they were used to. It glowed instead of glittered, it spread fans of heat around their bodies but left their feet cool as they climbed the twisting tracks and entered the dark sandy buildings. It was mellow like the carvings around them. Mellow with time. Here, Laura felt, time was on her side.

At midday they sat under a black bedouin awning and drank sweet tea. Afterwards they climbed up to the highest point and looked back over the whole city. There was a slight breeze up there tempting Laura to open her arms and flap like a bird.

'Come live with me and be my love,' she sings out, then runs a little way. 'I expect it's a sin to be so happy!' she cries, feeling as pure and free from sin as a bird.

*

The next day they go back to London, flying through so many airports that Laura loses count. She wonders why Martin has not warned her that her postcard to Nicky would arrive days after herself. She begins to see that he judges her actions on a different plane from other people's. She is his dream, after all.

The journey is long and dreary, behind schedule all the way like a nightmare with feet stuck in glue. By the time the last plane lands with a nerve-racking bang and bounce and bang again Laura has begun to disbelieve in their holiday. The only evidence of sun and happiness seems to be her coarsely brown face and limbs. She has not thought of protecting her skin and now she sees that her hands have dried out and wrinkled like a much older woman's. She glances at Martin who has picked up an *Economist* at Amman which has somehow lasted him till now. He looks younger than ever, his hair bleached to yellow and gold stripes, his face dark against it appearing finer than it really is, his eyes bluer. He had fallen in love with her because, she was 'placid, certain, beautiful'. Now what was she?

The moment they were through customs, Laura looks for a telephone.

'Where are you going in such a hurry?' Martin smiles at her.

'I'm going to ring home.'

'Home?' he questions now, still smiling.

'I want to speak to Nicky.'

'Ah.' A pause. 'Home is with me.'

This is a consolation to be carried like a shield as she rings her own number. Maria answers. Laura finds she hates the fat innocent girl as much as she's ever hated anyone. 'It's Mrs Knight. Is Nicky there?'

'Ah, no. No one is here. They are away for weeks.'

'What do you mean weeks?' Laura is further irritated by her obvious nervousness. 'Where is he?'

There is a gulping noise the other end which makes Laura realise that Maria is obeying orders. She speaks harshly,

'Where is he? Tell me where he is? You're speaking to his mother!'

The only result is that Maria bursts into loud and ugly tears. All possibility of communication is cut. Laura puts down the phone.

She returns to find Martin at the TWA desk. He looks up at her face and asks no questions.

'What are you doing?'

'Flights to New York.'

Laura feels very frail indeed. 'When do you go?'

'You too, I hope. In a few days. You saw the letter.'

'Yes.' . . . *She is older than you and has a son and a good husband.*

'I must go into the office today but I could drop you into the flat first.'

'No. No. I can take our things.'

To be alone seems the only hope of sanity. Her mind whirls with thoughts of her family, her home, her job. She has no idea how they fit into this new life. She wonders if it was out of terror of a moment like this that she had stayed faithful to Miles, a good mother to Nicky. Now she is whirling into darkness. She thinks that if Miles appears, sombre in his black suit, judgemental in his grey-curled wig, she will go with him like a child, obediently. Was this virtue? Or cowardice?

Since Miles doesn't appear, she doesn't decide. Instead she feels a flood of warmth as Martin takes her hand.

'We'll share a taxi as far as Cromwell Road and then I'll hop out. Don't be too anxious. It was sure to be bad.'

Is it bravery, then, to overcome her terror? But why does she lose faith the moment he breaks contact with her?

'I must ring my office too. I might even go in. Show off my sunburn.' In her ears Maria's blubbing still resounds. 'I should go to the house to get my things.'

'Yes.'

Laura recognises, now, that although Martin is brief in the face of her domestic problems, it does not mean he's casual.

'Nicky seems to be away at the moment.'

'Have a rest today. That's what you should do.' Martin squeezes her hand and then drops it. They must be individuals now they're in London.

Laura rests. She lies on Martin's bed with their unopened cases around her. Outside the light is so grey and dim after the glare of the Mediterranean that she feels as if the curtains are drawn. She sleeps a little and then, waking up with a jerk, reaches for the telephone.

She dials Nell's number. Almost immediately her voice is there, talking enthusiastically, energetically. Laura feels her own lassitude banished. Just as Maria's voice had filled her with irrational hatred, now Nell's fills her with joy. And love. Friendship, she sees, is one of the most positive experiences of human existence. How glad she is that she had continued to work for this friendship, battling against Miles's disapproval and their own differences of outlook and way of life.

Meanwhile Nell is telling her about a courtship she was enjoying. 'He's far too old and not my type at all – he goes to an office every day and thinks I dress like a tart – but he's very successful and very rich and swears he's madly in love with me.' None of this Laura takes too seriously. She waits, knowing that for once she has the greater burden of news. Nell draws breath, 'So. Are you all right?'

'I thought you'd never ask.' They laugh together, a relief of laughter without any demands. 'No. Yes. Wonderful. Dreadful to be back. Dreadful. Glorious. Are you coming up to London?'

'Why? Do you need me?'

'I've got to go to the house.'

'You want me to come with you.'

'Nicky's not there. At least so Maria says.'

'Of course I'll come with you.'

They decide to go the following afternoon. Nell suggests the fortification of an alcoholic lunch.

*

Nell is dressed in a safari suit with a straw hat and dark glasses.

'You look like a spy,' says Laura as they approach the house, rather tipsy, rather hysterical.

'Oh, I'm used to creeping in and out of other people's houses,' she replies airily. 'I like to dress the part.'

'But this isn't other peoples' houses,' says Laura, 'it's my house.'

'It comes to the same thing.' This strikes them both as extraordinarily funny and as they reach the crimson front door they are stifling giggles like schoolgirls in church. Laura puts her key in the lock and Nell, in a theatrical gesture, crouches low, finger to lips.

The door opens on a small, low-ceilinged house. Laura is surprised by the drabness of it, so different from the image of jewel colours which she remembers. She goes into the drawing-room. It is tidy, flowerless, anonymous. The grey light from the street outside seems to fill the whole room. Nell has gone next door.

'Well, he's living here anyway.'

Laura finds her in Miles's study. The room is piled with papers, books, briefs.

'It always looks like this,' Laura finds the evidence of her husband's hard work distasteful. She retreats to the door.

Perhaps seeing her expression Nell cries out gaily. 'What shall we do with them, then? Throw out of the window? Tear them! Roll them into little balls! Trample them under foot!' She picks up a sheaf of type-written papers as if to suit action to words.

'No! No!' Laura protests, smiling. She thinks that her departure from hearth and husband was different from Nell's. She did not take a conscious step away, she had merely fallen in love. She feels no liberation. Yet there is another voice which echoes Nell and says that those thin papers and heavy books ran her life for ten years and if she is ever to be truly free of them she must do as Nell suggests and splay them round the room in derision.

'Come on. Let's go upstairs.' Miles is a good, hard-working man. He has done no wrong.

The first room they reach belongs to Nicky. Laura, who had been steeling herself against crumpled pyjamas, half-eaten biscuits and half-made pieces of lego, is almost relieved to find it as blank as the drawing-room. 'Nicky's definitely not here.'

She looks in his cupboard and sees his clothes mostly gone, only his school uniform pressed and orderly, waiting for the start of the new term. Even his books have been arranged in an impersonal line, no sign of a hand or a heart.

Laura goes up to her own room. She gasps with ridiculous shock. The bed gapes unmade, sheets and blankets rolling down onto the floor, her pretty coverlet crumpled under their weight.

'I sense the need for a woman's hand,' Nell says with satisfaction.

'Miles never made a bed during our whole marriage,' agrees

Laura who had never in their whole marriage considered this of any interest whatsoever. In fact, recovering from her shock, she had automatically bent down as if to start making the bed.

'I thought you had that Spanish au pair,' Nell says.

'So did I.'

'Perhaps she went with Nicky.'

'When I called.'

'Exactly, Dr Watson.' Nell's attempts to keep the air cheerful is failing. Laura feels her face slumping with the desire to cry.

She gets down a large case and begins to bustle around collecting clothes and other objects. 'What do I take?' she wails, giving her distress a more acceptably practical expression.

'Only the things you love.'

Laura thinks she loves only Nicky and throws in several old ropes of beads she doesn't even like let alone love.

'This room smells,' announces Nell. 'Why do mens' bedrooms always smell when they're left on their own?'

'Perhaps they don't open the window wide enough.'

'But it is open. I think it's something more hormonal. Which side does he sleep?'

Laura glances up from a pile of greying tights. 'By the telephone.' She throws the tights into the wastepaper basket.

'Aha. So he took some responsibilities.' She moves across. 'Let's see what he's reading. Agatha Christie. Some boring old legal mag. or other and, aha! what's this? *The Joy of* . . . Oh no, what a disappointment, *The Joy of Camping.*'

'Oh, Nell.' Laura begins to think, as she often has in the past, that Nell passes the bounds of good taste. But then what are the bounds of good taste when you're in the process of walking out on your husband?

'I think I will make the bed.' With great energy, Laura begins to pull up sheets and blankets. Nell watches, sighing exaggeratedly.

'I don't hate him,' Laura says, though this is not really true.

'I suppose you've always been more civilised than me.' Half-heartedly Nell goes to the other side of the bed and helps to straighten the bedclothes.

It is thus that Miles, wronged and avenging husband, finds them. A woman on either side of his bed turning back the none too clean sheets in time-honoured fashion.

Nell, of course, laughs. It is probably nervous laughter but the effect, combined with her safari suit, hat and dark glasses which she has solemnly retained, is dramatic. Laura decides definitely that there are codes of behaviour for every situation. 'I'm sorry,' she murmurs staring mesmerically at Miles.

Miles's face which, when he'd first appeared in the doorway had been fixed in a serious but impartial expression, now flushes a deep red and begins to move in angry folds. Laura has never seen him look like this.

Finally he manages to open his mouth and shouts, 'Nicky's not here. And I shan't tell you where he is! I don't want him ever to see you again. You're just a common whore! I'm ashamed I called you wife! I don't want him ever to see you again!'

'Oh, God, I'm sorry. I'd better go.' Nell, for some reason holding onto her hat as if the tempest of Miles's rage might blow it off, edges towards the door and then stops, barred by his presence. Laura, inappropriately literary in a moment of crisis, is reminded of the black-suited church-warden who refuses poor sinful Red Shoes admittance.

'And you,' he points an accusing finger towards Nell, 'are worse than the worst because you are not sinning out of any greater conviction than a love of fun!'

The anti-climax of this is lost on all of them for Nell, with another explosive splutter, literally pushes Miles aside, and flees down the stairs. It is only as the noise recedes that Laura realises she is not laughing but crying.

The front door slams and there is silence. Laura, still avoiding serious thought, begins to be worried by Miles's rigid stance. She says in a persuasive, almost conversational tone, 'Why don't we go downstairs and talk it over?' As she speaks she realises she is shaking violently all over. She sits down abruptly on the bed.

But her words seem to have cued Miles for he takes a step forward and says, still in the same strained high-pitched voice of doom, 'No. There is nothing to discuss. Nothing!' On which he too turns, blunders through the door, down the stairs and out of the front door. Once more it slams shut.

Laura, too shocked to cry, sits where she has been left, alone on the half-made bed.

Chapter Sixteen

Miles's dramatic outrage magnified in Laura's mind. Martin's reaction – 'Poor chap, facing you two across his dirty linen – no wonder he blew his top' – did not diminish it. It created a final barrier to her return. It made her aware that until now she had kept open the idea of repentance and reconciliation.

Laura had always believed in forgiveness as the most important Christian virtue. She couldn't understand those who saw the church as rigid in its praise of the righteous and its condemnation of wrong-doers. But now she recognised the black church warden with raised accusing finger would never let her cross the threshold.

*

Nell rings up to apologise for her behaviour. 'I thought it was better to get out, knowing his views on me but when he pointed at me and said all those things, everything suddenly seemed too dreadful. I mean everything in my life. That's why I cried.'

She goes on at some length, explaining that her caravan youth with the golden earring is pressing her to go on a long trip to Tunisia, and her ex-husband wants her to have the boys till the end of the holiday, and her rich admirer wants her to stay in his country house with the boys if she likes but it's so boring and she's suddenly had this tremendous order for mugs. If only she can find the energy to do them!

Laura, sitting in her office for she has started back to work again, doesn't listen too hard but congratulates her on the orders. Work, perhaps, is the answer. Men have always gained strength from it.

'If only I could really care about it,' sighs Nell. 'Really care. Not just feel stupidly proud or glad to have the money.'

'That's because you don't need the money with your alimony.'

Nell sighs again. 'It's not the style I was accustomed to. Before I was divorced. Now Peter. . . .' She breaks off for once, reluctant to describe her rich admirer. She returns to Laura.

'You're so lucky. So decisive. Either married, more married than anyone, or totally utterly unmarried with the most desirable, besotted lover in the world. You never muddle round like the rest of us.'

This speech seems so extraordinarily out of touch with the real situation that Laura feels no way of continuing the conversation. Is it possible Nell doesn't realise that by leaving Miles she has become one of the rest?

She puts down the telephone. Then on impulse quickly picks it up again, and dials Katie's number.

Ever since she had not found Nicky at the house she has been fairly certain he has been staying with Katie and Johnny. Even Miles, disapproving of her brother's private life and Katie's chaotic household, would recognise that was where Nicky would be happiest. On the other hand, if he wasn't there, she would be cast into the utmost misery, unable to imagine where else he could be. Moreover she dreaded a conversation with Johnny or Katie.

The telephone rings for a long time. Laura imagines Katie settling one crying child, shouting at another, pulling a saucepan off the stove. Even so it is a long time. Just as she's about to put the receiver down, it is answered.

'Hello.' It is a child's voice. Laura's body dissolves into watery yearning. She murmurs, 'Nicky.'

But the voice goes on louder. 'Hello, who is it? Mummy's in the garden. It's Maddy speaking.'

Laura recovers. She realises she has here a wonderful chance. 'Is Nicky there?'

'Yes. Somewhere. I don't know where.' She is bored, nonchalant. 'Do you want me to try and find him?'

'No. No.' That would be too sudden, too shocking. It is enough for the moment. He is there, safe, happy.

'Is he well?'

'What?' Maddy cannot cope with such a concept. 'Do you want Mummy? I think she's coming in now.'

'No. No.' Again Laura shies away hastily. She is not prepared. 'I'll ring again later. Thank you.'

'That's all right. Bye.' The little girl has not even asked who she is.

Laura sits over the telephone, smiling. Nightmare fears are pushed far away. Nicky is all right. In a normal happy setting he knows well. One of a gang. Maddy would have told her if there were any problems. She feels like dancing round the room with joy and relief. Instead she rings Martin.

'He's at Katie's. He's all right.'

'Then you'll come to New York? It's only for a few days, after all.'

Laura agrees, surging forwards still on a wave of optimism. She is surprised, later, when she goes to see Ben Casey and he says sourly, 'I thought you wanted to make a proper career of the job.'

'Yes, of course I do,' she says impatiently.

It is true that on her return she had talked intensely about the importance of work in her life. Although she had not told him about her separation from Miles, she was convinced that he knew and that it was essential, if he was to continue to respect her, that she emphasised her position as a strong determined career woman.

However now her mood is different. She knows where her son is safe and sound. She is flying off to New York with her adored and adoring lover. 'It's only for a few days. And, who knows, I might manage to drum up a bit of support for saving the old country. Farmyard follies are a much more attractive proposition than barns and tractors.'

This idea of lobbying for her new project while in New York captures Laura's imagination. To Martin's amusement she busies herself collecting introductions to the rich and well-disposed towards England and conservation. 'They could buy a dove-cote,' she explains gaily to one possible source of names. 'For enough money we'd even paint on their initials. Think of it, a personalised eighteenth century dove-cote.'

At first she'd found it hard to ring up people she knew, afraid of that moment of revelation when they'd say, 'And how's your clever husband?' And she'd say – what would she say? But in fact no one asks and she gives her office number and feels positive and independent.

Martin says, 'You'll be happier in New York with a project.' And she immediately realises this is true, unconsciously she is protecting herself against the memory of their last visit. Then she had been nobody, neither wife, declared lover nor worker. This time she would not luxuriate in bed, watching him dress like a girl in a harem, waiting unoccupied for the summons to lunch or dinner. She would bound out ahead of him, waving her list of the rich and famous.

This energetic image of herself lasts until their arrival in New York. The city lies under the pall of August heatwave. As their airport taxi crosses the East River and heads west over Second and Third Avenues, Laura, trying vainly to get air through the window, decides the scene on the streets looks like a goldfish bowl with pedestrians like fish swimming slowly by in the wetness.

'Humidity is high,' says Martin wiping his face and hands.

'How do they survive?'

'How will we?'

Martin, at Laura's request, has booked them into a different hotel. It is small, central, and decorated in a style said to be English. This means chintz. Through a whirl of pink and orange roses Laura spies the air-conditioning unit.

'Ah,' she says holding her skirt above its squirting cold. 'I spy a survival unit.'

Martin laughs, 'I thought no heat was too great for you.'

'Beaches are different. Whatever do people wear?'

'The usual things. Blouses. Skirts, pants.' Martin comes to Laura and starts undressing her. 'And they do the usual things, too.' He leads her over to the bed. 'In the usual way.'

Afterwards when they're lying together in a darkness that could be dawn or dusk, Laura thinks that her body's enslavement to Martin is what makes it so difficult to be independent. She wonders men don't feel the same. Or even all women.

She gets up shakily and walks to the window. It is dusk, their hot arrival at lunch-time.

She switches on a light and goes to her handbag, touches her New York address book. Tomorrow morning they will not make love and she will stride out confidently. It is easier to imagine this from the cool of their bedroom.

Martin stirs and sits up abruptly in the way he has. Laura is immediately drawn to him. The words 'practical resolution' flick into her mind. Is that why she loves him? She stands at his side. He looks at his watch.

'Time to dress. We have a dinner date.' He gets up and puts on the television. The room is filled with talking faces in an unreal technicolour.

'I would live in America were it not for bad television.'

'You don't watch much television in England.'

'Not when I have you. The newspapers here are very good, of course. Better than in England.'

Martin crouches down naked in front of the television set.

Laura admires his straight back and strong thighs. 'Where are we dining, if I may ask?'

'Of course you may ask. With a friend of mine, in his penthouse apartment. He has a new girlfriend he wishes me to look over.' Martin goes to Laura, kisses her and goes to shower.

Laura, waiting her turn, hangs out a dress and tells herself that life has never been so rich. An image of Nicky in bed slides through her mind. For a moment the pain of loss is so intense she bends double muffling her face in the soft folds of her dress. Then it is gone.

The penthouse apartment overlooks the Hudson River. It is not big but boasts a huge balcony. Martin's friend, Eddy, has laid a table out there with an elegant striped umbrella. They sit drinking white wine and admiring the view. To one side is the river and bridge lit up with golden lights and to the other a city of glittering turrets.

Martin, says little. The girlfriend is undisguisedly large with a flat pale face and yellow hair. She doesn't say much more than Martin. However she has a graceful manner and smiles attentively, offering them olives and home-made cheese straws. She is called Ellen. Laura can see that in a frantic city like New York she might represent a desirable style of calm and goodwill. Perhaps also her clean fairness represents a belle ideal of old America. Eddy, though also large, is dark and quick with a nervous excitable manner. He is older than Martin, in his forties, perhaps even fifty, but even so Laura is astonished when he suddenly refers to his third wife. She thinks he might be joking but clearly not.

'My mother thinks he's a blue-beard,' says Ellen. 'But I tell her he's a romantic.'

'Or a fool,' Eddy laughs. 'At least Martin brings down the average to respectable levels. Never married at all.'

Laura begins to wish this particular conversation would end. The friendliness and lack of intensity with which it is conducted troubles her particularly.

'So. Three marriages for me – coming up four,' he looks warmly at Ellen. 'Ellen one coming up for two.' She gives him a pleased smile. 'Martin none and Laura . . . How often have you walked the tight-rope so far?'

Laura, her face pinched and prim, stares at her plate. Can Martin share this attitude to marriage? Is it possible he doesn't realise how much she would hate all this? 'Once,' she answers raising her eyes to the night sky. It is hazy with heat but a blinking eye of red light moves sharply across. Laura imagines being in that aeroplane, able to look down on the scene round the striped umbrella. What would that God-like person think of their conversation? Letting her eyes drop lower, she fixes on the golden string of lights which mark the bridge.

She swears to herself that if Martin makes some fatuous remark about marriage, she will throw herself off the side of this fragile balcony, disclaiming even to take hold of the umbrella and use it as a bright parachute . . . Smiling at her silliness Laura takes a sip of wine. Martin says nothing.

The subject is changed. New York City politics, about which Martin is surprisingly knowledgeable but Laura knows nothing, takes over. She enters the conversation only once when she hears mentioned the name of one of her rich and famous. It gives her the opportunity to explain her reason to be in New York, to deliver her speech of the serious worker. It gives her some satisfaction until she catches Eddy's watchful eye and suddenly realises they have been invited to dinner not only for Martin to look over Ellen but also for Eddy to look over her.

She becomes silent again. In such a place, she decides, looking once more at the sky and the river and even swinging round for the turrets, there is a lot to be said for silence. She feels an even greater sympathy for Ellen for, even though she has now revealed her profession to be a teacher, she still seems always passive.

It is the men who argue energetically, crossing from politics to business. Eddy is a reporter in the business section of the *New York Times*. After a while, Ellen rises, 'I'll get coffee.' Laura follows her.

Inside the small, neon-lit kitchen, Ellen immediately starts talking as if either the presence of the men or of the great dome of sky had previously silenced her. She asks all the questions that a visitor expects and had been curiously lacking. She offers to enlist Eddy's help in approaching a couple of financial rich and famous. She asks whether Laura has children and in this unknown place Laura has no hesitation in describing the perfection that is Nicky.

'You obviously love him very much,' says Ellen, carefully laying out coffee spoons.

'But of course!' cries Laura surprised. Then catches Ellen's eye. A cruel flush starts up her cheeks. 'He's staying with my brother's family. He loves it there,' she says in the same hard bright voice.

Ellen has two children, she tells Laura, but wants another one with Eddy as soon as possible. Marriage, less important, will come sooner or later.

They step back out to the balcony. Laura, emotionally unable to separate herself from her own notions of guilt and duty, sees in Ellen another set of rules as serious as her own.

Ellen pours coffee with unexpectedly graceful fingers at the end of her strong arms. As Laura lifts her cup, a delicate drop of water falls into the black centre.

'It's raining!' she exclaims.

The rain comes down in tiny silver slivers, hardly water at all, more the condensation of the night sky. Quick silver from the stars, thinks Laura. Unwilling to go inside they draw their chairs close under the umbrella. Laura feels Martin's leg pulsing against hers. Then his hand grips hers on the table. She smiles at him, acknowledging this public ownership.

They sit there talking cosily with the rain tinkling above their heads for some time. Words, almost as lightly patterned, form around and about Laura.

'I think she's fallen asleep.'

'It is five in the morning our time.' Laughter. And Laura wakes up.

In the hotel Martin says, 'What did you think?'

'She was nice.'

'She might calm him down.'

'Yes.'

It seems they may have an ordinary friendship in common. The isolation of a grand love affair dissipating. Laura is more pleased than sorry.

'She said she'd help me increase my rich and famous list.'

*

The next morning the list becomes reality. Martin has left early, repeating, despite Laura's resolutions, the scene of man

215

dressing energetically, woman in bed lounging. She feels sick. Sick and exhausted. The prospect of city heat fills her with dismay. At least this has the effect of lessening to quite manageable proportions her dread of telephoning into the unknown.

The ease with which she makes appointments is, in fact, quite startling, making the point that this is not slow old England. The exhilaration of her own efficiency raises her from bed and into a neat suit. It is only then her sickness returns again, making her feel dizzy.

She goes to the window and stands above the cool air-conditioner looking at the busy street below. It is already nearly eleven, workers high in offices, so she sees only boys carrying brown paper bags from café to desk, or tourists, or late risers like herself. Sick and jet-lagged.

Laura strides along Fifth Avenue in her crisp red and white suit. She turns into a dashing modern building and after consulting the board chooses an elevator direct to the thirty-eighth floor. As she ascends she rehearses her introductory patter, 'Lady Southey, who's an old friend of mine (not altogether true) told me of your interest in the British heritage of land-originated buildings and artifacts. . . .' She sounds quite impressive to herself. Perhaps she should go into properly paid public relations. Of course the foundation is a charity with no profit motive of any sort. 'We're in the business of preserving and conserving (what's the difference?) the deserving without a hint of self-serving.'

The elevator stops. Laura gets out, swings through gold-lettered glass doors and approaches a neat welcoming receptionist. She glances at a slip of paper in her palm.

'I have an appointment with Mr James Hatfield III. . . .'

*

They meet again, Laura and Martin, in a Japanese restaurant called Robato. Laura, a little early, sits in the half-dark and thinks that four days will hardly be enough for her plans forming. James Hatfield III had not only promised to look at her case very favourably, but also suggested two other 'very good people' she should see, 'good' in the sense of virtuous, she understood, and had then invited her to Cape Cod for the weekend. All this in the space of fifteen minutes. Returning to the hotel on her way to lunch she had found several messages, one confirming an appointment for the afternoon with Mr Arthur Hellman, another from Ellen giving her a name and number she should ring mentioning Eddy's name and a third from Mr James Hatfield III who, she thought, must have rung almost as soon as she left his office. Ringing him back, she was told by his secretary that Mr Hatfield had left for lunch but he had left two messages. One to confirm there would be some funds available for the Agricultural Heritage and secondly that, if she was coming to the Cape, would she tell the secretary when to book a flight as they tended to be very full at this time of year, and his private plane was temporarily grounded.

All this spins happily in Laura's head as she waits, sipping a white wine and soda. She waits to offer it to Martin. She imagines how proud and even relieved he will be to discover that, wrenched from her natural surroudings, she can flower again. She remembers how he had described falling in love with her, 'secure, centred, beautiful'. Now she will be that again, the precipitous whirling sensation that had threatened her ever since losing Nicky and definitely leaving Miles will stop.

Martin arrives. He is very hot. Sweat stands out on his forehead. When he kisses her she feels it on his upper lip.

'God!' he says. 'What a nightmare. I need a drink. Brooklyn and back in this weather. I'd rather swim the Atlantic.'

'Poor you,' Laura smiles sympathetically trying to disguise her coolness and self-satisfaction. Let him get a drink first.

'At least I won't have to go back there this afternoon. Sorry I'm late, incidentally. It took me two hours to find someone who could understand a word I said.'

'That's all right. I couldn't have been happier.'

Coming-to a little, Martin looks at her and smiles. 'No, I can see that. Beautiful Laura. Always beautiful. Did you go back to sleep?'

Laura is startled. 'No. I. . . .'

The drink arrives. 'A large whiskey and soda,' Martin drinks, tipping back his head. 'I have it on the best authority that this is the only known remedy to the humid lowlands of southern India.'

Laura for a disloyal flash thinks how much better she seems to be coping with the temperature.

'Actually, I've had quite a productive morning,' she begins

modestly. 'This man, Mr Hatfield,' she watches Martin pick up the menu, 'looks as if he'll cough up some money.'

'That's great. I should get it in writing straight away. What do you want to eat?'

'You order,' Laura examines his lack of enthusiasm and sees it as due to heat and a bad morning.

'Was your morning productive?'

'Oh, yes. Yes. In the long run. No commitments. Always problems, of course. Nothing for nothing.' He doesn't take his eyes off the menu and Laura sees he doesn't want to talk about it.

'Mr Hatfield also invited us to Cape Cod.' She hesitates a moment over the 'us' but then pronounces it bravely. In New York she feels every woman is assumed to have a man.

This news causes more interest. 'A proposition already?'

'No, no. It wasn't like that. He was old.'

'They're always old. Were you tempted?'

'No, of course not. What do you mean?'

'Now you're no longer a respectable married woman. No ties. Sun and sea in smart society.'

'I've had enough sun and sea.' Laura speaks bravely but feels bewildered. Is that how he sees her? No ties. Is that what has happened? Perhaps that is what she was feeling as she confidently approached the neat, welcoming secretary. 'Anyway I'm here to do a job.'

'Are you?' This seems to surprise Martin more than anything. At this point the waiter arrives and while Martin orders, Laura has time to consider. She doesn't, however, merely continuing where her thought had broken off.

'I've got another appointment this afternoon.'

'Ah.' Martin approaches his second whiskey and soda. 'Good for you.' A pause. 'I've got the afternoon free.'

Laura is truly amazed. She at last realises that her work is not giving Martin the pride and joy she expected. It is almost as if he is jealous. This is so ridiculous that she is tempted to joke. Instead she is apologetic.

'I could cancel it.'

'No. No. There's someone I should see anyway. That NBC producer. She's still dithering whether she wants me as an advisor. If I see her this afternoon, we might be able to get away sooner.'

'From New York?'

'Yes. You don't want to stay in this furnace, do you? Or is it the lure of Cape Cod?' He laughs.

And Laura smiles.

Yet, after that lunch, Martin does not try and stop Laura keeping her appointments with important people whose offices look over the the whole of Manhattan. He even seems to encourage her, helping with addresses.

Soon it becomes clear that she will actually do better business in Cape Cod or Southampton or Martha's Vineyard where the rich have gone to avoid the heat. But she says nothing to Martin, thinking perhaps next year.

The thought of the future is frightening to her, so adapted is she to living in the present. Planning for the future will be like sinning in cold blood. When Martin, after three days, says, 'I've managed to change our flights to tomorrow morning,' she accepts it without question. She retains, however, the image of herself in her crisp red and white suit, playing the worker's game as well as any woman.

'I suppose it's the weather,' says Laura as they leave their hotel for the Kennedy airport at some unimaginably early time. 'But I've never really got over my jet-lag. Not in the mornings anyway.'

'Change is on the way.' Martin picks up his inevitable English newspaper. 'Fog and rain sweep across the South. Clash of the Titans, says weatherman, Roy Hidgeley.'

'It seems impossible,' says Laura looking out of the taxi's rear window. Behind them the spires and pinnacles of Manhattan are already clothed in a golden haze of heat.

She thinks it again as their aeroplane sways upwards into the clarity of perfect blue. It is easy to make the present perfect, she thinks.

Homeward journeys are always quicker than the outward bound. But this flight is even shorter than usual. The pilot, an American since this is T.W.A., announces that owing to weather conditions at London, Heathrow, they will be landing at Shannon Airport.

'Where is Shannon?' enquires the American lady on Laura's left, quite politely she thinks under the circumstances.

'In Ireland.'

'Ireland, Ireland?' In a voice of disbelief. 'I.R.A. Ireland.'

'I'm afraid so.' Taking a look at the woman's shocked face. 'It's not dangerous.'

'It's not London either.' Martin peers crossly at the still unbroken blue sky outside the window. But even as he speaks, they begin their descent, lumbering downwards through piles of ever-thickening cloud. When they pierce through, it is into the cool clarity of driving rain. Below them is the sea, the River Shannon flowing inwards and near its reedy shores, a small airport.

'Nowhere,' says Martin gloomily.

Laura who has always had a special affection for Ireland, tries to think of some positive aspect to the situation. Passing through the cloudy greyness seems to have already undone her New York sense of time-serving. Timeliness waits for her in that flat river expanse and wet green fields.

A bus takes them from the strangely empty airport to an even emptier hotel. It is there they are told that they will not be leaving till the following morning. At once Laura sees what she had been looking for.

'We must go and stay with Roy!'

Martin smiles at her conviction but says, still dourly, 'I've arranged a meeting for the morning.'

They are shown their bedroom. It is extraordinarily cold with water-colours of wet grey castles on the walls. Rain batters against the windows. Laura sits on a bed which is draped by a single thin coverlet and looks at the telephone.

'I might at least ring him.'

Martin comes and sits beside her. He puts his arms round her.

Roy is over-joyed to hear Laura's voice. It is seven-thirty in the evening Irish time, such as there is. He will uncork a bottle, put lamb in the oven, dig up some potatoes. They will have a feast, wipe out all mean moments.

This reference startles Laura until with a most unwanted jolt she remembers that their last meeting had been at that fish restaurant in Soho when he and Katie had tried to dissuade her from Martin.

She realises, then, that she has not mentioned he is travelling with her. 'Of course Martin's with me,' she says stiffly.

There is a brief pause and then Roy's voice even heartier than before, continues, 'There's no shortage of beds here.' This is followed by another pause as Roy clearly realises the implications of his remark. 'Nor potatoes either.'

Laura laughs. 'It'll only be for a brief night.' She thinks what a puritan Roy is. There can be few men who at the age of forty still find the subject of beds capable of shock. Yet she supposes it was odd of her not to have realised what she was asking of him. Perhaps it was the effect of skyline standards. Perhaps she wanted to shock him. It does not strike her that, up to a few months ago, her attitude would have exactly mirrored his.

By the time they arrive, driving a hired car in the rain through unknown winding roads, any awkwardness is lost in the relief of warmth and peace.

Roy talks, of course, as he always does. The rain, to Martin and Laura, merely irritating, is to him a disaster. Two days ago he had started bringing in the corn. Now the combine harvester, hired for a vast sum, stands idle, the corn already baled turns to sponges in the fields and the unharvested crops are beaten into the ground. 'You were sent here to save me from suicide and madness.' His eyes behind their ever-broken glasses leave Laura for a moment and flicker sideways to Martin. 'Computer boffs don't have problems like this.'

'They have other problems.' At last Roy and Martin talk directly. Laura, exhausted, leaves them talking and goes up to bed. Roy has made no further mention of rooms so she chooses the one with a double bed and trusts Martin to find her there.

The next thing she knows is an ungallant shaking.

'Time to get up.'

'I feel ill.'

The shaking stops. 'I suppose you could stay.'

'What?'

'Stay here with Roy. He'd love it.'

'Stay.' Laura tries to think, but finds it too difficult. 'Is that rain?'

'Yes. But Roy thinks it'll clear by the afternoon. He's been up all night watching the needle on the barometer.'

'I like Roy.'

'You should have married him.'

'What?'

'You're alike. If you're not staying, you'll have to get up.'

'Don't be so cruel.'

Laura stays.

At about eleven she puts on a dressing-gown and goes to look for breakfast. She finds Roy making himself coffee.

'It's stopped!' he cries grasping the same shoulder that Martin had shaken earlier.

'What? The rain.'

'Yes, yes. And there may be sun.'

'I am glad. I hope you don't mind me staying.'

'Oh, no, no.' Roy can think of nothing but the weather. 'You've brought the sun.' He peers anxiously through the window.

Laura, very hungry now, looks almost equally anxiously for food. Roy turns back to her. 'Brand. There is some soda bread somewhere. I'm afraid it's pretty hard though. Mrs O'Dwyer's given up appearing before midday and then she feels too depressed to do much. She's pregnant for the tenth time, poor woman. If you damp it and put it in the oven it's not so bad.' He goes on. But Laura is no longer listening. Nor does she take the proffered lump of grey and freckled rock.

She sits down on a chair. The moment Roy had pronounced the word pregnant with that ignorant sympathy, she'd known without the slightest doubt. The most up-to-date method of birth control notwithstanding, she is going to have a baby.

Chapter Seventeen

Laura dresses in her bedroom. The walls are painted a vivid blue as if to encourage clear skies. Roy waits impatiently for her downstairs. She can hear him pacing up and down the hall in his large gum-boots. Every now and again there are two or three brisk taps as he attacks the barometer.

Remembering Martin's remark about Roy being a suitable husband for her, she wonders what it would be like to be his wife. He was a good man who behaved out of principle rather than instinct. That was rare. It set him apart, made him unhappy. What would he think when he knew she was pregnant?'

'Are you sure you want to come?'

'Yes, yes. I'm ready.' She runs down the shiny oak stairs.

She has to run most of the way to the farmyard to keep up with Roy's urgent strides. The sky is speckled all over like a thrush's egg. But every moment the white breaks further apart to show the blue beneath.

'It's a miracle!' cries Roy.

His exhilaration is catching. Laura has a sudden moment of great joy when she remembers she is carrying Martin's baby.

At the farm the two great combines are already making majestic war-like progress to the track leading to the fields.

Roy stops the front one, waving his arms like a child, and turns out the driver. He jumps up himself, ungainly but determined, and the procession moves off again. The combines are followed by two tractors and trailers to collect the grain. The noise of so many powerful engines is colossal.

Laura is forgotten. She stands in the middle of the muddy farmyard and watches them go. The noise never dies completely, but soon it is far enough away to become a dull background roar. She wanders round the sheds, admiring the old prettily tiled ones and noting the new far bigger aluminium ones as signs of Roy's industry and prosperity.

She sits down on the crumbled remains of a stone wall. The sun at last breaks through, warming her face and hands. She lifts her skirts so it reaches her brown legs.

Cape Cod. The name spins into her head and makes her laugh out loud. It is simply impossible to believe in its existence. Or at least in its existence for her. Was she really seriously considering going there? Could she have been there now? Was that confident woman striding down Fifth Avenue in the crisp red and white suit the same woman who sat in the middle of a muddy Irish farmyard? Pregnant, moreover. Impossible. It is all impossible. So she laughs.

This is the reality. The other side of guilt. Every woman knows it. Even those whose wardrobes are stacked with crisp suits. Pregnant by a man you are not married to and who has shown no particular signs of wanting to marry you. Sitting in mud. Worse than mud. Dung. Dung and slurry. With the distant sound of other people working.

The sun goes in again and Laura pulls her skirt over her knees. What will she do about the baby? Poor Mrs O'Dwyer had nine babies already. A tenth on the way. Well, that is not her case. She has one beloved son.

Laura begins to feel sentimental and rather weepy. She had never particularly wanted another. They had tried for a year or two and when nothing had happened she had returned with a strange sort of relief to her excellent modern contraception which had now let her down so shockingly. Children demand such passion.

She shivers. Where is Nicky now? This instant. What is he doing? What is he feeling? Who is looking after him? Blackness and cold pain.

The sun comes out again with a new stronger force. She has been so long in Mediterranean and then American sun that she has almost forgotten this changeable variety. How can one make any plans with such a basic fluctuation? Does it make for inconstancy among its tribes? To live beneath a winking eye.

'Would you be liking a cup of coffee?'

A young woman stands in front of Laura. She has short dark red hair and a white freckled skin. She wears a heavy shrunken sweater and trousers baggy everywhere but round her stomach. In one hand she holds a huge silver thermos flask which she extends in a friendly way. 'I'm taking it out to the men in a while but there's enough for you first.'

Laura stands up. 'Good morning, Mrs O'Dwyer. I'll walk along with you and get something then. That thermos looks heavy.'

'It is that.' Mrs O'Dwyer is married to one of the farm workers. They have a farm cottage which barely holds all their children and they live mostly off produce from Roy's garden. It is a way of life profoundly out of keeping with the twentieth century, Laura thinks.

The two women walk slowly along the track carrying the thermos flask between them.

'I hear you're expecting again.'

'That's true enough.' Mrs O'Dwyer's voice, although hardly enthusiastic, doesn't sound as bitter as Laura expected.

'I thought the last one was to be the absolute last one.'

'No, no. That was the one before. I never feel so badly about the even numbers. It seems to shape up the family. It's the odd number that gets me down. It's like starting all over again. I know there'll be another after.' Mrs O'Dwyer smiles at her own foolishness but Laura sees that she really means what she says. She thinks how talented women are at making sense of the senseless. Why should this woman be burdened with ten human beings to care for?

'I thought there was talk of a new priest in the parish, who held more modern views.' Laura treads carefully.

'Father Gorman. Oh, yes. He's a good man. He came to tea and we talked. The children were all around but I was determined to ask him. So I said I'd heard there were changes in England. About birth control. And a difficult word that was to get out to a priest I can tell you. But he smiled sympathetically. He asked me had I tried the rhythm method. And I said yes – ever since I was married. And that made him laugh. With all the children around. And then he said had I tried abstention. So I said I had but Pat wasn't too keen. So he laughed again and said he was a fine manly fellow, which he is.

'Then he took another fresh-baked scone and sat back a bit. "It's a fine home you have here," he said, "a fine family."

'Well, I had to agree with him there because they're great kids and I'd made them all wash and brush and put on their best to see him. "A fine healthy family too."

'Here I could disagree with him a mite because Jo, our fifth, was born with a bit missing from his lungs, so he's always chesty and it's affected his brain too, I think. So he called up Jo and gave him a special blessing and said God favours those he loves most with a cross to bear.

'Then he turned back to me. "So which would you be regretting, Mrs O'Dwyer? You'd have to do without some if you followed those people in England."

'He couldn't catch me that way, of course. I said I wasn't regretting any of those I had, God's souls as they were – I played his game there – but I was worried about the future. How could I look after these if I was always pregnant, sicker as I am each time? And what if I had another Jo? Or worse? How would I look after him?

'This made him uncomfortable. I could see it in his eyes. He didn't say anything for a while. He looked at me and he looked at the children. Elsie who was the smallest then had crawled onto my lap. Three of the others were stuffing in scones knowing I wouldn't scold them in front of Father. The oldest two girls were in the kitchen pretending to clear

225

up and the boys were kicking a ball in the garden.

'"You're very busy, Mrs O'Dwyer?"'

'"That's true, Father." I waited for more.

'He sighed, a sad deep sigh that made me look away. It's embarrassing to see a priest thinking of himself. "Never lonely."

'"Far too busy for that, Father."

'"And the children say prayers at night, thanking God for the day."

'"Yes, Father." I was startled. We were not talking about prayers.

'"And you should too, Mrs O'Dwyer. Thank God every night for the blessings he has heaped upon you. For it is not man's right to regulate the gifts of God."

'So there it was. No change.'

'That's terrible!' Laura stops walking and takes Mrs O'Dwyer's arm.

'Oh, but it wasn't at all. You see at first I was bitter and angry. But then I did what he said. I prayed at night. I thanked God for all his blessings. And then I began to see how lucky I was and that I had been looking at everything from a wrong angle. I hadn't been able to see that I was part of a pattern in God's design for us and that I had this wonderful blessed role which was bearing new life. So even when Patrick came who was an odd one and now this new one I feel happy in my heart. If you know what I mean. Peaceful. And I truly don't envy women who have to choose when to have a baby just like they would a new frock. I mean for them having a baby means nothing – outside themselves. And for me it's part of everything.'

They begin walking again. Laura can say nothing. In her years of visiting Roy, Mrs O'Dwyer had never spoken to her like this before. It was almost as if she has sensed that Laura had a special interest. Laura had seen her swell up and down – more up than down – and never thought of her further than Roy's poor Mrs O'Dwyer, intensified to poor miserable Mrs O'Dwyer after the unfortunate Jo's birth.

Now, rock-like soda bread or no, she seems to Laura the nearest thing to a saint she is ever likely to meet. Yet she knows that all over Ireland there are women with views just like hers.

They are nearing the cornfields now and the sound of the

226

combines following each other round in narrowing circles is already loud enough to make conversation difficult.

Just before the gate, Mrs O'Dwyer takes Laura's arm. 'I'm sorry to go on as I did,' she says apologetically. 'It does good to say what's in your mind, once in a while. Helps you to stay firm.'

Laura suddenly understands that the saint-like statement of faith has been expressed as much to convince herself as her listener. This realisation makes more sense of the inefficient irritable very unsaint-like occupant of Roy's kitchen. 'You've helped me,' she says warmly and leans forward to unhook the gate. Everybody has doubts.

The two women stand together on the edge of the wide sloping field. The vast red machines pass very slowly, lumbering one after the other like two elephants in a circus ring. Laura no longer sees them as fierce instruments of war. They have already cut several circles so they are quite far away, smaller, even though the noise is still overwhelming.

'We'll go over to the tractors,' says Mrs O'Dwyer. 'The mugs are there.'

Laura wonders if she has really been helped by this Irish Catholic case history. What relevance did it have to her, a sophisticated woman who has discussed politics eye to eye with the Empire State Building?

The tractors are drawn up side-by-side under the shade of three large oak trees. Already their trailers are half full of flowing golden grain. As they watch, the leading combine, driven by Roy, turns off its track and comes towards them. When it reaches the first trailer, a long elephant-like trunk swings sideways and begins to pour out grain with the speed of water.

'That's a lovely sight!' exclaims Mrs O'Dwyer. They all watch the men driving the tractors.

'My Pat's driving the second,' says Mrs O'Dwyer. 'My eldest begs him for a ride and he might let him when they've got on a bit. It's a serious business at the beginning. With the weather and all.' She looks at the blue sky nervously and crosses herself.

Laura smiles at the gesture indulgently and then wonders what right she has to patronise.

The grain slows to a trickle, the engine stops and Roy jumps off. He strides over to the men and picks another driver who snatches up a helmet and goes immediately to the great machine.

Roy comes to Laura. He takes off his glasses and rubs first them and then his eyes with a large turquoise handkerchief. His hair is stiff with ends of corn, his face thick with dust.

'Why ever don't you wear a helmet?'

'I can't make the visor work with my glasses.' He grins happily at Laura. 'Besides, I have this image of myself leading my troops bareheaded into battle. Thank you.' He takes a cup of coffee from Mrs O'Dwyer.

Behind them the other combine begins to pour out its grain. Roy instinctively turns to watch. 'We'll go on all day now,' he says.

'No lunch?'

'Mrs O'Dwyer will bring sandwiches out here.'

'What about her children?'

'Her children!' Roy's surprise makes Laura laugh. Children had as much reality for him as the Empire State Building. Laura has been planning to tell Roy about her pregnancy. But now she wonders. Perhaps it will not seem shocking but merely unimportant against his greater harvest of Nature's fertility.

'I want to see how another field's ripening. Do you want to come?'

'Of course.'

They walk round the edge of golden fields already marked for cutting and across fields of long juicy grass. In one of these, Roy stops. 'Do you remember this?'

'What?'

'The field.'

Laura looks round. She sees the field of action now reduced to a model scale. She sees Roy's house half-hidden by a distinguished copper beech that she had hardly noticed from near at hand. She sees the farm track leading into a coppice and rising behind it varying levels of hillside. The field they are standing in is green and square.

'No,' she says. 'Should I?'

'It's where your St Anthony found me my bit of steel.'

Laura remembers now. The whole scene comes back to her with total clarity. She remembers the pale sun breaking through the mists of gentle rain. She remembers Roy's appeal to her to explain her faith. 'I wish I could believe,' he'd said.

228

And she'd said, 'If you want to believe, then you will believe. It's as simple as that.' But he'd not been convinced so she'd admitted that it was easy for her because she was a cradle Catholic and that her faith was 'emotional'. What had she meant by that?

And then she'd prayed with a prayer that filled her whole soul and seemed to lift her up to God. And though in theory she was praying to St Anthony to find a piece of old metal, she was really asking to be given the grace to resist temptation and stay within her marriage vows, with the belief in something beyond herself. And the moment she had returned to England she had run away with Martin.

'Yes. I remember this field,' she says without emotion.

Roy fishes about in his trouser pocket. 'You know I never put that bit back on the harrow. I keep it with me. A symbol or something. Hope. Faith. Good luck.'

Laura looks at the little metal loop and is reminded irresistibly of the little metal loop that has failed her so totally. She sees this thought as the ultimate reduction of great thoughts to the absurdity of practical ones.

'I'm glad,' she says gently. She will tell him about the baby another day.

*

Time is counted in days in Ireland, rather than hours as in England or minutes in Manhattan. Laura speaks to Martin on the telephone but she doesn't tell him about the baby. He seems glad she is in Ireland and say he'll hardly be in London for the next few days so why doesn't she stay there and he'll pick her up at the weekend.

It is only then that Laura remembers Ben Casey waiting with eager anticipation for the results of the work in New York. She finds her file and telephones him, poised to be efficient and eager. But he is out to lunch and out at a meeting and when she finally catches him seems only moderately interested. Perhaps it is just as well. For she can hardly enthuse about the urgent need to tap wondrous sources of support in New York and then announce she is staying in Ireland for a week. She promises him to be in the office next week but feels she is promising herself.

'I might be too old to start a proper career. There's no ladder for women like me. At least in England.'

229

'Quite probably.' Roy nods agreeably, seeing no tragedy in such a statement.

She will tell him about the baby after the weekend, after she has told Martin.

Martin's arrival breaks apart her sense of suspended time. She had forgotten the strength of his physical presence. This had been their first separation since Italy. She looks afresh at his youth, his blond good looks, his confidence, his extraordinary love for her. He dominates everything, blotting out what now seem vague womanish ramblings. She makes herself look beautiful for him, turns old beetroots into borscht and once more overlooks Mrs O'Dwyer.

'We're going to have a baby.'

It is Martin's second night in Ireland. Laura lies in his arms in the double bed belonging to the blue-painted bedroom. They have just made love. She whispers in a soft contented way.

'We're going to have a baby.'

Martin snores a little just on the edge of sleep and then puts his lips to her cheek. 'Did you say baby?'

'Yes.' She smiles. It is part of their love, their romance. A recreation of Viareggio, Petra, less perhaps of New York. Although she remembers Ellen. Ellen will be pleased. 'Yes. A baby.'

'Well.' Martin kisses her, his lips brushing across her face to her mouth. He says no more. He hardly seems awake. But Laura, wrapped in his body, baby wrapped in hers, is content.

The next day three events, unrelated but all equally unexpected by Laura, occur. Lizzie, Katie's sister, arrives on her way back to England from a holiday in the west of Ireland. Martin's mother telephones from a house twenty miles away where she is spending a week. And Martin, with a concerned and loving face, asks Laura if she's considered having an abortion.

Laura is pleasurably surprised by her reaction to all these events. Instead of screaming and tearing her hair for which she feels ample excuse, she becomes particularly calm and sensible. She even welcomes Lizzie warmly with a kiss on either cheek and asks her to throw her dirty washing down the stairs.

Lizzie responds in an equally matter-of-fact way, although it must have been as great a shock for her to see her once good, now wicked, older sister's sister-in-law scrubbing potatoes while her lover does the *Telegraph* crossword puzzle in the garden, as it is for Laura to see Lizzie's innocent pink-cheeked face.

Martin, apparently delighted to see her (and after all, what is he but the conquering hero?), puts up another deckchair and asks her what she thinks of County Kerry.

Roy, arriving back for lunch, plies her with sweet sherry and looks round at the assembled company with the munificence of a man who knows he has 200 tons of corn safely in his shed and that the weather forecast looks good for the remaining five.

It is then the telephone rings. Laura, being the only one in the house, answers it.

'Inchcape 213.'

'Ah.' A slight pause. 'I wonder if I could speak to Mr Keane?'

Laura recognises Martin's mother's voice instantly and feels sure she recognises hers. She says, 'Just hold on a minute and I'll see if I can find him.' She puts down the receiver and goes to the window. 'Martin!' she calls calmly. 'Your mother on the telephone.' With a feeling of rebellion she goes back to the telephone.

'He's just coming,' she says in an excuse to talk. 'Are you well?'

'Ah.' Mrs Keane repeats in what Laura sees could be an irritating affectation. 'I have a summer cold.'

'I'm so sorry,' responds Laura politely. 'Summer colds are so hard to throw off.'

There is a longish pause which Laura decides not to break though she breathes loud enough for Mrs Keane to know she's still there.

'And how are you?'

She is tempted to respond with one devastating word. *Pregnant*, Mrs Keane.

But at that moment Martin appears and with a slight frown takes the receiver. 'Hello, mother, I said I'd ring you.'

Laura moves away. So he had spoken to her in London. She knew he was coming to Ireland. Perhaps even knew she was with him. Laura goes out to the garden. There Lizzie sits with a bright expectant look. The world is closing in.

'Are you nervous about university?' she pours Lizzie another sherry.

'Not really. It's been such a long wait. In fact I'm not sure I

231

haven't gone off the boil. I can't really remember why I was so keen to go.'

'To learn something presumably.' Laura notes a sharpness in her voice which could never have been there in the past. In the past she was a plaster figure to be adored and to dispense unexceptional wisdom. Now Lizzie looks at her differently and she cannot be the same.

Roy sits watching them talk, smiling with barely repressed excitement at Lizzie. Eventually, unable to contain himself any longer he bounds towards her, crying out in almost supplicating tones, 'But you have the whole world in front of you! So bright, so clever, nothing spoilt, with so much time in front of you! You must feel wonderful!'

'I don't know.' Lizzie, embarrassed as much for him as herself, bends down to hide her flushed cheeks. Her thick chestnut hair parts at the nape of her neck and swings on either side of her face.

Laura looks at Roy standing above with fixed gaze and wild gesture and then again at the young girl withdrawing nervously from such passion. It reminds her of some Victorian engraving in which a lover, hand to heart, presses his suit while his beloved withdraws with maidenly modesty.

She has always seen Roy's admiration for Lizzie and thought it nice for both of them. But then too she had known Roy was half in love with her. Now she is the fallen woman, she sees his glowing looks are too extreme, quite silly. He must be nearly twenty years older than Lizzie.

Martin comes out from the house. Still frowning. 'I've promised mother to go over there for tea today.' He looks at Laura though avoiding her eyes. 'No one need come who doesn't want to.'

'Oh, I will,' says Lizzie quickly. 'I love visiting strange houses.'

'I'm afraid I must get back to the farm,' says Roy. He wanders over to a border and peers hopefully at a large bunch of nettles. Perhaps, Laura thinks, to his short-sighted eyes they resemble delphiniums. She says nothing.

Martin sips his sherry. 'It's a bore, I'm afraid. On my last day.' He gives a general smile.

'I'd better see about lunch.' Laura stands up and goes inside briskly. She pulls out the joint and puts the pan on top of the stove to make gravy. She hears footsteps approaching which she assumes without turning her head to be Martin's.

'Do you want me to come?' she asks with her admirable calmness. She had said *She's older than you, has a son and a good husband.*

'It's me.'

'Oh, Lizzie.'

'Can I help?'

'Finish laying the table if you like.'

Lizzie plods in and out with knives and forks. She shares with Martin and all men that unhousewifely and irritating habit of carrying only one thing at a time. She also, Laura notices, wears the same sneakers as Martin which is why she had confused their footsteps. She wears the same jeans too. In fact they seem to be far more of the same generation than she is. She can pair off with Roy, with his silly patched tweed jacket and his silly patched tweed ideals.

She realises the fumes from the gravy are making her sick. She sits abruptly down on a chair.

'Are you all right?'

'Perfectly, thank you.'

'Can I say something?'

Lizzie hovers nervously.

'That usually means you're going to,' Laura tries to smile.

'I just want to say I'm glad you're happy. I mean that's what's really important, isn't it? Being honest, being true to oneself, being happy. At first I have to admit I couldn't understand. After all you'd done to keep Katie and Johnny together. Do you remember that weekend? When she wanted to go and you persuaded her. And we talked about marriage, about its importance. And duty. And responsibility. It took me a while to understand. But then I saw that you and Katie are so absolutely different. She's not strong like you. Her whole life revolves round the children and the home and the husband too, however badly he behaves. But you make your own world wherever you go. You make things perfect just by being yourself. So you couldn't live with lies, with hypocrisy. When you stopped loving Miles, you simply couldn't stay with him any more. It would have been like someone singing a bit from *My Fair Lady* in the middle of *Cosi Fan Tutte.*'

Lizzie stops, laughing at herself, but then continues, still intensely, 'Everything has to be perfect for you. When you fell in love with Martin,' she pauses again, gulps and continues, 'it wasn't like other people, ordinary people, I see that now.' She looks at Laura who says nothing. 'Do you see I'm on your side?' Laura smiles. She is troubled. Of course she is touched and surprised, by such a recital of love and affection when she thought it was all gone. Yet she is curiously detached, too, and depressed. Lizzie's arguments don't sound very convincing in her ears. She remembers with nostalgia that bright week when they had walked without men among the daffodils. Everything had seemed very clear then.

'There is one more thing.' Lizzie wears the hot look of the confessional which Laura remembers from childhood. 'I think perhaps you guessed I was half in love with Martin. Well, I want you to know that I'm not at all now and I just hope you can be married and everything wonderful as soon as possible.'

Lizzie has finished. She darts to the stove and starts stirring vigorously which absolves Laura from a need to react.

'And now that that's out of the way,' she says after a moment, 'why not call in the men and we'll have lunch?' Lizzie goes, tripping lightly with unburdened soul. Laura thinks that she has left Nicky out of the picture altogether. Or perhaps that came under 'you can be married and everything wonderful'. She pours the gravy into a jug.

At four o'clock Martin, Lizzie and Laura set out for tea with his mother. Roy's car is old and smells of manure and weed-killer. After a few miles Laura says quietly to Martin, 'I'm afraid I'm going to be sick.'

He says in an equally unassuming tone, 'Have you thought of having an abortion?'

Instead of grabbing the wheel and heading the car for the wall running conveniently close to the road, Laura replies, 'No. What do you mean?' A third and final restraint which she immediately spoils by being violently sick all over the car.

'Oh, God.' Martin stops the car. They all three get out. Laura begins to shiver uncontrollably. 'I'm sorry.'

'Don't be silly,' Martin takes off his sweater and hands it to her.

'It'll smell.'

'I love you.'

Laura bursts into tears. Martin puts his arm round her, sick and all.

Lizzie goes round to the back of the car and pushes old boxes around noisily. 'There might be something here to wear.'

So they appear at the nice Anglo-Irish house in which Mrs Keane is staying with Laura dressed in Martin's jacket above and an ancient sack below. Tea, delicate sandwiches, a heavy cake and much china is laid in a small dark room. The windows are stuffed with newspapers and are obviously unopenable. As the temperature rises, an aroma of cowshed begins to surround Laura and spread outwards. She and Lizzie exchange conspiratorial glances.

Their host, a retired English army officer called Major Drummond, clears his throat. His wife, an anxious perspiring lady in a large cotton frock, offers more tea.

Mrs Keane, her beautifully boned face set in lines which Petra could have envied, sits next to her son. She is dressed in a pale blue knife-pleated skirt and an exquisite blue and mauve hand-knitted sweater.

She says to Martin, 'Next time you go to New York you must look up my friends, the Partridges.' She drinks a little tea. 'They will introduce you to all sorts of nice people.'

Martin unlooses himself from his mother's gaze and turns to Laura. 'Mother used to go to Martha's Vineyard every summer.'

'I never enjoyed it so much when one no longer had an excuse to travel by boat.' Mrs Keane addresses herself to the major. Who clears his throat again but says nothing. He does not seem very comfortable with his elegant guest. Perhaps he is wishing she still did go to Martha's Vineyard instead of gracing their normally humble home.

'I remember. Every year. One could tell July 26th by Helen's departure,' Mrs Drummond enthuses.

'Oh, darling. Do you really remember? I am touched.'

'I remember everything about you. While I was going to dreary postings in Bulawayo and Borneo, where the wet heat brought me out in rashes, you were always going to such glamorous places. And Martin too. What a lovely childhood Martin had!'

Mrs Keane softens in memory of glamorous places and Laura feels a twinge of sympathy. Perhaps it is sad to be old, and a widow. It is hard to believe she enjoys staying with the Drummonds. Despite Mrs Drummond's obvious awe and admiration.

Notwithstanding her interesting aura, Laura is beginning to feel very well. The heavy cake, dark and burgeoning with fruits, seems to suit her unreasonable digestion. Martin's jacket, such a warm intimate part of him, makes her feel as if she is clasped in his arms. Moreover it proclaims in the most satisfyingly obvious way, their relationship. Poor elegant, scraggy Mrs Keane not eating a morsel. She has had her Martha's Vineyard. Now it is her son's turn. And Laura's.

After tea they go out for a constitutional round the garden. It is designed with many gravel paths and narrow flower beds neatly planted with annuals. The major becomes animated over these, explaining the loss of the Empire and the failure of British Rail as due to lack of appreciation of the annual.

Laura and Lizzie stifle giggles, choking and huddling like schoolgirls. The relief of escape from the stuffy room and the antics of Laura's sack which writhe and rustle round her legs make them feel quite light-headed. Martin, walking ahead with his mother, turns once and smiles too.

Luckily it begins to rain. Slow lingering drops that hang in the air and catch in the trees. Enough, however, for Mrs Keane to exclaim and move towards the house. And for Laura, who has said so little, to say she thinks they should be going.

The theatre followed by dinner. Laura hears Martin promise this to his mother when he returns to London. Well, it is not much. *She's older than you, has a son and a good husband.*

She kisses him when they get into the car. 'I'm sorry we behaved so badly,' she says. 'I'll forgive your mother's letter soon.'

Martin looks surprised. 'What letter?'

Lizzie gets in the back and slams the door. Laura lowers her voice. 'The one in Italy. Filled with hatred.'

'But darling, she's old. She loves me. She's jealous.'

'Who's jealous?' cries Lizzie curiously.

'I'm jealous.'

'What?' Martin, ignoring Lizzie's presence, gives his bellowing laugh. 'How old do you think I am? I haven't cared what my mother thought for twenty years. I just try and be kind to her. You must be too.'

That evening they play bridge. Only Martin and Lizzie have any real grasp of the game. Roy was very good twenty years ago. He tells Lizzie he won his school championship. Lizzie laughs disbelievingly.

'Did you have rain here?' asks Laura sleepily. She is so sleepy that the hearts and spades rise off the cards and dance in front of her face.

'Not enough to worry. There's only a couple of fields left to bale anyway. After all that we'll have fire.'

'Fire?'

'A huge conflagration bursting across the fields.'

'What do you mean?'

'The straw's cheap now,' Roy is enthusiastic. 'Almost worthless. So we burn it up. It's good for the ground. It's dry too. It'll go up like fire-works, crackling and roaring, the end of the world. We'll stand at the edge and dare the flames to get us. I love it. It's terrifying!'

'Oh, do shut up, Roy. We're trying to play a game.' Lizzie's voice, loud and mocking, sends the hearts and spades tumbling back to their proper places. Laura sits up straighter.

'Three clubs.'

'Oh, no, Martin. Not again. Why are you so lucky!'

That night Laura wakes up screaming. Martin sits her up trying to wake her from her nightmare.

'Ssh. Sshh. What is it? Tell me?'

'No. I can't,' Laura trembles, terrified. She can't tell Martin. He wouldn't understand. It was the fire. A huge fire racing across the fields. Towards Nicky. Nicky standing alone in his pyjamas. Roy was behind the flames, lighting the ground with a torch, building a wall of fire to encircle Nicky. And she was with Roy.

'Nothing,' she says. 'It's gone. I can't remember.'

But Martin has heard her say something. ' "Baby". I heard you say "baby". You were dreaming of the baby, weren't you?'

Laura can't explain. Nicky is her baby. Her only real baby. 'It's nothing.'

Martin perseveres. He kisses her cheeks and neck. 'You want to have this baby very much, don't you?'

Laura mumbles. The dream is still so vivid that she can think of nothing but Nicky, standing alone, so small and frail in his

237

pyjamas. Until she can talk to him, hold him, she will only see him like that.

'You must have it, then.'

'Mmm.' What is this other baby? Nothing. A worm in her body. A product of lust. No reality. No importance. No existence. *I want Nicky! I want Nicky!* she cries, inwardly.

But Martin begins to caress her, keen to celebrate this brave decision of new life. He strokes her shoulders and her breasts, running his arm down her body. 'You're so tense,' he murmurs.

'Yes. Yes, I'm sorry.'

He smiles. 'Don't be sorry. I just want to make your nightmare go away.'

Grateful, Laura tries to kiss him. But her lips are stiff, insensitive. Even so, he responds, pulling her on top of him. It seems best to pretend.

Tears of loss are no different from tears of passion.

Chapter Eighteen

Laura telephones Katie. It is three days since she returned from Ireland. She can't understand why she's waited so long. The telephone is picked up instantly.

'Katie. It's me, Laura.'

'Oh. Laura. How are you?' Katie sounds horrified.

'Very well. I want to come down tomorrow and see Nicky.'

'Oh, you can't!'

'What do you mean, I can't? I'm his mother. I haven't said anything about your part in this kidnapping.' Laura becomes excited and begins to shout accusations.

At the other end of the line there is a gulping sound and Katie bursts into tears. 'I'm very sorry,' she hiccoughs. 'I was only trying to do the best for him, for you, everybody.'

Laura calms down. 'I'm very sorry, Katie. It's all my fault. You've only tried to help. Now, what time shall I come tomorrow?'

'But you can't. I mean you can but Nicky isn't here any more.'

Wild ideas race through Laura's mind. Miles has fled to South America, emigrated to Australia, taken a cruise to Bulawayo or Borneo.

'He's gone to school.'

'School!' September already. Laura even laughs. 'Then he's in London?'

'No. No. He's gone to boarding school.'

Katie rushes on nervously, explaining that Miles had thought it would be better for him at the moment. That Nicky had seemed very keen. That it was a small kindly place recommended by several of her friends and that soon they would take girls and then Maddy and Honour could go too.

Laura is so angry that she can hardly breathe. She feels her face puffing redly. Miles has dared to alter the whole current of her son's life. She thinks of the little day school, with its dark crowded cloakroom, with unaccustomed affection.

'I'm sorry, Katie. I'm too angry to speak. Give me the name of the school and I'll ring back later.'

Laura paces up and down Martin's flat. There are not even her own objects to fling.

He comes in and she bursts out in fury. He makes himself a drink. She is drinking nothing but orange juice at the moment.

'Clearly you must ring the school,' says Martin. This is the first time he has entered her old life. Or perhaps this new school is part of the new.

'My name is Mrs Knight.' Three days later Laura gets through to the school. Again she cannot understand why she lets so much time pass. 'I am Nicky Knight's mother. He started with you this term. I would like to speak to the headmaster.'

'I'm afraid Mr Stuart is teaching. Can I take a message?'

'No.' Why should she be polite?

'I'll get him to ring you back then. We have the number, I presume.'

You presume wrong. 'No. It's 435 8868.'

It is the following day before Mr Stuart rings back. He is apologetic and sounds extraordinarily nice, far nicer than the acerbic headmaster of Nicky's last school. Laura is made crosser than ever. Besides he calls Nicky Nicholas.

'His name is Nicky. He was christened Nicky. He is as little Nicholas as you are Smith.'

This rudeness only draws forth more and even more charming apologies. 'Such an even-tempered sensible child. So adult in his approach.' This is clearly nonsense. Nicky, as Laura knows well, is a highly-strung, sensitive, emotional child. Perhaps Mr Stuart is muddling him with someone else? Such a suggestion is greeted with a jolly laugh.

Laura is goaded into saying her piece. 'I do not want my child at your school. He was entered without my consent and I now wish to take him away.'

'Ah, I see. Well Mr Knight did indicate that there were, er, problems.' Mr Stuart's calmness is set in iron. 'In fact he seemed to think that while these, er, problems were being sorted out it might be better for your son to be at a school like this where he has his own life as it were. We're such a small school that we like to think of ourselves as a family. In fact you might say we've won rather a name for ourselves in helping the child whose family background is going through a bit of a shake-up.'

Hating every moment, Laura listens to the kindly voice. She imagines him, quite young with tweeds and a pipe. She hears about his own four children and wife, Jacqueline, with no surprise. She pictures at his description the friendly Georgian home with added wings, the well-mowed lawns, cosy Mrs McFaddon, the matron, and Dr Runyon, the excellent Classics master. She sees that against such things she can offer nothing at all.

'Is he really happy?' she says eventually.

'Oh yes. But I wouldn't suggest a visit before half-term.'

Now that Laura has invested all faith and trust in Mr Stuart, she must take his advice.

'It's a little disturbing for new boys, we find, and slows up their total adjustment.'

'Ah. I see.'

'By half-term it should be fine. I've said the same thing to your husband. It's a very short term as it is.'

Short term, long days. Laura wonders about Nicky each evening at about seven. Who is putting him to bed? No kisses. Again she dreams of the burning fields of stubble, the small pyjama-clad figure. Then the days begin to pass more quickly. She is working again, feeling pregnant in the mornings, changing the flat to make it suit two. It will never suit three. She begins to see a few friends outside Martin. Martin loves her.

She writes to Roy thanking him for their visit and telling him, as she has failed to his face, that she is going to have a baby. The length of the letter that comes back is daunting. His thoughts about marriage, motherhood, fatherhood, so honest and self-critical yet so generous to others, are painful for Laura.

He has moved her from one pedestal to another. Now she is the Mary Magdalen when before she had been the Mary of all Womanhood. He, on the other hand, is still Doubting Thomas, the Laodicean who blew neither hot nor cold, the intellectual with mud on his boots who has not even found the road to his Pilgrim's Progress. His humility is either tragic or absurd.

On impulse she writes and invites him to London when the farm is bedded down for the winter. All he needs, she thinks with simplicity, is a nice wife and several children.

Towards the end of October, Laura writes to the school announcing her arrival on the Friday of half-term to pick up Nicky. Two days later the telephone rings. Martin and Laura are eating by candlelight on a card-table set up in his living-room. Laura's digestion has recently returned to normal. She sits looking at the crimson wine gleaming against the candle's flame while Martin answers the telephone.

'It's the school.'

There is that voice again, so nice, so sensible, so apologetic. Nicky has been removed a few days early from the school to accompany his father to Hong Kong where he is adjudicating. It had seemed a unique opportunity so he'd agreed although normally he is strict about school dates.

Laura feels completely helpless. Out-manoeuvred. She says nothing. Quietly she goes back to the card-table, so foolish it looks to her now.

Martin says, 'You'll have to find a good lawyer.'

Laura laughs, 'Miles is the best lawyer I know.'

Laura rings up Johnny and asks to have lunch with him. He responds in a nervous effusive way. He suggests a date ten days away and a very expensive restaurant.

Laura knows how much Johnny cares about appearances, and chooses a smart suit. It is alarming to find the skirt won't do up. She is four months pregnant. She pulls the jacket down hopefully.

Johnny sits warmly glowing in a corner seat. No trace of

nervousness. He has already finished one gin and tonic.

'You look wonderful, fabulous, better than ever!' he greets his sister.

'Yes,' Laura sits opposite, noticing that with his usual charming selfishness he has not offered her the seat against the wall. 'I feel well. You look well too.'

'Too fat, too fat,' Johnny pats his stomach. 'Shall we order straight away?'

Laura catches a flash of his terror. What will this newly wild sister say to upset his calm? She thinks affectionately that her brother is not only selfish but a coward too. Yet just sitting here with him makes her feel happier, she is almost tempted to do what he would like, have a delicious lunch, too much wine, and part, without raising any disturbing question marks.

In the end she puts it all in the simplest form. 'I want to see Nicky,' she says.

'Lovely boy,' responds Johnny with an air of a connoisseur.

'No, Johnny, that won't do. Miles has more or less kidnapped him. I haven't seen him since July.'

'Ah.' He sips at his pink Sancerre, smiles. 'I suppose one of mine wouldn't do? I can tell you I see a good bit too much. . . .'

'Johnny!' Laura interrupts angrily.

'Sorry.' At last his bonhomie is wiped out. He looks shame-faced and then serious. He puts his glass down regretfully. He frowns. Laura says nothing. For a few seconds there is silence. Then Johnny's brow clears again. He gives Laura a cheerful smile.

'If you want to see him, let's go and see him.'

'What?'

'My afternoon is yours.' Johnny picks up his glass again with the virtuous look of a man who has solved all problems.

Neither Johnny nor Laura has a car but this doesn't deter him. They take a taxi to Waterloo Station, catch a southern region train to Woodfield and there pick up a local taxi. It is only as Laura bends to get into this car that Johnny, perhaps for the first time seeing her without the benefit of life-enhancing alcohol, remarks, 'You seem to have put on a bit of weight too.'

'Oh, Johnny,' Laura settles herself into the seat, far too concentrated about the coming meeting to concern herself with anything else. 'Surely you can see I'm pregnant!'

Johnny gives the direction to the driver and gets in beside

Laura. 'Yes, I can see that now.' He looks more serious than he has at any time. 'Does Nicky know?'

'Of course he doesn't know. I haven't seen him for months. It's nothing to do with me and him.'

'Ah.'

'What do you mean "Ah"?'

'Little boys are quite sharp-eyed. Particularly when he hasn't seen you for so long.'

'I haven't come all this way to turn round without seeing him.'

'No.'

Laura stares obstinately out of the window. She supposes the countryside with its neat woods turning red-gold in the autumn light is pretty. There are those, she imagines, who admire small red-brick houses with thatched roofs set in a patch-work of green and yellow fields. Personally she finds the whole picture claustrophobic in the extreme.

They turn in a driveway thickly bounded by rhododendrons. The car stops in front of a house very like the one Laura had imagined except the flowerbeds are less tidy and the lawns less well-mowed.

'Old Stue's quite a mate of mine,' says Johnny, smoothing back his hair. 'In the same house at school.'

'What?' Laura holds the handle of the door.

'"Mr. Stuart. The head. Yes. Won't have any trouble with old Stue. Good chap though a trifle hearty for my tastes.'

Laura gets stiffly out of the car and draws her jacket around her. Should she thank him for his help or scream at him as a conspirator? She does neither.

'Do I really look very pregnant?'

'Maybe he'll just think you're fat. After all, I did at first '

They pull a door knob set in the wall which rings with shattering loudness. After a very long wait a young woman appears carrying a bare-bottomed baby. She stares behind her with a harassed expression.

'Oh dear. I'm afraid there's a match on. My husband's down at the playing fields. They're all down at the playing fields. Did you have an appointment?'

'It's all right, Jacky. It's only me.'

The woman, presumably the headmaster's wife, sights Johnny behind Laura. 'Oh heavens, I am glad. Stue's made me promise not to open the door with a baby. He says it give such a bad first impression to prospective parents.'

'This is my sister, Laura. We were passing by so we thought we'd get a cup of tea off you. Her son's here, actually.'

'If you don't mind the kitchen.' She immediately turns back into a corridor from which noises of other children come. She stops for a second at the door of a brightly lit kitchen filled with the smell of toast and bacon. She looks more closely at Laura. 'Did you say you have a son here?'

'Yes. Nicky.'

'Oh, I see.' Laura feels herself flushing but Mrs Stuart is friendly, finds a spare arm to draw her forward. 'Please forgive the mess. When they're all out of the way with a match I tend to let everything go and enjoy myself with the children.'

As she speaks, Laura sees her eyes drop to Laura's waist-line and flicker recognition of a state she knows well.

'I'm sorry to burst in like this.'

'No. No. Johnny's an old friend.'

Johnny stands in the middle of the room looking with obvious distaste at the three small dirty children, the used potty and the half-eaten tea. 'I think I'll stroll on ahead to the playing fields. You can point my sister the way after she's had her tea.'

Laura sits at the table. Mrs Stuart darts about the room wiping faces, making drinks. Laura is reminded of Katie except that whereas Katie is always on the edge of chaos, this woman, despite the mess, is in control. She talks as she moves around the room, telling Laura about Nicky, about his work, his sleeping, his playing. She obviously knows him very well already.

Laura listens and at last cannot resist the question. 'Has he talked about me?'

'Oh, yes. He misses you.'

'Ah.' Laura's eyes blur with longing.

'But he's not unhappy. Children are astonishingly adaptable, you know – I've seen it so often at this school.'

Laura looks at her surrounded by her children and thinks for a bitter moment that she can never understand. But that is not fair. 'I'm very grateful,' she says.

She stands up. 'Where will I find him?'

'Oh, yes.' She pauses doubtfully. 'You want to see him.'

244

'That's why I came.'

'Of course.' Again her eyes flicker to Laura's midriff. 'It will be rather a shock for him.'

'I'm going to find him.'

'Yes. I'd go with you if I didn't have this lot. . . .'

Laura sets off through the garden towards the playing fields. It is a perfect autumn evening, long sloping shadows crossing the green lawn, a few black crows flying through an orange streaked sky. Brilliant colours in the last glow of the sun.

She finds her way by the sound of cheering. It comes from beyond a thick band of rhododendrons, such as edged the driveway. As she nears it there is a sudden louder cheer resolving itself into a more organised hip hip hooray. She guesses the match must be over and sure enough in a few seconds a stream of boys breaks through the leafy barrier and comes running along the track which she is following.

Laura steps aside with a curious sense of being invisible. Indeed none look at her as they pass, big boys, small boys, wearing open-necked navy shirts and white shorts. This is the first she has seen of her son's uniform. They have a healthy country air, with rosy cheeks and loud confident voices. Their hair tends to be rather long and they hurry along as if to somewhere nice. Perhaps supper, she thinks, hot soup and toast in a dark-beamed hall.

Now a group of the younger boys comes more slowly. Barely trotting, sometimes dropping into a walk. They talk harder than the others, swinging their arms about in demonstration, clearly reliving every moment of the match. The home team must have won, Laura thinks, smiling.

She sees Nicky. In the middle of the group. So much part of these jolly swaggering boys that for a moment she wonders if it is him. Next to him she recognises another face and realises, with a throwback to when she had last seen her son, that this was the English boy from Viareggio. How odd. How very odd. As she thinks this, the boys pass so that she must run if she is to catch them. She starts forward but her smart high-heeled shoes have sunk in the grass as she stood watching. She stumbles, half falls, leaving one shoe behind.

Suddenly she has an image of herself, gaping skirt, red-faced, shoeless. She stops abruptly, turns back and pulls her shoe out of the lawn. She puts it on, tidies her jacket and skirt and smooths down her hair. She stands quietly watching the rest of the school pass.

Soon boys dressed in red shirts and navy shorts join the flow and eventually masters and a few parents. Among them she sees Johnny. She walks to him, perfectly composed. She puts her arm through his.

'I saw Nicky. He looked radiantly happy.'

'Good.' He appears only moderately interested, as if that part of the affair was not his business.

'I didn't speak to him. It seemed better not.'

'No. No. Quite. Wait a moment, if I can divert old Stue from his great victory for a moment I'll introduce you.'

*

That night Laura lies in bed as Martin strokes her round belly. She feels her skin rise under his touch. She takes his hand and guides it all over her body round the under parts of her shoulders, thighs, buttocks.

'You're so soft, tonight,' he says, 'I feel as if you've come back to me.'

'I haven't been away.'

'Yes.' He kisses her, smooths her all over so she cannot move.

'I'm sorry.' She admits it now. 'It was Nicky. It's better now. I've seen him.' Rosy cheeks, thick curly hair. Laughing, chattering. Not her baby any more. 'I love you,' she says, eyes closed. For here is the whole present.

*

Laura became magnificently pregnant. It rather startled her, this majestic matron so ready to burst forth. It was like being taken over by a whole new persona. She was quite capable of sleeping twelve dreamless hours and then rising still heavy-lidded for a dreamlike progress through the day. What the sun had worked on her in Italy, now pregnancy worked even more thoroughly.

Late in November Martin had to go to America for a few days and asked Laura if she wanted to come. The blank stare he received was so uncomprehending that he didn't bother to press her. When he was gone she thought of their last visit and could find no point in which the present her, the heavy charger caparisoned in gold and velvet, met the high-stepping trotter fluttering along in scarlet and white. She had sent her love to Ellen.

Christmas was one of the few things outside her private world that came to her real and vivid. She had always loved Christmas, the celebration of ritual, the restatement of the meaning of family.

A week or two after her visit to Nicky's school she had received a letter from him. She had seen his writing with a normal heartbeat and read it with pleasure not desperation. She had already become that slow-feeling magnificent mountain. He was writing, so he said, at the suggestion of the headmaster and he hoped she would write back. He also informed her that he would be at Aunt Katie's for Xmas and daddy had said she would visit him there.

They began a correspondence. A low-key affair in which day-to-day events were untinged with regret. In the middle of one of these lists of walking, shopping, working, Laura was able to write without trumpets, *Of course I shall come to you at Christmas and if you notice I seem to be fatter it is because I'm going to have a baby. A half brother or half sister for you. You will feel grownup!*

*

Martin returns from New York. He has caught flu and is depressed. The television series has still not been finalised and a deal he was counting on has been put off till the New Year. He goes to bed and allows Laura to bring him hot cups of bovril alternating with whiskey and lemon. She loves him sitting against puffed-up pillows in his striped pyjamas. He looks like an obedient child. After a day or two he revives and asks her to bring skiing brochures from the travel agents. He spreads brilliantly coloured pictures round the bed and begins to make animated telephone calls to agents and friends.

Laura sits on the end of the bed watching. He puts down the telephone and seems suddenly aware of her.

'I always go skiing,' he says. 'You'd like to spend Christmas in Switzerland, wouldn't you?'

Laura doesn't answer at first, still watching Martin as he shuffles the brochures about. He picks out two. 'Davos is best if we're a group of eight or ten. We can take a good chalet then. Anything less we'd be best in a hotel at Klosters. There're no cars allowed there.'

'I've promised Nicky to visit him at Christmas.' Laura speaks mildly. There is no issue in doubt.

Martin also is quiet. 'Couldn't he come skiing? Best age to start. He'd have a great time.'

'I thought you'd be with your mother.'

'I'll give her a slap-up lunch before I go.'

Laura realises Martin's greatest attraction for her was his certainty. Miles, despite his ambition and success, his cleverness, was not strong. In their marriage she had been the rock who held their lives together. But Martin didn't need or want her in that way. It was all love with him. Nothing more, nothing less. He drew nothing from her but love.

She says, 'If the worst comes to the worst I can always follow on.' She knows Miles will not let her, with her fat belly from another man, take his son skiing.

Laura travels by train to Katie and Johnny's house. It is Christmas Eve. The train is crammed with people and very hot. Outside the countryside is cropped and grey with a heavy colourless sky as if it might snow. The children will like that, Laura thinks and notes that it is no longer automatic to think from a child's point of view. She puts her hands up to her burning cheeks. Who will meet her at the station?

Laura steps off the train. She is a fine-looking woman. She wears a deep crimson cloak and black suede boots. Her dark hair is longer than before, caught up at the back with combs. Her eyes flash about expectantly, although her body is slow.

'There she is!' A boy's high-pitched voice shouts. She sees him, running towards her, a tall confident boy in anorak and gumboots. She is surprised by his maleness, his complete lack of the feminine softness that little boys have. Already, he seems to be what he will be in ten years' time.

'You're so big!' she says, as he stops suddenly, almost gravely, in front of her.

'So are you.'

They look at each other. Please God, don't let him hate me, Laura prays swiftly, almost unconsciously.

Behind Nicky come two of Johnny's children and then Johnny himself, tweed cap pulled low over rosy cheeks. 'Welcome! Welcome!' he cries.

Nicky throws himself forward, kisses his mother, smiles at her, 'I'm glad you're here,' he says and then raising his voice so the others can hear, shouts, 'We're going to have a wonderful Christmas!' He grabs Laura's case standing beside her and begins to drag it down the station. 'Aunt Katie's given me the biggest stocking ever,' he shouts as he goes.

Laura has forgotten about children's energy. She feels as if she is being buzzed by an aeroplane. She sits, centred immobile, while Nicky flies over her, round her, beside her, tossing little bombs of conversation. She speaks into the air, unsure whether anything she says ever catches him up. Perhaps it doesn't matter anyway, she thinks. It is her presence that counts. On their next meeting he might come closer but if he does not, she must say he has grown up, become independent and be proud. It is not her needs that count.

When Christmas is over she is going to stay with Nell. She had seen no point in joining Martin. She cannot ski. She thinks of taking her turn at kidnapping and taking Nicky with her. But Nell's boys are older. She rememberes their silent blondness, their books under their arms, and cannot fit Nicky into the picture. He is happy with this merry gang.

'I've bought you a new kind of construction kit,' she tells him.

'Oh, great! Dad's bought me roller-skates. I never used to have two presents.'

Laura unpacks in her cold bedroom. She lays out Nicky's redundant stocking presents in a neat circle. She had always taken pleasure in choosing the smallest of objects but now the sight makes her feel infinitely lonely.

Katie comes up with a glass of sherry. 'Do you want to go to midnight mass?'

'No. No. I'll take Nicky in the morning.'

'The thing is, I had promised the children. . . .'

'I see.' Laura hands Katie a small packet, 'I bought some charms for the cake.'

Katie looks at them with dismay. 'Actually, I already. . . .'

'It doesn't matter.' Laura sips at her glass of sherry.

*

On Boxing Day morning Laura sets out for Nell's house. Everybody stands outside the house to see her off. It is very cold. 'Too cold to snow,' somebody says. But at that moment huge white flakes begin to waft lazily downwards. They fall so slowly that sometimes they seem to stand still or move sideways making patterns in the air.

The children scream with delight. They run about with hands cupped, mouths open trying to catch them. Laura looks at Nicky. 'Come on Johnny. Let's go to the station.' She rubs her hands together briskly. 'Let Nicky stay here. I'd rather remember him like this.' It is too cold for tears but something sharp like icicles digs into her eye-lids.

She catches Nicky, himself whirling faster now as the snow-flakes begin to whirl, and crouches down. Her cloak hangs round them like a bell. 'Don't forget to write and remember I can visit you any time you want.' Then he's off again, skidding, falling, running in an ecstasy of abandon.

Laura, smiling, looks at him out of the car window. Johnny sounds the horn and they are off. One more look and there behind them the children have lined up, waving and shouting, dark figures in the whiteness. 'I feel as if I'm leaving my wedding, confetti falling all around,' murmurs Laura.

'Your wedding?' Johnny cries in sharp mocking call, 'Now there's a subject worth talking about!'

Laura pats the sleeve of his coat. Not even Katie had dared ask her about that.

Chapter Nineteen

Snow had settled over Nell's moorland like a thin white sheet. It was a frail disguise for the stubby grass, the furze and dark sharp-ended trees. When you walked on it it stuck to the soles of your feet leaving a dark imprint behind. If you laid your hand on it, it was hard like ice. It made people seem huge, gave them a black silhouette like Victorian cut-outs.

*

Nell's boys are large anyway, tramping away from the house with carefully composed faces that at a distance look like sullenness. One of them carries a gun under his arm, the more usual book transferred temporarily to his pocket.

'Thank God they're out of the house.' Nell and Laura stand in the low doorway watching them go. 'Now we can talk.' She turns inwards. 'I should think there isn't a bird or beast that hasn't seen them coming.' Laura watches them still, reluctant perhaps for Nell's talk.

'I'm putting on the kettle. You put your feet up.'

Laura goes slowly into the small sitting-room. Nell, inspired by the whiteness outside, has decided to paint it. She is doing a wall at a time, quite undeterred by the amount of bodies to be moved from corner to corner. The whole cottage is impregnated with the smell of paint and turpentine. Nell wears dungarees splashed over like bird-droppings on a rock. Her red hair is permanently tied up in a brilliant pink and gold scarf.

'I had to find something for the boys to do over Christmas,' she explains.

The boys seem to do little beyond moving furniture. They spend long hours in their bedroom playing music, descending occasionally to eat huge self-cooked meals of spaghetti or rice larded with tomato puree. Laura imagined they came out at night for in the morning the sitting-room's smell of paint is temporarily defeated by a boyish smell of little-washed viyella and secret cigarettes.

They have never left the house before.

Nell lies on the floor, posed elegantly on her back as if sunbathing on a green lawn.

'How is your admirer?' asks Laura since Nell, unusually, didn't open the conversation. 'Still pressing?'

'Ha! Ha!' She jumps to her feet and stands with determined theatricality against a dust sheet. 'Why should I grind my fingers to the bone? For what?' She picks up a paint-brush and waves it around her head. 'Cleaning, painting, cooking. Struggling, always struggling. Fighting for beastly commissions for my mugs and then fighting to get them done. What's the point? What's it all for? Other women don't do it. Other women have husbands, servants, lovers. Other women do not spend their Christmas slaving for two teenage boys in the middle of a God-forsaken moor. Do you know I have to chop the wood myself? And this,' she sweeps her arm round the draped and disturbed room. 'Who else spends Boxing Day covered in white emulsion?'

Laura drinks her coffee. Nell's rhetoric, continuing still with a parade of her responsibilities, seems to have little reality. Nell had always created what she wanted for herself. Perhaps she will tell Laura later what she really means.

'Why don't we finish this wall and then we can put the room straight again?' she suggests eventually.

251

'If you want,' agrees Nell with no particular interest, confirming Laura in her view that it is the state of painting she wants rather than the clean walls. Product has never seemed so worthwhile to Nell as the process. Living has always been her pleasure.

The two women face up to the wall paint-brush in hand. They begin to paint rising and bending as if performing some Eastern dance. Laura who has taken no exercise for so long, finds the movement soothing, the stretch she feels in her stomach good. 'I've let myself become fat and lazy,' she murmurs during a break in Nell's laments.

'Yes. You are big.' Nell stops, brush to hip. 'Does Martin like it?'

'I don't know.' Laura does not pause in her ritual slapping. She thinks that Nell, with her caravan lover, her rich admirer, her feminist strength and crudeness, can never appreciate the sort of indescribable passion she and Martin share. Their love is wreathed in purple mists, she thinks with romantic yearning. She will not tear through them even for Nell.

'I may throw it all in!' cries Nell reaching to the cornice with the tip of her brush. But Laura, up and down, up and down, has no idea what she's talking about. At least with Katie she could exchange views about demand feeding.

That night, lying in her narrow cottage bed, Laura feels a sense of restless excitement which she hasn't known for months. Perhaps she has caught it from Nell, perhaps it is the unusual exercise.

She lies awake picturing Martin's face and letting the silence buzz around her. The two seem to fit together, a vibrating electronic kit, creating his face as if it was on a television screen.

She sits up. At once her unusual state is explained. For a liquid warmth begins to gush from between her legs. She does not cry out or move, keeping her place like a sat-up doll, for quite five minutes. Then she lowers herself slowly back again.

Still she is not tempted to call for help. She is gripped by fatalism. No action seems possible or necessary. Gradually the flow begins to diminish. Then Laura begins to think about praying. She thinks about sin and punishment and the new life that she had started to create. She cannot tell whether she believes in any of these things. Even the baby for whom, presumably, she lies now so rigid, seems hardly possible.

The black night buzzes round her but Martin's face has gone, replaced only by a mounting noise of nothing. She thinks of reaching out, and switching on her bedside light. That will dismiss it. But even that action seemed too bold. If she turns herself into pure vessel, hard casing, good for nothing but containment and protection, then perhaps God will overlook her sinful heart and stop up the hole.

Or perhaps he wants her to drain away, leaving nothing but shell. Perhaps that was what she has become. A blown egg.

Laura dozes. A rigid death-like sleep which never cuts out awareness of the gentle slide between her legs. Yet she awakes so she must have slept, there is light behind the thin curtains. A grey light but still strong enough to speckle the walls with the flower pattern of the curtains. Light reflects off a white country-side, she thinks, and has a sudden image of blood on snow.

'Nell!' she calls cautiously. 'Nell!'

The day comes to life. Nell with towels. The boys with books to raise up the end of her bed. A doctor.

'No pain? No pain at all?' Young and thin, he stands in the middle of the room. Behind him, Nell peers curiously, even in her anxiety unable to conceal a childlike excitement in the dramatic.

'No,' says Laura, surprised that she hadn't thought of this all through the long night. 'No pain at all. And now I've stopped bleeding altogether.'

'In my view,' says the doctor heartily, 'what we've got here is a classic case of placenta previa.'

'Is that good?' askes Nell.

'It depends if you like lying around?' the doctor smiles questioningly to Laura.

Laura thinks she has brought it on herself, this sentence to lie around for three months. It is the logical culmination of her self-created inertia over the last few months. The medical reason seems hardly to convince her. 'You should go to our local hospital and stay there in case of further haemorrhaging,' says the doctor who Laura cannot help thinking of as a vet. He has such a simple open face and his tweed jacket smells of hay and iodine.

But the next day he suddenly relents saying she can go to a London hospital if all is well in a few days but then she must not move again. Laura wonders, without much emotion, whether he has been informed of her unmarried state.

'I do want the baby,' she says mildly. She supposes she must since she had lain so still that whole night through.

'It's you I'm worried about,' says the doctor without looking at her. 'If you've got to move around at all go on your hands and knees.'

'Like an animal,' says Laura.

'Yes, animals are far better designed than humans, to carry their babies.'

Less efficient than an animal, thinks Laura. I'm glad Martin's skiing. I don't want him close to me now.

*

The hospital was not very large. It was built of red-brick and stood between one of London's widest and noisiest roads and a prettily designed church whose clock struck every quarter of the hour. Laura felt herself caught between the twentieth century on one side and the eighteenth century on the other. She was in a no-man's-land, a lady in waiting, with no roots to anything but the baby inside her. Martin had not returned early from his holiday but he had insisted on a private room. This rose-patterned luxury increased her sense of isolation. When he did return she would persuade him of the pleasures of a general ward. There, she imagined, she would find life again with other women in the same sort of position as herself.

*

One evening about six, when it is already dark outside, and she is staring unhopefully at the tin dishes covering her newly delivered supper, there comes a firm rap at her door. The window flap is open so she can make out her visitor's face enough to know she or he is tall and wears glasses.

The unusual prospect of someone to talk to other than professionally cheerful nurses brings immediate colour to her cheeks. She sits herself further up on her cushions.

'Come in.'

Miles walks through the door. Then stops abruptly. 'Can I come in?'

'Would you go, if I told you?'

He indicates the tray from which a faint aroma of peas and gravy arises. 'It's your supper.'

Laura sees that he shows no signs of anger, of a need for confrontation. While she lies trapped, that might have been tempting. In fact he looks extremely uneasy as if the excuse of interrupting her supper would have sent him fleeing away.

She pushes aside the table and tray. 'Oh, don't bother about that. Find a chair. Sit down.' Is it possible that, on this neutral ground, he has come to talk reasonably? Nicky, her heart says, but she looks at him calmly enough although the colour in her cheeks deepens further.

Miles sits down. He is wearing a fawn mackintosh which she doesn't recognise, over one of his dark suits. He has a large briefcase which he lifts onto his knees and opens. He takes out a heavy bunch of grapes swathed in tissue paper. 'I don't think they've got crushed.'

'They're beautiful.' Laura takes the grapes and places them on the mound of her stomach in front of her. They rise like great purple carvings out of a hill-side. Such a vulgar unimaginative peace-offering. Laura sits waiting. He has come to her. Let him speak. She takes a grape and breaks it against her teeth. The juice trickles almost like alcohol down her throat.

'Perhaps I should wash them?'

Laura starts. She had fallen into a kind of daze. 'Yes. Perhaps you should.'

Miles takes the purple bunch and runs fast-spurting water over it. He returns it to its nest of tissues and goes back to his seat.

There is a bustle at the door and a nurse enters briskly. She picks up the tin covers. 'You haven't even started.'

'No. I'm not hungry. You can take it away.'

'Coffee, tea or horlicks?'

'Coffee, please.'

The nurse leaves with the tray. Miles who has stood up during her visit sits down quickly and begins talking.

'I'm so very sorry to hear you're unwell. Johnny told me. And Katie, of course. It must be dreadful for you. Here all the time.'

'I'm pregnant.'

Miles blinks painfully and looks away, making Laura ashamed of her cruelty. 'Yes. I know.' There is a small pause. Laura takes another grape.

'I'm glad you've come,' she says.

'Yes. Johnny said. . . .' Laura thinks that Johnny must have

255

told him that Martin was out of the country otherwise he'd never have dared come.

'I miss Nicky horribly. Horribly,' Laura says suddenly and finds to her dismay that her eyes have filled with tears.

'Yes. Yes. I can imagine. He's very well. He likes his new school. I've just taken him back there. He gave me something for you.' He rummages in his case again and produces an envelope bulging untidily. 'He put a lucky stone in it.'

Laura takes the envelope and puts it by her side, half tucked under the sheets. She thinks that this quiet opening of communication is worth all the sacrifice of not seeing Nicky. Miles has lost his anger.

'I'm sorry you're having such a bad time.' Miles leans forward and puts one hand on the bed. 'I don't feel vindictive, you know.'

Laura can think of nothing to say. Her swollen belly, close between them now, as he comes closer, begins to seem an embarrassment. He is her husband after all, looking at her, she suddenly notices, with something quite like husbandly warmth and affection.

'I wanted to take Nicky out at half-term,' she says nervously. 'But now of course I can't.'

'No. No. I'm sorry.' Miles seems to listen but Laura realises he is not thinking about Nicky at all. He has a speech prepared in his mind which he is gearing himself to deliver. A ghastly premonition makes her slant sideways.

Too late. Miles catches her hand between both of his. His chair scrapes along the floor behind him.

'I'm prepared to forget everything. Everything! Even the baby. I would learn to love the baby if it's born. I've talked to the doctor. They say if you go back to a home with staff, nearby, they'll let you out for another month at least. It's all still there waiting for you. Everything you had before that made you so happy. I love you still. I don't even blame you. It's natural for women of your age to feel restless. Too much temptation. I spent too much time with my work. I didn't take your work seriously enough. I thought Nicky was everything to you. Enough. You'd make him so happy. Me so happy. I am your husband. You believe in marriage. I know you do. You know it. Catholicism. Your church. Your friends. Roy, Katie, Lizzie. It wouldn't hurt him. He would survive. He doesn't need you like we do. And you need us. Look at you now. Where are you? What are you? What's it all about? You're not real any more. You're lost. Lost. Your house is still waiting for you. Oh, Laura, my poor darling misguided Laura. . . .'

Overwhelmed by the strength of his feelings and the passion of his delivery, Miles throws his head into what remains of Laura's lap. There it lies set apart from the neat black body by the disarray of the fading locks and sweating brow. Laura, ice cold now, feels herself like Judith holding the head of Holofernes.

She strokes the hair back from the temples. Counsel, she thinks, has spoken in his own defence. Was this the speech of a lifetime, sweated over night after night? Was its climax and appeal planned to catch the ever sympathetic jury? Was she no longer the accused as he'd tried to convince her? No. That was false. He thought she'd learnt her lesson and now he wanted her back, poor misguided Laura, sack-cloth and ashes big enough for the baby – if it was born. He doesn't believe it will be born. It is all words. She takes her hands off the hair.

'I love Martin,' she says.

The head raises itself slowly back onto its shoulders. The mouth gapes. The face sags. 'I see.'

Again Laura feels shamefaced as she did at the beginning. But she says nothing. Miles hauls himself onto his feet. He hardly seems able to bear the weight of his briefcase. He walks to the door. Laura thinks he will go without speaking again or turning round. She says, in an agitated voice, 'I want a divorce.'

He looks at her and she has time to notice that his eyes are red behind their glasses. Perhaps he had been weeping as his head lay on her lap. 'Yes. I expect you do.'

He goes out shutting the door carefully behind him. Through the window flap Laura sees his fawn-coloured back disappearing down the corridor.

The day after Miles's visit is a Sunday. Laura has not thought any more about his terrible proposition but when a pale face above a black suit appears once more in her window-flap she shivers as if it is death. The knock when it comes is quite without threat, so lacking in confidence that it slides rather than taps.

Nevertheless, the shiver remains, pinching her face.

'Come in.'

The door half-opens. 'I wouldn't want to disturb you.' It is a priest, torso leaning round the door, legs lurking behind. 'It says Roman Catholic on your form.'

'Come in, if you like.' Miles's agent, she thinks, come to frighten her with a crucifix. Except this priest would frighten nobody.

'Is there anything I can do for you?'

Laura considers. Should she tell him her story? How her life before had been unreal, a child playing games and now she has entered the real world. Would he understand? Or would he merely see it as excuse for lust? Virtuous before, sinner now. 'I'm going to be here quite a long time,' she says, smiling.

He takes this as the dismissal it probably is. 'I'm only in on Sundays.' He takes a pace backwards. He is more used to dismissal than welcome.

The telephone rings. Laura answers it, still looking at the priest's face. It is young, round, despite the lack of confidence, hopeful.

'Laura, my darling. My darling.' It is Martin. He has rung before from Switzerland but Laura knows at once he is back. He will be with her very soon. The priest's face disappears. He might not be in the room at all. Even to talk to him was playing games, passing the time. Now she exists again. Martin will banish the shadow of Miles.

'I'll be with you in half an hour. How are you?'

A door closes just inside her consciousness. 'I had a priest in my room.'

'A priest in your room.' Martin's voice sounds lightly amused as if she'd said she was playing snakes and ladders.

'He's gone now. Come quickly.'

Martin hadn't understood that Laura must lie still till the baby is born. The strength of his sympathy makes Laura feel brave. 'You can come in when you finish work,' she says, 'we'll have delicious smoked salmon picnics and bottles of wine.' As she speaks she begins to see that after all the private room may be a necessity.

'But how can I do without you for so long?'

Laura, adapted after a week to her own role, realises she has not fully considered his.

'It will be like before,' she suggests with unconvincing generosity. 'You'll be a desirable bachelor, giving elegant

258

dinners in your club and receiving scintillating invitations to the rich and famous.'

'Then what about our picnics?'

'We'll have them every other night.' Laura lies back in her bed. Tears of self-pity roll down her cheeks. It is the first time she has cried since her haemorrhaging in that cold winter night. 'It's so cruel,' she murmurs. 'So cruel. And unfair.'

Martin puts his arms round her and rocks her gently. 'It isn't so very long.' She sees he likes her more like this. It gives him more to do. Really she was ridiculous to try and encourage his independence. He would have enough, whatever happened. In his arms she feels weak and secure and enjoys wetting his anorak with her tears.

He stays all day, leaving to get the Sunday papers and then returning again. This time Laura is calm enough to notice how well he looks and handsome. He is like some giant dragon fly caught in her flowery little room. She feels proud and subdued and only a little anxious. She cannot imagine the world outside.

As the weeks pass this feeling of unreality increases. She has more visitors. But their experience of an English January and February seem so remote from her cosy cocoon of ever-lasting roses as to be almost unbelievable. When they first burst in, noses red, hands stiff and cold, coats usually wet from rain and snow, she finds herself shrinking back. She cannot imagine how other pregnant women battle out amidst the noise and dirt and cold. Her baby is in one womb, she in another. At night she sleeps curled up, hands near her mouth.

Martin is outside of all this. He is part of her. But even he coming one day straight from the airport after a trip to New York, seems to her foul-smelling and gross. She lets him hug her and touch her ever-growing lump but she looks over his shoulder with blank eyes. Nor does she ask him questions about his work or the people he has seen.

The doctor, a tall distinguished man who wears elegantly cut suits and pale silk ties is, on the whole, more attractive to her. He is brusque but in the most comforting way. His hands are so clean that the nails look as if they've been varnished. Laura gets into the habit of casting surreptitious glances at her visitors' hands. She is amazed at the dirt under the fingernails.

One occasion Martin arrives at the same time as the doctor. Laura is slightly disconcerted as they swop information about ski resorts. Afterwards Martin, perhaps prompted by the expensive silk tie – grey spotted with yellow on that occasion – asks if Laura is under a medical insurance scheme.

'Insurance?' Laura who has started doing a little light embroidery, looks up from a twist of cherry silk, 'Miles took care of all that.'

'So that's no help.'

For most of her life Laura has been a kept woman. She is so far from independence that she has never felt the slightest embarrassment in taking money from Martin. Up to now her own small salary has paid for her personal needs.

'I'm afraid I'm a terrible drain on you,' she says now without much conviction.

'Money is the least important thing in the world.'

A few days later Martin tries to arrange for her to be moved into a public ward. Laura does not object but she no longer feels any aptitude for cheery mixing and her wan lack of enthusiasm shames Martin. She stays where she is. The baby is due in eight weeks.

Two weeks later Laura feels a slight pain in her stomach, no more than if the baby had moved a little more energetically than usual, and she begins to bleed. She immediately rings for the nurse.

'Is the baby coming?'

The nurse, friendly though she is, gives Laura a reproving look. 'The baby's not due for six weeks.'

'Will you call Mr Lovell?'

'There's no need to get excited.'

All during the day Laura bleeds on and off. By evening it seems entirely off. Martin arrives carrying wine and salami. It is one of their now rather rare picnic evenings. Laura drinks and eats and says nothing, despite her absolute conviction that she has started the baby. The pain in her stomach lessens with the wine but does not go away.

Martin leaves, kissing her lovingly, although his eyes, she notices, slide eagerly ahead of him toward the door. His world is outside. He has another big job.

The bleeding starts again. As she is restless the nurses give her valium as well as sleeping pills and switch off her light. The bleeding stops. At midnight she is woken by a pure sensation of loss only felt before in nightmares. She screams out and a black

260

nightnurse who has not seen her before appears immediately. She puts her head to Laura's stomach. For a moment Laura is reminded of Miles's dark decapitated head on a lap. The image fades quickly.

The nurse stands up with a startled urgent expression. 'You're having contractions,' she says. 'For how long?'

'All day.' Laura is relieved to speak the truth.

'And bleeding?'

'Yes. On and off.'

'I'll ring Mr Lovell.' The nurse hurries away.

Laura settles back, despite everything calm, even complacent. She has proved her case to the medical world. Now they will take over. She feels no fear and does not think of wanting Martin.

Some time not long after the anaesthetist arrives and asks her whether she has eaten or drunk anything in the last eight hours. When she reaches salami and a bottle of wine his shocked expression makes her smile.

She smiles still as they take her along rainbow-coloured corridors to the operating theatre. The round and glistening lamps in the ceiling seem curiously like the winking faces round her. All woken from sleep, she thinks, to attend on me.

Then, just then, she entertains the idea of Martin. His face never glistens palely, even in the middle of the night. His face glows red with youth and energy.

They go into the operating theatre and all Laura's hopes are pushed into a black rubber nose filled with gas.

It is dawn when she awakes. That fact impresses her more than any other. Night had been so strong before, as if it could never be defeated. Then she hears a voice saying in a quiet patient tone as if something repeated over and over again. 'You have a daughter. You have a daughter.' Several times she falls back into blackness but each time she wakes this voice repeats the same message, gradually becoming louder in her ear.

Laura opens her eyes fully, raises herself and sees Martin sitting on a chair beside her. 'Martin.'

He takes her hand. 'I've seen her. She's in an incubator. But she's quite big. Five pounds.'

Laura vomits. Martin holds up a silver basin with a tender solicitude. When she stops he says, 'I've been here most of the night. I saw you wheeled out of the operating theatre.'

Laura looks up and sees a bottle hanging above her head. 'I've got a drip.'

'Nothing's too good for you. You've had three pints of blood too.'

Laura vomits again and feels the pain where she has been cut. 'I'm glad the baby's all right,' she says unable in her exhaustion to choose more exalted words.

'Oh she is. I wanted to be the first to tell you. That's why I stayed. They said you'd sleep for hours.'

'Thank you.' Laura slips away again. Still she is just conscious of Martin's leaving. She imagines he talks of breakfast and work although that may be just her image of him. He is always self-sufficient.

The baby is perfect. She is out of the incubator the second day, crying as lustily as any of the others in the nursery. Everybody congratulates Laura on having a premature baby that is so well and sturdy. But Laura looks on her with all the fear she hadn't felt before her birth. She is so very much smaller than Nicky had been, so light that she seems hardly more than a bundle of clothes. The nightdresses Laura had bought need a wide fold at the back and the sleeves of the cardigan turn back to her armpits. Laura is terrified to hold her for more than a moment. She passes her to a nurse as soon as possible. She will not bath or feed her.

The ward sister approaches her on the third day with a stern headmistress expression, 'It says on my list that you wished to breast-feed your baby.'

'Yes. I did think,' Laura mumbles and bends over her wound protectively. It is still painful to stand upright.

'I'm afraid you'll have to be harder on yourself, Mrs Knight.'

'Tomorrow. I thought. . . .'

'This afternoon I'll have a nurse give you a warm shower,' the sister interrupts briskly, 'and then your milk should flow nicely for the six o'clock feed.'

Laura is far too weak to object. Tears of self-pity only make her head ache as well as her stomach. The most satisfying emotion she can sustain is a dull hatred – of the sister and the nurses and indeed the whole hospital. The many contented weeks she had spent there are obliterated in her present misery.

Martin arrives soon after six. He smiles at the lovely sight of mother and daughter clasped in the embrace of first feed.

'That's worth a five hour journey from the North.' He had been to Newcastle that day.

Laura gives him a baleful look. 'They're all sadists here.'

Martin laughs cheerfully. 'You are feeling better.'

Laura looks down at the baby's head. Although so small, she has a greedy, determined suck as if sensing her mother's reluctance and determined to get her rights. It arouses no love in Laura, such as she remembered feeling for Nicky, but a curious feeling of cold admiration. Sister and baby are in league to bully her into proper motherhood. At least it lessens her terror of the baby's vulnerability.

'We must think of a name for her.' Martin pours himself some wine into a tooth-glass. 'I suggest Emily.'

'Oh, no!' Laura is horrified. 'She isn't at all Emily.'

'Daisy? Kate? Clarissa? Rose? Chloe? Charlotte?'

'She isn't that sort of baby at all!'

'Ah.' Martin waits.

'Not so pretty.'

'She looks very pretty to me.'

'Not so old-fashioned.'

'So what do you suggest?'

But Laura won't commit herself. Secretly she has a plan to discover the sister's Christian name and call her that. Laura is a little unbalanced, unable to say what is in her mind. Martin and she have been apart a long time.

When visitors come she shows off the baby as if she loves her. Nell comes and Katie and a few other friends, who Laura had almost forgotten, lured by the attraction of a new-born baby.

Nell bends over the cot with a calculating air. 'Of course I haven't given up the idea of having a daughter.' She eyes Laura. 'Though I wouldn't want your dreadful experience.'

'No.' Laura agrees. In her more rational moments she thought that it was her 'dreadful experience' which made it impossible for her to love the baby. It was as if she'd used up all her emotions on her before she'd even been born. Now there is only emptiness. Her feeling of being bullied persists.

Katie comes in with her hands over her eyes. 'I mustn't look! I mustn't look. I'll want another. I know I will.' She goes to the baby irresistibly and takes her from her wrappings and holds her close. 'Oh, she's such a darling. So tiny. So fragile.'

'Actually, she's much tougher than she looks.'

263

'I didn't mean that.' Katie bends lower. 'I always have such big loutish babies. She's so beautiful!'

Laura smiles. She accepts her beauty.

One unexpected visitor is Martin's mother. Laura, prepared for her arrival, puts herself and her baby into their most elegant robes. She re-arranges her flowers and turns off the overhead light. She gulps down a glass of wine five minutes before she is due. Then she sits back expectantly. For all she knows she is coming to denounce her.

Mrs Keane comes into the room ahead of her son carrying a slim white box. 'Congratulations, my dear,' she says with a small smile. She lays the box on the table beside the bed.

Laura gives her a small smile back. 'Would you like to sit?'

'No. I. . . .' She looks round the room until she sees the cot on the far side of the bed. She goes over immediately, pulling the coverlet back from the sleeping baby to see her better. Laura finds her eagerness a little embarrassing from such a controlled woman. She decides to open the box.

Martin joins his mother and they stand together, staring down proudly. 'My first grandchild,' Mrs Keane murmurs. She turns her head towards Laura and flashes her a wide altogether unrestrained smile.

Laura is taken aback. She holds up the embroidered dress she has taken from the box. 'Thank you. It's exquisite.'

Mrs Keane turns back to the baby. 'I always wanted a little girl.' Her voice is wistful. She comes back to the bed again. 'Thank you for letting me see her.'

Laura realises she must make some further overture. 'Would you like to sit?' she repeats.

Mrs Keane looks at her watch, but takes the chair pulled out by Martin. 'I mustn't stay long.'

There is an awkward pause.

Martin says, 'We can't decide on a name for her.'

'It's so very difficult.' His mother gives Laura a sympathetic look. Laura does not trust this gentle humility but is quite unprepared for her next remark delivered in ringing almost challenging tones, 'But I gather she will bear my son's surname!'

Laura gives Martin a stupid look. In the confusion of the moment she cannot even remember whether they've discussed such a thing. She thinks not.

But Mrs Keane does not seem to expect an answer. She is standing up, gathering her things. Martin puts his arm round her. 'I'll come with you and find a taxi.'

While they are gone the baby wakes and cries noisily. Laura rocks her cot and decides she cannot mention surnames if Martin doesn't.

Martin returns. He says, 'My mother is thrilled. I've never seen her so excited by anything. Poor old thing. She's very lonely.'

Laura says nothing. She feels herself surrounded by enemies and aliens. She suspects even Martin.

Martin talks enthusiastically about the little house he has rented for them. It is in a mews backed by grand town houses, faced by garages. It is temporary only. Laura thinks 'temporary' is the most terrifying word in the language.

They move in a few days later, Laura carrying the baby with nervous resignation. Martin's attitude is disguised by the amount of fetching and carrying he is called on to do. The baby, this first day, is quiet. By evening Laura is left with enough energy to find a clean dress and face Martin across the supper table.

'Welcome back!' he raises his glass to her.

She understands. With an enormous effort she looks directly at him. 'What have you been doing while I was gone?'

'Earning my living.'

The spark of communication gives Laura courage. 'We must register the baby or we'll be fined. I want to call her Matilda.'

'Matilda!' Martin's beneficient expression is broken, giving Laura an odd sense of pleasure.

'You can call her Tilly.'

Her voice is so final that Martin, who has been about to argue, changes his mind.

'Mat is another alternative,' he says weakly.

Matilda was not the name of the sister but Laura had fixed on it with a feeling that Irene, her real name, was truly insupportable.

The next day Martin sets out to register Matilda on his way to the office. Laura, bathing her baby with slippery hands and beating heart, tries to think calmly about such a step. Presumably it means that Martin is giving her his surname. Above Matilda's wails, who had as little confidence in the bath-time experience as her mother, she tries to understand why they did not talk of such things. She suspects it is her fault.

She allows herself to remember that moment of pure happiness when she had registered Nicky's birth. Stuffing tiny unwilling arms into tiny unwilling vest, she remembered her insistence that he should be registered by the diminutive, Nicky. She had loved him so much. Loved herself in relation to him. A new young mother receiving congratulations, so confident, so different now.

Laura sits in her small bedroom furnished by someone else and drops tears over her feeding baby's head. Tears and milk flow at much the same rate.

Nicky had been christened in the village where her mother lived till her death a few years later. The priest had been old but infinitely tender, treating Nicky as if he was the first baby he'd ever baptised. Afterwards they'd had lunch of cold chicken and courgettes from the garden. Nicky, large and complacent, had lain in his pram with eyes drooping but not quite shut. She'd felt sure he'd enjoyed it all as much as her. Miles must have been there too.

She had never loved Miles.

Laura puts the full sleepy baby into her cot, and lies on her bed. This attitude after so many prone months comes more naturally than any other. When she stands she feels dangerous, even with a sense of vertigo. Desultorily she goes through her post-natal exercises. It hardly seems worth it with so much weight hugging her vice-like round the middle.

Perhaps Martin's touch, so long forbidden, unwanted, will like a fairy wand, magic it all away. Perhaps she will return to that state of heightened awareness for which she had left her husband. Love. Love passes. Even the most ignorant know that.

> *Georgie Porgie, pudding and pie,*
> *Kissed the girls and made them cry;*
> *When the boys came out to play*
> *Georgie Porgie ran away.*

She and Martin have nothing to put in its place.

Laura had been planning to ring Ben Casey and convince him of her willingness to start work from home at once. Instead she dresses herself and Matilda in their outdoor clothes. Since she has no pram yet, she takes the baby in her arms.

It is a cold day but the sun shines. After the white-veiled windows of the hospital the streets glare with icy ferocity. The noise, too, seems to direct itself at her like an attack. But she carries on with shaking legs and bursting head until she reaches a church. Not caring to look at the denomination, she goes inside and sits in a back pew.

What is it all about? What does it mean? Why I am here? Or anywhere? Why do I have this baby? That man, house, job?

No one troubles her and after a while she gets up and wanders back to the house again.

That evening she tries to make a funny story out of it for Martin. But he says 'Don't!' and takes her hand.

So they sit quietly together and she feels her affection for him returning.

Later he programmes his computer with Matilda's genes and proves she will be both beautiful and a genius.

Chapter Twenty

Laura's life took on a brisk cheerful look. She had the little house, the pretty baby, an interesting but not too demanding job and Martin. In the eyes of the world, the advent of Matilda seemed to have turned them into a family, Martin into a husband. Their running away together had lost all scandal value. Except to Miles who still would not give Laura a divorce. He did, however, let Nicky visit. He arrived, clean and handsome, and admired the baby. As he leant over the cot Laura saw Miles in his deliberation. The energy which had so impressed her over Christmas was apparently now reserved for the playing-fields. He talked for most of his first visit about his ambition to be in the Rugger XV. She went to buy a pair of shoes with him and his feet were nearly as big as hers.

It is Nicky who tells Laura that Miles has a girlfriend. 'She's quite nice,' he says, with a bored lack of interest, 'but he makes Maria cry.'

'Oh really. Why's that?'

'She's allergic to dust. It makes her sneeze.'

Laura tries to look only reasonably interested but sees by Nicky's side-long glance that he knows he has a perfectly enthralled audience.

'Actually, she's allergic to all sorts of things. Flowers, animals, corn-flakes. In fact I sometimes wonder how she survives at all.' He pauses reflectively. 'She bought me a scalextric set.'

'That's nice. And nice for Daddy to have a friend.'

'He's not that keen on her. Not as much as her anyway. She says she's always been crazy about older men.'

Laura manages a casual laugh but can't resist asking, 'She's quite young then?'

'Oh, yes. She has long hair which she's always messing about with.'

'She certainly doesn't sound Daddy's type,' says Laura who'd been prepared to consider a middle-aged asthmatic.

She goes into the kitchen and starts buttering bread in a fussy motherly way. Nicky turns on the television. It comes to her loud and clear from the other room. A programme she doesn't disapprove of quite enough to forbid.

A few days later, time to assimilate, time to defuse, she tells Martin about Miles's long-haired, asthmatic friend.

He smiles, 'That's progress.'

Laura considers his meaning. Does he really want her to get a divorce then? Is this understood in their relationship? Are they not at a plateau, at the top, but another plateau, on the way to a summit?

Martin says, 'I once knew someone with dreadful asthma. It did make her very clean.'

But Laura isn't really listening. She decides to talk to Katie.

*

Katie likes coming to Laura's mews house. She treats it as if it were a doll's house, poking about the shelves and moving furniture around. She can't get over the fact that everything has been designed for the purpose it's used. Secretly she finds this gives it a feeling of unreality as if that which had been created in one sweep could disappear in another. But to Laura, she enthuses, 'So extraordinary not to have one dusty corner, one patch of rot.'

'It's in the contract,' smiles Laura, 'repairs and maintenance.'

'What a dream!' sighs Katie. In fact over the last year her life
has taken on a new sense of order. She has at last found a nice
country girl who comes in on weekdays from a nearby village.
She rides a moped. Johnny's expression at his first sight of her
plump body in crash-helmet on wheels made it clear that even
he drew the line somewhere. The last baby is eighteen months,
walking, nearly potty-trained.

Katie draws breath and looks around her. It is a long time
since she'd had the energy to think about other people. Before
coming up to London, she had gone into the garden with little
Toby at her heels and picked a large bunch of creamy daffodils.
As she looked at them she felt the sadness usually associated
with home-sickness. Then she remembered. It was that week of
desolation when her life had seemed finished and Laura had
come to her, persuaded her to stay with Johnny, to start again.
Then Laura had filled the house with those same creamy
flowers.

Yet the nostalgia Katie felt was not just at the memory of her
own unhappiness then. It was a hardly understood feeling that
Laura was unhappy now. That the bright strong woman she
had been then had changed into someone else, remote, shadowy.

This feeling was completely contradicted, as usual by actually seeing Laura. There she was, larger than before the baby,
but still beautiful, calm, competent.

So Katie admires the doll's house and the quietly sleeping
baby, while Laura lays the table.

They sit facing each other in a peace which Katie has only
lately got used to. They talk about children for Katie has
nothing else to talk about, unless it is the mist above the hills
when she takes them early to school and that would make her
self-conscious. Laura tells Katie about her work and Martin's
work and his decision to do more and more in New York. 'He's
always been a bit of a maverick here. He gets on better with
Americans.'

Katie is a little surprised by Laura's manner, her vivacity
and conversational tone. It is not like her. Laura stands to clear
the plates. 'Nicky tells me Miles has a girlfriend.'

Katie, dull in some matters, is not slow to get the point of this.

269

She doesn't have to disguise sympathetic understanding since Laura now stands at the sink with her back to her.

'Philippa's hardly a girlfriend.' She manages a matter of fact tone, 'More friend, if anything. She likes attaching herself to clever men if they'll let her. Miles lets her cook and clean and organise outings for Nicky. Nothing else as far as I can make out. Johnny's known her for years.'

As Laura turns round Katie blushes suddenly. 'Nothing like that with him either.' But Laura is far from thinking of her brother's infidelities, 'Philippa,' she repeats. She goes to put on the kettle for coffee. She stops, holding the kettle in one hand and faces Katie, abruptly. 'Miles begged me to go back to him, you know. When I was in hospital waiting for Matilda. He wept over my pregnant stomach.'

'How dreadful!' Katie is horrified by the image conjured up by these words. Miles, usually so controlled, so stately. After such a humiliation, it was no wonder he would not even mention Laura's name. She, hardly wants to know more but feeling Laura who never confided anything must be needing to say more, asks, 'What did you do?'

But Laura turns away again, as if she'd lost interest. 'Oh, I sent him off. What could I do? It was all ridiculous.'

There is a silence while she makes the coffee and brings it to Katie. 'So you don't think he's planning on marriage?'

'Oh, no,' says Katie decisively, and then adds with one of her sudden flashes of inspiration, 'The only thing he's planning on is being a judge.'

Both women stop, considering this idea and each without speaking further realises this is the whole truth of the matter. Miles will not divorce Laura for fear it affects his chances to become a judge.

Laura picks up a pile of clean nappies from the side, 'It's time for Tilly's feed.' She hesitates for a moment and then says more or less to herself, 'I wish I could remember what the point of marriage is.'

Katie stares at the fluffy cotton nappies and says vaguely, 'I'd expected you would use disposable.'

*

'Your breasts are so heavy.'

'It's the milk. Shall I stop nursing?'

'Who wants small breasts?'

270

'I'll never have small breasts.'

Laura, lying alongside Martin, thinks that a man's body is so infinitely more desirable than a woman's. A young man's body, that is. Hard unchanging lines. Ever since the baby she has felt disgusted with her body. The mountainous quality which had supported her before Tilly's birth now seems soft and squelchy. Self-disgust makes a barrier to her love-making.

The next day Laura stops nursing Tilly and announces she is going to look for someone to come in three mornings a week so she can go back to the office. Martin seems pleased as he does with all her decisions. Sometimes she feels he sees her as some kind of beautiful stage performance, unalterable in its ways. She even begins to wonder whether he has another life outside theirs. She knows so little about him. Yet she is frightened to find out more. Besides, he is a very private person. She had known everything about Miles.

*

In June they go to New York. Laura had planned to leave Tilly with Katie but at the last minute she decides to bring her after all. She thinks this is cowardice. Her protection against living. The morning they leave she receives a letter from Miles's solicitor saying he is planning to sell the house and would appreciate her removing any of her remaining possessions at the earliest possible date. Strangely, this makes Laura happy. It puts her in touch with the reality of undeniable objects. Besides, she had always felt disturbed by the thought of that house, which had been so much her creation, left either uncared for or cared for by another. She would far rather it was dismantled, put out of reach. It was hard for her to admit that in that house she had often been perfectly happy.

She passes over the letter to Martin who reads it carefully as he always does anything to do with business. 'It'll have to wait till we get back.'

'Yes,' agrees Laura regretfully. She longs to rush round that minute and tear pictures off the wall. 'We'll have to find somewhere to put the stuff.'

'How about New York?' Martin smiles mysteriously. Laura knows he is on the verge of a big American deal but has not yet faced the implications.

*

This time New York was not having a heat-wave. The days were exhilarating. Clear blue skies with light crisp air. Martin had rented an apartment from a friend. His talent for managing life never ceased to impress Laura. She thought it was probably a difference in generation. But because she distrusted all those easy friendships she looked on the apartment with qualified appreciation. It was featureless in an expensive part of the upper East Side. The doorman always helped her with Tilly's basket. But one day she caught sight of herself in a long mirror in the hall. She saw a large pale woman struggling with late motherhood. She began in a fairly desultory way to look for somewhere to live which could be her own. It seemed almost certain that Martin would want to settle in America. He had lived there for several years immediately after university and several years later come back again for a training stint with a computer programming company.

*

'You've developed quite a New York twang.' Laura and Martin sit side by side on their sofa. He holds the baby.

'Nonsense! I speak in pips and squeaks.'

'It's because you have so many American friends.'

'Oh, do I?' He begins to count on Tilly's fingers. 'There's Hal and Jeannie. But I haven't seen much of them since they moved out west and Hal came out of the closet. Poor Jeannie. There's Eddy and Ellen, and Eddy and Ellen and Ellen. . . .'

Laura laughs. She has become very friendly with Ellen. She is pregnant and balloons along the streets in a jovial contented way which reminds Laura of her pregnancy with Nicky. In fact Ellen already has two children and is two years older than Laura. But she is practising motherhood with proselytising fervour. She has given up teaching for the last month and, being an extraordinarily energetic woman, has lots of extra energy. She goes up and down to vast unconverted lofts or chic little apartments exclaiming at the area, the floor-space, the light. Laura, far more tentative, can't get used to a grand overall design. She realises that she had never advanced beyond the idea of a regular house with regular box rooms. She admits this, rather shame-faced, to Ellen who replies cheerfully, 'You'll never afford a brown-stone so you'll just have to adapt.'

Laura is meek. This is not her country. Sometimes she catches Ellen looking at her with a kind of admiring bewilder-

272

ment. At first she thought this merely a reflection of Atlantic barriers. But then she realised it was remarkably like the look Martin gave her when he came home and found her tucking Tilly into her cot or simply lying on her bed reading a book. It was the same look that Miles had given her when he found her sitting quietly in her pretty glowing drawing-room.

Was she always to be remote?

Laura had begun to drink more. Martin seemed to like its effect on her, pouring wine generously and smiling if her cheeks became flushed, her voice loud. It increased her enthusiasm in bed.

Shamed by Ellen's energy, Laura puts on her prettiest dress – the red and white suit no longer fits her – and returns to Fifth Avenue. She makes pilgrimages to the same sky-top glass offices and tells the same blue-shirted executives about eighteenth century dove-cotes. But the magic has gone for her. Not that they are unreceptive. The magic might have gone but they still direct her to the appropriate executive channel. And one even ask her to Martha's Vineyard.

Remembering Martin's mother's annual visit, Laura tells him this, smiling. Last year the invitation to Cape Cod had seemed like a glorious dream, utterly unobtainable, utterly desirable. This year Martha's Vineyard seems equally unobtainable for quite different reasons. And really not desirable either. She imagines Ellen's scorn at such ridiculous fantasies.

But Martin immediately takes the idea seriously. 'Who was he?' he asks. 'Bearable for a weekend?'

'Oh yes. Youngish. To be so rich anyway.'

'You don't have to be so rich to go to Martha's Vineyard.' He speaks quite sharply.

'No, no. I suppose not. Just an English country weekend.'

'I should take him up on it anyway.'

The next day Henry Cartwright telephones and repeats his invitation. Laura accepts for herself, her baby and her 'very good friend'. The mention of her very good friend clearly causes no disappointment, which is hardly surprising when Laura considers herself, large and slow, bound as a mother, bound as a mistress. She thinks she will not swim because she cannot bear to wear a bathing costume. It is unbelievable that last year she had spent all summer in a bikini, brown and straight-limbed.

273

To her surprise Ellen sighs with envy. 'I wish I could get away.'

'It's only for a weekend.'

'Oh to lie in the sun! Instead of fighting to avoid it.'

Laura wondered about herself. Where had she lost that placid contentment, which would allow her to lie easefully in the sun? Ellen had it still. She could see it in her broad pale face, the clear blue eyes, the way she walked and talked and sat. Yet her life offered no more than Laura's. Also, her very good friend Jack was far more demanding than Martin.

Martin seemed a very simple sort of man to Laura. His aims, his ambitions, his feelings about people, his estimations of their character, so clear and simple. For example he didn't seem to have noticed any change in Laura's behaviour or appearance.

She supposed it must have something to do with his clean computer life which she would never understand. But her own theory was that having entered a state of love for her, he was literally incapable of seeing her objectively. This had an odd effect on her for although in one sense it gave a total sense of security, in another less recognised way, it pointed to the abyss in her path. Just as he had fallen totally in love with her so he might fall totally out of love with her, suddenly, without warning. Sometimes her terror of this seemed the explanation for her inertia. Not that this inertia was particularly obvious to anyone seeing the bustling mother. It was much more a feeling inside herself and therefore more dangerous.

*

On a bright clear morning Martin and Laura and Matilda take a plane to Boston and then a smaller plane to the island. There they are met by their host who is immediately recognised by Martin as an old acquaintance. Laura, relieved of the responsibility of introductions, looks round in the fresh morning air and takes a great breath of relief. Perhaps it was the crowding towers of Manhattan which had been oppressing her. She looks down at Tilly sleeping quietly and thinks with straight-forward motherly pride that she has nearly out-grown her basket. She does not even suppress the thought as she normally would, that Nicky would have loved this island. She will fill her weekly letter to him with descriptions.

As they get into the large rather battered convertible, she gives Martin a smile of excitement. He takes her hand in a warm clasp. Their host, catching this gesture, smiles too. 'There're three other guests,' he says, 'but unfortunately my wife is away. In Mexico. She's always preferred Mexico to Martha's Vineyard. But my daughter is here with a friend.' He looks over his shoulder at Laura. 'Perfect babysitters.'

The house is a cool white, each moment served assiduously by a Philippino couple. One wall of the main room is filled with a view of blue sea rising about billows of pampas grass. Occasionally the grass waves gently as a breeze passes over. Otherwise there is complete calm, as if it were a still painting.

The other three guests, lounging around in tennis whites, consist of a couple in their fifties, about the same age as their host, called Jack and Alice, and a dazzling and youthful blonde, called Mary. Laura, prepared to be jealous, is disarmed by her overwhelming admiration for Matilda. 'But what skin! What eye-lashes! What a smile!' The teenage girls, Cissie and Louisa, join in this chorus also making Laura think that perhaps a beautiful daughter is fair swop for beautiful long brown legs.

Henry and Martin disappear to play tennis, the young woman Mary to swim, the couple Jack and Alice to visit a friend. Laura, deciding the sun is too hot for Tilly, sits playing with her on a white rug by the glass windows. Cissie and Louisa stay with her for a while, tickling her stomach and rolling her over. Then they run outside to join Mary in the sea. Laura sits alone with her daughter. After a while Tilly falls asleep. Laura cradles her, hardly awake, almost content.

Martin and Henry return with a sweating self-satisfied air. They look at the pretty picture of mother and daughter with approval. 'That's what I call a real woman,' says Henry.

Lunch is served on a wide shady terrace. After lunch they talk about business, theatre, politics, people. Mary, Laura notes, despite her looks, is not stupid at all. She works in Washington for a young senator.

Later she helps Laura bath Tilly. She explains that she is the eldest of six children and until she moved away from home used to bath the youngest regularly. This does not fit in with Laura's stereotype of the independent, long-legged beauty and she finds herself oddly taken off balance. 'Of course, you'd guess my family was Catholic,' says Mary laughing.

'Oh, but I wouldn't!' Laura doesn't know why she cries this so impulsively. Mary looks surprised. She realises she was

275

reacting to her own image of Mary as middle-aged rich Henry's young beautiful girl-friend. 'You're not Catholic any more, are you?'

'I wanted to be a nun for years, then I decided to get into politics. That's the way I think I can effect things most easily. At the moment. I might always change my mind.'

Laura finishes bathing Tilly, feeds her, puts her to bed and then goes to get herself ready for the evening. All the time she has the idea of Mary with her. A young beautiful woman from the same sort of background as hers who with no pretensions or display of conceit is running her life so that she can 'effect things'. The 'things' Laura does not define too clearly, as Mary didn't, but assumes them to stand for a kind of general good, of cleaner homes, cleaner clearer air, cleaner morals. It is the confidence which staggers. Laura, who has always been treated as a queen among women, now finds herself bowled over with admiration.

When Martin comes in for a shower, she says, 'I think Mary is remarkable.'

'Certainly her legs are!' shouts Martin turning on the taps.

Laura, cut off from further conversation by the noisy rush of water, considers Martin's remark with displeasure. She sees it as further evidence of the simplicity of his character. When he reappears she looks at him coldly, 'She's a very serious person, you know.'

'Who?' He towels himself energetically and then, turning to look at Laura, bursts into laughter at her face. 'I'm sure she is, darling. It's just that her legs are more obvious.'

Laura accepts his kiss with an obstinate lack of grace. Not only simple but superficial, she decides.

Supper consists of two huge lobsters. They are laid on the stone floor of the terrace. Henry crouches over them with a hammer. In the darkness lit only by midge-repelling candles he looks like some Wagnerian Niebelung. Laura has never seen so much lobster, the flesh so fat and pink. They eat it with bowls of mayonnaise and lettuce, licking their fingers energetically. White wine is poured into huge goblets with which they quench their thirst like water. Eating makes them hot, sweat starting on their foreheads. Martin takes a turn with the hammer, cracking the shell with neat accurate taps. Laura now looks at him with silly womanish pride.

He hands her a smooth pink claw, perfectly shaped. She dips it into mayonnaise, pops it into her mouth. But this time she doesn't enjoy it. The flesh is too rich, she thinks of it adding to her own bodily over-abundance. She only manages to swallow it down by swilling white wine after.

Her head begins to ache slightly and she realises the midge-protecting candles are not protecting her at all. Surreptitiously, she scratches an ankle with a toe, and then grasshopper-like begins to rub both feet together. This has little effect. Soon the midges come up from under the table and begin to attack her neck.

She looks at the others but no one else scratches. Mary, all in white, white cotton shirt, white jeans, white bangles, sandals, band round her head, face and hands only golden, is talking about the old Martha's Vineyard. 'My mother,' she says, 'would never have swum between midday and three, nor sat outside after six. The midges figured in her mind as man-eating monsters.'

Before Laura can pick up this sensible line of argument, Martin responds by telling Mary of his mother's annual visit. She knows the name, in fact she's sure she met her. In a moment they're in animated conversation.

'But why didn't you come?' says Mary. 'I fell in love with all the handsome men. I was a horribly romantic little girl.'

'Devastatingly pretty too, I'm sure.' Martin offers her more mayonnaise.

Laura scratches furiously. Henry turns to her with a kind expression. 'Oh dear. They always find the English skin. Cissie, go and get some "Off".'

'What a very good baby you have!' says Alice.

The girls reappear with several spray cans and a tube of ointment.

'In India,' says Jack, 'we used snakes. Not live snakes. Little green powdery one. They were most effective.'

Martin and Mary carry on talking.

Laura uses every spray she is offered. One for her head, one for her legs, one for where she is already bitten. She puts a band of mixed insect repellants all around till she feels no creature great or small could bear to come within ten yards. This gives her a curious sense of satisfaction. She sits back with her weapons arranged like nuclear warheads in front of her.

Her mood, in defensive belligerence, is however less like a beleaguered nation, than a teenager who makes herself as unattractive as possible in order to deter any demanding friendly overtures and to create an excuse for why there are no friendly overtures.

'I don't think marriage would be an absolute disaster,' says Mary brightly, 'but it would take up time.'

Laura sips her wine which has a distinct flavour of insecticide, though not enough, she presumes, to be lethal.

'So you're really settled in for a good long stint in New York now!' Henry bends so attentively that, were it not for her warheads, Laura would actually have suspected him of a pass. This gives her more spirit.

'Oh, no!' she says flashing Martin a mean look. 'I don't think I could ever stick it for long. Besides I have a son who needs me in England. This is just a sort of jolly interlude!' She throws back her head, crying out the last word with a perfect flourish of pleasure.

It has the desired effect. Henry leans away nervously and Martin and Mary stop talking.

Martin looks at the row of cans, as if he's just noticed them. 'What ever's that? Castles on the table?'

'No.' She glares at Mary. 'Just protecting against the man-eating monsters!' Laura surprises herself with her cruel ironic tone. She feels her mouth and face curl into crimped and bitter lines. At least, she thinks, they will not confuse me with a warm and comfortable earth mother.

There is a silence. When the conversation starts again, Laura notices she is treated with a sort of deference as if she is a dangerous quantity. This gives her satisfaction. She sips her wine and lets the talk rise round her.

Martin and Laura leave for their bedroom together. After looking automatically at the cot where Matilda sleeps soundly, Laura throws herself onto her bed. Her full smock-like dress floats and then settles round her in waves. She thinks of herself romantically as a Victorian doll. Her legs, pink and well-rounded, are almost china-like in their smoothness. She caresses one calf appreciatively.

Martin throws off his clothes in his quick manner. He glances at Laura. 'Whatever made you behave like that?' His tone, though casual, is critical. He has never made any criticism of

278

her. This was one of the things that had seemed to give their relationship an unreality. But now she is horribly shocked. She lies still for a moment testing the waves of shock and then, since they don't recede, sits up straight with an angrily defensive glare.

'Whatever do you mean?'

'Shouting about our "jolly interlude". All that nonsense.'

So that phrase had hurt. Laura feels pure joy. 'What about you? With Mary. It was disgusting. Slobbering all over her. She must have thought you the most awful fool.'

Martin picks up his pyjamas from the bed and then turns his back on Laura. He stands still for a moment as if considering and then goes into the bathroom. He reappears wearing his pyjamas and sits quietly on the bed.

Laura has not moved. Time seems wonderfully unimportant to her. She could sit there upright and glaring all night. She now feels less like a Victorian doll and more like a china Buddha with fat white stomach. There used to be a life-sized Buddha outside a jewellery shop which had a sign hanging round his neck, *Rub my tummy and wish*. As a child she had often rubbed.

'Rub my tummy and wish,' she says to Martin looking somewhere above his left eyebrow. Distances, like time, have melted.

'What's the matter?' He takes her hand. 'Too much wine?'

She snatches it away. 'Nothing. I had a marvellous evening. Quite fantastic!'

Martin stands up again. He goes over to the cot. He bends over and puts his arm out to pick her up.

'Don't!' says Laura sharply.

'Why not?'

'She might wake.'

Martin cuddles Matilda up to his face. Her eyes are tight shut but her fingers curl round his. Laura looks at them as if they are quite remote from her.

Martin puts Matilda down and comes back to Laura. 'Why don't you get ready for bed?'

'Because I don't feel like it.'

Martin begins to look exhausted. Laura notes with pleasure that he is not as young as all that. His hair-line is receding and his nose juts, redder than his cheeks. She has done that to him. He does not look strong and brave and confident.

279

'Why won't you tell me what's the matter?'

'Nothing's the matter. It's all perfectly wonderful. I have a perfect lover, perfect baby, perfect job. Perfect.'

'You look at me as if you hate me.'

'Nobody could hate you!'

'Do you want us to separate?'

At last he has said it. She has made him say it. Words that can never be tidied away or forgotten. Now she has got what she wanted. Laura gets up and passes Martin in a stately way. She changes in the bathroom as he has and reappears, still moving slowly, in her nightdress.

Martin has got into bed, huddling down into the clothes. She feels a Lady Macbeth of the night. Blood of guilt on her hands. She goes to the window and looks through the curtains. To her surprise she sees beyond the blackness a silver sea shining in the light of the moon. She stares, straining forward. She treasures this ice-cold moment of dread as if it was the greatest joy. The stillness which had so impressed her in the day holds the image clear. For a moment she remembers that windy English sea-side where Martin and she had first made love. Then his love had pin-pointed her into silence and peace while around the clouds and grass and birds and waves bustled energetically. Now the stillness is all around and she is the one who flapped and cawed and tripped.

Turning suddenly, she goes to the bed. She puts her arms round Martin. 'I've never loved anyone like you.'

'You're not happy.'

'What's happiness?'

'You used to be happy.'

'I've changed.'

'I don't understand. If you love me.'

'I'm different. I'm sorry. I think there wasn't a me before at all. Just a shell. Perhaps you fell in love with me on false pretences. I wasn't that person at all.'

'I still love you.'

'Oh Martin!' Laura puts her face to his and finds she is crying. She sees that everything she's been thinking, everything they've said is nonsense. All she wants, the whole of life is in his words. He loves her still. 'I love you so much. So much.' She cries.

They make love. Falling apart only into sleep.

Later in the night Tilly wakes Laura. She comes into consciousness spasmodically as the baby cries. Used now to testing her emotions, she waits for a moment before moving. But all is well, Martin sleeping beside her, their legs still crossed as if in token of continuing love. She slides out gently, picks up a bottle she had ready and goes to Matilda.

Laura sits with the baby in her arms. The chair is by the window but she is not tempted to draw back the curtains. Here in this room is everything she wants. She thinks: If the rest of the world, even my Nicky, didn't exist, there would be no problems. They would live, like primeval man, in a cave with no windows.

Matilda takes her bottle greedily but looks not the slightest bit sleepy after it. Laura changes her nappy and tries to put her down. She cries. This happens several times. Laura is afraid of waking up the rest of the house. The room has holiday-home walls, very thin and not at all like a primeval cave.

Laura walks up and down. Martin stirs. He puts out his hand for Laura. She sees this and smiles. It gives her courage. She wraps Matilda in a blanket and opens the curtains and then the window beyond.

She steps outside, her head bent to the baby. She walks up and down on the grass beyond the terrace, rocking and singing softly. Gradually Matilda calms, her eye-lids drop lower. Laura looks up now, feels the night air around and with a sudden shock realises she is completely naked.

She looks round nervously and then smiles at herself. There's hardly likely to be anyone round to see her at three or four in the morning.

Tilly is sleeping now and she turns to go back inside. But the night air on her skin is too refreshing. She looks up now at the silver sea, still unmoving but now seeming so close and so desirable.

Not daring to leave Matilda in case she wakes again, she cuddles her closer and walks briskly sea-wards.

*

So Mary, returning from Henry's bed, slipping along the terrace like a thin white ghost, sees, silhouetted against the silver sea, an unusual vision of mother and child. Mother, large, pale, naked, hurrying towards sea and moonlight, while child wrapped enough for an English winter, sleeps.

Mary, having as her life's precept that everyone should do exactly what they want and finding what they want is often fairly strange, is not particularly surprised. However, used as she is to be dramatic, the idea of suicide does cross her mind. She stops to watch.

She watches Laura place her daughter very gently on the sand and then walk slowly into the water. When the water is to her knees, she stops, puts her arms above her head and stretches in such a luxury of delight that Mary feels almost envious. Slowly she sinks, glistening porpoise-like, into the water. No need to watch any more. Mary turns and goes back into her room.

Chapter Twenty-One

When Laura arrives back in New York she finds a fat envelope waiting for her. The ink of the address is smudged as if from tears. When she sees the stamp is Irish she smiles. Rain in Ireland seems a long way away from tears in New York. She imagines Roy tramping to the post box in his green wellington boots.

'A letter from Roy,' she says to Martin and puts it into her pocket. She will read it later that evening.

I wanted you to be the first to know because for all kinds of complicated reasons you have been the cause of it. Without you I might never have understood. I might never have had the courage. . . . Roy's writing is small and black, like tiny coiled springs pulled out across the page. Laura looks at it without understanding. The neatness is so unlike his large rambling person. The intensity is there, however. *In fact I've been under instruction for some time now but I never dared to hope that it would end properly as it should. I'll be received in three weeks. I would be so happy, so very happy if you could be there for the mass. I know it's a lot to ask but apart from what you are yourself to me, you also happen to be the only Catholic I know well in the world!*

Laura cries out, 'Roy's going to become a Catholic!'

Martin puts down his newspaper. 'Why do you sound so amazed?'

'I don't know. He always seemed incapable of making up his mind about anything.'

'He must have found a good priest.'

'What do you mean?'

'He said something about it when we were staying.'

'Oh.' Laura is taken aback. She cannot imagine why Roy should have confided in Martin, her bold, simple, computer man and lover. The subtleties of Roy's nature are for her alone. 'He wants me to go over. For a special mass. In London.'

'When is it?'

Laura looks at the letter. 'Three weeks' time. I could see Nicky. I could sort out the house.' She doesn't raise her eyes in case Martin should see her eagerness. She is getting into the habit of hiding her deep emotions from him.

'Of course you're a Catholic.'

Laura glances up swiftly. 'I was baptised one.'

'Once a Catholic always a Catholic.' Martin gets up and walks over to Laura. He crouches down and puts his arm round her. 'I think you're very Catholic.'

'What do you mean?'

'The way you think. Right and wrong. Guilt. Guilt especially.'

Laura shifts uneasily. 'You must have been brought up in some religion?'

'Actually I was baptised a Catholic too.' Martin laughs as Laura jerks upright almost in horror. 'My mother was French, remember. She had me baptised but then my father made sure I was taught good old C. of E. Until I was thirteen. Then I lapsed from everything. My boarding school was very progressive. It didn't make children go to church. The headmaster was an agnostic. He used to boast about it to the Sixth Formers.' He kisses Laura's cheek. 'Of course you must go back for Roy's big day. I'll try and come myself.'

'I don't know where we'd stay?' Laura masks her absolute determination with a vague humour. But then she lays her cheek against his. 'Are you an agnostic, then?'

'Oh, no. I believe in God.' Martin stands up. '"For now we walk through a glass darkly", in the words of the good book.'

Laura tried to imagine what it must be like to take a major decision about your spiritual life. She supposed before she had left Miles she had lived by a set of principles. But it had been so natural and easy that she had hardly noticed it. Her life was entirely selfish, her only opportunity for Christian behaviour in her relationship with those she loved. No form outside herself.

*

One sunny afternoon Laura is pushing Tilly along Fifth Avenue in her pushchair. The baby's skin is protected by a frilly red and white parasol attached to one of the handles. To the left a wide row of stone steps appears. She turns and bumps the pushchair up backwards. She goes through huge dark doors.

It is a strange sensation turning off the wide busy pavements filled with shoppers moving from Tiffany's to Bergdorf's to Saks and entering the large ornate church. Laura half expects to see racks of hats and scarves instead of rows of empty pews.

She sits in one at the back oddly unwilling to kneel. If she kneels she will have to pray. And what will she pray? But the cool of the church is nice, even the darkness after the harsh brilliance outside. And the quiet is wonderful. Tilly sits happily waving her pale fingers in front of her face.

It strikes her that she could thank God that Roy had found the faith he wanted so much. This she does, head in hands, with a happy feeling of self-abnegation. After a few seconds Tilly makes a little mewing sound and she looks round. The baby smiles showing off her single whole tooth. It is impossible not to smile back and as she does so Laura decides that she will not only go to Roy's mass but also arrange to have Tilly baptised at the same time.

Filled with energy and good intentions, she makes a quick sign of the cross, genuflects and then wheels baby, pushchair and parasol quickly out of the church.

Her feeling of virtuous decision-making is only slightly dented by Ellen's surprise and Martin's doubts. 'I thought your church liked married parents.'

'It's not like that any more,' she says confidently. 'In a perfect world may be. You don't have any objections to her being baptised, do you?'

'I don't want you to be upset. I'd like Tilly to be baptised.'

'Oh, would you? Good.' Laura scurries around cleaning and tidying. Ever since her decision to go back to England she has been filled with organisational energy. Her weight seems not to hang so heavily. She follows up three American contacts so that she will have something to take back to Our Agricultural Heritage.

She writes to Nicky's school, to Miles's solicitor, to Katie, to Nell and to Roy announcing her arrival and her intention of having Tilly baptised. The pattern of her English life which had seemed so impossible to shape when she was there now seems clear and manageable.

She is obscurely pleased when Martin says he can't manage to come with her although he will follow later. Without him she will be able to operate more freely. Unable to imagine the time when she will return to New York she gives up looking for a new apartment. She finds herself faintly surprised when Ellen shows signs of being hurt that she will not be around when her baby is born. She says to Ellen. 'If I'm not back by September you'll have to bring the baby over. I'd love to show you around.'

Ellen says, 'But Martin's living in New York.'

Laura turns away. 'Yes, of course.'

She leaves Martin late at night. The warmth and heat of Kennedy Airport, the excitement of the unknown gives their parting clasp a special poignancy. 'I don't want to go.'

'Yes, you do,' Martin says this nicely. He lets her go and pats Tilly's face. 'Come back soon.'

'But you're coming over.'

'Yes. Yes. I love you.'

Tilly starts to whine a little, holding out her arms. But Laura doesn't want to cry. She takes a step back and looks over her shoulder. 'I love you too.'

They kiss again. Mouth upon mouth. Tender flesh pressed together. Tilly cries out, whining turned to wail.

They walk away from each other, a brisk duelling stride, only slightly hampered by the pushchair. But after ten paces Laura is into customs and only Martin turns. He thinks he can hear Tilly's wails, but an airport announcement blots it out. He walks slower than usual. He has lost the habit of being alone.

*

Laura stands outside Mrs Keane's house in Chelsea. She is to stay there. The little mews house is no longer available and Martin's flat is still rented. In New York it had seemed a good plan, in keeping with her new confidence and taking the bull by the horns. She is, after all, Tilly's grandmother.

But at eight o'clock in the morning with rain casting a grey sheen over pavements and roads, it feels unreasonable. Mrs Keane hates her. The taxi moves off from behind her, black and shiny. The rain falls heavily on her hair, making it drag round her face. She pulls Tilly's hood down to her eyes. Their baggage, not much of it, stands at her feet. She feels like an illustration from a Victorian illustration of desolation.

The door opens and Mrs Keane faces them dressed in a long candlewick dressing-gown. She stares at them with such a surprised expression that Laura wonders for a moment if Martin had got it all wrong. She had not pressed them to stay. But then she takes Laura's arm and pulls her in.

'You're soaking!' Her voice is shocked, disbelieving, as if this is the sort of bad management she did not expect from Laura. Her grip is boney. Laura feels it hook into her soft flesh. She smiles weakly and shifts sideways. Mrs Keane lets go and pulls the suitcase and pushchair over the threshold. She gives Laura a little push in her back.

'Come on now, upstairs. We'll come back for these later. You need drying out. Breakfast is all ready.'

They go up red carpeted stairs. Mrs Keane has the top two floors of a small house.

Laura sits in the warm kitchen giving Tilly her bottle, while Mrs Keane bustles about with saucepans and coffee-pots. The unlikely candlewick dressing-gown and kitchen efficiency give Laura a sense of a scene replayed. She strokes the baby's soft head. Then she remembers the occasion after the opera dance in the country when she had found her making cocoa in this same dressing-gown.

She turns now from the fridge. 'You'd better call me Helen.'

'Thank you.'

'I've lived on my own so long I'm afraid I've turned into rather an old maid.'

'It's a terrible imposition.'

'Not at all.' She puts a pot of beautiful home-made marmalade on the table. 'And now I'll get dressed.'

'Aren't you having breakfast?'

'I had coffee earlier. I'm not very good at sleeping.' She goes away, her neat slippers slap on the lino.

Laura can no longer avoid seeing she is old and lonely and afraid. She sighs and spreads a thick layer of marmalade on toast. She doesn't really want to be intimate with this woman.

She wants a rest from all that sort of thing.

Helen comes back again and begins to clear the table. Laura watches her for a moment and then says quite to her own surprise, 'I don't know what will happen to Martin and me.'

Helen puts down a plate, comes over to her and places one hand on her shoulder. There is a silence.

She is comforting me, thinks Laura.

Then Helen moves away, saying briskly, 'Then we won't talk about it. I haven't been close to Martin for a long time.' She swills the plate under the tap. 'Now tell me about this lovely christening. I expect you know I'm a kind of Catholic. The longer I stay in England the more French becomes my attitude. And my grammar.'

The two women smile a first smile at each other.

That afternoon, Laura goes out, leaving the sleeping Matilda in Helen's care.

She goes to her house. It is still raining, but she notices that the front garden is well cared for, the lavender neatly clipped. More neatly than she ever managed. Although she still has a key she suddenly decides to ring the bell. The door opens almost immediately. A girl stands there, jeans and long hair.

'Laura. I'm Philippa. Come in.' She has a small face, with neat features and straight fair hair. She says, 'We met before, you know.'

They stand face to face in the hallway. Laura decides not to admit it. 'I don't think so.'

'At Martin's dinner. In his club.' The girl is more determined still.

Laura understands how she has pressed herself onto Miles. 'I don't think so,' she repeats.

'Oh, yes. At the same dance in the tent too.'

Laura slides past her into the house. This asthmatic Philippa was Martin's girlfriend, her flowered dressing-gown hanging on the back of his bathroom door, her demanding voice pleading over the telephone. That evening at the club she'd seen no one but Martin.

'I wrote to the solicitor from New York.'

'Yes. That's why I'm here,' Philippa follows her and stands close again. 'I live here now.'

Again Laura moves away. She goes into the drawing-room. 'I'll start here.' She will not question Philippa but she longs to know if Nicky is there. She looks around for signs of a small boy. But the room is orderly, perhaps unchanged though it seems to Laura totally different. She wants none of it.

'Shall I get you a paper and pencil?'

'Thank you.' At least it will get her out of the room. Laura sits down on a chair she has never sat in before.

'Nicky's with his aunt.' Philippa is back already. Martin's live-in girlfriend. Now Miles's.

'Thank you.' Laura takes the paper without getting up. Tomorrow she will take a train to Katie and see Nicky there. She scribbles on the paper.

Philippa sits down opposite her. She has a lively expectant air. Laura remembers her face at the Agricultural Heritage dance. She writes down 'six cushions' and then crosses it out. Whatever could she do with six cushions? She remembers with what extraordinary concentration and excitement she had chosen them. They had made her happy for weeks. Even years. She crosses them out more heavily.

'You've always got exactly what you wanted, haven't you?'

Laura looks up, surprised. Philippa's voice is shrill and filled with hatred. She sits on the edge of the sofa, hands clasped tight. Laura wonders whether to answer her. She doesn't feel hatred, only a bitterness at her freedom to see Nicky.

'No,' she says after a long pause. She stands up. 'I'd rather do this on my own, if you don't mind.'

Philippa bends her head and then starts gnawing at her pale knuckles. Laura stands waiting.

'Everybody always falls in love with you. Everybody!'

'I think I'll start in the bedroom.' Laura moves to the door but before she can go through Philippa has jumped up and runs around to block her way.

'Martin and I had a perfectly good arrangement! Perfectly good. Till you came. And you were quite happy with Miles. He worshipped you. He does still. It's not fair, you know. Not right. You don't know how I hate you. How I hate you!'

Laura feels as if a curse is being put on her. She thinks: This woman lives in the same house as my son. She says calmly, 'Why are you here?'

'Because Miles needs me!' The words jump out like witch's frogs. 'Your husband needs me.'

Laura makes up her mind. She thinks the girl is mad. She

pushes past her, 'I don't want anything in this house. You can tell Miles that.' She hurries to the front door. Outside it is still raining.

Philippa stands in the doorway shouting, 'You're a wicked wicked woman! A destroyer!'

Laura turns round for a look. She can hardly believe this is happening. On her own doorstep. Then Philippa begins to cough. She bends double, pulling desperately for breath. Her eyes close and stream with tears. Laura's flight is prevented. She cannot let her die. She goes back and puts her arm round her. She leads her into the house. 'It's the lavender.' Philippa chokes out the words.

'In the rain?' says Laura doubtfully. Privately she thinks it's hatred. Nicky had said she was allergic to dust. She leads her into the kitchen and finds her a glass of water. Everything is very clean, much cleaner than when she was there.

Philippa subsides. Her face which had turned red and puffy resumes its normal shape and colour. Laura prepares to go again.

'I'm sorry.' Philippa blows her nose.

Laura wonders which outburst she is apologising for. 'That's all right.' Taking advantage of Philippa's weakened state, she goes to the door.

Philippa stands up and follows her but this time with the utmost politeness. She holds open the front door to let her pass. At the hallway she says as if paying Laura a compliment, 'Miles is such an admirable man. I feel so privileged to be able to help him.'

'I'm so glad,' Laura nods graciously and passes once more through the front door.

At last the rain has stopped. But there are still puddles to be sloshed through and leaves dripping on her head. Feeling she has nothing much to lose, Laura goes and sits on a bench beside a bus stop. It is not cold, only very wet. An Irish day.

She has just had this thought when a large figure rises from the pavement. 'Ha! Ha! Caught up with you at last.'

It is Roy, face red and beaming. As he bends to kiss her his glasses slide off his nose and land in two pieces on Laura's lap. 'Oh Roy! I am glad to see you.'

'I should think so. Sitting on wet wood like a tramp. Come on, I'll buy you a cup of coffee.'

Raising his glasses in one hand like a lorgnette and holding Laura's shoulder tightly, with the other, he marches her briskly along the pavement. 'This will do.' He turns into a coffee bar that Laura had passed for ten years of married life but never thought of entering.

'First I got Martin's mother dragon who told me you'd gone to the house. And then I found this extraordinary yellow hissing thing. She asked me two dozen questions in the time it took me to say "Where's Laura?" Whatever is she?'

'Miles's girlfriend,' says Laura with a glorious kind of relief. Philippa was a snake. 'She has terrible asthma.'

'Ah, that could explain the hissing. I keep grain in my pocket to use like worry beads. Wonderful crop this year.'

'I've never seen you so cheerful.'

'Ah well. I've never taken so many decisions.' A slightly shifty look comes over his face as if he's unwilling to expand for the moment.

'I'm so happy for you. I really am.'

'Yes, yes. And the baby too. Such a treat. The day after tomorrow.' But now his tone is really perfunctory as if there's something far more important on his mind. 'How are you?' he says as if for diversion.

Laura feels let down. Their meeting is not the centre of his attention. 'I'm very well. You must meet Matilda. She's sweet.'

'Oh, I don't doubt that. With such a mother.' Even his flattery is half-hearted.

Their coffee comes, reviving Laura into greater strength. She smiles across at Roy. 'The snake attacked me, you know. Accusing me of all sorts of things. Called me a destroyer. She had been in love with Martin, I think. I know. Actually she was his mistress. She lived in his flat.'

'Oh, well. A woman scorned.' Laura can see Roy doesn't want to hear this. It embarrasses him, upsets his idea of proper order. It brings forth the old confused Roy.

'She telephoned him once when we were in bed together.'

'I think women are different from men,' Laura had hardly paused before Roy spoke in a loud almost hectoring voice. 'They like all that sort of thing. All that sort of ugliness.'

'Oh, Roy.' Laura is taken aback. She can hardly believe this is the vicious criticism it seems to be. 'I don't like it, I can assure you.'

But an obstinate fixed look has closed over Roy's face. 'Women are pragmatists,' he says sullenly, 'incapable of understanding a principle, let alone following it.' He pushes his undrunk coffee away and stares at the tablecloth.

Laura can think of nothing to say. She supposes this is her day for being attacked. And she had been so pleased to see him.

'I asked Lizzie to marry me.'

'What?'

'I asked Lizzie to be my wife,' Roy gives the tablecloth a sheepish smile. 'After I decided to become a Catholic, I felt so pleased with myself. I felt all-conquering.' In sudden emotion he shakes his head which sends his glasses flying to the floor. He continues unnoticing. 'I suddenly saw that she would never find a better husband than me. I could offer her the things any wife needs to make her happy: love, health, intelligence, a home and a belief in the married state. So I went down to her room in that horrible college and told her so. I wasn't a bit humble. I told her she needed me and if she didn't know it now she would later.'

'Oh, Roy. What did she do?'

'Gave me a disgusting drink from a tin can and told me to sit down. She said she had a tutorial and would I wait till she got back. When she came back she had another girl with her, a particularly silly girl with red frizzy hair, who apparently knew all about it.'

'Poor Roy.'

'Not really. It just convinced me further I was right. She'd never do better than me.'

'What did she say?'

'She said she had to finish her degree.'

'That was all?'

'Roughly speaking. I didn't listen very hard. Once I realised nothing I'd said had made any impression there was no point. Women are pragmatists.'

'I'm sorry.'

'No need to be. There're much more important things in life. The mass and baptism is at midday. And afterwards there'll be a lunch.'

'I'll look forward to it.' Laura bends down and picks up Roy's glasses. She feels this is no moment to talk about her own position.

It is raining again when they come out of the restaurant.

It is still raining the following day. Laura telephones Katie and speaks to Nicky. He says, 'I've just written to you in America but I'm glad you're back. Tilly must be huge.'

After all, it seems more sensible to wait to see him until the christening. 'We've all clubbed together and got her a super present.'

*

Laura telephones Nell who is apparently living in London. She sounds mysterious, happy. 'Let's meet at the Tate. I love talking in front of pictures. It gives everything one says an extra depth.'

Laura who prefers looking at pictures doesn't feel strong enough to refuse. She arrives late, confident in the knowledge that Nell has never yet been on time for anything. To her surprise she finds Nell standing already rapt in the semi-darkness of the Blake room. Although she still wears her tart's high heels and tightly banded waist, although her hair is still long to her waist and burns with the same improbable red, Laura immediately realises there is something different about her. Her clothes no longer seem a protest. In fact in her own way, she looks actually elegant. Even respectable.

'Laura!' She turns and runs to hug. That is no different. They stand apart for a moment and then Nell drags Laura to the bench in the middle of the room. 'I've got something to show you!'

She opens her bag. It is leather, new looking and that, Laura realises with a start, is the difference. Nell is dressed expensively, leather instead of plastic, tight black trousers tailored instead of held together with safety pins.

'Look!' Nell thrusts a large white envelope into Laura's hands. Even then she doesn't guess. 'Go on. Open it.'

A wedding invitation. Laura looks at it stupidly. It is not so much the idea of Nell getting married that amazes her but the thickly embossed print, the formality of *Eleanor Gray and Sir Peter Potter invite you to celebrate their marriage on September 12th.*

'Sir Peter?' she says aloud in a wondering sort of voice.

'Oh yes. That's nothing. Nell sounds impatient. 'Everybody who can sell more than a pack of cigarettes is knighted these days.'

'Not cigarettes, surely.'

'That's not the point. You will come, won't you?'

Laura feels more and more bewildered. She looks at the Blakes. *Satan smiting Job with sore boils, The Serpent attacking Buoso Donati.* Naked bodies flaming, bodies falling, twirling, rising, flying, sleeping, dying. Is this the depth to their conversation Nell wanted? 'I thought you liked being independent,' she says.

'I did. I do. That's not the point. I want you to meet Peter. He wants to meet you. It's so extraordinary to have someone really in love with you. Of course you've always had that. He's so good too. So honest. Although I could never really be in love with him in the star-spangled way, I do admire him. In fact, the whole thing's a sort of miracle.'

Nell crosses her legs, closes her handbag with a sharp snap and stares ahead with a look of satisfaction.

Laura stares at her profile for a second and then feels impelled to say, 'I thought you didn't believe in marriage.'

Nell turns with a look of surprise. 'I don't. Not like that. I refused Peter for ages. He proposed almost at once, you know. But then he was so keen and the boys were so keen – he's got two girls about the same age, you know – that it seemed ridiculous to refuse. Think of making no more mugs ever. Ever!'

Laura stands up. She mutters congratulations. 'I'm so happy for you.' She goes to look at more Blakes. *The Good and Evil Angels struggling for possession of a Child, The Blasphemer, God judging Adam.*

She remembers how Miles disapproved of Nell. He saw her as the temptress who would lead Laura out of the honourable course of marriage and the family into the primrose path of independence and fornication. He felt his whole self threatened by her short skirts and sheer black tights. It had been even worse when she had started her pottery and had, at least, modest success. Miles hated anyone who broke the rules of his life.

Yet here she is proposing to marry Sir Peter Potter (Laura now thinks she has seen admiring articles about him), a Captain of Industry, a man of whom Miles too would speak with admiration. The wedding celebration is to be held at a very select Club in Piccadilly.

'How about something to eat?' Nell calls from behind her.

Laura takes her eyes from the flames of hell. Nell takes her arm again. 'Peter likes me plump.' They walk from the darkness of Blake to the light of Sir Joshua Reynolds.

Laura doesn't want to have lunch with Nell. She has a great longing for Tilly's soft warmth. She doesn't want to talk about Martin who she can't see too clearly at the moment. She thinks of Helen's unquestioning sympathy with longing. She doesn't want to hear more about Nell's future contentment. She says, 'Oh dear, I've got a working lunch with Ben Casey. I am sorry.'

'But I've hardly seen you!' Nell's disappointed wail strikes a note of guilt with Laura but no repentance. She looks at a sugary painting of a little girl called *The Age of Innocence*. A reproduction of it had hung in her bedroom as a child. She turns back to Nell, 'Come and see Tilly being baptised tomorrow. It's happening after Roy's been received into the church.'

Nell makes an ironic grimace either at the painting or at Laura. But Laura won't stop to explain. 'Twelve o'clock at the Church of the Assumption in Cromwell Road. I'd like you to be there.'

*

Laura can make no sense of her life. Nor anyone else's. She dresses up Tilly in a long white christening robe presented to her by Helen. Martin had worn it for his baptism. Helen doesn't ask why Martin has not come over for the baptism. Since Laura understands nothing she naturally cannot explain even if she'd wanted to. She thinks dimly that she and Helen may turn out to be very much the same sort of woman.

It is raining again. Laura's month of clear New York skies make this continual dull wetness seem a frightful burden. One of the things she can't understand is how people carry on without screaming. Helen puts up her elegant pearl-handled umbrella without complaint. To Laura it seems a sort of insanity.

Laura had spoken to the priest who will baptise Tilly but not met him. This, too, feels strange to her. But Roy had arranged it all when she was in America. She had taken the decision, she couldn't really remember for what good reason, and now it is being carried out. Were all decisions, she wondered, made in this haphazard way? It seemed, yesterday listening to Nell, that it was so. Yet not for Roy. Roy had spent twenty years deciding to become a Catholic. There was no aspect of the situation that he hadn't considered. It is a real and admirable change of direction.

Cheered by this thought Laura says goodbye to Helen who will follow shortly with the white-robed baby and starts on her way to the church. She is to be met there by Katie, several of Katie's children, and Nicky.

She sees Roy first standing on the steps outside the church with a look of terror. His ears seem to stand straight out from his face leaving it looking as small and pale as a child's. As Laura comes closer she realises this is partly the effect of a very close hair-cut and new steel-rimmed spectacles. In fact when she reaches him he smiles broadly and she sees the terror expresses joy. His hand, shaking slightly, grips hers. 'Would you ever think I could come to this? Would you think it possible!' Behind his geriatric glasses his brown eyes glitter as if with tears.

'I'm so happy for you, Roy. So happy for you.' Laura's eyes slip away. Such unrestrained passion seems indecent on a street in day-time. She imagines him falling to his knees beside his bed and the image mixes with herself lying with Martin in naked embrace. She says, 'Has Nicky arrived?' She thinks of Blake's Nebuchadnezzar, naked on his hands and knees.

'No. Katie rang. They'll be late. Come with me. I want you to meet Father James.'

The church is large and empty. Laura, somehow expecting a wedding scene, is surprised by this. But Roy hurries her forward eagerly. From the vestry comes a tall young priest smiling broadly. Laura thinks what a celebration this is for the church, capturing a soul like Roy's.

'So you're Matilda's mother,' says the priest, confusing Laura with his directness. 'Roy told me all about you.' He looks around. 'And where's the child herself?'

Laura smiles. His Irish accent seems appropriate. 'Her grandmother's bringing her later. I didn't want her to spoil Roy's service.'

'A child never spoilt anything. You have another child, I understand. A big boy.'

'He's nine. He was baptised where my mother lived.' Laura feels herself blushing guiltily and is angry with herself. 'He's coming soon.'

'Is that right. Now I need a servor. Perhaps he would like . . . ?'

'I'm afraid he hasn't. . . .' Laura stops confused. It hardly seems right to tell the priest who is about to baptise her second child that her first hasn't been brought up a Catholic. She looks at Roy appealingly.

But before he can speak, although Laura wonders if his euphoria takes notice of such niceties, the priest has turned away. 'Now don't worry about my over hasty ideas.' He starts back up the aisle. 'I must robe up or we'll have a queue forming in the confessional.'

He has understood, at least. Laura wonders if she is disappointed that no flaming sword has been waved over her head. Yet she knew the church had changed since Blake's satanic threats. She had told Martin so.

Suddenly the pews begin to fill up: a sister of Roy's whom Laura has never met with her husband; Nell, once more unusually punctual, with her new expensive look; various men friends of Roy all wearing dark suits and the same bewildered expression. Two wear black ties as if for a funeral.

Then Laura sees Katie, arriving like a princess on stage encircled by pages. One is Nicky. He comes to her, tall and strong.

'Hi, Mum. Where's Tilly? How long will it all take? You're not sunburnt at all. I thought you said it was very hot in America.'

Laura sees he has a cold. His nose is red and his voice nasal. She takes his hand, constrained from kissing by the church.

'I may be pale but you've got a cold. It's so good to see you.' She squeezes his hand.

He neither returns the squeeze nor rejects it. 'Where are we sitting? We go to church twice a week at school. For hours.'

The front pews are nearly full. A verger lights two candles on the altar. Roy has given up receiving his guests and now kneels, swaying a little, near the centre aisle. Laura directly behind, sees that the collar of his suit is not turned down properly. She longs to lean forward and straighten it but feels Roy should not be interrupted in prayer. She would like to pray herself but is far too distracted by the whispers of the children and the whispers inside her head. What is she doing here? Anywhere?

She is here as Roy's friend by his invitation and for the

baptism of her child. Again she fixes on Roy's faith but this time the uneven flap of collar acts like a devil to upset her calm. She can think of nothing else. Eventually she can bear it no more and leans forward. But at that moment the priest enters the church and Roy leaps to his feet. She is thrown backwards, the collar unchanged.

'What's the matter?' hisses Katie, catching something of her movement.

'It's Roy's collar,' whispers Laura despairingly.

Katie follows her look and smiles. 'Dear Roy,' she mouths at Laura.

'In the name of the Father and the Son and the Holy Ghost,' begins Father James.

I have no inner life, thinks Laura. Nothing at all. I am not a serious person in any way. I existed a little before when I was part of the structure of marriage. But now I am nothing. I believe in nothing. And what is it all for? Why did it all happen? For love. Because I fell in love. And what is the point in that? What good has that done anyone? It's certainly done a great deal of harm. Besides, what sort of love was it? Here am I with the child of that love separated from her father by an ocean. And why are we separated? There's no real need for it. He wants to work, I want to baptise Tilly. But those aren't real reasons. So why are we apart? Because we don't love each other any more. Because it's all over. All gone. Hollow passion.

Laura, standing arms folded, thinks such things and the priest, finishing the introduction to the mass, begins the confiteor.

'I confess to Almighty God, and to you, my brothers and sisters, that I have sinned through my own fault in my thoughts and in my words, in what I have done, and in what I have failed to do. . . .'

Chapter Twenty-Two

Laura has a sensation of falling down a black hole very fast. After a timeless period this is interrupted by a loud noise behind her. Her vision returns and she sees in sharp silhouette a tall man. He is standing against the light of the door. He takes a small step forward and she sees he is fair and handsome, quite young and athletic-looking.

A feeling of déjà-vu threatens to return her to the black hole. Where before has she seen that man in his padded anorak standing so still, as if waiting? She then realises it is Martin as she had first seen him at the railway station.

She goes to him carrying the baby in her arms. As she gets closer the stillness and strangeness is broken.

'Martin, how wonderful! You've come.' Her voice welcomes him.

'Yes. I couldn't resist.'

The breaking process continues and Laura has a curious sensation of going through that Martin whom she'd first seen and never lost and on to some quite different man. This man, standing in front of her. A man with a reddish face, tired and kindly. A man who is neither young nor old but nearer old. A man who has travelled the Atlantic to see her and has a small split in his anorak.

'Have I missed the baptism?'

'Yes. But it doesn't matter,' Laura smiled and took his arm. 'We're all done. Come and meet Father James.'

Laura felt as if she'd stepped out of the flare of a great stage production into ordinary life. Martin looked ordinary, like any other man.

She had hit the end of the tunnel with a soft bump and found herself sitting in a nice cosy living-room.

'Have you just arrived?'

'I came straight from the airport.'

'You must be exhausted.'

The words were so simple, affectionate. She looked at him with affection.

'This is Matilda's father,' she said to Father James.

'Ah. Congratulations. This is a good day.'

A good day. Laura looked round at this church filled with old friends and relations. Roy took Martin's hand and shook it emotionally. Laura, hardly thinking what she was doing, leant forward and straightened his collar. Roy didn't notice.

'Now we've dealt with the soul,' he said, 'we mustn't forget the body.'

A buffet lunch had been arranged in a small restaurant nearby. The children raced about snatching asparagus rolls and brandy snaps. Tilly sucked a sausage. For the first time Laura saw some resemblance between Tilly and Nicky. She realised she had never been able to bear to see them in the same room before, one so loved and so discarded, the other such a creature of misrule. It had never seemed remotely possible that together they could make a family. She looked at Martin. He was not eating or drinking, he was listening to the priest. He wore a calm serious expression, of which romantic heroes are not made. He felt Laura's eyes on him and looked up. He didn't smile or stop listening to the priest.

Laura thought: He no longer loves me as he used; but the idea did not destroy her. It made a dull ache. They still loved each other. Perhaps now they could talk.

Laura continued to watch him and soon he began to talk back to Father James. She saw he was an intelligent man and that in itself is a revelation. For before she had cast him into the role most unlike Miles. He was to be a man with energy but few brains. Miles had brains, but no physical reality. Laura almost laughed at her idiocy. Perhaps she had wanted to despise him.

She remembered how she had once seen his mother. Like a mother in a wicked fairytale. Cold, hard, pitiless. Beautiful. Now she knew her to be a sad lonely woman in candlewick whose husband's death had left her alone in a foreign country. Who had hardly managed to make proper contact with her only son. Who had warned her son against a difficult love and not liked it. Matilda had made her generous.

Laura wondered if it was too late for her. By leaving Miles she had broken herself apart. Was there anything left now to put together? The image extended in her mind and she saw those she loved around her like fragments of a precious vase. Nicky, Matilda, Roy, Nell, Katie – Martin, Martin's mother even, the priest, Johnny arrived in time to eat and drink. All gathered round her like a grand finale of some foolish pantomine. It only needed Miles and Philippa, coughing at the flowers, to walk through the door.

'What are you thinking about?' Martin came up to her and despite everything her heart beat differently at the sound of his voice. He put his arm round her. 'It's a lovely party.'

He didn't expect her to answer his question but Laura said slowly, 'I was thinking what a mess I've made of everything.'

'What do you mean?'

'I just did things. Without understanding them. Like a child. I had no control. You can't if you don't know what you're doing. I fell in love with you, that was the start of it all.'

'And now you've fallen out of love?' Martin's voice was calm but Laura didn't want to think of him. She wanted to follow her own train of thought.

'It's not that. At least not exactly. I can't explain. Not here.'

'Later.'

'Yes.' Laura looked at Martin and thought that, in a sort of way she has never loved him as much as she did at this moment.

'In church, I wanted to die.'

Martin said nothing or perhaps he was thinking what to say because at that moment there was a loud banging behind them.

'My Lords, ladies and children, no party is complete without speeches, particularly when I'm a guest!' Johnny was standing on a chair, his thumbs stuck into scarlet braces. Groans and claps greeted him.

'Thank you. Thank you. But on this occasion I only take the chair to introduce another. . . .'

'Shame! Shame!'

'Which does not mean my introduction will not be exceedingly long and filled with witticisms . . .' More groans. '. . . for never let it be said that I have missed any occasion for airing my opinions. Particularly when I know nothing about the subject in question. . . .'

'Here! Here!'

'Although as it happens I too went through the great waters of Catholic baptism. And if some of you are thinking that I'm not a very good example of what the holy waters can do, let me put this to you: what would I have been like without their help?'

This point, greeted with ribald laughter, caused Laura to look at Father James but he too was smiling.

'Yes. yes. I, too, like my beautiful sister may appear a somewhat fallen angel. . . .'

'Here! Here!'

'But let me remind you in the words of that great atheist and nautical expert, HMS Voltaire "Every man is an island." In other words the inner life is known to God alone. For who would have guessed that our good friend Roy, more of an atheist than HMV himself, was harbouring such spiritual ambitions? And here I ask you to prime your glasses. For let us drink to those two new souls, today fresh and white, tomorrow . . . ? Roy and, er – Mary!'

'Matilda!' hissed Laura.

But Johnny had already jumped off his chair and with a satisfied air was trying to persuade Roy into speaking.

'Poor Roy,' said Laura to Martin.

Roy stood in front of the chair. A large missal was stuck into either pocket of his jacket so that his hips bulged like a fat woman's. Laura saw tears in his eyes although he smiled widely. Then the smile went. 'I only want to thank you all for coming here and to the church. And to thank Father James and the Catholic Church for allowing me to join them. This is not just the happiest day of my life. This is the only happy day of my life.'

Abruptly he sat down on the chair behind him and bowed his head. A silence followed, of awe or embarrassment. His attitude is one of prayer. Then Laura, with tears now in her own eyes, found she had taken up his speech.

'Matilda is too young to speak for herself so I will say thank you. Thank you Father, thank you everybody. She may become what Johnny calls a "fallen angel" like her uncle and her mother. But I know one thing, it is better to be a fallen angel, than no angel at all.'

Chapter Twenty-Three

At last the rain had stopped. Suddenly it was summer again except the grass brushed wet marks like paint across their shoes and the heavy trees dropped globules of water the size of pigeons' eggs. But the sun, even though it was evening, was strong enough to lengthen the trunks with black shadows and pierce through the umbrella of trees. Bright lozenges of colour danced at Laura's feet.

Martin and she walked briskly through Hyde Park.

'What do you want to do?' he said. He took off his jacket and hung it round his shoulders. 'It's really quite warm.'

Laura thought of Matilda snugly in her cot and Nicky travelling back to Katie's house, 'It's not just me.'

'If it helps you to make your mind up, I might as well tell you that I had an affair in New York. After you left.'

'Oh. Oh.' Laura had a dissolving feeling of terror that she would drown in tears and not be able to say anything after all. 'It doesn't help,' she managed after several minutes.

'I'm sorry.'

'No, please.' There was no doubt in her mind that it was that girl, Mary. She tried very hard not to think of her long golden limbs. Such a cliché. 'That's not the point at all.'

'I was lonely.'

'Please. I don't blame you.'

Martin stopped walking. They stood facing away from each other. A beam of light struck Laura's face making her screw up her eyes but she didn't think of moving.

'I didn't know what you wanted. I thought perhaps you even wanted that. If I had a girlfriend you could go off. You seemed so unhappy.'

'I'm sorry.'

'And that's not quite true either. I did it because she was available and I wanted her. I don't feel as you do. I'm just not the same. No angel at all.'

Laura put up a hand to shade her eyes but still didn't think of moving. 'I behaved very badly to you.'

'I tried to give you everything.'

'Yes. I know.'

'I'm still in love with you. I don't know why. Did you mean what you said about wanting to die?'

'Yes.'

Martin suddenly started walking again very fast. Laura had to run to catch up with him. As he strode ahead his coat flew off behind him. Laura bent to pick it up and then followed again, folding it close in her arms.

She caught him up on the edge of the Serpentine. He glanced at her over his shoulder. 'I think we'd better part,' he said.

'I don't know. It's not about guilt any more. If you could wait. . . .'

'We've had a good run for our money.' His voice was rough. 'At least we did to begin with. It was like,' he paused, staring out at the smooth water, 'like nothing else. Now the world's come in.'

'When are you going back to New York?'

'Soon.' Again Laura fought off visions of golden limbs, crossed in ecstasy like angels' wings. 'I'd been a bachelor a long time before I met you.'

'You mean you could be one again?'

'I've got my machines.'

Now Laura stared at the Serpentine. She thought of the ice-cold sea where she had washed after they had first made love, the green waters of the Mediterranean they had swum at the height of their love, the silver night sea at Martha's Vineyard. Dreams of glory and death reduced to this shallow stretch of muddy water.

'If only there was more time.'

'I don't have to go immediately.' For the first time he turned to her. 'We're both perfectly free, after all.'

Laura wondered if he meant from each other. 'I don't know what you mean.'

Martin seemed surprised. 'Free to do what seems best.'

'What about Tilly and Nicky?'

'You can't please both of them. Or perhaps you can. If you go back to Miles, Tilly will never know she had another father.'

'Is that what you want?' Both their voices had become ugly and bitter.

'I'm trying to think what's best for you.'

Laura went right up to the edge of the water and watched the white ripples tickle the ends of her shoes. She was very slowly beginning to feel very angry. 'Miles has a girlfriend!' she said in a loud voice.

'Well, that's a surprise,' Martin didn't approach her. 'Not serious, I'm sure.'

'Actually, you would be more likely to know than me. She's one of the remnants of your bachelor days. Philippa, with the asthma. I did mention her before, if you remember.' Laura took a real pleasure in her anger now swelling into sublime hatred.

'Philippa. Poor old Philippa. Well, she's no rival, I'm afraid. She's one of those girls men take in when there's nothing on the television.'

'How disgusting!'

'Not at all. She knows the score. She's perfectly willing.'

'You make it sound like some game.'

'I'm just being realistic.'

Laura noticed the clipped viciousness of his tone with satisfaction. 'And I suppose making love, if you can call it that, with a girl you hardly know in New York is being realistic too.'

'Right.'

'Well, I don't have much interest in that sort of realism.'

'Fantasy is more your game.'

'If you want to call it that. Although it is not a game. I never play games.'

'Pity. You might have more fun if you did.'

Laura looked round at the curve of parkland, dark trees, light water and sky going pinkish now. She remembered the affection with which she'd first seen Martin a few hours ago. Now she saw him just as clearly but with loathing. She realised she was still cradling his coat.

Words failing her, she took it in her right hand and threw it high in the air. As it made a flapping ascent followed by a speedier descent towards the muddy water, it struck her it was a more apposite action than she could have hoped.

'Now look who can play games!' she cried joyfully.

The jacket which was an expensive grey linen suit-top landed on the surface of the pond causing consternation among several large green ducks. Laura looked at Martin's face and burst into laughter. 'Have you never seen the greater two headed sea-gull before?'

'Only in dreams.' Martin watched mesmerised as his jacket filled with water in the middle and began quite slowly to sink.

Laura was impressed by his calm. The wild action had quite wiped out her anger, leaving her in an excellent humour. But she could hardly expect it to do the same for him.

'Inside that jacket,' said Martin deliberately, 'are my keys, my wallet with large sums in both pounds and dollars, at least six credit cards and my passport. Oh yes, and my diary which encloses a picture of us taken on the sea front in Viareggio.'

To Laura's surprise, he walked over to an iron bench facing the pond and sat down. 'An interesting experience to sit watching your life go down.' He looked at Laura. 'You certainly have changed.'

Laura was overcome by a slightly exaggerated remorse. 'Oh, Martin, you can't let it drown!'

Martin said nothing. Laura didn't hesitate. Pulling off her sandals, she waded into the water. It was warm and slimy underfoot. She held out her arms to keep her balance and shouted, 'Shoo, shoo!' to the ducks, returning now with quacking curiosity.

The coat was almost submerged, only one shoulder still upraised like the bow of the Titanic. She pulled on this, heaving with some difficulty the wet weight. She stood to face Martin holding up the dripping cloth in an attitude of victory. 'Saved from the spirits of the deep! Saved from destruction!'

She felt the hem of her dress drag wetly against her knees. Her hair was loose and wild, her arms muddy, her face hot and red. She knew she must look ridiculous. She shouted again, 'Don't I even get a round of applause?'

At last Martin laughed. He got up and stood with his arms open at the edge of the water. 'Come on, I wouldn't want you to slip and drown.'

'You're just thinking of your cash.' Laura splashed her way happily towards him.

'Don't you know, money always rises to the surface.'

Laura and Martin sat side by side on the bench. The sun had dipped behind the rim of the park, beyond the red-brick mansions that bordered it. Strangely, there seemed more people now in this moment before dark than there were when the sun still shone. Or perhaps it was just that Laura had become aware of them. Or it could be that their rather odd appearance, surrounded by wet notes laid in strips across the bench was attracting passers-by.

'Go away,' said Laura to a dog snuffling curiously. Behind came its owner, an upright old woman with furry grey hair and a stick. As she came level with them she pointed her stick at the bench.

'Is that place free?'

Apologetically, Laura began to shuffle the notes. But Martin without moving, looked her in the eye. 'No,' he said firmly.

'Well, I must say.' Defeated, the old lady moved on, grumbling.

'I know a nosey old lady when I see one,' said Martin, smiling.

'There must be masses of empty benches,' cried Laura, spreading the notes back again and thinking how silly she had been to move them in the first place.

They both looked round automatically. But strangely, although there were many benches at the edge of the pond, and beyond among the trees, every one seemed occupied by dark evening figures, huddled close and quiet.

'It's like slugs after the rain, crept out from their burrows.'

'Loving couples,' replied Laura. The thought was slightly chilling as if they had found themselves part of some unhealthy underworld.

As she watched, all round the park, couples shuffled up from the seats and started in a slow train to the gates.

'We should go.'

Martin began to gather up the money. Laura waved her still damp skirt about and they both stood up. Martin took her hand. They headed for the gate in Kensington High Street.

Laura thought how often she had pushed Nicky through these gates when he was a baby. Their house was only a short walk away.

As she thought this, she saw a tall dark figure ahead. He carried a heavy briefcase, walked slowly. A man alone, returning home after a long day's work. With hardly a blink of surprise, she said to Martin, 'Miles is ahead of us.'

Martin stopped. 'What do you want to do?'

'Say hello.'

'Shall I disappear?'

'No.'

They walked faster. Laura almost ran. She tapped Miles on the shoulder. Miles turned round. His eyes were empty, expecting no one. 'Hello Laura.'

It seemed appropriate to kiss, a restrained peck with bodies well apart.

'You remember Martin.' They had not met since that tennis game in the hot sun.

'Getting some air,' said Martin. The two men shook hands formally.

Miles turned back to Laura. 'I'm glad to see you looking so well.'

This was said with a kindness and sincerity for which Laura was unprepared. She couldn't help remembering their last two meetings. On the first occasion he had raised his arm and condemned her to eternal damnation. On the second he had wept over her pregnant stomach in utter humiliation.

'Thank you,' she said. 'You look well too.'

This was not true. Miles had a chalky complexion in particular contrast to Martin's sun-bronzed glow.

'I haven't been too good as a matter of fact.'

'You work too hard.'

There was a short pause and they all started walking.

'I heard you were seeing Nicky today,' said Miles.

'Yes. He was very sweet. So grown-up.' Laura decided not to elaborate on the circumstances. Of course Katie might have told him. 'It's far too long since I last saw him.'

'You're living in New York?'

'Yes.' Laura wondered if this was any longer true.

'Philippa tells me you don't want anything from the house. I find that a little surprising.'

'Why?' Laura said this without thinking and regretted it immediately. Dangerous ground. She saw that Miles was also taken aback but with a lawyer's training could never resist answering a question.

'You loved the house so much.'

This was too direct. Laura ducked her head. She mumbled half hoping he wouldn't hear. 'Perhaps that's why I don't want anything.'

'Actually you can have the whole house, if you want. It's no use to me. Although I suppose if you're in New York. . . .' He stopped and a look of suffering crossed his face.

'I don't know about New York,' said Laura, trying not to see his expression, although she couldn't stop herself thinking with a kind of triumph: He still cares. 'Everything's so complicated.' She saw that she must not lose this opportunity to ask about a divorce. Whatever happened between Martin and herself she should have that possibility open to her. But before she could think what words to use he turned to her, taking her arm and smiling in a way quite sinister in his drawn face.

'I've had some good news today.' He paused.

Laura bent attentively, nervously. What made him hesitate? Did his news concern her?

'I saw the Lord Chief Justice today.'

This statement, clearly supposed to reveal everything, revealed nothing to Laura. She waited expectantly.

'The Lord Chief Justice?'

'I've been made a judge.' Now the pride and pleasure were clearly displayed. 'In the Family Division which is perhaps not exactly what I'd have chosen.'

'That's wonderful. I'm so pleased!'

'Of course it does also mean a cut in salary to begin with.' He gave her a strange sly look. 'At least you've never asked me for money.'

'And I don't intend to,' said Laura sharply. Would she end up marrying Martin for money?

Martin came level with them. Laura realised they were at the turning to the house. She looked at Miles. He nodded.

'Come and have a drink?'

Martin's face was expressionless.

'All right.' They became silent.

When they reached the house she thought with painful nostalgia of that afternoon when Martin had kissed her on the doorstep. His love so great that it had made his voice hoarse.

The door was opened by Philippa. Miles led them in, putting down his briefcase in the hall. 'They've come for a drink.'

Philippa didn't look at either of them. 'I'll see what we've got.'

Head down, she went to the kitchen.

Laura went straight into the drawing-room and waited to be served. Miles and Martin followed her.

She smiled at Miles. 'Actually we had far too much champagne at lunchtime.'

'And I'm jet-lagged.'

'Ah.' Miles leant back in the chair he always chose. He seemed much more at ease now he was in his own home. His face had lost its deathly pale and his body seemed more substantial in the heavy cloth. In the kitchen Philippa clattered glasses and bottles.

'Philippa's a very efficient woman,' said Miles.

'Is she working at the moment?' said Martin in the polite tones of casual acquaintance.

'She's very interested in training for the bar.'

'Ah.' He nodded agreeably.

'Miles has been made a judge!' shouted Laura unable to bear such idiocy.

'Congratulations!' said Martin, looking first at Laura with some surprise and then at Miles with clear admiration. 'Sir Miles Knight. It sounds very distinguished.'

'What?'

Miles turned kindly to Laura. 'All judges are knighted as a matter of course. It's really no great honour.'

'Oh, come on now!' expostulated Martin good-humouredly.

Philippa arrived with the drinks. She looked round smiling. 'I see Miles has told you the wonderful news?'

'Do you mean I'm a lady?' Laura gave a bellow of laughter. 'Lady Laura Knight.' All things considered this seemed the appropriate climax to the day. 'Only Miles could manage to be a knight twice over!'

Philippa put down the drinks but otherwise there was a background of searing silence. Laura laughed on regardless.

'I haven't yet told you my other bit of good news.' Miles's voice sounded like the bearer of imminent disaster. Laura stopped laughing. Martin put his head back on the sofa and stuck his legs out. Laura thought, he has never been in this room before.

'While I was with the Lord Chief Justice I took the opportunity to discuss my marital situation with him. In fact I felt it my duty to declare it before accepting. Particularly as a judge in the Family Division presides over cases where there is a marital break-down.'

At this Laura gave another snort of laughter, although quickly stifled. Miles paid no attention.

'In fact I raised the question of divorce. My divorce, I mean.'

Here he faltered, the magisterial delivery seemed to fail him and he gave a wild glance to the long windows as if planning escape. 'So to cut a long story short, he had no objection to you,' quite clearly agitated now, he jumped to his feet and stood in front of Laura, 'to you sueing me for a divorce. There you are. There's your good news!'

As if worn out by emotion he sunk away again and collapsed back into his chair.

Laura looked down at her legs and feet. She noticed they were slightly streaked with slime from the Serpentine. She guessed she should say something. Thanks, perhaps. But felt most unwilling to commit herself at all. She looked at Martin but his eyes were actually closed either in sleep or to indicate a total dissociation from the events taking place in front of him.

Philippa said in a bright voice, 'So what are we all drinking?'

Miles, talking as if to himself, said, 'Since I don't intend to marry again, I have no particular interest in anything about it except for one thing. That I have care and control of Nicky while you have reasonable access. And, of course, I should like it all to be done amicably with no fuss.'

Here there was another more dramatic interruption as Philippa dropped a bottle on the tray and ran from the room. She thought he was going to marry her, thought Laura. I could have told her that would never happen. Really, he doesn't like women. He just happened to love me.

Martin heaved himself to his feet. 'I'm sorry. I really am most terribly tired. I hope it won't seem very rude.' He walked slowly to the door.

Laura watched him. He didn't look at her at all. She watched him all the way out and a moment or two later heard the outside door slam.

'Where's Philippa gone?' she asked after a moment's pause.

'Oh, I don't know,' Miles passed a hand over his head. 'She has a sort of bed-sit downstairs. She's very helpful with Nicky. With all sorts of things.'

'Yes.' They sat in silence. Laura remembered how he always made her feel like a naughty schoolgirl. Now she felt sorry for him.

'I've made a mess of everything,' she said.

'Oh, no.' He looked up with a dazed blinking look. She realised he had taken off his glasses which he held in his right hand. 'I don't blame you any more. I did. But I see I was a lot to blame. I didn't give you enough attention. I thought you were happy, you see. You always seemed so happy.'

'I was, I was!' Laura felt herself near tears. 'Please don't think anything else. I could have gone on being happy with you for years. It was just, it was just.' It seemed too cruel to say, it was just because I fell in love. But she said it all the same. Perhaps it was less painful than other reasons. 'It was just that I fell in love.'

'Oh, yes. I see that.' He rubbed his eyes and put his glasses back on. 'I understood that from the beginning. Right from the beginning. But I didn't believe you would run away like that. I thought I was more important. Nicky was more important. Our marriage was more important.'

'You were! You were!' Laura sat on the edge of her chair, arms out-stretched, pleading. 'I was mad. Can't you understand? I wasn't rational. It wasn't me at all. I was taken over.'

'Yes. Yes. I see that.' Miles got up and poured himself a glass of whiskey. He sat down again. Laura watched mesmerised.

'And what about now? Are you still mad?'

'No. Yes. What do you mean?'

'It's been a long time. You've got a baby by him. You've got responsibilities there. New responsibilities, duties.'

'Yes.' Laura whispered. She thought of Tilly draped in white receiving drops of holy water on her head while she battled with the angels of death.

'You've changed too. You're quite different. More like other people in a way.'

'Oh.'

'I don't mean to be rude. It may be a good thing. I know people always thought I was pompous, complacent. I've changed a lot too. I'm not so sure any more. Do you know I actually thought of turning down becoming a judge? I thought how can I sit in judgment on other people when I have failed so totally to understand my own family?'

'But you haven't. I told you. I fell in love!' Least of all could Laura bear him to be pathetic.

'Love. You make it sound like some magic potion.'

'I think it is a bit like that.'

'So you still love him?'

311

'Yes.' Laura's voice sounded dull and unconvincing even to her own ears.

'And you want a divorce?'

'I suppose so.'

Miles looked at her now, half-questioningly. He got up again. 'Do you want a drink?'

'No. Oh, all right. A brandy.'

He handed the glass over silently. She answered as if he had questioned her. 'It's just that I can't be sure of anything any more. When I was with you, I had so many beliefs. I dealt in certainties. Now I don't know anything. I don't know who I love or who I hate. I don't know where I want to be or what I want to do. I don't know what I feel about you for example. Love, hate or nothing. It's almost the same, not quite, with Martin. He doesn't love me like you did, you know. No end of it. Total. He's had one affair already and he'll have others.

'There're all sorts of things I understand now. People. Roy. Do you remember how he swung so wildly from one belief to another and could never believe in any of them? And Nell. Living in a kind of vacuum. Only allowing the present to exist. I understand both of them in a way I never did before.

'And the irony of that, of course, is that both Roy and Nell have settled now. Roy to Catholicism, Nell to the most conventional of marriages. Her future husband's a knight too. You wouldn't believe her if you saw her. And here's me, here's good old reliable me. . . .' Laura felt herself starting to laugh again.

But Miles said sharply. 'Don't!' She stopped immediately.

'I'm sorry for you,' he said. 'I never expected to be that. But I can never forgive you for what you did to Nicky.'

'You took him away,' Laura protested half-heartedly.

'You would have found a way to see him if you had wanted to. You didn't want to.'

'You can't make an omelette without breaking eggs.'

There was a very long pause. Laura's words echoed vulgarly.

'So what will you do?' His voice was quite kindly.

'I don't know. I suppose I love Martin more than anyone else. And it wouldn't work with you any more. You can't put the clock back.'

'No.'

Laura got up and walked round the room. She touched the objects that had given her so much pleasure in the past. She put on a light so the cool dusky room became warm and golden. Once more her cushions glowed, her pictures in rich patterns on the wall, the red candles on the mantelpiece, the little marble-topped tables, the rugs she had collected over the years. Each object a part of herself, the self she had been.

She went and sat on the chair she always sat in. 'Do you remember that weekend I went to sort out Katie's marriage?'

'No. No, I don't think so.'

'You didn't come. You went away somewhere. Manchester, I think. You were working.'

'I had a big fraud case in Manchester.'

'Yes. That was when it started. When I first saw him. We went to a dance. An opera.'

'Don't tell me, Laura. I don't want to know.'

'It's interesting. You won't be able to be so squeamish in the Family Division.'

Miles stood up angrily, 'This is my life!'

'Sorry.' Laura thought how badly she behaved now.

Miles stood at the mantelpiece fiddling with the little china ornaments there.

'I just wanted to say,' Laura began again, 'that it could so easily never have happened. Do you know that old Catholic phrase, "Occasion of Sin"?'

Miles looked at her but said nothing.

'I know you don't like Catholicism, you don't like religion at all if it comes to that, but this should appeal to you. To your precise legal mind. The Catholic Church teaches that if you put yourself in a position where you know a sin is likely to follow then you have already sinned. So I was lost, you see, the moment I decided to see Martin again. The war was fought on the first battlefield and lost.'

'Lost!' Miles shouted, spittle flared across the room. 'Lost! Lost! What do you mean? What ridiculously emotive words you use! It's all nonsense. Nonsense. There's no need to bring sin into it at all. As far as I can see you're just using it as an excuse to wallow in your pigsty!'

Laura was pleased at his anger. She assumed it would make him feel better. But it didn't touch her at all.

'Anyway, that's the way I see it. I thought you'd be interested.'

'Illogical dangerous madness!' Miles stamped up and down

313

the room two or three times and then sat down again.

Neither had anything left to say. Outside the tall window it was now completely dark. It struck Laura that anyone looking in from the street would see a cosy domestic scene, husband and wife resting together after a busy day.

In fact the window seemed less protected from the public gaze. No flowers on the table. She always used to put a large vase of flowers in front of the window. Instead something heaped and grey lay there. For a moment Laura couldn't identify it and then she saw a drop of water falling from it to the carpet below. It was Martin's wet jacket.

Chapter Twenty-Four

The train slowed down and then stopped. The rain which had been running horizontally across the window, drops fleeing after each other in impossible chase, now fell vertically, fast and full, as if in relief.

Laura watched it, her face close enough to the glass to feel the coolness of moisture. She thought of nothing. She was not in despair but in a kind of vacuum that was much the same.

Beside her, Tilly slept, head lolling forward in abandon.

They were stopped at a disused station. Weeds sprang among the concrete. Tiles, fallen from the roof, scattered the floor with broken remnants. A hedge sprouted in unshaven liberty. Amidst it there was the merest glimmer of pink roses struggling for light.

Suddenly Laura wanted to get out. Just for a second. Just stand for a second in that middle of nowhere. It seemed important.

She propped Tilly against the seat and went to the door. She pushed down the window and looked out. Immediately she was overwhelmed by the smell of warm wet countryside.

She jerked the door open and jumped out. As her feet touched the ground, she almost laughed. Her sensation of freedom was so great that she wanted to run, laugh, cry. It seemed to her that this touching down in the middle of nowhere was the first free decision she'd ever made in her whole life.

But since there was Tilly, she held open the door and didn't move further. Only her face tilted upwards, letting the rain drops wash across it.

The train gave a slight lurch.

It was enough. She was on her way to Katie's. Nicky would be there. Even without Tilly's sleeping presence she would have stepped back on as she did now, shutting the door sharply behind her.

The train moved forward.

315

About the Author

Rachel Billington is a member of that illustrious writing family the Longfords. Her mother is Elizabeth Longford, her sister is Antonia Fraser and her brother is Thomas Pakenham. Rachel Billington is a regular reviewer for the English *Financial Times* and a writer of novels, short stories, and plays for radio and television. She is married to the director Kevin Billington, and with their four children they divide their time between London and their five-hundred-year-old house in the Dorset countryside.